Dedalus Europe
General Editor: Timothy Lane

THE DEDALUS BOOK OF FAROESE LITERATURE

THE DEDALUS BOOK OF FAROESE LITERATURE

edited by Malan Marnersdóttir

translated from Faroese by
Lindy Falk van Rooyen and Marita Thomsen
and from Danish by
Paul Russell Garrett

Dedalus

This work has been published with the financial assistance of The Faroese Culture Fund, FarLit and Arts Council England ACE.

Published in the UK by Dedalus Limited
24-26, St Judith's Lane, Sawtry, Cambs, PE28 5XE
info@dedalusbooks.com
www.dedalusbooks.com

ISBN printed book 978 1 912868 99 5
ISBN ebook 978 1 915568 43 4

Dedalus is distributed in the USA & Canada by SCB Distributors
15608 South New Century Drive, Gardena, CA 90248
info@scbdistributors.com www.scbdistributors.com

Dedalus is distributed in Australia by Peribo Pty Ltd
58, Beaumont Road, Mount Kuring-gai, N.S.W. 2080
info@peribo.com.au www.peribo.com.au

First published by Dedalus in 2024

Printed and bound in the UK by Clays Elcograf S.p.A.
Typeset by Marie Lane

The Editor

Malan Marnersdóttir was born in Klaksvík in the Faroe Islands in 1952. She studied Nordic languages and French at the universities of Copenhagen, Aarhus and Odense before completing her doctorate at the university of Aarhus. She was a lecturer and later the Associate Professor of Nordic Literature at the Johann Wolfgang Goethe University in Frankfurt. She returned to the Faroe Islands in 1983 and was appointed to the chair of Nordic Literature at the University of the Faroe Islands in 2004. She has written extensively on different aspects of Faroese literature and collaborated in the three-volume *Faroese Literary History*. Malan is the editor of *The Dedalus Book of Faroese Literature*.

The Authors

(in the order they appear in the text)

Venceslaus Ulricus Hammershaimb (1819-1909) was born in Sandavágur on the island of Vágar. While studying theology at Copenhagen University, together with others, he contrbuted to the development of the Faroese written language. In 1846 his collection of legends was published, in which 'Kópakonan' (The Selkie) featured. Hammershaimb was the parish priest and rural dean for the Faroe Islands from 1855 to 1878, and later served as a priest in Denmark. He published a Faroese grammar and collected a number of Faroese ballads, rhymes, riddles, proverbs, and legends which were published in *Færøsk Anthologi,* along with one of the first Faroese-Danish dictionaries edited by Jakob Jakobsen. "Kópakonan", *Færøsk Anthologi*, Volume 1, 1891/'The Selkie', translated by Lindy Falk van Rooyen

Jakob Jakobsen (1864-1918) was from Tórshavn and the first Faroe Islander to be awarded a doctorate, training as a philologist. His doctoral thesis was about "Norn", the Norse language on the Shetland and Orkney Islands, published in *An Etymological Dictionary of the Norn language in Shetland* (1928). He aided Hammershaimb in his work on *Færøsk Anthologi*. He collected legends and folktales, which he published in *Færøsk Folkesagn og Æventyr* in 1898-1901. Jakobsen wrote the first literary monograph in Faroese, about the poet and rebel Poul Nolsøe. He developed a phonemic alternative to Hammershaimb's etymological orthography, but it was not accepted. Jakob Jakobsen also translated short stories by Guy de Maupassant into Faroese.

"Kálvur lítli", *Færøske folkesagn og eventyr* (1898-1901) 2009/'Little Kálvur', translated by Marita Thomsen.

Johanna Maria Skylv Hansen (1877-1974) was from Nólsoy on the Faroe Islands. For most of her adult life she was a lighthouse keeper and wife of a lighthouse keeper at various Faroese lighthouses, and only began to write when her children had grown up and moved out. Her writings describe life in old Faroese peasant society—the first about men's work at sea and in the mountains, later dealing with women's areas of work. The stories deal with women's preparations for marriage, though not the marriage itself, and about widowhood.

"Gomul søga", *Gamlar gøtur* II, 1967/'An Old Tale', translated by Lindy Falk van Rooyen

Regin í Líð (1871-1962) is the pen name used by **Rasmus Rasmussen**. He was from Miðvágur in Vágar. Rasmus Rasmussen was a teacher at the Faroese Teachers' School and one of the two founders of the Faroese Folk High School in 1899. He wrote the first Faroese novel *Bábelstornið* (1909), and published his first collection of short stories *Glámlýsi* in 1912. He also translated Pierre Loti's novel *Pêcheur d'Islande*. He also wrote a series of textbooks on nature, including *Faroese Flora*. Rasmussen was co-founder of the Faroese Fishing Union and editor of its official magazine.

"Rakul", *Glámlýsi,* 1912/'Rakul', translated by Marita Thomsen.

Sverre Patursson (1871-1960) was from Kirkjubø on Streymoy. Upon completing his schooling, he went to Vallekilde Folk High School in Denmark, and travelled to Norway where he became acquainted with the language movement and youth associations there. Back home in Kirkjubø he established a discussion club. Sverre Patursson was the Faroe Islands' first journalist, published the newspaper *Fuglaframi* (For the Good of Birds) 1898-1902. For a number of years, he was the Faroese correspondent for Ritzau and the Norwegian News Agency. Patursson's articles about nature and ornithology, his lyrical prose and stories are found in two anthologies published in 1935 and 1971.

"Ábal", *Fuglar og folk,* 1935/'Abel', translated by Lindy Falk van Rooyen

Andrea Reinert (1894-1941) was from Norðradalur and studied at the Tórshavn's Folk High School. She became a dressmaker, travelled to Copenhagen in the 1920s to study as a nurse, but did not complete her training. She had her own dressmaker's shop and married an engineer. She wrote poems for the literary journal *Varðin,* and the story "Dreymurin" was her contribution to a Faroese short story competition in Copenhagen in 1936. It was first published in 1949.

"Dreymurin", *Søgubókin*. 1949/'The Dream', translated by Lindy Falk van Rooyen.

Elsa við Á (1892-1975) is the pen name used by Petra Djurhuus. She was from Nólsoy. Together with her husband, the popular poet and teacher Hans Andrias Djurhuus, she worked for the establishment of the Faroese National Museum.

She wrote stories and translated plays by the Icelander Jóhann Sigurjónsson.

"Bekka", *Varðin*, vol. 23, 1944/'Bekka', translated by Lindy Falk van Rooyen.

Maria Mikkelsen (1877-1956) was from Tórshavn, but moved to Copenhagen at a young age, where she trained to be a registrar at the national archives. She was a central figure among Faroe Islanders in Copenhagen in association activities, including with the Faroese journals in Denmark, and offered authors on the Faroe Islands assistance with editing. In addition to her own writing she translated Norse and German literature into Faroese.

"Fyri fyrst", *Útiseti* (Exile), 1945/'For Now', translated by Marita Thomsen.

Heðin Brú (1901-1987) the pen name used by Hans Jacob Jacobsen, was from Skálavík on Sandoy. He went to Folk High School in Tórshavn, trained as an agronomist at the agricultural college in Copenhagen and worked as an agricultural advisor. The first of his six novels was published in 1930. His novels deal with the shift from the old agricultural society to a fishing society. He also published four short story collections, some poetry and his memoirs, in 1980. Heðin Brú translated a number of folktales, Shakespeare's *Hamlet*, Dostoevsky's *The Brothers Karamazov* from Danish. Along with William Heinesen and Martin Joensen, he is one of the great Faroese prose writers of the twentieth century.

"Krokið", *Búravnurin*, 1971/'*The Refuge*', translated by Lindy Falk van Rooyen.

Martin Joensen (1902-1966) was from Sandvík on Suðuroy. After attending the Folk High School and the teacher training college in Tórshavn he taught in several villages on Suðuroy. He wrote his first stories in the 1920s for the student teacher magazine and later for the Social-Democrat newspaper. His novels *Fiskimenn* (*The Fishers*, 1946), and *Tað lýsir á landi* (*It Shines Ashore*, 1950), are realistic and marked by social criticism. He also wrote fiction for children.
"Heimkomin", *Útrák*, 1949/'The Homecoming', translated by Lindy Falk van Rooyen.

Jørgen-Frantz Jacobsen (1900-1938) spent his early childhood in his native Faroe Islands, then went to High School and university in Denmark. He worked as a journalist for the newspaper *Politiken*, but in 1922 he developed tuberculosis which led to his early death. He worked to the very end, and while *Barbara* was his only novel, it was preceded by a work entitled *The Faroes, Nature and People*, which has the dual quality of being informative and a work of considerable beauty. Although written in Danish, his work is intensely Faroese. He left *Barbara* unfinished at his death and it was completed by his great friend William Heinesen. It has become one of the most successful novels in the Danish language and has been studied in Danish schools and turned into a film by Nils Malmrose in 1997. It has been widely translated and has been translated into English for Dedalus by Glyn Jones and published in 2013.
"Kundskabens Træ", *Den yderste kyst og andre essays*. Ed. Jógvan Isaksen, 1999/'The Tree of Knowledge', translated by Paul Russell Garrett.

William Heinesen (1900-1991) was born in Tórshavn, the son of a Danish mother and Faroese father, and was equally at home in both languages. Although he spent most of his life in the Faroe Islands he chose to write in Danish as he felt it offered him greater inventive freedom. Although internationally known as a poet and a novelist he made his living as an artist. His paintings range from large-scale murals in public buildings, through oil to pen sketches, caricatures and collages.

Dedalus has so far published six of his seven novels in translations by W. Glyn Jones: *The Black Cauldron*, *The Lost Musicians*, *Windswept Dawn*, *The Good Hope*, *Mother Pleiades* and *The Tower at the Edge of the World*. They range from social realism with elements of magic realism to his last lyrical elegiac novel *The Tower at the Edge of the World*. He also published six short story collections. He was awarded the Nordic Council Literature Prize in 1964 and is generally considered to be one of the greatest, if not the greatest, Scandinavian novelist of the twentieth century.

"Don Juan fra Tranhuset", 1970/'Don Juan of the Cod Liver Oil Factory', translated by Paul Russell Garrett.

Jens Pauli Heinesen (1932-2011) was from Sandavágur on Vágar and was the great Faroese-language prose author of the twentieth century. He trained to be a teacher in Copenhagen and published his first work, a short story collection in 1953 followed by his first novel in 1958. Art and the artist are important themes in his writing, which depict Faroese society, including fascist forces and the brutality of the political arena. In 1980-1892 he published his great artist's novel in seven volumes *ferð inn í eina óendaliga søgu* (*On a Journey into a Neverending Story*). His short stories, like the one included here, are often small, concentrated insights into contemporary society. Heinesen was awarded The Faroese Literature Prize four times as well as Tórshavn Council's M. A. Jacobsen Cultural Award.

"Rógv, sonurin, rógv!", *Aldurnar spæla á sandi*, 196/'Row, My Boy, Row', translated by Lindy Falk van Rooyen.

Oddvør Johansen (born 1941) is the daughter of a craftsman from Tórshavn. She trained as an organist at The Royal Danish Academy of Music and moved back to the Faroe Islands in 1987 and is the organist at Tórshavn Cathedral. Her first novel *Lívsins summar* (*The Summer of Life*) was published in 1982, and with her novels and short stories she has raised Faroese women's literature to rival the best work published in the Nordic region. She has received Tórshavn Council's literary prize, M. A. Jacobsen Literature Prize and Children's Culture Award.

"Niður við nakkanum", *Vencil* 14, 2013/'Heel!' translated by Marita Thomsen.

Hanus Kamban (born 1942) is the son of a teacher and spent his first years on the island of Skúvoy before moving to Tórshavn with his parents in 1956. He studied English and German in Copenhagen and is a trained nursing assistant. He published his first work, a non-fiction book in 1979, followed by his short story collection *Dóttir av Proteus* (*Proteus' Daughter*) in 1980. His translations, mostly from English, include Shakespeare's *Othello* and works by Graham Greene, Orson Welles, Ray Bradbury and James Joyce. The short story here is from the collection *Hotel Heyst* (*Hotel Autumn*) 1986.

He has received Tórshavn Council's M. A. Jacobsen awards for fiction and non-fiction, the Christian á Brekkumørk merit award, and has won several short story competitions.

"Hanarnir gala", *Hotel Autumn,* 1986/'The Cocks Are Crowing', translated by Lindy Falk van Rooyen.

Gunnar Hoydal (1941-2021) was the son of a politician from Tórshavn. He was a poet, novelist, short story writer, essayist and songwriter, including songs for his sister the singer Annika Hoydal. He was the city architect for Tórshavn Municipality. He published his first book in1982 and one of his three novels *Undir suðurstjørnum* (1991) was translated into English as, *Under Southern Stars* (2003). He was very active in various aspects of Faroese cultural life and a winner of Tórshavn Council's M. A. Jacobsen Cultural Award.

"Hjartasorg", *Av longum leiðum*, 1982/'Heartbreak', translated by Marita Thomsen.

Magnus Dam Jacobsen (1935-1978) was a fisherman, publisher and author from Tórshavn. He published his first poetry collection in 1975. His other works included a diary of his fishing trips to Greenland, two novels and short stories that were published posthumously in 1985. He wrote about men's experiences, feelings and relationships, stressing the importance of writing as close to the spoken language as possible.

"Seinasta útróðrarferðin", *Seinasta útróðrarferðin,* 1985/ 'The Last Fishing Trip', translated by Marita Thomsen.

Arnbjørn Danielsen (1947-1980) was from Tórshavn. He went to sea as a fisherman, received an MA in Nordic

Language Literature and Cinematography from Copenhagen University and for a short time was teacher at the secondary school in Tórshavn. He was a poet and short story writer, with his first poetry collection published in 1966. The short story included in this anthology comes from a collection he put together from fellow members of the commune where he was living. Danielsen was politically active, and was one of the founders of the Republican Party's youth division and during his student years was a frequent contributor to Faroese left-wing publications in Copenhagen.
"Á eini kaffistovu", *Roynd 1*, 1971/'At a Café', translated by Marita Thomsen.

Oddfríður Marni Rasmussen (born 1969) from Sandur on Sandoy is a schoolteacher and poet who studied at the author's school in Copenhagen. Since 1994, he has published thirteen poetry collections, two children's books, and the novel *Ikki fyrr enn tá* (2019), for which he won first prize in a novel competition. It was translated into Norwegian and Danish and nominated for the Nordic Council Literature Prize. Rasmussen was for some years the editor of the literary magazine *Vencil*, which published new and translated poetry. He has twice been awarded Tórshavn Municipality's M. A. Jacobsen Cultural Award.
"Ljósið í røddini", *Gráir týdningar* 2003/'Breath of Light', translated by Lindy Falk van Rooyen.

Carl Jóhan Jensen (born 1957) has a degree in Nordic philology and literature. He is a poet, novelist, translator and literary critic. His work was first published in 1977 and he is the author of five novels. His acclaimed *Ó-, søgur um djevulskap* (O, Tales of Devilry) was published in 2005. He was awarded Tórshavn Municipality's M. A. Jacobsen Cultural Award and has been nominated five times for the Nordic Council Literature Prize.

"Endurkoman", *Mentan og mentaskapur* 1999/'The Return', translated by Marita Thomsen.

Tóroddur Poulsen (born 1957) is a highly prolific poet writing at least one collection of poetry every year since his first collection in 1984. He has written two genre-defying hybrid works, of which *Reglur, eitt brotsverk* has been published in Swedish. He has been described as the Punk Poet of the Faroe Islands. As well as lyrical poetry and prose, Poulsen has published experimental music and is a graphic artist. He has received Tórshavn Council's M. A. Jacobsen Literary Award and has been nominated for the Nordic Council Literature Prize.

"Til tey ið halda seg skilja alt", Útvølir, 2008/'To Those Who Think They Know', translated by Lindy Falk van Rooyen.

Sólrún Michelsen (born 1948) published her first children's book in 1992. She writes poetry, short stories and novels. The popular *Nornan spinnur* (The Norn Spins) is a three-volume historical novel. She has been awarded Tórshavn Municipality's Literature Prize, Children's Book Award and M. A. Jacobsen Literature Prize, and has been nominated for the Nordic Council Literature Prize.

"Morgunfrúa", *Morgunfrúa*, 2018/'Marigold', translated by Marita Thomsen.

Marjun Syderbø Kjelnæs (born 1974) published her first short story collection in 2000. She has also written books for children and young adults, as well as novels, plays, poetry and a film script. She has won many literary awards, including the Thorvalds Poulsen av Steinum Award, Tórshavn Council's Children's Book Prize and the Nordic Children's Book Prize NFS in 2011. In 2015 she won the Bookseller's novel competition.

"Kópakonan", *Mjørki í heilum*, 2001/'The Seal Woman', translated by Lindy Falk van Rooyen.

Katrin Ottarsdóttir (born 1957) has written and directed a number of feature films. She published her first poetry collection *Eru koparrør í himmiríki* in 2012 (Danish edition 2016). She is also the author of three novels and short story collections. She was awarded Tórshavn Council's M. A. Jacobsen Literature Prize.

"Á upptøku". *Aftanáádrenn*, 2016/'On Location', translated by Lindy Falk van Rooyen.

Firouz Gaïni (born 1972) was born in Norway and grew up in the Faroe Islands with his Faroese mother and Iranian father. He is an academic, with a PhD in anthropology from the University of the Faroe Islands with his specialism being masculinity, children and young people's culture. His published works include short stories, essays and travel writing.

"Horvnir menn", *Horvnir menn*, 2011/'Disappearing Men', translated by Lindy Falk van Rooyen.

Lív Maria Róadóttir Jæger (born 1981) is from Tórshavn and has an MA in philosophy from Copenhagen University. Her first work was "Sjey stuttporsatekstir", seven short prose texts, 2013. The collection of poems Eg skrivi á vátt pappír (*I Write on Wet Paper*, 2020), saw her awarded the Torshavn Council's M. A. Jacobsen Cultural Award and a nomination for the Nordic Council Literature Prize in 2021. The collection has been published in Danish and French. *Gult myrkur* (2022) a co-production with the singer-songwriter Guðrið Hansdóttir.

Two of "Sjey stuttprosatekstir", *Vencil* 14, 2013/Extract: 'Seven Short Prose Pieces', translated by Marita Thomsen.

Annika Skaalum (born 1958) from Vágur on Suðuroy, trained as a gardener, has an MA in history and political science, and works as a secondary school teacher. She has written a number of short stories for the literary magazines *Vencil* and *Varðin.*

"Fennika", *Vencil* 15, 2015/'Fennel', translated by Marita Thomsen.

Malan Poulsen (born 1963) from Hov on Suðuroy is a secondary school teacher of Danish, Faroese and Cultural Understanding. She published her first poetry collection *Lát/ Sing* in 1988.

"*Kongabomm*", *Vencil* 19, 2018/'*Kongabomm*', translated by Marita Thomsen.

Trygvi Danielsen (born 1991) is a musician, poet and film director from Tórshavn. He published his second collection of poems, *Silvurbók* (*Silverbook*) in 2018. He has been awarded the Faroese Cultural Award for young artists, numerous music and film prizes, along with the Ebba Award for Literature in 2019.

"Væna lív, sum er mær givið", *The Absent Silver King*, 2013/'Beautiful Life I Have Been Given', translated by Marita Thomsen.

The Translators

Lindy Falk van Rooyen is a literary translator of Danish and Faroese fiction. She holds an LLM in Commercial Law from the University of Stellenbosch and an MA in English and Scandinavian Literature from the University of Hamburg. Her translations have appeared in *Blue Lyra Review*, *Asymptote* and *Lunch Ticket Magazine*. Book-length translations include *Transfer Window* by Maria Gerhardt (2019) and *What my Body Remembers by Agnete Friis* (2017). Falk van Rooyen was awarded a PEN Heim Translation Grant for *HOPE* by Danish author Mich Vraa in 2018, and a Faroese Arts Council Grant to translate *Óendaliga Vera/Infinitely Vera* by Marjun Syderbø Kjelnæs, one of the authors appearing in this anthology. Other current book-length projects include the true-crime novel, '*The Nurse*' (2022) by Kristian Corfixen, and the first two volumes in Michael Katz Krefeld's award-winning crime series, *Derailed* (Ravn #1) and *Missing* (Ravn #2), forthcoming in 2023 and 2024, respectively.

Marita Thomsen grew up in the Faroe Islands and lives her life in stories between cultures and languages. She has translated a wide range of Faroese fiction, poetry and plays into English, including the bilingual poetry volume *Myrking/Darkening* by Sissal Kampmann (2018) and the novel *On the Other Side is March* by Sólrun Michelsen (2023). She has translated Latin American and Faroese children's books for younger readers. Marita has also taught interpretation and translation in Peru and the UK. She is a member of the International Association of Conference Interpreters, AIIC, and works as a conference interpreter from Danish, Norwegian, Swedish, Spanish and French into English for various European and international institutions. Marita is also a mentor for the 2024 NCW Emerging Translator Mentorship. Her most recent translations are *Dead Men Dancing* (2023) by Jógvan Isaksen and *Sólgarðurin/The Suntrap* (2024) by Beinir Bergsson.

Paul Russell Garrett is a literary translator from Danish and Norwegian, with drama holding a particular interest for him. He has translated a dozen plays and heads the translation programme at Foreign Affairs theatre company in London. He has also translated a score of books, most recently Michael Strunge's punk poetry collection, *Speed of Life*. In 2020, his translation of Christina Hesselholdt's Vivian was longlisted for The Warwick Prize for Women in Translation. Paul is chair of the association of Danish-English Literary Translators (DELT), a founding member of the translator collective, The Starling Bureau, and a mentor for the 2023 NCW Emerging Translator Mentorship.

Contents

Contents

Contents

Contents

Introduction

by

Malan Marnersdóttir

The Faroe Islands are a self-governing country in the Danish realm situated in the middle of the North Atlantic Ocean.

From 1816 to 1940 the Faroes were a Danish County and Danish was the official language whereas people in the country spoke Faroese. After WWII the status as a Danish County could not continue. During the war no relations were possible between the Faroe Islands and Denmark because of the German occupation of Denmark and the resulting British occupation of the Faroes in order to prevent Germany from taking over these strategically important islands in the North Atlantic.

The Faroese self-governing status was created by the Home Rule Act of the Faroe Islands 1948. Many people still feel a lot of frustration because this law followed a referendum in 1946 that showed a majority in favour of total independence from Denmark, but the Danish government decided not to recognise the vote. Instead, the Danish authorities insisted on the continuation of the negotiations that led to the Act of 1948. These events have had a traumatic effect on Faroese politics.

However, preparations for independence had already been ongoing for a long time and one important element was to get Faroese to be the official language. In order to prove that Faroese was a language in its own right an orthography was created in 1846 that slowly came into use. Faroese students in Copenhagen started to write poems in Faroese in 1876 and the Faroese Association established in 1889 published newspapers in the Faroes in the 1890s.

The Faroese language was introduced in Faroese schools at the beginning of the 20th century, but did not have the same weight in terms of lessons and skills as Danish. In addition, in the period 1912-1938 teachers had to teach in Danish even during Faroese lessons—Faroese was allowed in classes for the youngest pupils. After 1938 Faroese and Danish have become parallel subjects on the curriculum in primary and lower secondary school.

There is a vast range of oral Faroese poetry going back to the Middle Ages consisting of heroic ballads and songs about faraway historic events. The comprised works about *Sigurd the Dragon Killer* and *Charlemagne* and other historic figures and they are still being sung today during the Faroese chain dance. These compositions are the oldest preserved Faroese poetry. They were collected with legends and other oral forms in the 18th and 19th centuries and provide the basis from which Faroese literature has developed.

The idea that the spoken language of the people created the identity of a nation was at the heart of the national movement in the Faroes in the late 19th century. The new poems written to existing, primarily Nordic melodies helped foster this sense of national identity. The new patriotic poems mapped the country by describing the Faroese landscapes and took on the role to define and describe the Faroe Islands and develop this growing national identity. The aim of the national association in the end of the 19th century to make Faroese the language of the Faroe Islands continued within the cultural discourse that urged people to express themselves in Faroese. However, due to the lack of Faroese literary tradition in the first decades of the 20th century meant that some Faroese poets wrote their first poems in Danish.

Literature was the main tool in the promotion of Faroese identity as it describes the Faroese landscape, life and thought. Also, the development of the Faroese language itself has been important, therefore "language purification" has been essential. The ambition has been to remove as many Danish words and concepts as possible and replace them with Faroese. However, today this struggle is more or less over, even though much popular literature and subtitles in films and TV-programmes are in Danish, English is about to overtake Danish in having the most influential role.

Repeated discussions about the internationally known Faroese authors who wrote in Danish, William Heinesen's and Jørgen-Frantz Jacobsen's role in Faroese literary history, led to their exclusion from the literary canon and to their books not being read in secondary school until their works were translated into Faroese in the 1970s.

Post World War II Faroese literature became monolingual with the generation of authors that started school in 1939 and published their first books in Faroese in the 1950s such as Jens Pauli Heinesen. A brief comparison of the number of novels published in two periods can be taken as an indicator of the development towards a monolingual literature in the Faroes: from the first novel in Faroese, which was published in 1909, to 1969, Faroese authors published forty-seven novels, thirty-two were in Danish and fifteen in Faroese. In contrast, between 1970 and 2005, out of sixty-nine novels only six were in Danish with sixty-three in Faroese. From a national and a purist linguistic point of view, monolingual high literature proves the success of the language struggle: now writers can concentrate on aesthetics and the development of literary genres in their own language, Faroese.

Today all official communication in the Faroes takes place in Faroese. However, Faroese culture is still bilingual or multilingual, but Faroese is the dominant language in the country as it has taken over in many areas where Danish was previously used. However, Danish is still dominant in the huge realm of popular culture, as for instance TV programmes and films in cinema are subtitled in Danish. Also, advanced school text books in school are often in Danish or English.

This anthology contains newly translated Faroese short prose texts from the end of the 19th century to the beginning of the 21st. The oldest texts are legends, oral narratives which have been written down. The other texts are works of fiction and short stories by authors who developed Faroese literature and created a modern Faroese fiction.

The Selkie

by

Venceslaus Ulricus Hammershaimb

translated by Lindy Falk van Rooyen

In the dawn of time seals were people who had transformed their shape and cast themselves into the sea. Once a year, on the Thirteenth Night, they shed their skins and became just like other human beings; they loved to dance all night in the pale moonlight which shone over the rocky shores, illuminating their caves.

Now, according to legend, a boy from the southern slopes of Mikladalur got wind that the seals would gather in the cave outside his village. So, on the Thirteenth Night, he stole down to the water's edge, determined to find out once and for all if what he had heard was true. Hiding behind a rock at the mouth of the cave, he waited till the sun disappeared below the horizon. At last he saw a host of seals swim in with the tide, and when they reached the shore they shed their skins; and yes, now they looked just like ordinary people.

The boy from Mikladalur was fascinated by these naked beings who danced in the moonlight, and as he watched from his hideout, one of the seals shed its coat and transformed into the most beautiful human being he had ever seen. He fell in love with her instantly. Now, whilst the seal girl was dancing in the moonlight, the boy snatched her seal skin from the rock where she had left it and crawled back under his rock. All night long the seal creatures danced before the cave, but at first light of dawn, they collected their skins and returned to the sea, except for the selkie whose skin had been stolen. She began to sob desperately because her skin was nowhere to be found on the rocky shore. At last, just before the sun broke the line of the horizon, a light sea breeze brought the familiar scent of her skin—which the boy from Mikladur had taken along with him—and she was compelled to follow it.

In words strange to her tongue, the selkie begged the boy to return her skin, but he would not listen, and when he made his tortuous way home through the gorge, it was all she could do to follow.

The boy inherited the farm and took the selkie for his wife. They lived together as any other married couple, except that the farmer had to take great care that his wife never found her seal skin; he locked it away in a chest, and always kept the key strapped to his belt.

Then one day, when the man was out fishing, his hand caught on his belt as he drew up the nets, and to his surprise, he found that the key was not where it was supposed to be. Realising that he must have left it behind, he broke down and cried bitterly. Wracked in sorrow, this is what he said: "Today I will lose my wife!"

As fast as he could, the farmer drew up his line, grabbed his oars and rowed back to shore. When he came home he discovered that his wife was gone, but their children were quietly sitting at the kitchen table, and to ensure that they would come to no harm on their own, she had snuffed out the fire in the hearth and locked away all the knives and sharp tools out of their reach.

Once the selkie had taken care of her children, she ran back through the gorge and down to the shore. On the rocks, she slipped back into her seal skin and threw herself into the sea. When her husband had been out fishing, she had found the key and unlocked the chest. The moment she saw her seal skin inside, the selkie could not hold herself back any longer; hence the expression: "...cannot control yourself any more than a seal who sees its skin".

No sooner had she cast herself into the sea than the male seal, who had been her mate before, came up to her side, and they swam into the deep together; all these years he had been waiting for the day that she would return.

In Mikladalur, whenever the children from the southern farm come down to the water's edge, you see the seals come up to the surface and linger by the shore; everyone believes that their mother is amongst them, watching over her children.

Many years passed without news of the man from sunnara garði and the selkie's children; not until the day he heard that the Mikladalur men were planning a seal hunt in the cave on the outskirts of his village.

The night before the hunt the selkie came to him in his dreams: she warned him not to kill the bull that would be at the mouth of the cave because this seal was her soulmate, and she warned him not to kill the two seal pups that the men would find at the very back of the cave because these were her sons; the selkie gave the Mikladalur man strict instructions and careful descriptions so he could recognise the patterns on their seal skins and spare their lives.

The farmer took no heed of the dream.

The next morning, he joined the hunt with the other Mikladalur men, and they clubbed all the seals in the cave to death.

The selkie's mate, as well as the paws and flippers of her pups were part of the farmer's bounty from the hunt. For dinner that evening, he cooked the head of the bull and limbs of the pups in a cauldron. When the meal was cooked and the table prepared, he heard a loud banging at his door, and then—in the guise of the ugliest troll alive—his selkie wife burst into the kitchen. In a furious rage she sniffed the air all around her, then she went to the stove and took a long sniff at the boiling cauldron: "Here is the snout of my husband, the hands of dear Hárek, the feet of my little Fríðrik. "Vengeance upon all the men of Mikladalur!" she roared. "May they drown at sea and plunge to their deaths from the mountains and bird cliffs till the dead can make a ring all around Kalsoy!" And without another word the hideous selkie troll stormed out of the door.

She was never seen in Mikladalur again.

The years went by and the tragic tidings from the north kept coming over the mountains: so many Mikladalur men were lost at sea; so many men who went onto the cliffs to tend sheep or catch birds simply plunged to their deaths. Before long, Mikladalur lost so many men that if the dead arose and joined their hands they could make a ring all the way around Kalsoy, just as the selkie had said.

Now on Sandoy, near the village of Skálavík, there is a seal cave known as Bláfellskút, and it is here that the legend of Mikladalur lives on: Tróndur and Niklas, father and son, were the first men to settle in this gorge, in the hamlet known as Hamri. Nikodemus, who was the son of Niklas, went to the cave near the village on the Thirteenth Night. He also stole the skin which a beautiful seal girl had left behind on a rock. He returned home with it, and the girl followed him (although some say that Nikodemus carried the girl over his shoulder). Whatever happened on the way home, the boy from Hamri was sure to hide the seal skin in a box which he kept locked with the key that was fastened inside the pocket of his trousers. But one day, when Nikodemus was out fishing he wore a different pair of trousers, and he forgot to take the key with him. And so in this way Nikodemus lost his wife: when he came home she had transformed into a seal and was standing on the edge of the cliff.

It is believed that in the village of Skálavík there are people who descend from selkies.

Little Kálvur

a traditonal oral account written down by
Jakob Jakobsen

translated by Marita Thomsen

Little Kálvur[1] was the last of the Catholic priests on Sandoy in the Faroe Isles. Terribly greedy by nature, he was a bloody-minded scornful man and tales of his character still abound.

The fields of Klettabøur[2] and Skarðsbøur[3] bordered on Kálvur's presbytery, Todnes. Whenever Kálvur passed through them on his way home to Todnes he was inconvenienced by the grazing cattle. This was not to his liking. So he set traps just inside the gate, leaving it open so as to lure the neighbouring cows into his field. Come morning when he peered out of the window, he had the thrill of seeing the herd ensnared right by the gate. Laughing at the success of his exploit, he went into the *roykstova*[4] and boasted to his farmhands, "The beasts of Bø are sprawled hoofs flailing inside the gate this morn!" The priest strutted up to the gate, looking to savour the sight of the trapped bovines, only to realise with horror that the fallen cattle were his own, and most were already dead. Little Kálvur cried at the spectacle. And those were both the first and the last tears he is said to have shed.

Kálvur had a stone storehouse built on an islet in Lake Sandsvatn, and there he kept meat and other foodstuffs. For ease of access, he had stepping stones put down leading from the spit in Todnes out to the islet. But his sons were bent on stealing their father's meat. One winter they braved the ice and tried to follow the stepping stones, but they must have lost their way. They came upon a thin patch and when the ice shattered beneath them they drowned, six in all—only the seventh son remained; never one to join in their rogue ways. When these tidings reached Todnes, Little Kálvur shed no tears (though his eyes did mist up, or so the story goes).

One year later Kálvur's farmhands had driven his flock down from Fjalshagi mountain field, Kálvur had gone to meet them at the sheepfold—it was the Klovarætt fold within the village walls under Hamri (near the ridge that links the lakes). As Kálvur was handling the sheep one of the farmhands, who bore a grudge against his master, swung the ram he was holding in the priest's direction and let go. The ram butted Kálvur in the chest and knocked him over, his arms and legs splayed. Kálvur got back on his feet without a word; but as he left the sheepfold, he said to the farmhand, "You shall be repaid with the choice cuts of Slavansdalur!"[5,6]

The following summer Kálvur's lad, Haraldur Kálvsson, went fowling with the ill-fated farmhand on the towering cliff known as *á Drangi*, where the pair descended the narrow ledges. On the day they were to be hauled up again, Kálvur could be seen pacing the cliff edge. Haraldur then said to the farmhand, "Today father is surely minded to repay you for the trick you played on him at the fold in autumn, the deed may soon be done. Swap clothes with me!" The farmhand did as he was told, and Haraldur tied himself to the rope first. When the son had made it far enough that Kálvur thought he recognised the farmhand by his garb, he pulled out a sharpened axe, which he had concealed under his mantle, peered over the edge and readied to cut the line. Haraldur, who had his eyes on him, called out at that moment, "Swing if you will! I am your son still." Kálvur recognised his son's voice and hid the axe. But such was Haraldur's fury, that once he had made it up unscathed and freed himself from the rope, he gave his father a good beating. And so the farmhand made the ascent unharmed never to return to Kálvur's farm.

Árni lived in Nes north of Hersá. One day Kálvur sought him out, and asked him to come and catch shag chicks in the scree below Árnaberg. They travelled there by boat, but no sooner had Árni stepped ashore than Kálvur rowed back out and left him stranded. The scree was not passable in those times, though the crashing waves have since cleared many a boulder and today a path leads back to the village. Árni drew his last breath among those rocks, and Kálvur took his possessions. To this day the Árnatoft ruins[7] mark his lost dwelling.

After their father's death, Árni's children would stalk the landing, begging for fish. One day the Todnes boat returned from a fishing trip—Rasmus Kálvsson was the foreman. Kálvur came and instructed the crew to carry the fish to his stone store; he told Árni's children to climb into the boat, moored at the landing, and get themselves a little bait. As they sat in the boat, Kálvur came down and pushed it out to sea. Rasmus Kálvsson heard their cries and got ready to go after them in another boat; but it was stormy, the wind blew them offshore, and it was a long way to go to drag a boat from the boathouse. Thus delayed he arrived too late to save them. He watched as the boat carrying them drifted towards Árnaberg and shattered in the surf. But Kálvur dared not show himself for two days, he feared his son's retribution so.

One day a housemaid of Kálvur's was kneading malted dough for *drýlur*[8] loaves. She had taken a little bit off and was baking a loaf for herself. Kálvur came through the door, saw what she was up to and slipped out again. Moments later he returned (surely it would be baked by now, he thought) and in that instant the maid took out the scorching hot malt bread and hid it in her bosom. Kálvur noticed as much, but pretended not to. He ordered her to follow him immediately and to carry him across the river (this was in Sandur at Náðinsgarður[9]). Unsuspecting, she did his bidding. When they had reached the river—he hurried there—she let him ride piggyback to ferry him across. He crossed his hands where he suspected the loaf was hidden and pressed with all his might. She cried out, and he asked what made her squeal so. In that moment of peril she confessed her deed. The hot bread seared her chest and inflicted a fatal injury.

There was bad blood between Kálvur and his daughter-in-law (Haraldur's wife). One morning when her husband was out fishing, the old man enquired about the weather. She replied, "'tis glorious today; gold crunches underfoot!" It was the frost she was referring to. "Mock you me, and I shall scorn thee," said Kálvur, irate that she made fun of him. Then he bade the Todnes housemaids light a great fire north of the presbytery. He intended to burn her alive. But the housemaids tasked with kindling did so only grudgingly, and they gathered soil, manure and all manner of rubbish for the fire, so rather than ignite it would smoke excessively; and the plumes spiralled so high that they could be seen from sea. Kálvur's son was fishing the grounds known as Grynnan, found just off the Salthøvdi headland and the tip of Skúgvoy Island. The fumes billowing over Vørðan Mountain made him ill at ease, "The old man is surely up to something today!" he said and told the others to row ashore. He spurred them on, and all as one they pressed their feet against the thwarts and lengthened their strokes. They made landfall by the Grótvík scree, and the very moment Kálvur and his men were undressing Haraldur's wife to throw her into the flames, Haraldur arrived with his crew and flogged his father with a leather strap. And so she was saved. "Were you not my father, you'd be the one on the pyre," he said to Kálvur.

One time Kálvur complained that the black pudding he was served by the lady of Húsavík, when he lodged with her, was too lean. The next time he visited Húsavík, she placed before him a piece of horse tripe, which she had filled with leaf tallow. Then Kálvur quipped, "Moderate sausage is better fare, whether it be of cow or mare."

Many years after Kálvur's death Reverend Klæmint, then priest in Sandoy, strolls one evening through the undir Skarði quarter in Sandur village. He spots three men heading north along the church path, one in clergyman's robes is leading the way. The other two resemble no natural people of any kin. Klæmint enquires who they are and where they hail from. The one robed as a priest replies, "I am Little Kálvur, former priest of Sandoy, and the other two are devils from hell that follow me." "Where do you intend to go?" Reverend Klæmint asks. "We are headed for undir Skarði, men there have oft called on us in card games, and now we have come to find them."

"Wait for me here a while, I must hasten home!" the priest

replies, hurries home and dons his cassock. They wait for his return, and then all proceed together. Undir Skarði men are amusing themselves with card games, their play peppered with foul oaths and curses. A stranger has joined the fray, winning hand after hand. A player drops a card under the table, bends down to pick it up and notices that there is neither rhyme nor reason to the stranger's nether parts. The priest makes his entrance, admonishes the card players, takes the deck, throws it in the fire, and swears that for as long as he is priest in Sandoy, undir Skarði shall never see another card game. Then he bores a hole in the wall and casts the devil out through it. People wail or swoon, but the priest proclaims the Lord's peace and blessing upon them and then departs to find the trio waiting for him outside the door.

"You will follow me to the place where I met you," he commands and they follow. "Now stop," the priest commands, and begins to recite a prayer and drives the demons down through the rock. At first with ease. But Kálvur remains, with his eyebrows still above ground, he's reluctant to go, and the priest's strength is waning. Klæmint lifts his gaze heavenward and calls for the Lord's help; with that Kálvur starts sinking below the flat rock. As he vanishes the priest bangs his heel on Kálvur's head and commands him to return to hell from whence he came. To this day that heel mark is preserved in the stone. But when the priest returned home he was drenched, as though he had been hauled from the sea.

Little Kálvur grew bored of the Faroe Isles. He heard rumour that the king's chaplain was dead, so he journeyed to Denmark meaning to seek this position. But he was too late, a replacement had already been found. Kálvur then posed as a barber, and the King took him on. One day as he was shaving the King, his Majesty told Kálvur that if he bled him, he would pay with his life. The spot yet untrimmed was under the royal chin. As Kálvur shaves the Adam's apple he asks the King: "Who now rules the land?"

"Thee and we," replies the Monarch.

"Had you not spoken thus, I would have been minded to relieve you of your apple," Kálvur exclaims.

"We thought you might, had we replied otherwise," the King retorts. And with this exchange Little Kálvur was arrested and sentenced to death.

An Old Tale

by

Jóhanna Maria Skylv Hansen

translated by Lindy Falk van Rooyen

Once upon a time a pretty girl was engaged to a lad who was studying to be a pastor. He wished to marry her just as soon as he had taken his oath. But the girl was afraid of bearing children. And she had never confessed her fears to her betrothed.

By and by, the pastor became impatient, and one day when the girl was walking through the village she met an old woman in the street: “Why such a sour face, my girl? You ought to be glad that your husband-to-be has found a suitable post, so that you can marry soon.”

The girl was so unhappy she decided to confide in the old woman.

“I see,” said the old woman. “Follow me to the grinding mill.”

“Turn the handle three times against the grain,” she explained. “The number of cracks you hear will be the number of children you will be spared.”

When the girl returned from the mill the old woman told her: “Now you need not delay your marriage.” And the next time the pastor asked, she no longer made any protests, and soon after they walked down the aisle in church.

The girl and her pastor were happy as only young married couples can be; the pastor's wife was cheerful and carefree, and nothing and no one ever caused her any pain.

Many years passed, but the marriage produced no children.

Then, one beautiful summer's day, the couple were out walking together in the glorious sunshine. But the girl kept her distance, and the pastor noticed that his wife seemed troubled, so he asked her: "What have you done?"

She said that she was sure she had done no wrong. But then she recalled the day in the grinding mill and decided to tell her husband about the old woman.

"You will pay a harsh penalty for this," her husband said. "How many cracks did you hear?"

"Three."

"Then you shall spend three nights in the church on your own. It need not be three nights in a row, but as from now until the penalty is paid, you shall not utter a word to anyone."

The pastor took his wife to the church himself and opened the door for her.

The wife was terrified to be alone in the church, and in the middle of the night she was visited by a big, white ram that molested her, over and over. And this is what he said to her: "Were it not for you, I would have been a respected man in this land today."

The next morning when the pastor came to collect his wife he found her more dead than alive, and he took her home with him. His wife crawled into bed immediately, and after a few days rest she began to recover a little.

So her husband took her back to the church to do a second night's penance. This time she knew what awaited her, and sure enough, in the middle of the night, she was visited by a large, black ram that had a white collar around its neck. Also the black ram molested her brutally, and he reproached her severely: “If it weren’t for your wicked deed, I would have been a bishop by now.” And the next morning when the pastor came to collect his wife, she was in a similarly frightful state.

Then came the third night. This time, a crippled girl paid the pastor’s wife a visit. The girl caressed the wife’s cheek and said she need not have any remorse, for had she been allowed to be born, her life would have been a misery.

At last the day came when the wife could tell the pastor what had happened in the church.

First she told her husband about the crippled girl. Then she told him about the white ram.

The pastor was deeply distressed, but when his wife confessed what had happened with the black ram, he flew into a rage. He pointed to her shoes standing by the bed, and this is what he said to her: “Not till the day that roses and lilies grow out of your shoes will you be shown any mercy,” he vowed.

Then the pastor stormed out and slammed the door behind him.

He returned a little while later and found his wife stone cold dead.

But tall roses and lilies had grown out of her shoes by the bed.

Rakul

by

Regin í Líð

translated by Marita Thomsen

I

Klipfish under the icy glint of tiny salt crystals lay fanned out to dry on barren coastal rock swaddled in the sun's embrace. The air was saturated with heat and not a breeze would stir it, so it quivered and clung to the shore.

All living beings yearned for rest, only a puppy snapped at a hen scraping in an ash heap; but when the canine saw that the fowl in its zeal paid no heed to its yapping, it too had a lie-down in the warm slags, and a long lazy yawn signalled that the bedding was to its liking.

The merchant had long since gone for his lunch; noon had passed and he had yet to return.

The fish were laid out, every last one, so what were the fish women to do other than sit and wait.

Though before they sat down, they had laid out a little stack while bickering furiously about whether the merchant before leaving had told them to leave the skin or the flesh facing up; in the end they had turned the fish upwards.

Now they were letting exhaustion melt away, hardly bothering to part their lips. The older ones, who claimed to have experienced the world, slumped, elbows on knees, and pulled their headscarf forward across their brow with both hands to create a little cover from the sun.

The younger ones, as yet unaware of what the world held in store for spinsters and housewives in a Faroese village, tried to start a chat about last Sunday night at the dance when all those trawler men had been there. Though this was one of the weightiest topics one could think of, the words withered on their lips in the stifling heat.

In the end some sat and others stretched out on the ground letting the sun bake them at its whim.

Below the road, a rope's length from the others, stood a brunette, her scarf had slipped down revealing two thick braids, and a keen eye would have noted a comely white neck through the short hairs at its nape so delicately curled between the pleats.

An abrupt dip in the terrain below the road concealed her to her shoulders; but had she appeared in full, it would only have been in her favour, as she was both well built and beautiful. Her gaze followed the bay out to sea. It was as if she had been waiting for an arrival to glide into view.

Though there was nothing to do, a commotion rippled through the women lounging in the sun, when the merchant reappeared from his lunch.

Osvaldur (such was his name) was not young, no, he would probably be more aptly described as old, certainly well past forty; but he was of the ageless sort, fresh until they run to seed overnight.

His had been a bold manly face and an agile body, but Osvaldur's appearance betrayed that he had not rejected any of the pleasures life can offer a real man, who needs not count every shilling that leaves his hand.

Now, after an enjoyable mealtime, he felt vitality rush to each fingertip, and so he strutted down swinging his walking stick. Osvaldur had never been a man of many words in the morning, but after his food he was given to chitchat and could not be accused of weighing on a gold scale every word addressed to his workers.

Osvaldur did, however, always deploy sufficient jest to avoid dislike.

Fish drying was a task he oversaw in person for two good reasons: he wanted his fish to be better than anyone else's, as this made for a good reputation and bags of money. Plus, he gladly kept an eye on the girls himself, because, second to cold cash, he considered pretty girls among the greatest treasures the world holds; and he was not entirely devoid of prowess, when it came to making acquaintances with the weaker sex. The calamity was that he would soon have enjoyed everything there was to sample in this village. He did, however, harbour one long-held desire, and that was to get his hands on Rakul, Niklas' daughter, she was the most delicious morsel he had ever seen. Osvaldur often pondered how he would make it happen. It would be easy enough for him to persuade Niklas, if that should prove necessary.

Rakul was the girl standing below the road; and she was not unaware of Osvaldur's desire, although he had yet to make any advances.

Young women are mostly very shrewd in such matters, so they are rarely caught off guard; still, they are more often won over by a bold and unexpected approach than by patience.

This was as known to Osvaldur as anyone, but he dared not manoeuvre suddenly, lest he frighten her away, as he suspected she was made of better material than ordinary fish girls; and then Rakul also had a firm suitor, but this could both hamper and assist him. At any rate, Osvaldur had promised himself to proceed steadily, he wanted this conquest.

Rakul spotted him making his way down, and she would dearly have liked to get back up to the others; but the road was so high that she would have to crawl up. And he was now so near that he could easily be by her side before she could get upright again, and she would not be seen crawling at his feet, so she stayed where she was.

As Osvaldur strolled past her, she felt his eyes on her neck and felt the light touch, it was no accident on his part, of his stick against her skirt.

The other girls were all watching them and whispering to each other.

Whether Osvaldur suspected that they sensed what he was thinking or not, he pivoted on his heel, a move that brought his eyes to the fish laid out that morning.

"Oh, the devil take the lot of you, I told you to leave the skin up on the little stack, and you have bloody well gone and done the exact opposite. Will you hurry the hell up and turn every tail!" He swung his stick violently as he lectured them.

They just gawked, they were so used to these tirades that he sounded like the politest of courtiers.

When he paused and pointed with his stick they all, including Rakul who had now made it back up, went about turning the fish.

II

A light westerly breeze sighed across Iceland's eastern shores, Austurland.

Beyond the Langanes Peninsula the sea was dotted with rocking fishing ships. Rising on each crest the vessels floated, a picture of endless patience.

Dreamy tranquillity suffused the surface, but the deep seethed with life, there fish travelled in great shoals from line to line judging the bait, sniffing warily at hooks. Now and then one got too close and was caught, but it made no difference to the multitude.

Out here shoulder to shoulder on adjacent decks stood the cream of Faroe youth waiting for the fish to bite.

The distant horizon was festooned with mountaintops and glaciers; it was the ancient saga island with all its intellectual treasures and old memories.

There it rested in its sense of self-worth, knowing it was the bosom from which all the Nordic nations had drawn nourishment for their cultural life.

Such a sight would have warmed the cockles of the most pitiable Icelander's heart, and every man of culture would celebrate it. The men on the fishing vessels saw nothing but russet mountains known to spew ash clouds seawards on a whim; they also knew that along the shores of that land lived a people, whom they, Faroemen, had taught how to fish along with other good customs. Oh, and up in the valleys feeble wretches without a krone to their name.

*

Silhouetted against the main sail stood a capable youngster. His face had a melancholy air as he stood hauling the handline back and forth, with such force that the grooved wooden block carrying the line across the gunwale wobbled. There was little bite, so the crew frequently abandoned lines to go below deck. He was content standing there, or at least he seemed to be, and he was working up a little pile of fish.

Steadfast and unhurried, much in the same way as he pulled up the handline when a fish bit, his thoughts were working and it was not cod he was pondering.

He had no interest in this, though he worked the line so diligently, but the regular seesaw back and forth seemed perfectly suited to his musings.

Were he rich. Had he two thousand, ah yes, then life would be sunny.

He thought this with such ardour that he could picture stacks of gold skillings piled high. A sight he had glimpsed only once when the shipowner was counting out money at his counter.

Alas, this grinding work just led into a void.

He was stuck. Oh the despair!

Were he rich, ah yes, then life would be sunny.

Every time his thoughts had gone around once, they restarted the circle. And each time he heaved a fish up on deck, he sighed, "Huff! huff! it's all the same."

One time he hauled in four in one go, and when he looked set to lose one, the captain came forward to his aid.

"That's quite the catch Pætur. My word," the captain remarked. Pætur just sighed, "Huff! huff! It's all the same."

"All the same if the fishing is good or the fishing is poor, Pætur? Bloody hell!"

"Well, where does it go? For years I've caught plenty, and still I haven't even enough for birch bark to keep my old mamma dry in her shack back in the Faroes!"

"Ah, well, Pætur, you shouldn't have signed that paper!"

"Huh! That devil, God forgive me! Osvaldur, the shipowner, threatened to sue me, what was I to do?"

The captain shrugged, "Pfff!"

With conditions looking right for a good haul, the captain bellowed down the hatch at the shirkers to get themselves back on deck.

*

Pætur was Rakuls' suitor. His father had passed away when he was a boy, squalor became a long-term companion, as the children were many and all sickly. Eventually death had the decency to take the weakest pair. Now only Pætur was left with his mother, two sisters had married and left home and one was in service.

In such circumstances it was no surprise if the man fared badly; but everyone was still shocked the day word came that the widow, upon the husband's death, had been sent a bill of 1600 kroner from the merchant Osvaldur. Many held that it was not right, but the widow could make neither heads nor tails of it, and what option did she have other than to accept the merchant's record. He did not seem unreasonable either, because he let her continue to buy on credit from the store as before.

As soon as Pætur was grown enough he signed on with Osvaldur's ship, but what he could bring home made no dent in the debt, which always seemed to grow. And then one year when he returned, the shipowner called him in to have a private conversation. When he came back out, he had signed a deed wherein he acknowledged owing a large sum, over 1600 kroner, to the merchant Osvaldur, and on this he had to pay six per cent interest per annum.

Pætur only later realised the yoke he had strapped across his own shoulders, and he could make no sense of why the merchant Osvaldur wanted to bind him like this.

His understanding did not venture beyond sensing this as a burden he had inherited, along with poverty, from his parents.

Since childhood Pætur and Rakul had been in love. She was a blossom so fresh and so pure that he was far from capable of fully appreciating her womanly virtues; but he loved her, and he yearned to be rich for her sake. Rakul was the fount of his joy and his despair, ever since he had broached with her father, Niklas, the topic of marriage.

Though Niklas was by no measure rich, and so not in a position to consider Rakul too good for Pætur, he still snapped that the suitor would have none of Rakul until the debt was repaid and he had built them a new house.

Niklas said that he was not minded to let his daughter live her days in that hovel of his.

Pætur had not yet truly taken the yoke of poverty and debt to heart, but this exchange left him mired in a gloom he could not escape, except in his dreams, both asleep and awake.

III

Summer went and autumn came. The ships returned from Iceland and a new life began in the villages.

Fun and games, a dance every Sunday eve and often midweek too. The young folk travelled the land to visit each other and make merry. Now was the time to take pleasure after the toil and drudgery over all the summer. Pætur did as the others, but it all seemed hopeless to him, even when Rakul and he were together and she rested her head on his chest like a caress and he took the kisses she gave—even then he despaired feeling no thrill at what many a rich man would have given his fortune to possess.

He could dream better when he was on his own. Rakul was more precious to him when she wasn't too near.

Returning after such nights to his hovel, where rain had dissolved the earthen floor, the bedclothes were sodden and humidity pearled the walls, then every hope sank so low that he long lay sleepless, feeling oh so empty, his brain a void, until eventually dreams revisited and his thoughts started trudging that little circle.

People were beginning to think that Pætur might not be in his right mind the way he behaved that winter, and there were times when his thoughts spun so quickly that he really was in danger of forcing them to stop.

Were I rich then life would be sunny! And then he would see that big heap of money, so vividly that it was blinding, then Rakul and himself in a new house; but then it all shattered in despair and started over again: were I rich…!

As winter set in, relations also cooled between Rakul and Pætur. Rakul was fiery and warm-blooded, she demanded true passion like she used to find in Pætur, but now! Now he was as glacial as his hovel when even the embers went out.

By the time spring came around neither of them knew whether there was something or nothing between them, and in that state Pætur set out to sea. He went, though he had often calculated that it was no use. The debt would never be repaid with what he earned as a seaman, and he was not about to study to be a captain. No, he was born to be an underdog. Still he went and if he should explain why, it was probably because the sea was the best place he knew to be and to dream. Pætur was a capable young man and did everything effortlessly, so he rarely had words with anyone.

There was one person who relished Pætur's servitude, and he was the merchant Osvaldur; not that he wished Pætur ill, far from it, but he had long since executed his plan to get Rakul, and now that the tables had turned he would be mad not to strike while the iron was hot.

Who knew whether Pætur by some chance would wake up and cast off his shackles, popular education was all the rage now, and then all would be lost.

Osvaldur was not unfair either, when his whims were satisfied. No, he was a charitable man, so they said. It was also his genuine intention that Pætur should want for nothing, once he, Osvaldur, had his fill.

IV

One early summer evening the fish workers thronged into the general store for their daily pay.

The girls had to wait, because the women needed to do their shopping. The store was full of people, so the clerks were in full swing selling provisions, while the merchant paid out wages.

Rakul stood in the doorway without jostling, so she wound up last. The others left as they got their pay, and in the end only Rakul and two other girls were left inside.

When they too have their money, the merchant tells her in a quiet tone to please wait, there is something she is to bring home to her father, she may wait in the 'bureau'.

It is closing time and the clerks are readying to leave. The lingering pair wink at each other. They have both visited the 'bureau' in their time, and they know what it means. But, God knows there has to be a first time, and they have no complaints. And should misfortune strike, well, then the merchant was not the man, who had to penny-pinch in hushing matters up.

Rakul was not afraid, but she was apprehensive about entering. Still, she went when she saw that the girls stayed put, pretending they wanted to buy something, even though the sales clerks had gone by now. When Rakul crossed the threshold the two girls left the shop, and she did not hear the merchant locking the front door behind them.

*

It had been a stifling hot summers' day, one of the rare ones in these latitudes, and it was still muggy by evening.

The breeze was warm and soft, caressing the sea which mostly remained stock still, the air was like treacle in the lungs.

Below the landing a flock of eiders bobbed, most were hens though there were a few drakes about. They busied themselves diving to the seabed, though there was not much food to be had here.

A bulky drake had long displayed his affection for a hen by swimming to her side and placing his beak across her back up by the neck. It was obvious what he wanted, but she did not want him, she was fond of another drake, who was away tonight.

This plump drake grew more and more insistent, and tried every trick to lure her away from the others; he knew that away from the flock his force would let him conquer. He succeeded in the end. The eider tried with all her might to turn this way and that and make it back to the others, but it was impossible. All she could do was swim away. Out into the fjord she went her breast parting the waters rippling to both sides, but the drake was right on her tail. Again and again he buried his beak so deep in her shoulders that she nearly fainted; she dived, but he was there every time she re-emerged. She felt her strength wane, and she would no doubt have given up had not something big and black come between them and an almighty thump hammered the drake's beak.

The big black object was a trawler that sailed into the bay and cast anchor. It arrived with the crew of a Faroese fishing vessel, which it had found drifting, near-sunk, at sea. Another ship had collided with it in the night and fled.

The lost ship was precisely the one Pætur was on.

When the crew came ashore they were required to meet with the district administrator without delay, but word had to be sent to the merchant first, and Pætur had been entrusted with the message.

When he reached Osvaldur's store, Pætur saw that the basement door was open, so the merchant had to be there, though it was past eleven. He also thought he could hear something and went to the shop door, it was locked.

Was someone shouting?

Yes! The cries grew louder: "Leave me be, I said!"

Pætur felt his blood congeal, it was Rakul's voice he heard. She was angry.

He realised what was going on. Osvaldur, that dirty bastard who held him down in poverty, wanted to steal his girl too.

An emotion, it had to be rage, he had never felt before came over him. He felt capable of tearing the house down to come to her aid, and rammed his seaboot against the wood, but the front door was so strong that it made not the slightest difference.

Fortunately the basement door came to his mind, and this lumbering boy made it into the basement like a tomcat, set his shoulder against the trapdoor to the shop, and lifted it with such force that he toppled a beer barrel that was weighing it down.

All at once he was at the bureau door. It was locked but no match for his seaboot, the door shattered inwards as if it were nothing but storeroom slats.

Pætur darkened the doorway, crimson cheeked and fists clenched, but the sight of Rakul in the locked room with

Osvaldur enraged him further.

Many a time later in life Pætur would reflect on this moment, never understanding how he did not lay his hands on the merchant and end him.

Perhaps he did not think he had such a claim to Rakul, given that they parted so coldly. Or did he in that instant glimpse an opening through which he could steal away from misery and bondage? In any case, Pætur stood still.

Osvaldur turned once towards him intending to say something, but fear bridled his tongue when he took in the bulging seaman's fists and his wild expression.

Pætur remained still for a long time, as if reluctant to move for fear of sealing Osvaldur's fate.

Only when he appeared calmer, did Osvaldur dare approach the door to get out; at that point Pætur grabbed him by the shirt and told him that he would stay here now, as it was time to settle their accounts.

Osvaldur went over to the window and saw the captain and crew of his ship standing in the road. His eyes scanned the bay, but the only ship he could find was a trawler.

Then Pætur recalled his errand and relayed in short what had occurred.

Rakul was now by Pætur's side—she gazed at him, and he understood her instantly. All was well again between them.

*

What was decided in the bureau between the three of them, nobody would know.

In the autumn Rakul and Pætur married and moved into

a house built that very summer. Meanwhile, to everyone's astonishment, age tightened its vice on the merchant Osvaldur overnight.

Abel

by

Sverre Patursson

translated by Lindy Falk van Rooyen

They were young and healthy and oblivious to anything other than being happy together till the end of their days.

But before long, when a man and his bride settled in a remote village where work was scarce, clouds began to gather and want and worry knocked at their door. It was as if they wished to challenge their fate because the less food there was to go around, the more children they brought into this sinful world.

Abel was the fifth child to arrive. By the time he was born, his mother, who had been brimming with the beauty of youth when she got married, was already wilted, pale and ravaged by constant hard work. Abel should have been their youngest child, or perhaps he shouldn't have been at all, because their dinner-time broth was thinner for every child that was born. Nor did it help that their fifth offspring was so 'unusual'. Even so, the number of children in their household increased at regular intervals—just as regular as humanly possible—till Abel received no less than eight more siblings.

With every new mouth to feed the want under their roof increased; their clothing became more threadbare, their mother increasingly hollow-cheeked, the number of words uttered by their father fewer and further between.

By the time Abel was nine years old he had found a place to spend his days in a cleft of the rock face high up behind their house. From here, he could watch the villagers passing below. But most of all, he could not tear his eyes from the clouds which hurtled over the mountain peaks—and the ocean which was alive with neverending waves crashing against the shore and ships which sailed in and out of the fjords.

He was well hidden in the cleft. Indeed, only his head stuck out of the top, and should anyone come past, he could duck out of sight. Although, once 'the danger' had passed, he would peek out again.

Whenever a thunderstorm blew in you could be sure to see Abel on the precipice. Rumbling through the north-facing cliffs, the sound of thunder roared like a stone avalanche, striking terror into the hearts of the villagers. But the boy did not leave his rock. Like a latter-day prophet of the Old Testament, Abel stood tall on the ledge, facing the howling wind with outstretched arms, staring wide-eyed into the storm, waiting to see if this was the day that the world would burst into flames upon the arrival of Judgement Day: his mother, who was a God-fearing woman, had told him that, one day, the world would go under in a roaring thunderstorm. *Why should that day not be sooner, rather than later?* thought Abel.

Sometimes, when Abel was standing at his post with his hair flying in the wind, vicious convulsions would make him hunch over and curl up, as if he were a thread of yarn suddenly furled into a ball. And then, with his clenched fists beating against his forehead, Abel would start to babble in strange tongues that no one else could understood, but the villagers believed that his words foretold the terrible things which would befall them in the future.

After his confirmation Abel was taken into the home of a farmer and pastor that owned land on the northern coast of Esturoy.

He was an overbearing man, the pastor, but he let the boy be with *The Lord's Prayer*; it was the only thing he succeeded in drumming into him, despite all efforts to the contrary. It was not for lack of trying on Abel's behalf, because from an early age Abel had always had a fondness for pondering the world which existed beyond the one that everyone else knew. It was true that he could rattle off the *Our Father* without taking a breath, but apart from that, he understood little of whatever the pastor tried to teach him. Nor was it for lack of respect for the man; in fact, Abel was in awe of this pastor from Denmark who had come all this way to teach them his language. But the boy could simply not contain himself when his classmate, Haraldur, repeated those silly words after the pastor; he looked ridiculous when he tried to be all hoity-toity.

The day he arrived at the farmer pastor's door, Abel had little luggage with him: in his hands he held a single bundle that was wrapped in his long-sleeved shirt.

The farmer asked for his name.

"I don't know," said Abel.

"Surely you must know your own name, my boy."

"I think so."

"Are you not 'Abel'?"

"I think so."

At first, this was all you could get out of him.

As I mentioned before, everyone knew that his mother had once been a beautiful woman in her youth. But his mother was also a proud woman, who tried to hide the poverty of her family from the other villagers, and her children had been given strict instructions to reply with the words: 'I don't know,' to any questions they were asked. Her children knew that if they did not do as they were told—and she found out—there would be hell to pay.

The dread of disobeying his mother had left deep scars on Abel's mind. If anyone asked him a question, anything at all, he would simply reply with the words: 'I don't know.' Just to be on the safe side. And no manner of interrogation or casual conversation with the villagers could coax anything other than 'I don't know' or 'I think so' from his mouth.

Abel's shyness stayed with him for many years. But when he grew older and realised that his mother was far, far away, he was no longer afraid that she would throttle him if he said too much. Besides, fresh produce was a rare commodity in her kitchen, and when the farmer's wife put fresh milk, warm bread and dried mutton on the table his eyes nearly popped out of his head.

One thing that boy could do was eat till he was stuffed to the gills.

The only thing that could get Abel almost as excited as wholesome farm food was the misfortune or imminent death of others; news of this kind usually sent him into the mountains, muttering and clucking to himself as he pondered their fate all day long. And if he heard that someone on the farm had been gravely injured, for example, a broad grin would spread over his face; this usually annoyed the hell out of the wretched person concerned. But people were exasperated rather than angered by Abel's behaviour, because everyone knew that the boy didn't have a malicious bone in his body. And when you asked him why he was laughing, the answer was always: 'I don't know.'

Not long after Abel was taken in by the pastor on Esturoy, his father died, so Abel went home for the funeral; it was expected that he would join the funeral procession, just behind his mother and his siblings in the entourage.

Two teams of pallbearers—six and six—were appointed to carry the coffin over the mountain in turns, till they reached the graveyard in the neighbouring village on the other side.

Abel's heart went out to his dear father; always so grave and silent, now he lay in a black coffin that six men were jostling along a rocky cattle track, even if he hardly weighed a feather, the poor man.

Once the first ridge had been breached, the pallbearers put the coffin down, and Abel sneaked up to his dad. Without moving a muscle, he stared at the coffin; those who noticed knew that the boy was now lost in thought because a tremor ran through the length of his body, just like it did when he fled to the cliffs in a thunderstorm.

When the shaking subsided Abel went to his mother, who had sat down on a large rock to rest for a moment. She was crying. Abel looked round at the other people; yes, they also had serious expressions on their faces. Abel did his best to restrain himself, but it was intolerable when he saw that Theodore—who teased him relentlessly at every opportunity—was just as snotty and tearful as everybody else. It was all Abel could do to sneak behind a stack of peat cuttings, where he burst into a violent fit of laughter. *What was it like for his father in the black coffin?* Abel wondered. *What did it feel like, exactly, when you were dead? Hi-iiii-hiii-hii.* It was all so weird and wonderful, he thought.

Abel did not catch up with the funeral party until they had reached the churchyard in the valley below. But as he approached, he heard the mourners begin to sing, so he stopped short a little distance away; Abel loved to sing, he learnt the melodies of hymns very quickly and his voice was distinctive. He didn't know the words, but what did that matter?

Rather than the actual lyrics he understood the mystical waves of emotions which swept him along with the melody, and in *his* mellifluous voice, he sang *his* hymns, which no other living person had been able to decipher so far. Besides, he was always careful to keep a safe distance, so that no one would hear him.

For a long time after he returned to Esturoy, Abel could not shake the image of his father descending into the grave, clods of earth thudding onto the coffin lid. He could not stop wondering what it was like to die and *be* dead. *Did people actually* know *that they were dead?*

It was Abel's job to tend to the cows and muck out the stables. Because the cattle were his father's most valuable possessions, the pastor's eldest son Heini always kept an eye on him, even though Abel didn't *need* Heini's supervision; he was always where he was supposed to be, unless thunderstorms drew him onto the ridge because he had to study the clouds for a sign that the day of reckoning was upon them. The good thing about having Heini around was that he could try and get some answers to the questions which were plaguing him: "You must remember to harness Whiteblaze for the outfield tomorrow morning, Abel."

"Heini, what does it mean to be dead?" Abel said in reply.

"Stop asking silly questions."

"Heini, do you think people *know* that they are dead?"

"How should I know?!"

"Do you think they feel pain when they're dead?"

"Shut your mouth!"

"Heini, is my father in heaven now?"

"Yes."

"So why was everyone crying at his funeral?"

"I don't know."

"Do you get something to eat when you're in heaven?"

"Be quiet now."

"Heini, what is hell?"

"Will you *stop* talking now?!"

"Where will *you* go, when *you* die, Heini?"

In the end it was all Heini could do to turn on his heel and leave. But Abel kept turning these questions over and over in his mind, long after Heini had fled into the outfield.

*

Summer came around at last and Abel was sent into the fields to watch over the cattle.

Everyone knew that you had to be wary of the big, red bull. But the bull was like a lamb around Abel, who could play and do whatever he wanted with the beast. The bull could not stand Heini for whatever the pastor's son had done to him.

One day, when Heini was on his way home from an errand in the village, he came upon Abel and the bull in the outfield. As soon as the animal recognised Heini, he lowered his horns and charged. Heini managed to jump behind Abel in the nick of time—just before the bull got his horns into Heini, and Abel simply brushed it aside, as if it were a chicken. The bull heeled in shame like a scolded dog. Ever since this incident happened, Abel liked to greet Heini with a smile and say: "Hello Heini the Afraid, scared-of-the-bull Heini."

This was easy for Abel to say for *he* had nothing to fear because *he* could do whatever he wanted with the bull. It was true that on the long summer days on the mountainside, when he did not feel like picking the wool which the farmer's wife always stuffed into his leather pouch, the two of them played about in the field: first Abel would duck in between the animal's front legs, then crawl out through his hind legs. Usually it was Abel who ended this game: grabbing the bull by the horns, he swung himself up onto his muscular neck, and when the bull got bored he gently shook his playmate off. It never occurred to Abel that the bull might hurt him; and it never occurred to the bull to hurt Abel.

Sometimes, Abel would go down on all fours, and from a suitable distance away, he snorted through his nose, hard. The bull knew what this meant and replied with a fat snort in kind, albeit much louder. For their part, the cows loved this game, and whenever they heard Abel's tell-tale sniffing and snorting they would lazily trundle over and troop around the boy. But this game always ended with the bull: he lowered his horns, and very carefully, rolled Abel over the grass till he lost interest and resumed grazing.

If Heini came into the pasture, Abel would greet him characteristically: "Heini the Afraid, afraid-of-the-bull Heini."

Then came the day that Heini could not take it any more; he was so sick and tired of hearing Abel's taunt—even if he knew that it wasn't meant as such: "If you were dressed in red you wouldn't dare come near the bull—because he would kill you on the spot!" Heini snapped.

"Kill me dead, oh no, no-no-no-noo," said Abel, bursting into a fit of laughter, the same, strange cackle which you could hear coming from the ridge whenever the thunderstorms tumbled over the mountains.

Now Abel couldn't stop thinking about this: *would the bull* really *get mad if he wore red?*

It was a day in early autumn and a storm was brewing so the cows had been driven home for shelter. Abel wandered into the room where the maidservant slept. He noticed a red skirt laid out on the bed. Struck dumb for a moment, he could not take his eyes off the skirt. Then he burst out laughing as usual.

The maidservant Magga got into a huff when she found him in her room.

"What are you doing in here?" she said.

"I don't know," said Abel, laughing even harder.

"Tell me why you're laughing, Abel!"

"I don't know."

At last Magga threw him out of her room on his ear.

But Abel could not get the red skirt out of his head. And every time he thought about it, he broke into raucous fits of laughter.

The next day was Sunday and Magga put on the skirt for church. But every which way she went, Abel followed her, on her heels. At last Magga lost her temper: "What do you want from me, Abel?!"

"I don't know."

"You're going to tell me, right now! What are you laughing at? Is it *me*?!"

"I don't know."

"Tell me what it is, you stupid mule," Magga wailed, close to tears now. But no matter how much she pleaded and threatened, all she could get out of Abel was: "I don't know."

The next morning the storm had calmed and the cows could be turned out to pasture. Abel was ready to drive them to the outfield, but making a split-second decision, he went into Magga's room and stuffed the red skirt into his treasured food pouch before darting after the herd.

The first thing he did when they reached the outfield was to dip into his knapsack; the farmer's wife always packed enough provisions for two meals, but Abel usually ate it in one sitting. And it was a beautiful warm day, without a breath of wind, so he decided to take a nap in the sun.

It was only later, when he woke up, that he remembered the red skirt that he had brought with him.

Ducking behind a haystack, he pulled the skirt over his head. Then Abel clambered to the top and let out a long, drawn-out bray.

The bull lifted his head when he recognised Abel's call; it was playtime, and he knew it.

But then the bull noticed a red figure standing on top of the haystack. His hide began to twitch. He raised his muscular neck, sniffed the air and glared at the haystack. Then he lowered his neck, snorted fiercely and began to paw the ground in front of him.

Abel was nonchalant. He scampered down from his perch and crawled over to the bull on all fours as always.

At first, the bull stopped his pawing. Retreated a few steps. Abel advanced, grunting in good spirits as usual. The bull bristled, his tail shot up into the air, and with a loud roar, he charged headlong at the red skirt.

The first blow struck Abel between his ribs and sent him flying high into the air. He came down hard on the rocky pasture, somewhere behind the bull—and he was bleeding. Badly.

The bull spun round. When he saw the blood he was enraged and charged again. This time he impaled the red skirt and shook Abel's body as if it were a threadbare mitten stuck on his horns, and then he tossed the lifeless body into the river which ran through the valley.

The bull stood motionless on the bank, staring into the water. Burying his snout in the grass, he snorted one last time, his breath a strangled wheezing sound in his throat.

The cows gathered behind the bull on the bank. Their coats shivering as they bellowed over the water.

The tattered, red skirt floated on the surface, but Abel had sunk to the bottom like a stone.

*

It was late and Heini was surprised that Abel had not yet returned from the outfield. At last he saw the cows approaching the edge of the pasture. But something was wrong: the cows were moving too fast, bleating as they charged towards the stables. The bull brought up the rear, and also he was braying loudly; unsettling calls, devoid of the familiar yearning after the warmth and comfort of their stables.

Heini waited for a long time. But Abel never came home.

Four men from the farm—including Heini—initiated a search party. Not long after, their dogs stopped on the bank of the river and started to bark loudly. Something that looked like seagrass was floating on the surface—but it was red!—not the colour of Abel's clothing, so it couldn't be him. But the dogs kept barking at the river, so the men sent them to fetch whatever was bothering them: it was a piece of woman's clothing.

How did an item of woman's clothing land up in the river?

The men were confused. They decided to wade into the water to investigate. Heini went first and he was the one who found the body of Abel.

That the bull had killed Abel was clear to everyone.

But what about the tattered red skirt? Who did it belong to?

And why did Abel put it on?

Heini wiped the sweat from his brow, but said nothing. *He* knew what had happened.

Abel was carried home on a stretcher. There was a contented smile on his lips, people noticed. Perhaps he had reason to smile? Maybe over there, in the kingdom of the dead, he was able to find some answers to his nagging questions? Neither Heini, nor anyone else for that matter, had been able to answer them after all.

When Magga heard that Abel and a red skirt had been

found in the river, she ran into her room immediately. And sure enough, her skirt was gone! *But what in God's name had he been thinking?!* Magga wondered.

Neither Magga nor anyone else in the village could fathom why Abel took the skirt.

Only Heini knew. But *he* said nothing.

The day Abel was buried almost everyone in the valley turned out for the funeral procession. Mothers with their flock of children in tow; perhaps even the youngest people could sense that Abel, even if a little 'unusual', was a wise person, who spoke the language of wonder. But more than anything else, the children remembered that Abel was kind, and not once had he laid a finger on them.

Even Haraldur, who usually bored everyone with his constant bragging about how well he spoke Danish, followed the funeral party in silence. And Theodor, who had teased Abel mercilessly, had travelled the long way from his home village, accompanied by his mother and siblings, of course.

Out here it was not customary to send for someone to give a sermon as one did in higher social circles. But Heini had insisted on calling in the pastor to give a speech, so the farmer eventually had to bow to his son's wishes. The pastor's words moved half the congregation to tears. Although, in truth, it wasn't an actual *speech* because, standing by his graveside, the pastor merely retold all our stories about Abel; coming from the pastor's mouth, the anecdotes sounded strange, however. But the pastor was the kind of man who knew how to formulate the things which the rest of us struggle to express, never mind understand; perhaps we did not even notice them.

Indeed, in the stories we heard about Abel—now risen to that fascinating place which he had yearned to see with his own eyes—was a narrative that revealed the things that we tell ourselves throughout a lifetime.

As the pastor's long, black gown billowed in the gentle breeze, we lowered the coffin into the grave, and he brought his stories to a close, strewing earth onto the lid.

We sang Kingo's hymn—"Now we will let him rest in peace"—and then everyone dispersed to their homes in silence. Heini drew a bunch of heather and wild, red flowers out of his homespun coat and let it fall onto the lid of the coffin. Then he also made his way home; he was the last person to leave the graveside.

The next day, the farmer himself led the bull round to the back of the stables and shot him; he was well-fed and provided a bounty of fresh meat, but every time meat was served for dinner, Heini was away on some errand or another—in the outfields, on the cliffs, the village or some other place—and when he returned, he said that he had already eaten.

The Dream

by

Andrea Reinert

translated by Lindy Falk van Rooyen

"I'm so afraid, Ólavur."

"What has scared you, my love," he said, snuggling up to her in their bed.

"I had a terrible dream last night."

Ólavur felt her body shudder in his arms, and he pulled her even closer.

"Please don't go out today!" Her face was twisted in anguish.

"Don't be silly, Malan, you know I have to go fishing," he said, brushing a stray blonde strand out of her eyes. "Now, tell me about this terrible dream of yours."

Malan lay back in his arms and closed her eyes. Her words came haltingly at first, and her voice was quiet as she slowly began to recall the dream: "I saw your father, Little Kálvur. He was so angry with me, Ólavur, I thought he would tear me apart. We were in a room with a red interior. The walls, floors, ceiling—everything inside it—was painted blood-red. What appeared to be a dead animal was nailed to the wall. It was a carcass teeming with maggots.

'You must eat this animal,' said Kálvur. 'If you don't, I

will burn you alive,' he said.

Then he left and locked the door behind him. I couldn't bring myself to take a single bite. Every time I touched it, maggots oozed from the flesh and crept up my hands and arms. Kálvur was standing behind the door, peeping through the keyhole. His head had swollen to the size of his entire body, and his eyes were like glowing red coals.

'Now your time has come, and you will be burnt at the stake!' he said, bursting into his horrid laughter, which has always scared me half to death. Then I heard the front door slam behind him. I was left alone with the maggots. They had latched onto me, and I tried to brush them off, but they had burrowed into the threads of my clothing, so I took everything off, one item after another, till I was completely naked, and when I hung the clothes up on the hook on the wall, the room burst into flames, and I called for you desperately, but all I could hear was his vicious laughter. Then I started awake and found myself lying beside you. So I'm begging you, Ólavur, please don't go out today. If you leave me, I know something terrible is going to happen."

Malan opened her eyes; they were wild, terrified, and Ólavur could see it. He felt wretched. He knew that his father would kill her if he got the chance. Despite being a priest and a God-fearing man.

"My father will not do you any harm, Malan. You know he is afraid of me, my love," Ólavur said, doing his best to comfort her.

"Yes, I know. But I am asking you to stay on land today; if you are near, he wouldn't dare hurt me. If you are far out at sea, he will kill me, out of sheer spite. You know as well as I do that

Little Kálvur has destroyed every man who stood in his way."

This was true. And yes, Ólavur knew it. But a fisherman can't stay home just because his wife asked him to. But yes, something had to be done. He would go to Kirkjubøar and have a word with the bishop. He would tell him about the havoc Kálvur has caused all over Sandoy. He was merely a son born out of wedlock, but he didn't want to do his father any serious harm. If he could convince the bishop to threaten his father with an expulsion from the church, it might help: surely the fear of being excluded would convince Little Kálvur to abandon his evil ways? But how could his father be such a brute? It was ridiculous, so plain for everyone to see that Malan was not only a woman fair as a flower blossom on the mountain in springtime, but sweet, kind and loving of heart!

"Dearest Malan," Ólavur said. "You need not be afraid of such dreams. They don't mean anything. And you are a sensible woman, my love. I know you would not keep me ashore when the weather is tolerably good for fishing just because of a bad dream. If you don't want to stay indoors, you can go for a walk up to the ridge. Take your needlework with you, summer has arrived and the weather is splendid today. It's so beautiful up on the mountain. From the ridge you can see with your own eyes when I return, and you could come and meet the boat at the landing bridge when we are back in the fjord."

Malan sighed.

"My dear Ólavur, tell me that you won't go out so far that you can't see the shore."

"Alright. I promise you that I will not sail beyond the horizon."

Having Malan for his wife was a greater possession than all the wealth he had received from his father. He could not risk losing her. Malan was the joy, the light of his life; when she was around, it was like the sun peeping out from behind the clouds. But the clock had struck 4.00 am, and it was time to get out of bed. Ólavur looked out of the window; the weather was simply divine, he thought.

She did not have to, but Malan got out of bed as well. Every morning she made sure that Ólavur had enough provisions for the day; she soaked a fat slice of fresh bread in two fingers of milk, wrapped it in waxcloth and put it into his leather pouch. No husband of hers would go hungry at sea.

In the kitchen below, the farmhands could hear that the master and mistress were up, and everyone scurried into their boots by the door. They had prepared and eaten breakfast already; in the mornings, the master did not eat with them—Malan's idea, no doubt—and Ólavur was besotted with his wife. He did whatever she wanted him do. But the story was bound to end badly with Little Kálvur in the wings, biding his time to get his claws into Malan, and everyone knows that this woman has no respect for Little Kálvur, not like the rest of us on Sandoy. She's not from the island—she's not from the Faroes at all. Ólavur met her over on Bergen, on one of his fishing trips. He was completely taken with her, and by the time they sailed back home, that Norwegian woman was his wife.

This is true: Ólavur is the only man on Sandoy who is not afraid of Little Kálvur. And when he returned to Sandur a married man, all hell broke loose: naturally, Little Kálvur tried to dissolve the marriage, and of course Ólavur refused to give up his wife, but Little Kálvur had to have his son with him all the time, and he would not give him up for the sake of a woman. No matter where she came from.

Some say there was a time when Little Kálvur had been good to Ólavur's mother, until the day they found her cold in her bed. He killed her himself. Everyone said so. From that day on, the devil rode Little Kálvur. And the farm went to wrack and ruin because he failed to make good use of the land. His methods consisted of threats, beatings and shady deals with folks who feared for their lives, not just here in the village of Todnes, but in every corner of the islands.

Ólavur grew up on the farm. They say he always slept in the same room as his father; it was very odd that a man could not sleep alone at night. Besides, a man like Little Kálvur feared nothing and no one between heaven and earth. And everyone was concerned about the fate of Ólavur's lovely young bride.

After Ólavur set sail Malan decided to put on her shoes to go out. She could not bear to be indoors another minute; plagued by a sense of foreboding from the moment she woke, she had no peace indoors, and besides, it was time to gather the peat.

"Birita, Sunniva," she said. "The two of you will come with me to the peat fields. Get ready to leave at once."

Elspa and Elin could stay behind, thought Malan: there was that tapestry to finish. And they still had to knead the bread dough and prepare the dinner. Also, there was a pile of washing which they could dry when the girls had milked the cows in the outfields.

"No, wait," said Malan, changing her mind. "It will be a while yet before you are done. I'll go ahead and wait for you on the ridge."

She could not wait another second. Why was she being so pathetic? Today, the hill felt like the mountain it was. And why in God's name had she put on so many layers of clothing?! She was so distracted when she left the house. Bare legs would have been so much better. The stone path felt almost warm under her feet.

When she reached the ridge Malan sat down on a rock to pick flowers. The scent of thyme and other wild herbs filled her nostrils, soothing her heart. Earlier that morning there was a drizzle in the air, but now the sun was shining from the heavens in all its glory. The stony outcrops were rich with green moss as well, she noticed. She felt along the edges of her perch, delighted by the soft curvaceous tufts at her fingertips, and the brown patches of rim lichen which were scattered on other rocks about her.

Old Elin was the one who had taught Malan how to scrape lichen off rocks. It was a pleasant pastime, especially when they used it for dying cloth. Here, in the Faroes, there were so many shades of grey that it chilled the soul, Malan thought. No, every single day ought to be lived like this one; every living thing in luminous shades of green, and in the fjord below, the ocean glittered like flying silver ribbons.

As if a power unto its own, Skúvoy island rose out of the deep in the foreground; massive mountain, bird cliff and sheer rock face all in one. Further to the south, the islands of Stóra Dímun and its little brother Lítla Dímun seemed to float alongside one another, bathing in the sea. Dim and secretive, as if one of those otherworldly *huldrelands*[10] of Norwegian folklore, Suðuroy island was visible in the distance even further south, a fluff of downy feather fog lingering about its crown. Yes, it was a glorious day, Malan thought, so sweet I can taste it at the root of my tongue. Her soul could have danced for joy, were it not for Little Kálvur. There was no room for happiness with the devil lurking at your door. 'Tankalítla', the 'harebrain' he called her, just because he could not bear to see her happy, and now everyone in the village had adopted the nickname, as if she were slow-witted, or never gave a thought to anyone but herself. Kálvur terrified her, but she always tried to hide it whenever he talked to her. He might be a balding little man, but his entire being radiated evil, she thought, and she refused to let him get her down.

Now Sunniva and Birita were making their way along the path. Busily knitting as they walked, both of them were barefoot and their shirts were unbuttoned at the front. Malan caught herself wondering whether the rumours were true that Kálvur was sleeping with Birita. He often sent for her from Todnes. But there could be any number of things he needed her to do; everyone knew that Birita was a capable and hardworking woman.

As soon as the girls arrived on the ridge where Malan was waiting, she asked them to sit down with her for a moment.

"The peat is not going to get up and walk home on its own," Birita replied.

Malan burst out laughing.

"We will get the peat home soon enough, Birita," she said. "But look how exquisite it is up here this morning!"

"I don't have time to notice such things," said Birita, heading down the track to the peat fields without as much as a pause in her stride.

Sunniva stopped however, and waited for Malan to get to her feet. Then they followed in Birita's footsteps together.

"So what's gotten into Birita this morning?" asked Malan.

"Something has definitely upset her," said Sunniva. "But I'll be damned if I know what it is."

When they reached the peat field they immediately started stacking the peat sods. Birita led the way, cutting them into rectangles, and the three of them worked together swiftly. Here, on the edge of their outfield, the turf had an excellent quality.

It seemed as if someone had been there before them to prepare the peat sods.

"You're not the one in charge here, Birita," Malan said. "And we don't want to talk about the peat while we work, either. So why don't you tell us how Sunniva and I can cheer you up instead?"

Birita made no reply.

After gathering and stacking the peat for two straight hours, Malan was ready for a break. She threw herself down on the grass, but then she looked up in surprise. Why was there smoke rising over the ridge, she wondered?

"Come on, let's find out where that smoke is coming from," said Malan. "Perhaps Kálvur has made a bonfire!" she added. Without waiting for a reply, she jumped to her feet and set off at a run up the slope. Sunniva was at her heels, but Birita remained in the valley.

A bank of smoke had settled over the village north of Todnes, and from the top of the ridge, Malan and Sunniva saw a driftwood bonfire; this is where the smoke was coming from.

A posse of men was making its way along the cattle track up to Ólavur's house, but they returned to the village almost immediately.

"Dear God in heaven, what does this mean?!" Malan said. She gazed over the sea, squinting at the fjord, but not a single boat could be seen. Dread rose in her chest as she saw the Norwegian journeyman; she recognised the gangly shape of Sjúrður, Kálvur's right-hand man as soon as he scaled the cliff, and she knew at once that he was looking for her. What were they doing on the ridge? This did not bode well, she thought, because those rascals never set foot outside Todnes if they could help it.

"Come with me, Sunniva," she said. "I don't like the look of any of this."

They made their way into the hills, because the best place to lay low was the rocky dale leading to Skálavík, Malan reckoned, and when they reached the old mill they could take refuge there. But it was not long before the search party came over the ridge on their tracks and headed for the peat fields, where Birita was still working. And as soon as she saw the men, she pointed them towards the mill.

Sunniva and Malan held their breath as a shadow appeared in the doorway.

"So this is where you're hiding, Tankalítla," Sjúrður snorted. "Come with us. Now. Little Kálvur wants to talk to you."

The colour drained from Malan's face. "What does he want with me?"

"You'll find out when you come to the farm."

"I'm not going anywhere with you," said Malan, her voice

shaking, in spite of herself.

"Then we'll have to carry you there," said Sjúrður, trying to snatch her arm.

Malan shrugged him off. "Don't you dare touch me," she said. "I can walk myself."

Sunniva was crying now.

"Dear Sunniva, dry your tears," Malan said, taking the girl by the hand. No, she would not allow herself to cry, thought Malan, doing her best to swallow the lump in her throat. Her legs felt weak and her body felt strangely lifeless. And there was still no sign of a boat on the horizon. Determined to move as slowly as humanly possible, Malan walked ahead of the men, desperately hoping all the while that Ólavur would see the smoke, and hurry back to shore.

Did Kálvur mean to burn her alive? What else would he do to her? Malan concentrated on dragging her feet; when she trod in a hole or ditch she pretended to stumble, making every stone, rock or hillock into a mountain. Naturally, the men were not pleased.

"We are under strict instructions to bring you to the farm immediately. First you weren't home, and then we had to spend time looking for you, and now you're dragging your heels like a lost sheep on the path. Little Kálvur will be furious that it has taken us so long to bring you back."

When they reached the top of the ridge the men shoved Sunniva aside. Grabbing Malan by the arm, the men all but dragged her along between them. In Todnes, the villagers—mostly the women—had come out of their houses and gathered on the street. God knew what these scoundrels would do to Tankalítla; watching them haul the poor woman in between the courtyards and houses, everyone feared the wrath of Little Kálvur.

Malan was petrified, but she knew her only hope was to hide her fear from Kálvur. What was the bonfire for, she wondered, as he came towards them, rubbing his hands in glee, his wicked smile firmly in place.

"Tankalítla has kept her father-in-law waiting a long, long time," he said. "I've been burning my precious timber for more than an hour." Another devilish snarl twisted the corners of his mouth. "But tell us, Tankalítla, what has sent you flying out of doors at this ungodly hour of the morning? I made this bonfire just for you." He was staring at her face, drawing out each word as he spoke, her defiance enraged him, but he would break her soon enough, he thought.

Malan gritted her teeth. Her mind was racing. She must find a way to distract him!

"What have I done to deserve this?" she said.

"You will find out soon enough, Tankalítla. Why don't you come a little closer to the fire? Such a blessed and welcome heat for the soul, don't you think?"

"Tell me how have I wronged you, Father?" Malan asked again.

"You ate meat during fasting time, Tankalítla. I made it clear to everyone in the village that anyone who committed this sacrilege would burn alive."

"It is not true, Father. I did not eat meat during Lent."

"Do you dare to lie before death's door, Tankalítla? Mark my words: the driftwood on this pile will burn to ashes today, but the flames of hell will blaze for eternity."

"But you have no proof, Father," Malan said, her face

white as chalk.

Kálvur took her arm and drew her closer to the fire.

"Birita, your housemaid, said that you did. Both these good men have sworn an oath that she did."

Malan was grief-stricken. Birita had betrayed her! Her mind was racing. How could she delay her fate?! Kálvur was always so miserly and mean. Perhaps his eternal tight-fistedness could help her now.

"I understand that my dear clothing must be destroyed in the fire as well," Malan said mournfully. "But I suppose my body shall burn all the better for it."

Kálvur stared at her for a moment.

"That is true, Tankalítla," he said. "It would be a shame to waste your clothing."

He led her away from the fire and pointed to the urine barrel that stood behind the shed.

"You can undress here. And make it quick, will you!" he said. "Sjúrður, help me to stoke the fire in the meantime. It's a good thing I have gathered enough tinder—add more wood to the bonfire!"

Meanwhile, it was all Malan could do to play for time. She eased off her left stocking, then slowly began fiddling with the right. Kálvur had told her to hurry, of course, but as soon as he turned his back she pulled up the left stocking again.

But Little Kálvur was not a fool. He lost his temper and started yelling at Malan: "Tankalítla, stop your goddamned procrastination and get undressed at once! The bonfire will not wait all day for you!

Malan's hands were shaking, and her throat was dry as cork. Was this how her life would end? Never to see her husband again? Ólavur, Ólavur. Dear God in heaven, help me!

In Todnes word that Little Kálvur was going to burn Malan at the stake spread with the wind faster than a whale hunt signal. People spilled out of their houses and peered over the fjord. "May the dear Lord help us all, and send thunder for Ólavur," an old women muttered under her breath.

"I fear Ólavur will strangle Little Kálvur with his bare hands," said another by her side.

"Yes, you can be sure that Little Kálvur will pay with his life for this," agreed a third.

Ólavur hauled up the nets. He had found an excellent fishing ground, and it was a good catch today, but the dream that Malan had told him about that morning troubled him; this constant, nagging fear for Malan's well-being every time he left the house was intolerable. He cast a glance at the shore every so often, squinting through the fjords. He chided himself for having gone out so far; from here, he could barely catch a glimpse of land. But he was being foolish. On Sandoy Malan was not in any danger!?

But then, glancing over his shoulder once more, he caught sight of a grey haze hovering over the ridge; the weather was fine, so there was no logical explanation for it. So what else could it be? Smoke?! Now also the helmsman had noticed it; there was a dark cloud over the island.

"There appears to be a fire in the village," he said. His mates turned to look. They agreed: it was smoke, and it was coming from Todnes.

"Dear God, no!" said Ólavur, turning pale as a ghost. "Cut the lines at once! All men to the oars! Head for shore as fast as you can, my friends, my old man is up to something!"

The fishermen complied immediately, and bracing their feet against the bench in front of them, they rowed back to shore for all they were worth. Not a word was exchanged as the sweat poured down their faces. The sea frothed at the bow. Ólavur cast a glance over his shoulder once more; yes, the smoke was coming from Todnes. "Pray to God that I get there in time!"

Soon the fishermen ran the boat ashore. Ólavur jumped overboard and ran up to the village with the rest of the crew following on his heels. Ólavur was much faster than they were, but even before they caught up with him, they heard his voice roar: "LET GO OF HER!"

Malan was stripped down to her shift. Kálvur and Sjúrður were holding her tight between them. The bonfire was raging before them.

Kálvur started at the sound of his son's voice, immediately letting go of Malan. He stared at his son's face; Ólavur looked as if he would murder him. Sjúrður also knew that if Ólavur got hold of him, he was a dead man, and he turned and ran for the hills.

Kálvur was rooted to the spot, unable to move a muscle as his son advanced towards him. Ólavur's eyes were bloodshot and his face was purple with rage. He seized his father and shook his body as if the old man were an empty potato sack.

"You confounded dog! You will burn in the fire you intended for my wife, you monster!" Ólavur screamed. He had knocked his father clean off his feet and dragged him to the bonfire by his heels.

"Please don't kill me, my son!" squealed Kálvur. It

was no use; his son was beside himself with fury. He was determined to put an end to his father's life and protect his wife, once and for all. But Malan's voice beseeched him: "Ólavur, please calm down. Please do not hurt him, my love."

As if coming to his senses, Ólavur stopped in his tracks. He brought a hand to his brow. After a moment, he turned to face Malan. To him, she looked like an angel; she was clutching her white shift before her, trying to conceal her nakedness, deathly pale, her eyes shining with tears. Ólavur's heart bled for her. How could this woman plead for the life of the devil who intended to kill her?!

"He deserves to be burnt at the stake," Ólavur said, his voice low and hoarse. "But because you ask it of me, Malan, I will spare his life."

Ólavur turned to his father, who was scrambling away from the bonfire: "Get out of my sight before I change my mind," he hissed. "But remember who you have to thank for your life being spared today."

Kálvur sprang to his feet. Without looking back, he fled out of the village.

In the meantime, Malan had managed to dress, thanking God that Ólavur had not murdered his father; she was afraid of Ólavur when he lost his temper. But now he was his kind self again, the man she loved.

He put an arm around her shoulder comfortingly. "The danger is over, my love. You don't need to fear Little Kálvur any longer."

"Yes. But it would have been better if you had listened to me this morning," Malan said with a smile.

Ólavur merely stared at her in awe. Her smile could rival the beauty of sunrise, he thought.

Bekka

by
Petra Djurhuus

translated by Lindy Falk van Rooyen

Warm and red-gold is the sun that shines over the village. That rich and plush light which you only see towards evening when the summer draws to a close, and autumn takes hold; it's as if the sun, which has drawn in the lush green grass, colourful flowers and dizzyingly blue sea all summer long, wants to recall the beautiful soul of summer one last time, as everything pales and begins to wane. It is this frail moment of surrender that carries a scent of seeds and freshly tossed earth on the wind. The tide ebbs out of the fjord ever so slowly, and as the swell retreats into the ocean, brilliant streaks of brown seagrass break to the surface, but towards the east the air turns pale yellow, the sea grey as soft silk.

Now the first milkmaid appears on the ridge. Then the next and the next come over the mountain, one after another, their knitting needles flashing like lightning in their hands; nothing helps on a long walk as well as needlework. Not long after, all eighteen women are seated on the fence. As was the custom, they gathered here by the gate and took a seat on the driftwood planks, waiting. Then the entire group would make their way—knitting, laughing and talking as they went—like a dragon tail slithering through the gate and up the tortuous, trodden cattle track to the rocky outfields.

Not all the maids were light on their feet.

At the tip of the tail was Bekka. Hands behind her back, her head bowed and her body rocking with every, arduous step, she bore a row of milk cans hooked over her shoulders and arms. She was a curious sight, the old milk maid. Plump and ungainly as a haystack on unsteady legs just learning to walk. Her milkmaid's smock, bespeckled with umpteen threadbare patches like grey stone-moss stains, was heaving from side to side, side to side. On her hunched back, broad and flattened under its burden, rested Hálvdan's large and cumbersome milk can with its leather strap threaded through ram-horn ears, whilst the smaller, agitated milk cans along her arms thudded against one another as she tottered along the path. Yes, you could always hear Bekka bringing up the rear.

"She chugs like a motorboat in choppy waters," Elin quipped.

"And pitches like a peat boat loaded to the gunwales," Elsa called out from the back of the line. "Come on, Bekka, the cows are grazing in the far field."

Bekka looked up, and yes, they were right, she has lagged behind quite a bit. The clamour of milk cans grew louder and swung faster, and by the time she reached the driftwood gate, Bekka was back in the flock. As usual, the milkmaids held a short break here until everyone had come through the stile, so before they closed the gate behind them, Bekka had a chance to wipe the corner of her scarf across her sweaty face and brow.

Where Bekka got her strange, "Asian features" was anybody's guess. Coarse and protruding cheekbones with small, exceptionally dark—almost black—slit-eyes embedded on either side of the hollow bridge of her nose and flaring nostrils which startled many people the first time they saw her scuttle in-between the houses at sunset.

This evening many of them spoke to Bekka, as if she were in the centre of the fold, and this was because All Saints day marked Bekka's sixty-year anniversary of service at Hálvdan's dairy, and this year, her jubilee would be celebrated in conjunction with the annual milkmaids' fair.

Bekka seemed pleased—almost cheerful—and began chattering on about various incidents that had occurred over the years. There had been some bickering about her, but I agreed with most folks who supported her—unlike the sister of Súsanna—and when we lost our parents in the epidemic, both Bekka and I were taken into foster care; she went to the farmhouse on the promontory, slept by the hearth in the kitchen at night, always up at dawn, didn't even own a pair of socks till she earned her keep with the master. They gave her food to eat, but there was barely enough to go around. I never saw her again till after I was forty years old. When we parted, she was seven and I had just turned nine. So it was nice to see her again at the wedding here in the village. Even Súsanna was granted leave—her first day off after fifteen years of service—to join in the celebrations.

I remember it like it was yesterday. There was a stiff northerly wind, and a furious undercurrent with rough seas, which made the straight impassable. I had nothing with me but the clothes on my back, but Hanus from the courtyard was kind enough to throw an oilskin coat over my shoulders. I took cover in the front of the boat, screaming in terror every time the coal-blue breakers smashed over the gunwales. No one heard me though, because every man was at his post. The Lord knows I was happy to have solid rock under my feet again. Drenched to the bone, freezing cold and exhausted as I was, I couldn't face the thought of dragging myself all the way home again. That was sixty years ago. And I haven't been home to the other side of the fjord since. But I can't complain; I've always had food to eat, clothes to wear, and I like to think that I've aged gracefully alongside other folk on this side of the fjord.

At the foot of the mountain Bekka parted with the other milkmaids; her cows grazed on the eastern slopes in the far field, whilst everyone else was headed to the westward pasture. No one gave it a passing thought that Bekka would have to walk through the gorge alone. She was used to it and the weather was fine.

*

Bekka reaches the eastern ridge. She has descended a long way into the valley, but there is still no sign of her cows. Feeling her courage begin to wane, she takes a seat on a stone to rest. Soaked in sweat, her scarf is pasted to her forehead, so she loosens the knot at the nape of her neck and uses the tip to wipe her brow. After she has taken a moment to catch her breath, she starts walking again. The going has become more rocky, and it is difficult to keep to the narrow track between the scree mounds. Her legs begin to tremble under her awkward burdens, and yet, all at once, her feet seem strangely weightless, as if she were walking on thin air. Her mind is vacant, and it feels as if nothing is bearing down on her shoulders any longer, only the familiar rough texture of her scarf chafes against her brow. The next moment, she can feel the milk cans weighing her down once more. Bekka laughs heartily at herself. At last she catches sight of one of her cows; it's the speckled roan in the far field.

Bekka milks her cows steadily till the froth bubbles up over the rim of her tub, and before she knows it, she seals each one with a lamb-skin cover. She sits back on her haunches in satisfaction for a moment. Reaches out and runs her fingers over the light-green river moss. Dabs the beads of sweat on her brow. Then she glances up at the crag ahead. I'll be up and over in no time, she thinks. The sun has disappeared and dark clouds are rolling in over the mountain. The peak is no longer pitch black; the autumn light paints the rockface grey as newly-whet steel. In summer, the brilliant green of the grass and the charcoal grey of the pebbles seem to blanche, just as the deep dark hue of the sea fades into pastel blue; the waters were calm and quiet before, but now the swells seem so vast, as if stretching to the ends of the earth, engulfing her, and all at once the world feels infinitely huge. A shiver runs through her heart as Bekka lifts the milk cans onto her shoulders in haste, suddenly aware of a fear she has not known before; the first warning signs from an all-embracing mother nature, who sooner or later, will reclaim everything that she has bestowed upon us. A law unto herself that never fails.

*

Evening has shifted into night. Colluding with the mist, darkness has swept in and settled in the valley, and now Bekka has lost her way. It seems as if years have passed since she set out; an endless walk in amongst massive boulders overgrown with moss and rim lichen. The cumbersome Hálvdan's milk can is a nagging weight on her back; long since lost, the smaller milk cans tumbled down the mountainside, one after another, as she desperately tried to find her way back to the path. At last all her strength is spent, and the mist wraps around her, like a soft duvet of milk froth, tucking in the forlorn milkmaid and laying her involuntarily to rest on a patch of green in amongst the rocks. Far—in the distance beyond—the ocean waves thunder and crash against the cliffs, and high up above it all, the storm petrels are hovering, as if a thousand-strong buzzing mosquitoes like a blizzard over the gorge.

One by one, the images appear before her mind's eye: snapshots from a long and hard life, working from morning till night, day after day, without respite, for others; not a single day in Bekka's life was under her control. That time she came to the wedding—a moment like a warm glow in the dark—it was a given that Bekka would return to Hálvdan's farm at milking time. And of course she had seen to it that the dough was kneaded and the bread baked by the time she had to change into her good dress for the wedding feast that evening. And the next morning she was at her post, at the usual time, to muck out the stables in her oilskin apron.

Bekka is dreaming of languid days when you can just be: the late summer pastures in all their green splendour; men with puffin baskets strapped to their backs after bird-catching on the cliffs; peat boats, loaded to the gunwales, stealing away from the landing bridge in the black stillness of morning, whilst other people in the village were still fast asleep in their beds; the tart smell of cut grass and meadows; seagrass growing in the sea; cows napping in the fold; brown-coloured sea ducks lolling about on the waves breaking on the rocky seashore. Yes, your life is rich, if only you have an eye for the wealth of beauty which every day brings, even if you're just a humble milkmaid.

And now Bekka sees the difficult days when everyone fears for the lives of the fisherman who have gone out to sea, all the men tending livestock in the outfields, or hunting for birds in the cliffs; she sees the snow that covers everything; the vicious weather that whips up waves hurling sea spray deep into the mountainside shores; the sheds and boats by the landing bridge tossed about in huge swells; not least, those everyday little moments in your life, which hardly attract the notice of others, yet blur her field of vision, as if observed from a steep mountain track.

Bekka sees herself in the crowd of milkmaids who are celebrating her jubilee. These young girls are not content with a chat over a cup of coffee, they're always getting caught up in all sorts of nonsense. She sees a hefty bull before her, a baked cake, complete with patches and a wagging tail of blue tinsel paper and red ribbon around his horns—his name is Høgni—and Bekka bursts out laughing so loud she can barely talk when she catches sight of him; Høgni is a tribute to Bekka for what she did for the other milkmaids that day they encountered 'Høgni' himself in the far field.

Without warning, the raging bull charged headlong for the milkmaids in the far field, and everyone scattered in terror—except for Bekka—who deftly swung her Hálvdan's milk can right into his ugly mug. The bull was so surprised by the attack that everyone managed to get to safety behind a rocky outcrop on the hill. As for 'Høgni', he was left to take out his wrath on a mound of mud, which he scooped up with his sharp horns and tossed up and over his head. Meanwhile, the other milkmaids cowered behind the rocks, till a posse of men came to look for them. Høgni had seen the last of his days on earth.

*

"Here she is."

The dogs started barking, and men with lanterns spread out a blanket for her. They lifted Bekka up and carried her home, as if cradled in a hammock.

The rescue party slowly made its way back through the gorge, a path that Bekka had taken so many times on her own before, but this time, strong men were bearing her, and high up above, the storm petrels hovered, as if a thousand-strong buzzing mosquitoes like a blizzard over the gorge.

For Now

by

Maria Mikkelsen

translated by Marita Thomsen

Jákup leaned through the window frame. Across the bay smoke wafted from every chimney in columns silhouetted against the sky until a sudden wobble blurred them, fog came rolling in and the landscape was veiled.

He began to fiddle with a long telescope, attempting to sweep the horizon, there in a clearing he spotted a ship, glimpsed people on deck. And without warning the haze swallowed the view again.

He heard a clacking of clogs and patter of children below the window and voices from the eastern landing.

How soon would the captain of *The Refuge* make his way here, so he could be rid of this message he had been brooding over since noon, when he was fetched from the sail loft solely for this purpose, because the shipowner said that he had a meeting to attend. All Jákup had found to do was clearing out old papers, and eager as he was, he had done it so efficiently that someone poked their nose in to enquire whether the place was on fire, what with all the smoke.

Jákup waited in the doorway, someone was bound to pass with news of the arrival. Sure enough, a little mite sprinted past. It was *The Mandal* that had cast anchor, "...and *omma*[11] is so happy, because she is expecting Aunt Lena with the ship". So Jákup went back inside and lit up. And at long last came the captain, Per í Vik.

"So the shipowner is away, is he!"

And without so much as a blink, he launched into a whole lecture about *The Mandal*: it had been abominable on board, because that bucket was by nature intended to sail in sunshine with oranges and lemons in the Mediterranean, not to plough in darkness and fog with kerosene barrels and logs as deck cargo in the East Atlantic, and mark my words, with ships as with everything else, laddie, each to their own, but the captain of *The Mandal*, his good friend, he was made of the right stuff, aye, and next to the Good Lord himself, goes without saying, it was thanks to him that the dinghy was now anchored in this bay with its crew, and the remainder of its cargo, intact. Right, well, what about that salt ticket and that signature! Read it out! Aye, the shipowner was the right man for his post, under his hand everything was kept shipshape; he demanded his share, that he did, but was no miser and didn't begrudge others their takings... and Jákup was to pass on his warmest greetings and thank him... there was also much merit in how fluently Jákup deciphered the shipowner's scribbles. And then came a sermon on salt purchases, prices and insurance, and to boot Jákup was informed that he, Jákup, conversed like an old man and was far too good a lad to be pottering about on land from one thing to another... no, he should come sailing!

Not that Jákup got a word in edgeways, but he enjoyed listening to the captain and the praise that so effortlessly welled from Per's lips. Jákup knew when to add a pinch of salt.

"Right, time to head home," the captain declared, and Jákup locked up. He still had one errand to run, about a barge, and on the way he would pay Karin a visit to find out if her only daughter had indeed arrived with the ship.

It was rather dark and sludgy, hard to make your way through the slippery mud the cluster of houses known as á Hellu sat in, but Jákup knew every patch and passage. A stranger might break a leg were it not for the lamp over the door. He crossed the threshold and a strange mood gripped him, crikey what a malicious glow the lamp cast. Newly-laid boards in the entrance were caked with fresh mud and a filthy sodden mat lay kicked aside in a jumble of dirty clogs. In the kitchen by the window Karin sat at the uncleared table, and there stood Einar leaning against the wall chewing a cold pipe stem. Lena was hunched on a chest by the fire, which had gone out. She had her young son, Óli, between her knees. The boy was engrossed with a little red toy horse he was washing with a wet cloth, smearing both horse and himself crimson in the process. And the scarf Lena was wrapped in was a hideous mauve. They were a picture of utter dejection.

Jákup had on entering mentioned that it was Little Tummas, who earlier had said that '*omma* was so happy' (he suddenly felt bad, though he wasn't clear why, about mentioning happiness), and now that he had an errand with the joiner he was just stopping for a quick hello, but he was in a bit of a rush really. They had replied, "Good evening" and Lena had added, "Thank you, Jakke."[12]

That was as far as they got. And Jákup was back outside, perplexed. Passing the boathouses on his way home, he overheard men gabbing about the 'bloody miracle' that *The Mandal* made it to shore.

Two days later he came through á Hellu, and Karin, who was sitting by the window, waved for him to come in. This was the house he knew, it was cosy inside and every last board gleamed as usual. Óli was playing with the little horse.

"Listen, poor laddie, you were, I fear, ill received the night before last, but it was as if the place were bewitched. I'd been suffering with a scalded foot and the little one drags the children home to play, not that I get cross with the little angels, but that's why the place looks like a stable floor, and little wonder that Lena arrived in a foul mood, what with how terrible the journey had been. Then the first word Einar came to tell his sister was that his banns had been published and the wedding procession arranged, but why *that* should enrage Lena so before she even sat down, well, heaven only knows. '*She* would stay well clear of both the wedding and the bride, who probably didn't think much of having her, Lena, for a sister-in-law either,' and on she went. Einar tried to calm her down, but it was no use! And then he got angry in turn, the dear heart… and that moment Tummas told you I'd been looking forward to was ruined. Then yesterday they pretended nothing had happened, and she busied herself, washing diligently all day making this place liveable again, and she fussed over Óli. Today they are at the storehouse, she was sent for, they are drying fish inside.

Anyway, yesterday one of the crew called on us, Ole Olsen, is his name, who had been so marvellously kind to Lena on the journey, and I invited him to visit tonight for a cup of coffee and he thanked me and is coming. My foot is on the mend, and as I said, it brings me great joy that our Lena is back home."

It was April. One day Jákup came home for tea full of cheer, the kettle was hanging over a good fire. He could hear Karin's voice and that she and mamma were about to sit at opposite ends of the table between the windows, and he went in to join them.

Mamma told him to stay in the kitchen and stoke the fire. She would be out soon, Karin and her just needed a quick word. Jákup didn't like the look of Karin, and he hunched down beside the stove right next to the door, he knew there was no rush with the fire. They paid him no notice. Karin was not in her everyday garments, she was draped in a shawl and had a big black scarf on her head.

"Sanna, I'm on my way back from Reyni, from Essa's, my third-cousin. He offered his advice…

You know how I love our Lena. Not that I would complain about any of my children, but she has, truth be told, been the best to me. She was, poor soul, unfortunate when she had her Óli, she was never sharp, and the father-to-be was no less to blame, he would also have done well to remember that he had both a wife and a child… were it not for that it would have been easier to bear, less shame. But it was a blessing that the man and his family left the country, that we were spared the daily insult… her excuse is that she was fond of the man and he was handsome… little does that matter. I helped her as best I could and I have loved the boy, he has wanted for nothing. You know that she left and stayed away, I imagined that she was doing alright, and I had a feeling she was homesick; and I missed her and Óli also needed to know his mother, I might pass away, and so on. So I asked her to come back home, and she came."

Jákup was sitting up now. But he rested his arms on the stove and kept his head down, so as not to take up too much space. He was listening with both ears and couldn't take his eyes off Karin, who was grappling with her motions. Her face kept changing colour and a tremor came and went in her voice.

Mamma was sitting, facing straight into the room, keeping her hands around her elbows. She was looking sideways at Karin, who was gripping the table top with both hands, and then shot a glance at Jákup as if to shoo him out. She hadn't uttered a word in reply.

A brief pause set in.

Karin let the shawl slip from her shoulders, and from under the scarf she wore beneath the shawl she produced a little white bundle with meticulous care, just to then fling it on the table. She was sweating and resumed, "Well, and then there was that fright with *The Mandal* nearly lost at sea… and she was the same gentle soul she always had been, and just as hard working… and Einar married and moved out. Oh, Lena isn't fond of Einar's wife, I don't know why, I don't know if she thinks her brother too good for her… but it is what it is. Einar pays short visits and is besotted with the little one, so is his wife… Ole Olsen, who was now part of *The Mandal*'s regular crew, visited every time the ship was in port… and I won't hide that when Lena, aye, it hadn't been long, one day came and whispered in my ear that they were a couple now and had exchanged rings in secret… then I said that she mustn't forget her past disgrace and so reminded her to be careful, and she replied, "Good God, mamma, how can you bring yourself to say those words to me!" And I regretted not holding my tongue, and spoiling the moment for her, I who have never reproached her Óli. Oh, Sanna!"

Jákup reared his head. Their chairs scraped.

"Sanna! I blush to the roots of my hair knowing now they had already been down that road! For it will become plain that the child she is carrying was conceived on that voyage home, when the ship almost saw the bottom of the sea!"

These last words came out like a strangled howl. Karin was bright red and perspiring profusely.

"Surely you knew already, what with how heavy she is and all, it can't have escaped a soul."

Mamma shook her head and Jákup knew that it had escaped him too. But it was certainly clear now why it had been so disagreeable that evening at á Hellu when Lena came home, or why she was upset when Einar spoke of banns and nuptials.

"And what haven't I been through? We know what people are like. But they won't get the better of me. Like my pious brother-in-law, he had an errand for me, he did, but by the by he worked his way to *this wretched matter with Lena*. I just gave him a steady look, perhaps it was my silence that tied him in knots, making him stutter all sorts, '…that so much could happen… not everyone carried full term… and there was so many a child the Good Lord had called home… and we were all better kept in his bosom!' That was when the devil himself got into me. Why, I asked him, should Lena miscarry, or the child she bore not be granted a full life? It was true that we were all better kept in heaven, but had he yet asked Our Father to take the four children he had been given into His bosom?

He trembled when he grasped my words. I did too. But he shan't be darkening my door anytime soon as our Lord's appointed servant."

Karin's voice waxed and waned then faded to a croak. She was panting. Mamma was pale as a corpse now.

"Like at Stina's the other day. Dortia was sitting there when I came in. Naturally someone mentioned christenings, now that we have a priest back in the parish, many children are due a trip to the font, and then Tia asks me off-hand, 'if it's still the custom when several children are to be baptised in the same water that the bastards are brought forth last?' I could see that Stina, as a decent person, was embarrassed, because that was a barb aimed at me, but I ignored it and replied that in my days I had only ever born children in wedlock and had never been aware of any such custom, so she probably knew more than I did, about bastards. Can you imagine, Sanna, the like of Dortia, without even a blush on her cheek, has she no shame! But that shut her up. Oh Sanna, isn't it too much to bear? And yet I feel like less of a person for even deigning to respond."

Mamma finally interjected that Karin was on her way home from Reyni.

"Well, then Olsen signed on with a better ship and they corresponded. Six letters she received and a promise of marriage, oh, don't we know what men are like, and a house and a home. But then came the letter in which he called it all off and asked to have both his letters and ring returned. Lena was at her wits' end. But I insisted that neither letters nor ring must leave the house, so that the children, when the time comes, can see that their mamma was seduced!"

She made a sweeping gesture, and exactly how is hard to say, but her scarf snagged the stalk of a pot plant. Still she refrained from yanking it off, instead she untied the scarf under her chin and freed it most fastidiously from the stalk, then placed it on top of the bundle of letters.

Her neck was hot crimson and the sinews rigid. She was at breaking point. Jákup recalled from his recent confirmation sermon the words about sweat *as great drops of blood.*

Mamma had broken out in a cold sweat.

"But I'm in no mind to let him get away with mocking Lena, hence my visit to Essa today to enquire about law and justice, and I had the letters with me. And as he was reading, he muttered, 'that poor lass…' and 'aye, a right scoundrel this one'. He will try as best he can, write to the shipping company and the seafarers' hiring office. Come of that what may, our Lena won't be turning to the municipality for support for her child.

But walking home I was overcome, choking with grief and chagrin, and I thought to myself that it would be a relief to speak to decent folk, and now that I passed yours, Sanna, I came inside. What I have here revealed I won't be carrying to every doorstep, you know that. And thank you kindly."

She fixed her clothes in front of the mirror. No fluff and not a crinkle in sight, not a speck on her black leather shoes. Jákup had never noticed how beautiful, how tall and graceful, she was. And she had nearly recovered her usual complexion.

"Jákup, stay clear of women, laddie, when your time comes," she remarked over her shoulder as she crossed the threshold. Mamma followed her to the door. With a puzzled look, Jákup watched her from the window.

Mamma was slumped by the fireplace. She muttered something about how everything repeats itself, about Lena and poor children, about Karin, who was over the worst now, the contractions would relent in time. They were a particular folk…

Now Jákup understood why the scarf, and all those fancy words and preaching tone… what men are like… what people are like… beware of women. And out of the blue he remembered his *omma* always saying, 'then there won't be much left for brother's best!' And he felt bashful; hadn't he been scared witless moments ago, and didn't remembering 'brother's best' come close to aping Karin?

"Listen Jákup, does our kin care too much about goings on? …how much is a flash in the pan? …or does it care too little? Aye, I said our kin, don't you know how closely we are related to Karin?" Jákup kept mum, she probably wasn't expecting a reply anyway. She sat there pale as a ghost… like she was in another world.

"…but how about that tea?" Jákup had no appetite, though to comfort his mamma said that he would look in again later. And then he left, in a gloomy mood.

And so come Midsummer Lena bore another son.

Per í Vík had got it into his head that Jákup should join his crew. Jákup himself probably wanted to, but then there was his mamma and what she might think. Never mind, Per declared, talking to the woman was worth a try, and so one day in early spring, while Jákup was in, he strode up to their door.

"Good day, Sanna, I'm here on an errand. No, I shan't be coming inside, thank you kindly, I'll take my rest here on the peat crate. Let me get straight to it. I've come to ask if your Jákup can come aboard with us, come sailing on *The Refuge*? My question is: why not find out if Jákup, who had a sailor through-and-through, especially one with Sámal's fishing luck, for a father, well, if he hasn't inherited his father's gifts? Not that I'm one to meddle, Sanna, but where will it lead? Having the boy rove from sail loft to salt basement, and now even finding him in Dal's office morning, noon and night. I mention Dal, I've already conversed with him, Jákup has his blessing to go and his blessing to return should the sea not agree with him. Sanna! No arguing that you keep your hands cleaner sitting and chewing on a pen handle, strutting about with a middle parting and perfumed hair every day, and what's more, donning a cufflink shirt to parade on Sundays; compared to living in the stink of fish guts, scales and sweat, permanently soaked to the bone! But what lies between the two, Sanna, is a man! I'm being straight with you. The perils of the sea you say? Don't you think Our Father cares as much for us at sea as he does on land? Aye, He does, just as much, at the least! And has He not himself placed us, these islands in their entirety, here in the Atlantic? Peril and peril, aye, *between life and death is but a fragile plank*, but Sanna, we can help ourselves, and in no small measure, that's the truth! Like with a good vessel! It's no empty boast when I say that *The Refuge* is among the finest ships in the land, because she *is* the best, and I love her as much as any lady. And did you know, Sanna, what refuge means? A seal cave, a shelter, Sanna, could it be any lovelier or better, a shelter!

The crew is tiptop, our first mate, Billu-Símun, renowned for all his virtues… he knew Sámal, fished with him in his youth and still speaks of him… and myself as captain? I'd venture that, nobody thinks me inferior in the maritime arts, and I'm mild tempered in daily dealings, I'm no man of harsh measures. And yet another thing, Sanna, you, as the sensible person you are, must know that it can spoil a boy to cling to his mother's skirt. Besides, I'd be happy to take him off to sleep in my cabin, take him under my wing!"

Jákup had been stood there smiling. Blimey, the captain really knew how to handle his mamma, nobody had been that good. He liked Per.

Mamma probably did too, because she replied that if Jákup wants to go, she won't be standing in his way, and that she can tell the captain will take good care of him.

And with that Jákup was signed on.

There was no comparing darting between houses and rolling from gunwale to gunwale on board *The Refuge*. Jákup slept in the fore, he hadn't come out from under his mother's skirt to cling to the captain's coattails. And he found that Per's words were true about the vessel, Per himself and the crew. He was also told that the crew was no less tiptop with him, Jákup, on board.

When they returned from his first expeditions to land their catch, before heading to Icelandic waters, Jákup's mamma found him both taller and broader, but as Per said, "How else could it be, Sanna, good appetite, good sleep and good treatment and under my wing? Jákup is doing jolly well, he isn't scared or squeamish, but he is a sensitive soul, though quite where a scrap like him gets that from… once that's brushed off, and I shall do my best, then he'll be good; that he's a rascal and mischievous monkey to boot, so be it! And Dal is *not* having him back!"

But there had been so much for Jákup to assimilate in this new world, to learn, and be mindful of.

One such thing was having words on board. He couldn't stomach it, not only because he might easily regret it, but worse, he couldn't forget it. Not the good (he thought) or the bad, even after any anger had completely dissipated, something remained. How people appeared to him, to remember or forget, and how memory and oblivion manifested, that was the measure he considered them by. And people who took everything like water off a duck's back spooked him.

And then there was faith, religion. Here he met it in a new guise, only the readings from the book of sermons, which the captain read out, remained the same.

But the quarrels it bred between men! Jákup rarely caught any meanings, but many a turn of phrase stuck with him, like one evening a gabber was teasing someone, who otherwise never intervened, with a, 'and hear me now, that Our Lord created the world in seven days, that much we know.' Countered by, 'I wouldn't know what you know, but that he created it in six, that much I've heard!' And that settled matters for that evening.

Yes knowing… or having heard… and the hymns… some could sit and sing about crystal heavens, pearly gates and precious gems… others about the devil's mire, pain and darkness. The former brought him no comfort and the latter rather frightened him. He remembered one Sunday on his way home from church, that already on the doorstep a man was standing aghast, 'What's the world coming to, the vicar said in his sermon that hell doesn't exist!' And he could still hear his *omma*'s voice, a scoffing confirmation, 'Why does that anger you so?' And the man was speechless. Jákup never piped up and could find himself sitting between brothers of different religious communities, who in good faith sat through a, to his mind, half-mad, or tangled, communal worship.

But the routine at sea certainly didn't allow for wallowing in feelings. He couldn't complain, he had friends on board, and he harboured no desire to grumble about or find fault in people or censure their behaviour. Censuring himself he tried… to his best ability… and found no lack of cause.

And time went by. Five years. Jákup had fished in both Icelandic and Greenlandic waters, and been to foreign ports landing the catch. His home-trade-master certificate arrived this past winter.

The Refuge returned from the North Sea early one summer morning with a sick man. The crew was to restock supplies and under strict orders to be back at the landing at five in the afternoon to row the captain back on board.

Jákup managed to arrange his shifts so that he could go ashore.

The first he heard as he crossed the threshold back home was that Karin was lying on the bier and would be laid to rest the same day. His mamma was so wracked by a cough that she felt she would ruin the service if she attended the funeral, so she asked if Jákup would follow Karin to her grave, there was a suit hanging ready to wear and a dark hat.

As Jákup changed his clothes he thought about Karin, from that evening when he was told that '*omma* is so happy,' what a joy that proved! He recalled Karin sitting by the window pouring her heart out. No matter now… it was all over…

He felt so strange, so tired, though there had been nothing to tire him. On board they had been laughing at Ívar, who had declared that he was going ashore today *to make sure of his girl*. For a long time now they had been teasing him with this self same girl, who they said he would never have pursued were her father not a wealthy man, what the callous Ívar really wanted to secure was the rights to the pasture, and Ívar protested furiously. A couple of them were puffing out their chests, because they had a girl now, others were no less proud because their wives had born children. Jákup wasn't jealous, no that wasn't it… but could sometimes feel so single and detached… he couldn't quite bring himself to join in just to announce that his sister had had a daughter and that he was an uncle…

He looked in the mirror… remembering Karin… and that plant pot and the scarf. Why were the flowerpots so barren this time of year? Oh, laddie, the flowers were sent to Karin… Karin was always so fond of flowers.

When he reached á Hellu he felt a little embarrassed. People looked at him as if they were expecting to see his mamma, not him, they probably didn't know that *The Refuge* had come in.

Then the bells tolled, everyone gathered behind the coffin.

The men who sang over the body turned to face the funeral party and intoned the hymn

Go and let my grave be made...[13]

Her eldest son, Janus, and the vicar walked side by side, Janus' wife had Little Tummas with her, Hans Pauli and Einar walked each with their wife and next to Lena walked Petur, to whom they were probably related, or maybe it was just because he lived with the same throng on the slope. Lena's little boys were nowhere to be seen.

Jákup's prayers weren't exactly focused. Old memories kept disrupting him, and he noticed both this and that... wasn't Greta wearing grey socks with white soles in black leather shoes that were so big that a shining white rim was revealed every time she lifted her foot. The first time the stands were placed under the coffin, Jákup fled from Greta's side, at least that would give him peace from that distraction. It also helped that he knew the hymn by heart and it gave him comfort to follow the verses.

The first hymn ended. Again the three singers turned to the mourners. Then launched into the hymn:

Keep sorrow and lament in moderation[14]

and here Jákup only knew the first verse.

The party had reached the bridge over the estuary. The men rested the coffin here too. Bartals's wife, who had been rinsing out coal sacks, had stood up, she was crying, but glanced down at herself, and when she saw how dirty her apron was, dried her eyes with the back of her hand. He had ended up standing right next to her and could hear her, "But Jákup, laddie, you here?"

They put their shoulders to the bier bars again and the funeral party reached the graveyard.

The newly arrived parish curate had prepared his sermon from the verse:

I know of a little Paradise
so easy 'tis to find
where faith and baptism ne'er fully
abandoned heart or mind[15]

This dearly departed woman he had only seen and spoken to twice; when he first came to the parish and called on the parishioners, and now that she fell ill. And yet he could picture her clearly, a striking woman dignified in every manner, and he believed that she had preserved her childhood faith in the Almighty One, and she had therefore resided in the heavenly kingdom we possess here on Earth, and now she was kept in the Heavenly Kingdom to which we all once, by grace, shall return.

As the curate in his sermon reeled off every verse in the hymn, Jákup remembered Karin in difficult moments, *joyous we sense a soft whisper with divine traces,* had she heard that whisper? Had she sensed the traces?

The mourners stood in silence. Earth was thrown and the hymn:

Brothers and Sisters Here We Part[16]

was sung.

And each, as the hymn prescribed, parted on their

sanctioned ways.

Jákup walked with Greta. When they reached her home á Bakka, she invited him inside for a cup of coffee and he obliged, he was headed to his paternal aunt's house anyway and she lived nearby. He took a seat on the kitchen bench.

While she kindled and hung the kettle over the fire, she rambled, aye that was Karin released and we're left here... and there had been no drying anything this season... and croup was doing the rounds of the neighbourhood...

To say something, Jákup asked about his contemporary Pedda and whether the ship he was signed on with, *The Aldan*, had been in to land its catch.

She huffed at him not to mention Pedda. He had left *The Aldan*, washed up and blamed his health, but the truth was that he'd started chasing after Sigrið, the joiner's daughter, aye he, Jákup, and Sigrið had known each other since childhood, of course, wasn't Jákup's mamma her godmother? And Sigrið was friendly with everyone, but there was as yet no word of a suitor, but she'd never think that the girl would settle for Pedda. What did Jákup make of it? She had seen her and Jákup walk out together with their friend the Icelander in broad daylight. Was she waiting for someone perchance? She was a beauty. And Pedda was losing his senses. What would come of this! Pedda was in such a state, he had a good set of hands, he did. And in that he had a pretext for borrowing tools from both the joiner and the carpenter and his son, and then return them quick as... all to see that blessed lass...

Jákup didn't like to sit there listening to that drivel, he didn't like it one bit. It was as though Greta was being too forward about Sigrið. Was she to give her a character reference, or play matchmaker, or even consider, why… he had an impulse to defend Sigrið. Asking like this if Sigrið was waiting for someone… well, who knew, Jákup wouldn't mind having her for himself, he wouldn't mind that at all, though he thus far hadn't precisely set his sights on her. He really was in a strange mood today.

At long last he was handed his bowl where he sat, and in came Pedda, in a foul mood, bid good day and retreated to the back. Greta winked at Jákup, as if to say: there, you see!

Jákup thanked her and went to knock on his aunt's door.

His aunt had been expecting him, she had recognised the ship's boat at the landing.

The direction was north-north-east.

When was it that he and mamma had come up with this thing about the compass to convey what her mood was like? It was changeable, her mind was.

Oh, she never went to funerals. She'd rather sit and contemplate the departed, and counted more often those she had lost than those she had left. Karin and her had been friends since their youth, and it would be sad to sit alone reminiscing about what they had together. People remembered so differently, for some memories faded gradually, and for others they fell away… in chunks… not so with Karin and her.

What did the vicar have to say? Well, then he was one of the clergy, who let everyone flock to the top rung in heaven, the previous vicar barely knew if anyone ever made it across the pearly threshold. And on one's own one could sit and try to struggle through what one felt in one's own heart, but did a single soul know even a glimmer about what was behind death? And the hymns? Of the first one she said nothing, but Jákup couldn't tell if she was moved or shocked when he mentioned *Keep Sorrow and Lament in Moderation.* She squinted as if trying to recall it, then reached for her hymnal and read to herself. And then read it again aloud:

What of all grace was bereft
and became one with the dust
shall become a shining abode
for the soul in heaven above.

"Jákup! I saw Karin before she let go *of all grace bereft*, no!... Jákup have you ever considered how beautiful must be the earth from whence the children of men spring?"

She appeared to shrug something off and then returned to the everyday.

"That mild sermon the curate gave, aye, much has softened and smoothed. Karin had her troubles, she as so many. She didn't get the boy she wanted, and then that blow from Lena, her only daughter, who also could have fared better. But luckily, Karin knew before she died that Lena would cast anchor. He, Peter, the widower, and Lena would already have held their wedding at home had Karin not taken to her bed, and the boys would be taken in by Einar and his wife. Karin had full faith in this before she died. Lena herself loved them too. How will they fare, may fortune be kind to them, poor mites! Aye, here we sat discussing kinfolk and family traits, but how about that black lank Óli... hair as bushy as feathers, and that dumpling Luddi... like a licked calf, blond. The aunt barely knew where her own children had inherited their inner faults, and who they looked like on the outside, well, the hide revealed that plain as day… no, better to save oneself from speculation as regards such matters. But one thing had always helped Karin and that was that she had never uttered a word about her misfortunes! No hand wringing and no whinging!

But surely it was about time Jákup went on his way, what with the direction the wind was now taking, they would no doubt set sail tonight.

She walked him to the door.

"It brings me joy, laddie, that you behave so well. You gawp! Aye, you would, there's nary a whisper to be heard of you, nothing about the drink or chasing lasses. That you won't leave the dance floor whether there's a Faroese ballad to be chanted or a harmonica playing an English polka, well, there may be some who now think that's a sin too, still, it's not yet considered to be one. Oh, there goes Pedda, poor wretch, driven out of the house by Greta's prattling. If only some fine young man would take that lass for good, it would give Pedda a little peace, if nothing else then at least from his mother!"

She patted Jákup gently between the shoulder blades and shooed him outside.

"Go now, fare thee well and remember me to your mamma!"

Jákup picked his path home, so he wouldn't meet a soul. He didn't feel up to any more talking or listening.

What his aunt had said about Karin comforted him… also what she thought Karin had never breathed a word of. But Greta and her twaddle! His aunt would never have bemoaned

Pedda hadn't Greta filled her ears… it was probably whispered on every corner, and was Sigrið to be swept up in all that chatter! His aunt had sought a fine young man to go out with the girl, his aunt was right. Chase after skirts was something he, Jákup, would never do, but wasn't he a young man, one of the few, if there even was anyone else, who could enter the fray in earnest?

It brought to mind the past winter, when he and Halldór agreed to do a Faroese dance locking arms with Sigrið, one on each side… *troddu lættliga dansin,*[17] they chanted. Curious, she didn't tread lightly, not even the English dances… there were better dancers… such as Anna, a right tease that one was, you couldn't trust her, but dancing with her, my oh my… but the boys were at fault too… the way they milled about her… never mind that. Halldór would probably be back here soon, he was something else, what with the way he acted, he just *did* whatever he had his heart set on, like in play and without even trying, he was quite the merchant, knew how to buy and sell… what fun it would be to see his mug when he heard, from Jákup's own account, this thing about Sigrið… well, once there was a thing to be told, yes… now that it would soon be accomplished.

He felt his mind lighten as he walked here in peace…

He reached the doorstep.

"Jákup, love, where did you get to? Oh how I missed you!"

Jákup told her.

Mamma who sat with her hymnal and a Christian book in front of her, enquired first about his aunt, what the direction was, then she could assess for herself. And as that visit was recounted, the funeral was narrated too. She knew the hymns by heart and she could piece together the outline of the sermon.

When Jákup recognised the book cover it reminded him, as usual, of holding the books open in front of his eyes, while testing his memory, and that precisely those readings, *about the day after death*, those were the ones mamma would know by heart.

He knew that his mamma believed wholeheartedly in a life after this earthly one. And not in any hell, but in a cleansing and that 'God would finally be all in everyone and all would be one.'

When Jákup had retold what his aunt had added about the funeral, he cautiously mentioned the blow Karin had suffered from not getting the man she wanted, and then hinted at a question as to whether Karin had married badly.

Mamma refused to speak of any of this; his aunt and Karin had been in love with the same boy, and that neither nabbed him probably helped them remain friends for all their days. And neither one nor the other had married badly, as people like to call it. The men they got were smitten with them, and this much she would say of them that they never opened their mouths about their husbands to chastise them. Now it was all over... only his aunt was left to reminisce... such is the way of the flesh.

Jákup had to start thinking about changing his clothes. He declined to have any tea as food would be served as soon as they were on board.

He looked for the things that he wanted to bring along and stuffed them all into his sea bag. He suddenly found himself discontented with the various garments, as a suitor he had to be better dressed, he paid too little attention to clothes… this shirt in his hand… no, there was nothing of any use here…

And he chanted at the top of his voice:

And his finest shirt he donned
Green silken shirt richly adorn'd[18]

…the ballads tripped over one another… bugger that, the tune was the same…

Hr. Plov leapt o'er planks so broad,
and he said nary a single word.[19]

Aye, this was how it should be, go forth boldly without boasting… he knew his immediate design. The result?

…first he had to get back on board.

When he returned to the sitting room, he saw mamma sitting as if she were regretting something.

"Jákup, we are peculiar people, the pair of us. You know, when you broke into song, I sat here feeling like Dani-Meya, because I was so happy for you… how do these things come about? There was no rhyme or reason with what we were speaking of just now!"

Jákup said he knew how his turn had come about, it was because of the clothes. But did mamma remember the comedy about the other Jákup? Aye, she remembered, and not just by half.

And suddenly Jákup stood there hands on his hips singing the part of Meya:

My sweetest son, my heart's joy and my pride,
with your dashing looks you'll soon find a bride
My heart swells with the bliss of Paradise...

suddenly he felt bashful and faltered... he hadn't made it all the way to his namesake. Mamma just thought that he had forgotten the last line and declaimed it herself, smiling:

my darling Jacob heed this my advice,
on your voyage to seek her fair hand

but then added, that this wasn't precisely what, she as Meya, had been thinking about.

Again she asked him to please hurry up and have a little tea, he must be hungry.

Jákup teased her and asked if she sat there thinking that no one could take care of him the way she did, but she would have none of it... she wasn't thinking that far ahead, not until his advances had been turned down!

Now that tea was mentioned again, he recalled Karin once more and tea that day long since. Had she asked him to beware of women? And in the same breath he remembered his *omma*, would she not now have glimpsed something 'for brother's best'?

It was time to leave and he had finished packing his sea bag.

"Jákup, I'll miss you, I miss you every day... tell me, do you ever miss me?"

"Somewhat. And sometimes."

Jákup had replied in a drawling imitation of her rather

pathetic tone.

"Serves me right for asking… you're insufferable!"

She shoed him away and they both smiled.

Jákup caressed her hand, which was again resting on the book of sermons, and said his goodbye.

"Aye, fare well my blessed son and God be with you!"

He grabbed his sea bag and then he was outside.

On the way down to the landing Andras came sauntering along, face like a full moon, good day, good day! So, Anna had probably made up again for the seventh time and he had gone along with it, that dunce… not an ounce of pride. Then again, what was it to him, Jákup, whether Andras proposed, Greta jabbered or Pedda rambled! He had his own business to mind… he would, the very day *The Refuge* was back in the bay, ask for Sigrið's hand… today it would not be done! And how it had gone for Ívar and how they would tease him… that was between Ívar and them… nobody was going to taunt him, Jákup, who hadn't, and never would, make untimely mention of making sure of a girl; Sigrið was only to be mentioned once ha *had* made sure of her.

At the landing almost everyone had arrived except the captain and mate. That Ívar didn't get the girl was clear. Him and Mikkjal were standing over a sack of threshed barley and Ívar exclaimed that threshed barley would not cross the gunwale, he would sink the sack first; he could not stand or tolerate threshed barley. Mikkjal laughed. Ólavur just stood there silently pleased about his new gumboots, and oh, oh, there was that naive bovine Petur Jakke shooting his mouth off for the umpteenth time about the wonderful primus stove, which helped him escape untimely marriage when his mother passed and he and his father lacked a woman around the house. Jabber here and chatter there. Some were stowing cargo in the fore of the boat, Hans Pauli, tragic that he was half-deaf! Was idling on the stern thwart.

Jákup sat on a keg at the edge of the landing and across from the rear of the boat. His gaze fell directly on the sail loft across the bay and his thoughts again revisited that afternoon when *The Mandal* arrived in the fog, and what came after. And it was noon again today, in fair weather. So he turned and rose to look at the smoke columns, how they stood today; and as he let his eyes follow the contour of the boathouses, he took a step back… hearing Hans Pauli's voice,

"Oi, Jákup, let me by so I can move the boat before you tumble in backwards and kill yourself!"

…because in front of the boat houses he saw a couple come strolling, Halldór and Sigrið, him on the outside with his arm around her shoulders, and then he bent down towards her face… there was a white neck…

He never dreamed… he never thought… was there something he had forgotten and didn't want to remember… some dreadful experience he had lived, but forgotten, which now came back to haunt him… had he let go somehow… had something slipped through his fingers…

He took a step forward. They were out of sight now.

Wasn't it the captain's voice he could hear? He turned on his heel.

It was the captain. If only Per would keep mum for once. But no.

"Listen, Jákup! Can you guess who I met, and who I see

you haven't spotted, because you were busy gazing out to sea? Halldór, the Icelander, your friend, and her the lovely smiling Sigrið! We said our greetings! Congrats, congrats, I said because there was no mistaking anything there. 'But listen, Sigrið! I'd intended for it to be Jákup and you,' I said it in jest. He just laughed, but she has a way with words and replied, 'That can hardly have been Jákup's intention, I would have sensed it otherwise and I have not.' But congrats, I repeated, as I said!

Listen, Jákup, you seem a little off colour to me!"

But Jákup had just been to Karin's funeral.

Per looked at him knowingly, "Did you also attend the wake, laddie, officially or privately, eh? Had a nip? And if that's the case…!"

No, Jákup hadn't touched a drop neither here nor there.

Fortunately Per left him now, barrelling away. Everything and everyone found their place, even the threshed barley and Ívar too. The mate was also there now. And they pushed off.

Jákup sat on the stern thwart, Per in the rear, and again he searched Jákup, who Ólavur had already kneed once and told to bloody row! Might the captain now hold his tongue? Of course not! …Thank heavens that Hans Pauli was half deaf!

"Take my advice, don't bother with women… to hell with them! Not that I haven't bothered… no, dear Jákup, not that I haven't! Anything to do with love is just so complicated, love is a strange herb, that's what the man said, you know about the *tree of knowledge!* Aye, you know I've heard said, after a Swede, if memory serves, 'that in that chapter it's only the sin that wasn't committed that begets regret'… expressed in rhyme, such things always are, but *that* is a lie!

You're too inexperienced to know anything or suggest anything, luckily. *The Drink is foul*, Kingo composed, you'll find that verse in full in the hymnal."

It seemed to Jákup like Per was talking just as much to himself. They had reached the ship. As the captain climbed up he chanted:

The seal bull talks to his cow,
and tells her still to stay,
the seas are stirring round our cave;
no man can come hunting today!

Jákup came up behind him and the captain clutched his arm before intoning the second half of the verse accompanied by the steps.

The captain then grabbed Jákup's shoulders. "How old are you?—This is your twenty-second year you say! Twenty-one and unattached! Jákup, when we, God willing, come home again this autumn, then I want, nay, I'm telling you to pull yourself together, *hoist, hoist the sails!*[20] And join the merchant marine, sail the wide world… forget about them all, your mamma I shall take under my mantle… metaphorically speaking, of course, but forget, as I said, them all! And off you go to sleep, for now!"

Then the captain went bustling to the rear, while Jákup made his way to the front, keeping to the side so as not to be in anyone's way. He felt both heavy and tired.

How could, in this tangle or chapter the captain had just mentioned, his blunder be cleared up? He stood still and reminded himself of what had happened this day, blow by blow, and he returned to that sight. There they were strolling… did he wish himself in Halldór's place… his arm around Sigrið's neck and…?

Foggy brained and gaping he just stood there…

No! He would not want to make a spectacle of himself in public like that… embracing and… *No!*

He was awake.

But what was it his mamma had said and asked about that time… about the kin… and taking action… about the flash in the pan?

He had acted now! Karin had been in grave distress, but he? Was there something in his nature for which he had to suffer? He was more embarrassed than ashamed. So it was a relief that he had taken action within himself and for himself… the captain didn't count.

There was no tangle here, but probably a chapter. He had only begun to think about women, and Sigrið, whom he liked, whom he was fond of the way he was fond of his sister, Sigrið had been transformed into an initiative, an action… become the flash!

He had escaped, and he didn't have any energy left to muster, not for embarrassment or for shame.

But now he had made it to the sheltered cave and threw himself headlong into the bunk… in still seas… in this moment he was fonder of *The Refuge* than of any woman. In this moment…

Then he dozed off… for now.

The Refuge

by

Heđin Brú

translated by Lindy Falk van Rooyen

As far back as you can remember you felt unwanted.

You were a thin-skinned child, who believed that everyone held you in contempt, even your mother and father.

You played alone, from the day you could grasp a building block in your own hand.

And yet, you longed to fit in.

When the other kids played together, you watched from the sidelines, spied on them from a distance—from underneath a rock, behind a back, or a fence next to the field.

If the others asked you to join in, you ran away.

When you were a little older, you threw stones.

So they gave up. Stopped asking you to play.

Soon, no one took any notice of you at all.

You cried bitterly when no one was looking.

You begrudged the others the ease with which they were together, even as they squabbled, joked and hung around each other's necks. With the envy came the desire for revenge. You would get up in the middle of the night and go down to the playground. Destroy what they had built in the sandpit. You stole their toys and tossed them off a cliff and into the sea.

Afterwards, when you crept back into bed, you could not sleep. Tossed and turned in your dreams, your conscience plagued by the harm you had done. The day after you were miserable, your mind incrementally laden with guilt.

You were mean to young and old indiscriminately because you believed that they despised you.

But you were wrong.

Soon you were old enough to go to school. It was torture for you! The teacher hit you and the children teased you; they might have pitied you, but there was no doubt that you were a changeling, and there was nothing you could do about it.

You plotted your escape from an early age, determined to run away from home and make your fortune far away; once you had become a successful man in the big wide world, you would come home to the island and build a refuge on a lavish farm; and whenever the people from the village walked past, they would acknowledge your greatness—but the gardens would keep them at bay.

For you, the wide world was no farther than the other side of the Sound. And here, it was even worse: this world simmered and seethed—men fought tooth and claw in battles that required strength, dignity and bravery.

And you had none of the above.

You did not even have the courage to reach the ford, never mind cross the divide. Instead, on tender feet and trembling with fear, you took the long way around.

When at last you tentatively came forward to collect the crumbs that they had reluctantly offered, you were irascible.

You took offence. You believed that every word they uttered was in spite, every raised eyebrow was a slight or some kind of veiled insult, and every laugh they shared was at your expense.

So you left.

For a while, you tried to go it alone. Rowed out to sea single-handedly. When you returned to the harbour, you stayed on the fringe and tried to sell your fish on the landing bridge, just like other men. But before long, you noticed that the buyers didn't treat you the same as they did the other fishermen; it was clear to you that they preferred to trade with them, even if no one said as much out loud.

So you gave up trying to be a fisherman.

Besides, you were not happy in the small loft room near the harbour which you had rented. You knew that the landlady wanted you to leave. She had not said so directly, but every time you met her in the hallway, you could see reproach in her eyes.

As such, living with her became intolerable, and you decided to cancel the agreement, before anyone got wind of your landlady's wish to do so.

Now you had nowhere to live. So you decided to buy an abandoned house in town, and you only went out fishing to cover your own needs for fresh fish and food. Greeted only those people, who greeted you first, once in a while, when they passed you in the street.

The house in town offered some protection. You could simply close the door and draw the curtains, in your own home; although it was no more than a small cottage, it did have an inkling of the grand refuge which you had resolved to build. Of course, it was neither on the outskirts of your childhood village, nor was it located on the island where you had grown up, nor was it the magnificent fortress you had in mind, but it *did* exist—in brick and mortar—and *you* owned it.

So you gave up the idea of returning home to the island as a worldly, self-made man. But you remained firm on the idea of a refuge; you were absolutely determined to build a home which could keep people at a safe distance, so you would neither have to see nor hear them.

Then you got a woman in the house. A girl, whose incompetence, in your opinion, you indulged with great forbearance.

You and she had been co-lodgers at the old woman's house near the harbour: above your loft room was an attic with a bed where the girl slept.

The quiet girl had been living in the attic for some years before your arrival. But in all the time that you had lived under the same roof, you had never once heard her voice. Except for that one night, when you had climbed up onto a wall to get a better look at some young people enjoying themselves in the dance hall next door; when you came back you heard the girl snoring in the attic. Perhaps you had lingered on the stair, or just outside her door, for a moment, in desperate longing.

But when you moved to the cottage you missed her. So you decided to go back for her. Bring her home. She agreed when you asked. But it was no more than that: "Yes," she said. Then she put her meagre belongings in a battered old shoulder bag and followed you back home.

It was not long before you realised that the house in the village had been a mistake.

You could not stand being so close to your neighbours; the gaps between the houses that were clustered around the yard were much too small. No, it was essential, you thought, that your home be built under open skies, out in the fields, where there was space for the garden and the farmland that you wished to cultivate.

Besides, the townsfolk constantly invaded your privacy. If, for instance, you happened to pass someone on the cattle track, they always stopped for a chat. They asked questions and raised their eyebrows. It felt as if they were prying. And you didn't care for it one bit. You tried to stay indoors as much as possible. You rarely went to town. You stayed in the fields whenever the weather allowed. You avoided walking through the yard, or in amongst the houses, before your neighbours had turned in for the night.

All your efforts were in vain.

The townsfolk were adamant. They popped in for a visit. Sat themselves down in your kitchen and asked you how you were.

You had to lock the door and keep guard by the window. But this didn't help either. Now they pounded on the door, asking if you were sick or needed a doctor; when you didn't open it, they insisted, yelled through the door that they had brought you something to eat. This only happened once or twice, then they stopped. But there was no respite for you; you could still hear them loitering outside, day and night.

You tried to remind yourself that townsfolk were both kind and generous. And yet you lived in fear of your neighbours, suspected them of all kinds of malicious intent.

For her part, the Quiet Girl seemed unperturbed. Her face

lit up when they came, she even smiled sometimes, even if she never said a word.

Your agitation and anxiety grew, it was unbearable. You despaired!

In the yard, the children sniggered behind their hands. Rang your doorbell and ran away. The adults were bad enough, but the children were vicious; they leered and pointed, played tricks on you, peeped through the windows and wiggled the door handle.

When you couldn't take it anymore, you ripped open the door and stormed out like a hurricane, waving your arms, shouting and yelling at the children. But this only made things worse; it was great sport amongst the children. They went to great lengths to provoke you, taunting you till you burst out of the door. For a while, the villagers tried to shoo their children away, but never failed to peep through your window as they did, and you could tell that they also found it funny.

This was no way to live. Something had to done and soon. Your boat was no longer an option, either; you couldn't stand the townsmen, and you would not condescend to ask them for help. Besides, it was impossible for you to manoeuvre the boat over the rocks and down to the shore on your own.

But then your parents died, leaving you a generous inheritance.

You sold the boat and bought yourself a large piece of land, deep in the mountain gorge.

On Midsummer's Night, you locked your house, packed the necessary tools and provisions into a rucksack and set out long before dawn. You made a huge racket whilst everyone else was still asleep, and yet, as you made your way out of town, not one dog barked, not a single cock crowed.

You took the path north to the new building site, and when you reached the North Peak, you sat down for a moment to catch your breath and eat a bite of food.

The sun was just rising over the ridge, casting its golden glow over the landscape. Far down below, the village glittered. The Quiet Girl let out a sigh. To your surprise, she got to her feet and clapped her hands: "Look how beautiful the village is!" Then she sat down again, silent as before. Chewed on the slice of toast that she held in her hand. Her face revealed nothing.

You stared at her. It was the first time you had ever heard her speak without being spoken to first. But it only took you a moment to recover: "Silence, you bitch! It's a hell-hole, a filthy pit of a village, and that's my final word on the subject!"

You had jumped to your feet, brandishing your walking stick, but you kept your distance. In a rage, you backed away from her and threw the stick over the edge of the cliff. Then you gathered your equipment and set off down the cattle track. The Quiet Girl followed in your footsteps like a scolded dog.

You were so angry that your knees were shaking. You realised what a colossal mistake it had been to bring this woman into your home. You berated yourself bitterly. It was beyond comprehension that you ever could have wanted her presence. You had been certain that she had agreed with you on everything. *How could you have been so blind? How dare she have an opinion of her own?!*

All at once you realised that she had been on their side all along.

Once again the townsfolk had forced you to move.

Now you understood what had really been going on: all this time, *she* was the one, who enticed people to the house. You guessed that she had invited the other women over for coffee when you were away. They sat in *your* living room, talking behind your back.

By the time you arrived at the building site the Quiet Girl was exhausted. She could tell that you were angry, even if she didn't understand why. And she would not dream of asking; it was not in her nature to ask for explanations.

Now your grand design was to erect a temporary shelter where you could live whilst you built your refuge; once it was completed, you would dismantle the house in the village, bring the timber up to the mountain, and rebuild your home here.

As soon as you arrived, you started digging foundations for the shelter. By late afternoon, you were tired, so you sat down to eat, ignoring the Quiet Girl entirely.

She looked up, once, but then continued working. She said nothing.

You ate your fill, wrapped up the remainder of the food in a wax-cloth, packed it into your rucksack. Then you started working again. Not a word was exchanged; silence was ingrained in your relationship. Besides, if something needed to be said, *you* said it.

A few hours later, the Quiet Girl staggered over to a stream. She sank to her knees and drank some water. Then got to her feet and started digging again.

When the sun finally went down behind the ridge, you stopped working. Took out your food and ate your fill again. You pretended that the Quiet Girl did not exist.

This time she did not look up. Simply paused her digging for a moment, leaning heavily on her spade.

You sat down to rest. Lit your pipe and smoked for a while.

The girl let go of the spade and collapsed onto the ground, gasping for breath.

"Why aren't you digging," you said.

"Hungry," she said. "So… hungry."

You unwrapped the wax-cloth, found a half-picked chicken bone and tossed it at her feet.

She groped for the bone, brought it to her mouth and gnawed on it for a while. Crawled to the stream on all fours and drank a little water. Then she started digging again.

Late in the evening, when you were satisfied that the townsfolk would have turned in for the night, you gathered up your tools, packed your rucksack and set off down the hill.

You never spared the Quiet Girl a thought; not once did you look over your shoulder to see if she was behind you.

The townsfolk noticed that the girl was not with you when you returned. A muscular man, who everyone simply called Strongman, confronted you on the cattle track. Everyone knew that the Quiet Girl had accompanied you into the gorge in the early hours of the previous night, and Strongman asked why she had not returned with you?

You ignored the man, simply pretended you neither heard nor saw him, and kept walking.

But he came after you. And this time, he laid a hand on your arm. Now you *had* to stop.

"Tell me where she is!"

Still you said nothing. You simply stood staring at the ground, your face as if cast in iron.

You were angered by the grip on your arm. You did your best to hide your revulsion. Your fear.

Strongman tightened his grasp. He squeezed your arm so tight in his huge fist that you winced in pain.

"Where is the Quiet Girl?!" he demanded.

You said nothing.

Strongman squeezed your arm even harder.

Tears came to your eyes. Your knees began to shake. But not a word passed your lips.

Now Strongman's fingers dug into the bone and you squealed like a pig.

"Tell me!" he said between clenched teeth. He kept his voice low because he was reluctant to disturb the others, who had long since gone to bed.

The pain was too much for you, so Strongman got his answer: you told him that you had left her behind. He stared at you hard, for about five seconds, but they seemed to last for hours. And the look in his eyes terrified you. He could barely contain himself, all he wanted to do was… suddenly, he dropped your arm, as if it were red hot. Then he turned on his heel and knocked on the nearest door. Two men were dispatched into the mountains to fetch the Quiet Girl immediately. They would bring her home: not to your house, of course, he said. She would be returned to good folks, who would take care of her, he emphasised. In all likelihood, she would be sent back to the old woman's place near the harbour.

You stumbled back home in a daze. Leaning heavily on the frame, you managed to open the door. Inside, you threw yourself onto the window seat and wept like a child.

You could still feel Strongman's hand on your arm. It was as if the touch of another person had crushed every ounce of strength you possessed. Your dignity was in tatters. You could not deny that you had always felt inferior to Strongman—physically—but you had always taken solace in the fact that you did not *need* other people: living on your own had always been a conscious choice. But now you knew it was an illusion. The entire fallacy had crumbled.

Your life was a living death! Failure weighed heavily on your soul. Had Strongman laid a single finger on you in that moment, your knees would have buckled. No, it was impossible to face him again.

Your mind was spinning, you closed your eyes, and must have blacked out, because when you opened them again, it was late into the night. You were shivering with cold, utterly wretched. Now you noticed that the front door was open. You stumbled to your feet to shut it. *Had someone come inside?*

You staggered through the rooms, filled with rage and the lust for revenge—"If that woman thinks she can spend another night under my roof she is gravely mistaken!" you fumed. But your rage was all for naught; the Quiet Girl had not come home.

You crept outside and entered your tool shed. Peered through the wooden slats, trying to glean what was happening on the other side of the yard, perhaps you could catch a glimpse of her. At last, looking up towards the ridge, you saw a group coming down the mountain. Yes, she was with them, supported by a man on either side, as they made their way out of the gorge.

You decided to wait, keep watch from the shed, and get a hold on yourself. It was best not to be home when they brought her back. "They wouldn't dare break into my shed!" you muttered to yourself.

Just then they entered the yard, threaded between the houses, and you held your breath. But they neither stopped in front of your house, nor took the path to your door. Instead, they mounted the stairs to Strongman's house. You saw him open the door and invite the Quiet Girl inside. The door closed behind her. Heading back to their own homes, the two men who had brought her back disappeared between the houses.

"So, they will not condescend to knocking on my door!" you fumed again. You had a mind to storm over to Strongman's place and rip his head off his shoulders. But your bravado petered out like sand in an hourglass. You sank to your knees, defeated; you were still the same, timid creature that scuttled under a rock at the first sign of conflict in your life.

Your mind blank, your body numb, you stole back to the house. You locked the front door behind you. In the kitchen, you put on a light and fumbled for a glass to pour yourself a drink. But when the flask and a glass were standing on the counter, you no longer felt like drinking. You put the bottle back in the cupboard.

You were about to lie down when you remembered that the Quiet Girl had left her clothes behind. You found her battered little shoulder bag under her bed and stuffed her things inside. Once the bag was filled you took it into the kitchen. Yanked open a drawer, pulled out a knife and stabbed the bag viciously till it was riddled with holes. Then you opened the front door and kicked the bag onto the doorstep.

Then you locked your door, put out the light, and went to bed.

It did not take you long to complete the shelter and move in.

Toiling from morning till night, you immediately started laying out the grounds for the refuge. By Michaelmas, the foundations were ready. Till now, you had not been back to the village; if there was something you needed, you headed west over the ridge and went to the village on the other side.

Now you started taking apart the house in the village. You cursed the fact that you had to do it in the daytime; the nights were too dark to work effectively, and the townsfolk were insufferably impertinent. The men kept volunteering to give you a hand; the women offered to make you dinner or bring you some coffee.

You made it clear that you did not need their help. And besides, you had your own food.

But they still came. You declined their offers, shook your head. Never said a word in return.

Then you had some bad luck: on the first night that you started bearing the timber up to the new site, you stumbled under your burden, twisted an ankle and strained your back. On the final stretch, you practically had to crawl on all fours. Somehow, you managed to reach the shelter. After that, you were bedridden for a week.

As soon as you had recovered sufficiently to stand you got out of bed and set out to fetch the remainder of the timber.

Evening fell, the moon rose, but it was misty and dark, so

your walk down the mountainside was treacherous.

When you finally arrived back at the house everything was gone. Not a plank, brick or nail of your fortress remained, even the doorstep was missing. You had been robbed! Your refuge was stolen from you, just before you were about to make your dream come true.

The lust for revenge burned in your veins.

What to do? Set fire to the village, burn everything to the ground?! You looked around, but there was no light in the windows, no footsteps on the path, not a sound. You spun on your heels in confusion, you felt like wrecking the fishermen's boats, smashing their hulls with rocks. You felt in your pocket for some matches. Nothing. So you ran out of the yard and headed down to the boat house instead.

A dog started barking in a cellar. Another followed, others joined in the cacophony, and soon it was as if the entire village was barking. Windows opened in the dark, front doors clattered open, boots sounded on the path. You crept under a boat raised on stilts nearby. Footsteps approached, men talking in hushed voices. Someone grabbed your leg and nearly gave you a heart attack—but it was just the snout of a dog, checking to see if you were alive; that you were, so the dog left you alone, and didn't bark because you weren't a stranger to the village. The men passed your hiding place and continued to the landing bridge.

The dogs quietened down. Peace reigned in the village again.

No, you did not smash the boats. Instead, you scurried down to the river and out of the village, your heart in your throat as you made your way along the cattle track and into the gorge.

Clear skies above, the moon at its zenith, the going was easier now. You walked slowly, without any concrete plan. Your building project was useless, but you relished the fact that you had been right about the townsfolk all along. All things considered, and despite being robbed of all the timber whilst you were sick in bed in the shelter without the means to defend yourself, this was your ultimate victory, and you were almost happy that they had stolen your property.

Whilst you mulled this over, you came upon a flat, dry ledge near to your building site. And there it was. You staggered over to the pile of timber and sank to your knees in disbelief: everything was there, even the doorstep. Intact and at your disposal.

You were utterly flabbergasted. You spun round, looked down at your hands, surprised to see that you were not bleeding, despite the knife in your back. You clawed the air in front of you and blinked your eyes. Your face twitched and your lips trembled.

That the timber had been stolen was a rational explanation that you could understand. But this… that they would stoop so low as to drag every building block of your house into the gorge—for the sole purpose of humiliating you—was beyond every conception of human decency.

You were livid, stamped your feet like a child, threw your arms to the heavens. You would *never* give the townsmen the satisfaction of knowing that *they* were the ones, who had relocated the refuge to the mountain! This was going to be *your* achievement and *yours* alone! As if carried upon a gust of wind, you took a beam under each armpit and took flight down the cattle track.

But the timber proved too cumbersome to manage on your own. You had never been a man of great physical strength, and you struggled to stay upright. You tried dragging the timber down the path behind you, but this didn't work either. You abandoned all attempts to move the materials any further and sat down to rest. Wiped the sweat from your brow. Considered your next move. Whichever way you looked at it, you couldn't claim to have been the first man to bring the timber to the mountain. You had not been the one to realise your dream. And dragging the timber back down the mountain only made you look like a fool.

But there was something else that you could do. You could simply burn it where it lay. All of it. Every beam, plank and wood shaving. As for the doorstep, you could simply push it over the North Peak and watch it roll down the slope. And you could buy a new one in the west village.

You sprang to your feet and ran back to the shelter. Found what you needed and charged back to the spot where you had abandoned the timber.

Not long after, a massive bonfire was raging right before you. The flames could be seen far and wide.

You fed the blaze all night, and before the village rose in the morning, you had rolled the doorstep over to the edge of the North Peak. As the sun rose over the horizon, you set the doorstep in motion. But instead of bearing down onto the village, a ledge deflected its course; it bounded west, tumbled over a waterfall and smashed to smithereens on the rocks below. You were dismayed that your plan had not worked as you had hoped; you had so been looking forward to seeing it crash through the stone wall and gouge a big hole in the infield.

By late afternoon, every ounce of your refuge-to-be was reduced to ash. You returned to the building site in the mountains. Took out some whale meat and sat down to eat.

Thus fortified, you hobbled back to the shelter, closed the door and slid a beam across the entrance.

The Homecoming

by

Martin Joensen

translated by Lindy Falk van Rooyen

The ship gradually leaned into the breeze. One, two, three, four sluggish billows in the wind till the jib slowly filled with air. The foresail was more unruly; in a flurry, it lashed against the mast, as if a recalcitrant colt, playfully slipping out of its halter and jumping overboard in a frolic of its own. For a moment, as if in two minds which way to plunge—or simply disinclined to give up the tack that it had grown accustomed to—the bow rose and cleaved to the wind. But then it surrendered; one after another, the sails billowed out, and the ship reluctantly bowed to the orders coming from the hand at the helm.

"Release the foresail!" the captain's voice was like a cannonball shot over the deck. Eirikur, a young mate who was in his third year on the smack, undid the relevant rigging and hauled on the rope for that beast of a foresail which always had a mind of its own. He acted swiftly—quick hands were essential when the skipper snapped his orders—and prayed to God that this was his last trip for the year; the last time he would have to battle the Devil. At sea, Eirikur never had peace; no sooner had he completed one task, sunk to his knees to catch his breath, than the next order boomed and he jumped to his feet, grabbed a rope, ducked under a sail. Heaven knows the pure elation he would feel the moment he felt solid ground under his feet again.

The grey skerries and black cliff faces before them were a magnificent welcome. The yellow houses, the trading post's dark red roofs, the fishing warehouses, the ship streaking towards the rocky shore. Sheer bliss filled Eirikur's heart whenever he saw the autumn sun casting its glow over the buildings on shore. He revelled in the knowledge that soon he could gather his belongings and leap onto solid ground, buoyed by his comrades' excited chatter about all those treasures that awaited them on land.

"You're dreaming, Erikur!" shouts the Southlander.

Eirikur's seasoned comrade is lanky, so tall he teeters on deck in his long boots, as if he would topple over at any moment. He's always yelling in Eirikur's ear, but he's a good man, and always in fine spirits.

"Now's the time to get rid of those whiskers of yours, Erikur," the Southlander declares. "They may not be thick and wiry just yet—fortunately for you—but they soon will be, my friend. Look, I've managed to salvage a little water for my bristles. It's high time we spruce ourselves up—gentlemen in the making, we are—decent folks—the kind of men who know how to dress for a special occasion," he adds with a wink. "Stick with me, my friend, you won't regret it, I promise you. I know all the local joints, every nook, hidden path and cattle track in town." By the time Eirikur has turned his head to reply, the mouth of the hatch has swallowed the Southlander's bushy head.

Go ashore. *Of course* he'll go ashore. There's no point in skulking around on this rotting coffin, Eirikur thinks. "To the anchor!" the captain's voice barks, and everyone scrambles to their posts. The ship has whipped round in the wind again, the stern lets out a groan as the anchor chain rattles through its hold, and a shudder travels along the length of the keel as she grinds to a halt; the anchor has touched bottom. After protracted exertions and manoeuvring, the ship rests, dead still, as if she has yearned for this moment. The silence that follows is unfamiliar; it's not like the calm before a storm, or those moments when you're awake and can't tell whether you're at open sea, or not. No, this stillness is different; it feels more like a hush, and the tethering is quiet, so they must have reached the crook of the cove once more. They moor alongside the other ships that have docked by the trading post. As if cattle returned to their stables after a long trek from the pasture, the vessels huddle together, elongated skeletons resting near the landing bridge.

The skipper gives the order to sort the sails, furl them—and clear the hell up! "The rigging is tangled and scattered all over the place!" he snaps. "This place looks like a goddamned raven's nest—not a ship's deck!"

"Wherever I go, it's the same," Eirikur mutters under his breath. Everything I touch turns out badly, he thinks. I'm so goddamned sick and tired of scuttling about on this deck. It's been an entire year without respite. I need to comb my hair and scrape the worst of the dirt from my body. I'll go below and do what I can to clean myself up. And then I'll go ashore. *Of course I will.* I can barely wait another second to feel dry land under my feet!

Eirikur drags himself below. It always looks like a landslide down there: a pair of pants strewn on the stairs, a sweater crumpled on the floor. A duvet cover sticking out of one of the top bunks has torn. Its fleece stuffing is bulging from one corner, as if it were a slaughtered sheep; the owner is invisible, hidden in the farthest corner of the bunk. On the table—where the crew arc supposed to eat their meals—two dishes held the discarded bones of an American steak that is picked clean. Crumbling sea biscuits fill another bowl to the brim. Presumably intended as a tablecloth, the remains of an old hessian sack glitters—black as whale skin—in a congealed and unidentifiable mass entwined with rotting potato peelings, long since embedded in the threads. On the stove, a galvanised pot is covered in rust, as if it has been buried underground for years. The state of the galley is no better; grey as ash, giving off a black glow, as if a rock expunged from a prehistoric volcano, but it would have to do because it is all they have, dents, rust, rot and all.

The cook staggers into the room. His skin is grey underneath his shaggy, overgrown beard. He's carrying one black rubbish bag in the crook of his arm, dragging another along the floor behind him.

"Looks like the ol' sea dog is building a nest for himself," remarks the Southlander drily, looking up at the cook briefly. Trying to make his beard presentable, he's hunched over a shard of mirror that is wedged into a crack under the skylight,.

"Let me help you with that bag, cook," says Eirikur. "It's looks extremely heavy."

"Nonsense, my friend," says the cook. "Nothing but picked bones. So much goes to waste on this ship. I can't stand to see God-given gifts get tossed out with the trash. Got a house full of kids back home, I have, and not a single cow in my shed. Every morsel can make for a wholesome soup, and I'm saving these bits to make a broth."

"True, so true, my good man," the Southlander chips in. "The shipping company is rich. The shipowner pays us well. Next time, I'll be sure to leave you a tip after dinner. But you really ought to stop adding to your brood, old man. Children will only send you to an early grave. What's the joy in that?! There's no happiness in having a family, I say. Personally, I've no intention of getting married… hey, I think I saw one of your black bags lying around here somewhere… ouch… for f… now I've gone and cut myself—shitty, goddamned razor!"

"Yup, there's one more here," pipes up a voice from the corridor. "The old man's got two vats on the go under the table as well. You'll probably have to send for your own rowboat, cook, if you want to get all your stuff to shore in one trip."

"Mind your own bloody business," the cook mutters distractedly, as he tries to manoeuvre the bag into the gap between the vats under the table with the rest of his stash. "It's nothing. Just a handful of sea biscuits. All going to waste, I say. They're still perfectly good for dinner, if you dunk them into some milk. As I said: I got me a house full of kids."

"I thought you said you don't own a cow? Where're you gonna get the milk for your biscuits, then?" a voice chimes in.

"A good neighbour is kind enough to bring us a few drops, my friend," says the cook. "In fact, I'm saving these bones for his family as they've been so helpful to me, God knows they have…"

"Shattered goods in this one, I think," the Southlander

says, kicking his boot into the nearest black rubbish bag under the table. "I'm afraid you won't get a good price for this lot, cook. What have you got in there anyways? Stoneware—from Iceland, perhaps?"

"Shut your trap and stay the hell away from my bags!" the cook yelled at the Southlander furiously. "You've been such a bastard to me on this entire trip! Nothing but a thief who plays tricks on me, you are. I told you, it's worthless: crockery and a few chipped old mugs that no one is going to miss. They're just piling up here, and eventually, someone will throw them away, and I told you: I have many mouths that need feeding, and no cups to drink from."

"Yes, yes, so you keep saying," says the Southlander. "Many things pile up on a ship, just help yourself, clear it away, do us a favour, why don't you, make some space, by all means, we're living on top of each other in this hell-hole."

The cook ignores the Southlander's sarcasm. Instead, he clears the table, muttering under his breath, appalled by the filthy habits and untidiness of the crew—*as if they were wild animals rather than human beings*—he thinks, whipping off the tablecloth, which sent the sea biscuits flying, the naked bones clattering onto the floor.

"Do you think you could let me have that bowl of water and your razor when you're done?" Eirikur asks the Southlander. "With pleasure, with pleasure," he replies. "I'll pass them right over shortly. It's been a rough journey, I tell you. An unparalleled operation. But now it's over, and would you look at that: my face is pale and smooth as a baby's bottom and fit to kiss whatever princess might come my way," he adds with a guffaw, and immediately starts rummaging in his bunk, perhaps in the hope of finding a pair of pants that are slightly less grubby than the ones he's wearing.

More men come below deck. It's cramped as hell, worse than sheep packed in a fold and every man is asking for water and razors to trim their beards. The cook bustles in amongst the horde, wielding his broom, trying to brush the crumbs off the table and gain some semblance of order in the shambles. Eirikur is squashed in a corner with the Southlander's razor and a shard of glass which serves as a mirror. He's had little success removing the stubble from his chin, but despite the pain—cuts from the blunt blade bring tears to his eyes—he feels upbeat. *Come what may, nothing is going to get him down. Not today.*

On their approach, the moment he knew they were in local waters, happiness filled his heart, obliterating all the strife, hardship and drudgery—even the loneliness—that he had endured on their arduous journey to the East. *Coming home to the Faroes is pure joy*, Eirikur thinks. But the skipper's voice penetrates the hatch, interrupting his reverie. Every man is ordered on deck, he pulls on his sweater and sticks his feet into his boots, he refuses to be stuck onboard—there's no telling when he would get the chance again—if he misses the first boat to shore it might be a while before he can catch the next one.

Eirikur is quick on his feet, he's up through the hatch and on deck in no time, but finds the rowboat already packed.

"Hurry up, Eirikur!"

He leaps into the boat and moments later, they push off and head for the rocky shore. Most men onboard are young, Eirikur notices. Apparently, the older members of the crew are not inclined to go ashore tonight; perhaps they would rather stay onboard to sew on a missing button or mend a shirt, so they will be ready to catch a boat to shore and walk to their villages farther inland at first light.

The rowboat glides up to the shore. The skipper is the first man to leap onto land and stride down the bridge. He has a large book tucked under his arm—the Captain's Logbook—which contained all his navigational notes (south southwest, north northwest etc.), brief weather reports, a sailing log and anecdotes of events which he could show the Danish King's Commissioner to the Faroes. The captain is dignified and proud, a man utterly in tune with his calling.

"So, where would you like to go?" the Southlander whispers in Eirikur's ear. Naturally, *he* is not staying onboard with the other sea dogs. On the contrary, he's in his Sunday best, no less: a red silk scarf around his neck, a matching sailor's cap and brown gumboots, which reach halfway up his lanky thighs. "I have no intention of lounging about onboard, nor, for that matter, going to the trading post, yes, least of all, the trading post!"

He's such a ladies' man, well-known in most ports and no doubt a regular customer at the Castle, Eirikur thinks.

"I know," says Eirikur. "I've nowhere in particular I want to go. I don't know this place, but I always have to feel dry land under my feet whenever I get the chance, even if it's a foreign country, or a tiny trading post."

"Stick with me, my friend, you won't regret it, I promise you. I know all the local joints, every nook, hidden path and cattle track in town," the Southlander says again. "The best thing to do is to go to the coffee shop first. My throat is so dry, I tell you, I'd give my kingdom for a beer, and I happen to have a few kroner in my pocket, enough for a beer and a smoke. Who knows, you might bump into some better company," he adds under his breath. "If the shops weren't closed, I'd try to get a bottle of spirits from someone, but the coffee shop is usually not so bad; if you slip her a kroner, the hostess might find a glass of Schnapps for you."

Eirikur accompanies the Southlander down the bridge, follows his example and picks up a crate of fish from a stack stood on the edge of the landing bridge as they pass; a group of girls with wheelbarrows are carting them over to the warehouse. The girls' faces are crayfish-red, their arms and hands are swollen from the salt and cold, their bodies big-boned and enticing. A shiver runs down his spine when he catches the eye of one of them.

"Don't you know that tall one in the brown boots?" Eirikur hears the girl say to her co-worker, who is loading a wheelbarrow next to her.

"I remember him from last spring. I think he's from the southern isles."

Eirikur can't catch any more of the conversation, but he can't help noticing that several of the women stare after them. This is not unusual, unfortunately. He's been subjected to this before: people often stop and stare when strangers come ashore. Eirikur curses inwardly; he can't stand it when people look at him like that, peeling the skin off his back.

"Did you see that one?" the Southlander said. "What a filly, great pair of legs, I don't think I've ever seen the like before—wouldn't mind a piece of that—she's got some'ing to hold onto, my friend. We must find you a girl tonight," the Southlander rattles on. "It's simple, all you gotta do is strike up a conversation and keep talking, then everything happens of its own accord. We've been adrift in fog, mist and rain for several months in the East, and you ought to get a kiss on the first night you feel green grass under your feet again. The way I see it: you only have one life; you are only young once, there's plenty of time to be grumpy when you get back to your own flat—Good day, Maria!" he calls to a woman coming towards them on the road.

"A good day to you too, Torstein," she answers with a smile. "And welcome back! How've you been, then?"

"Oh, you know how it is. Worked like a mule to get over here to visit you," he looks over his shoulder.

"Quite a lot of girls on this island seem to know you," Eirikur says.

"I know, I know," says the Southlander. "What can I say? It's not entirely untrue."

It grates on his nerves, constantly having to listen to the Southlander's remarks about women. And they're completely infatuated with the man. *He probably thinks of nothing but women, day and night*, thinks Eirikur.

The Southlander has stopped in front of a house. It has dormer rooms on the second floor and gables on either end. The front yard is a mess. A clutch of chickens are pecking at scant patches of grass, ducks waddle about in the mud pools. In desperate need of repair, the outer walls are green and covered in slime.

At the foot of the front door, two crumbling rocks that have never actually been cemented into proper steps. The only decoration the house presents are the large, inviting letters painted yellow above the door—**K A F É**. A promise of hot cups of coffee, undiluted beer and cigarettes. The Southlander knocks on the door.

A woman dressed in mourning clothes from head to toe appears in the doorway. A large black veil covers her head, as it befits a respectable and God-fearing woman honouring the memory of her dearly-departed husband. She has a pinched face and an angular, slightly crooked nose. The only visible part of her forehead is a tiny, pale triangle centred over the bridge of her nose. As if Mother Nature had been particularly tight-fisted with her gifts on the day, the widow's bosom is completely flat and all excess fat is pared from her skeleton. Her hands smooth down the front of her apron continually, as if in a constant gesture demonstrating the hard fate she has to bear.

Their hostess greets the Southlander and invites them inside. Also her greeting has a mournful tone, as if bad news is the only kind she knows, bemoaning the ills in this world, not to mention the unreliable nature of human beings. She shows them into the room in silence.

The walls are green and two oil paintings hang on the wall, the colours so bright they sting your eyes. A few chairs are placed around an oval dining room table. A huge gramophone with a large, rusty spout has its place in the corner by the window. Their hostess announces that she has recently been to the second-hand stop, pointing to a pile of old records displayed next to the gramophone.

Only two other guests are at the dining-room table. They are smoking and each man has a beer glass in front of him, but they move aside graciously so the new arrivals can take a seat.

Her hands busily stroking her apron, the widow asks in her sorrowful tone what she can offer the gentlemen to drink. No more than two minutes after hearing their wish, she returns from the kitchen with two glasses of undiluted beer, all the while lamenting the heavy burden that all seamen must bear, battling with wind and weather on rough seas, only to return empty-handed.

"They have nothing to show for all their trouble," she mutters. "Of course, some men do make money," she adds reluctantly. "Some people can afford to dress themselves up in fine clothing, some people reap the benefits of the fishermen's hard labour—in spring as well as autumn—as Jákup used to say."

The mention of her dearly-departed husband by name only seems to make her appear more agitated, and once this black-robed and eternally disappointed woman has served her guests a round of excellent beer to quench their thirst and bring life to their limbs, she is satisfied that she has done her duty, and withdraws from the room.

The other two guests seem rather loud. Apparently, they've made good use of the excellent brew of the house, even if it actually isn't undiluted, thinks Eirikur.

One of the strangers is a broad and good-looking man of about thirty-years-old. He has a sharply defined face and body. He seems slightly less raucous than his friend and leans over to ask the Southlander where they have been.

"You probably don't know me," the big man says. "I'm the first mate of a smack called *The Rókin.* I originally come from Suðuroy, but when I got married, I settled in the west, on

Vágar. We had a pretty good trip in the spring but got caught in some terrible weather—not unusual in the bay east of the mainland—it's a devilish stretch of water—but I must admit I don't think I've ever seen such a storm. Waves crashing over the boat, churning foam everywhere, and when the wind finally dropped, the sea was so rough that the channel was impassable. I have to say, it was by the grace of God alone that we didn't die out there. In weather like that,"—he smashes his fist onto the table—"everything depends on the men you have on board. I've never ever seen such wild waters, and I didn't have the kind of crew onboard I needed. I couldn't believe it, grown men losing heart and calling for a wife here, a girlfriend there, you'd swear there was nothing to be done but let the ship go under. And the man who was supposed to be our captain was worst of all—sobbing in his bunk like a milkmaid with a headache. He told his crew not to go up on deck, we were in the hands of God now! The captain simply gave up all hope, he let us think we were doomed to sink like basalt rock to the bottom of the sea. You might think I'm blowing my own horn to say so, but I swear that if I hadn't been onboard that day, we all would have drowned. It's no picnic sailing a boat to Iceland—in any weather—but nowadays, any arsehole with cash thinks he can be a shipowner, even if he's never taken a piss in seawater in his life, but come, why not have a *real* drink with us?" he adds, taking a breath at last. "That beer you're drinking is not all bad, but it doesn't have the kick a man needs."

The Southlander nudges Eirikur in the ribs, lest he has a mind to protest; it's rare to get a drink the moment you put your feet on land. "Don't mind if we do," he said.

The Westlander promptly disappears into the room next door, where they can hear him talking to their hostess. A few minutes later he returns. He pulls a pint flask of Schnapps out of his pocket.

"The old lady keeps a tight lid on things," he says. "But she's not as pious as she seems. I've had a good many drams in this place at all times of the day and night. But she's not so generous to everyone. She doesn't usually serve people she doesn't know as she doesn't dare take the chance. If it ever came to light it would cost her dearly," the Westlander adds gravely. "But go ahead, drink your beer and chase it down with a drop of this stuff—that should do the trick." He pulls the cork out of the flask with a plop and pours them each a glass.

Eirikur raises a hand, admits that he's not used to Schnapps, says he'll only have a drop.

"Nonsense," says the Westlander, and promptly starts to sing a ditty in Danish—*i aften saa ville vi drikke, om vi kunne øllet faa*—"Drink up, my friend as long as there's beer to be had, and live your life while you're still breathing, we're only young once, I say, and this is the good stuff. Can anything beat a mouthful of Schnapps?! It sets fire to the blood, so whenever I set foot on dry land, I get me some," he declares. "And I love to listen to music," he says, pointing at the gramophone in the corner. "Just say the word, and I'll crank her into action."

The Westlander is talking so much no one else can get a word in edgeways. His face is angular, his eyes shining like molten embers, his long nose juts out of his face like a mountain peak. His every movement signals an irrepressible vitality that neither wind, weather nor anything else could ever hold down.

At last Eirikur relents, drinks the last of his beer and accepts a dram from the Westlander. The liquid burns his tongue, sends a trail of flames down his gullet, a pulsing heat like an alien being coming alive in his veins, growing stronger and stronger, till it takes control.

The Westlander has put on the gramophone, which churns out a tune in English that Eirikur can't understand. It's so loud you can't hear yourself speak. "Stop that bloody racket!" he bursts out, finding his tongue, for once insisting on taking a stand against the tide.

"Wait a minute, not so fast," says the Westlander, grabbing hold of the Southlander, and together, they strike up a waltz around the living room.

What a sight to behold! The lanky Southlander is twirling around with the rugged Westlander, their boots scraping on the wooden floor. The oblong dining-room table trembles on its legs, and their jaunt comes to its inevitable end: taking a final, flamboyant swirl in the corner, a boot gets caught on a leg supporting the table, the gramophone topples and falls to the floor with an almighty crash.

The hostess rushes into the room, her hands clutching the folds of her apron, as she fixes her eyes on the grandiloquent gramophone, now silent on the floor, its horn broken. The widow is calm, but obviously angry, which is not surprising. "This has always been a respectable house," she says with a sniff. For a moment, her busy hands fly to her face, only to continue their frenetic smoothing at her brow. She is dismayed that her guests should behave in this way. Her neighbours would like nothing better than to see her 'guesthouse' closed, leaving her without the means to earn a living, she explains.

"But of course," replies the Westlander, taking one of her hands in his, as she desperately tries to gather up the shattered pieces of the gramophone.

"Don't worry, ma'am," he says. "We are reasonable men, we were just having a little fun, and we got a little over-excited, that's all. You are an honourable hostess, and we would hate to bring ill repute to your house. Please tell me what I owe you for the drinks and the gramophone," he says, sticking a hand into his trouser pocket and fishing out his wallet. "And then we will leave you in peace."

"No, no, there's no need for you to go," says the widow. "I've no mind to throw you out. I never turn away customers—certainly not good folks that I know—I'm just saying, you know how it is."

"We won't trouble you any longer, ma'am," the Southlander chimes in. "We've imposed on your gracious hospitality for long enough, it's time to move on and see what's happening in town."

The men empty their glasses and stub out their cigarettes. The widow accompanies them out into the hall so they can collect their coats and hats, her plaintive voice imploring them not to misunderstand her: "I never turn away reasonable customers, and I'm not doing so now, but a woman in my position has to be careful, you know, my situation is precarious, and the world is such an evil place," she groans. "The world is going to the dogs. There's no respite for an old woman who is simply looking for a chance to make a few kroner, so she won't starve to death. I have nothing against music and dancing, but it makes such a noise, you know, and the neighbours…"

On the pavement outside the men escape the widow's

mournful waterfall of words. The Westlander takes the flask out of his inside jacket pocket and offers it around.

"Best we finish it," he says. "There's no point in saving it for later. You're all good men, I like you lot, let's go into town together."

Dusk has fallen in the interim. The moon is full, the autumn air crisp with a familiar scent of freshly-cut hay in the fields. In the streets passing through the village, people are milling about, lamps glow on the windowsills of the houses which light their way.

They stick to the street where the houses are isolated and still, as if huge monocles of otherworldly beasts that stare at them as they pass.

Eirikur is in high spirits, his heart indefinably blissful, delighting in the mere fact of being alive. With eternal patience, he is listening to the Westlander wax lyrical about the glory of manhood, the braves deeds of great men. Both he and the Southlander are talking much louder than one usually would on a public road. The Schnapps flask from the **KAFÉ** has loosened their tongues and thawed the distance between two strangers who are now conversing on familiar terms; they've become the best of friends with a bond that reaches back to the dawn of man.

The street brings them to an elongated fishery with a zinc roof. The sound of lively music and stomping feet spills from the windows; the fishery has an annex which the locals call 'the Castle'. It is here that girls from remote villages live while they are employed by the fishing merchants.

The factory workers like staying at the Castle; there are

no bolts on the doors and you can come and go as you please. Eirikur has heard that many of his colleagues from the ship frequent this place whenever they are in town, and they always have wild stories to tell of their exploits upon their return. The Southlander is a regular customer. He has mentioned—or rather, boasted—to Eirikur that he is firmly engaged to a girl: "A decent lass, unlike all those other girls who always complain when you are out on the town with your friends, so I can do as I please, and we're going to get married the first chance I get—if you meet a decent, moral girl who's tolerably pretty, there's nothing to wait for, but I like other women, especially at foreign ports, there's no harm in it after all."

"Let's go in," says the Westlander, as soon as he hears the dancing. "I'm in the mood tonight! Come on, follow me, my good men! Women are a gorgeous gift like brandy, offered by this earth, and you must be a stupid beast not to partake when you can. You have to *live* before you get old and end in your grave, my friends!"

"Very true, my friend," says the Southlander. "I couldn't agree more! Let's visit the Castle together," he declares merrily, starting to sing in Danish again—*I aften saa ville vi drikke, om vi kunne øllet faa, i morgen saa ville vi sejle, om børen blæse maa*[21]—as the sound of an old folk ballad and ring dancing beckons them inside.

The Castle is a relatively new addition to the fishery, even so, the cramped space between the roof, the ceiling and the dark wooden panels on the walls and floors bear the deep marks of time. Above their heads, a petroleum lamp with eight wicks spews smoke, creating a murky interior that is alive with people dancing in rings, as if ghostly folklore figures performing their ritual in a wood that is shrouded in mist.

Most dancers are young women: flushed with pleasure, the women twirl around the room; those with long hair toss their heads, sending tresses flying over their shoulders and down their backs, and those with shorter hair shake their curls about their faces, their arms in constant motion, soft and voluptuous flesh shifting in the dim glow.

Eirikur is captivated by the sight, not least by the girl leading *The Ballad of Marlbrook—the Prince of Commanders / gone to war in Flanders*: Marlbrook went into battle and left his sweetheart to pine for him. She waits for her lover in the castle, where she sits by the window, day after day, yearning for the return of her beloved, and the dancers sway to the rhythm of the ballad accordingly; the girl leads the dance with admirable skill, not unlike a helmsman inciting his men to take up their oars, and it's as if the Castle women are trampling their longing and impatience into the floorboards. Eirikur can no longer watch from the sidelines and leaps into the fray, jostling his way into the ring alongside the others, and soon he has danced his way up over to the leader. She has just come to the stanza where her lady-in-waiting brings the forlorn princess the news of Marlbrook's death; Eirikur falls into the role immediately, takes the broken-hearted girl in his arms, and she responds naturally, at once the picture of the sorrowful widow, she lets him stroke her cheek, comfort her body, and step into the rightful place of her lover.

Oh, dear God, what a feast for the eyes! Pale necks arched, naked arms beating the air like a divine spectacle that obliterates every dreary thought of stormy weather, blistered hands, spartan meals and insufficient sleep. The dance feels like the essence of living life, teeming vitality in every breath, and Eirikur is acutely aware of the girls large and relatively soft hand in his. Her arms are bare up to the armpits, and he can feel its damp heat through the wool of his sweater.

As if the tail of a whirlwind, the final stanza sweeps through the room, before running out of steam like a child who has over-indulged in a game and no longer wants to play. The dancing grinds to a halt for a moment, but then the Southlander steps in and strikes up the ballad again: Marlbrook is sent to his grave, but no sooner has the final graveside hymn begun to fade, than Valhalla's heroic deeds boom in the Southlander's rich baritone: the spirit of the legendary Viking warrior, Ragnar Lodbrok, looms out of the shadows—*Vi hugge med Kaarde i Striden hin haarde*[22]—and the dancers take up formation, as if conjuring the death throes of Lodbrok—bit in the heart by a snake—writhing in the murky pit of his prison.

The sound of music and dancing carries all the way down the road, and more people flock to the Castle. The ring of dancers is broken in several places as more and more people try to join in. There's a throng in the doorway. Some would clearly like to join the ring, but cannot get in, others are merely watching; hardy and weather-beaten seamen, who have neither washed nor shaven for months, standing around in their bulky scarves, socks, baggy breeches and boots.

But there is also a small contingent of slick, young men in the crowd, spruced up with combed hair and clipped beards, clad in nice blue sweaters and shiny gumboots, as if the last wave of Icelanders breaking on Faroese shores—once, twice, three times—before the seas are calm once more.

The Southlander picks up the tune again, exuding the sheer exhilaration of survival. He has conquered the storms that threatened his life at sea, unshackled from his lonely existence on endless dark nights and brooding days spent tending his handlines, and—as if swept along with his voice—the ring of dancers surge to life once more.

The Ballad of Ragnar Lodbrok is the ultimate personification of joy, it's rhythm like the swift blows of a sword wielded in battle—*Vi hugge med Kaarde i Striden hin haarde*—that pauses briefly in the air, before striking anew with double the force, till the grand finale resounds—*we head for Odin's hall*—and every nerve in the body tingles, flooded with the bloodrush of our Viking forefathers' courage and inspiration.

Eirikur is hot and sweaty, intoxicated by the dance and the passionate girl in his arms. For more than an hour, she has whirled round the room with him, her body pressed against his in the ring. At the far end of the room, he catches a glimpse of his comrades: the Southlander and the first mate of *The Rókin* are dancing together, the sweat pouring from their brows. The light in the room is faint, as if the oil lamp above is faltering, almost gone out, and the dancers are more like shadows, rather than actual bodies moving in the dark. And then a clumsy, or just exceptionally tall person on unsteady legs, gets his arm or head (you can't tell which is which in this light) caught on the oil lamp under the ceiling—a loud crash—and the room is plunged into absolute darkness.

His eyes are unfamiliar to the dark, and Eirikur feels for the hot arm at his side; a live, trembling limb that allows him to take the lead through the throng to the exit. He manages to elbow his way—or perhaps he is shoved—through the doorway, and finally he feels the cool autumn breeze on his face.

More people spill out into the night—dancing partners paired in the shadows—including Eirikur and the big-boned girl. With even greater zeal, some people continue the dance on the sidewalk, and those who have chosen to leave the party can hear the clatter of boots on the cobblestones behind them.

Eirikur and the girl he barely knows weave their way out of the dancing crowd that has lingered outside the Castle and head along the main road to town.

The weather is still fine. The moon is brilliant, fringed with feather-grey clouds. Eirikur has always loved this time of year. It brings fond memories of those fragrant autumn nights; coming home after an exhausting day's work, the scent of cut wheat, familiar lamps lit by human hands, one after another, the promise of happy hours spent indoors by the hearth in the evenings.

Now he has found a girl, just like the Southlander said he should. He has to find out for himself what everyone keeps talking about; it's worth trying once, and she's a lively creature, this one—everything about her testifies to the fact—and besides, she doesn't seem disinclined to the idea of being alone with him.

They continue down the main street and head for the outskirts of town. She asks him all sorts of questions about everything under the sun—fishing, his life, the sea—and she keeps repeating how much she has enjoyed the evening with him tonight and declares how wonderful everything *always* is, once the fishermen come home.

They walk a long way up the ridge, past all the houses and other people… her eyes are shining with laughter, her mouth is close to his… he kisses her, pulls her close, feels her body melt into his, an intoxicating heat, wet lips parting under his… a shiver passes through his body, a joy that surges in his heart, the same kind of elation he feels whenever he catches sight of the landing bridge, familiar houses on the ridge, when they sail back into the fjord after a long and arduous journey.

"I adore you, you're so sweet," says the girl, and he kisses her breathlessly. With neither rhyme nor reason, words strange to his own ears come out of his mouth, and for a moment, he seems to slip into oblivion, all his troubles disappear, he simply rests in the blissful knowledge of being alive, a tingle flooding every fibre, limb and bone in his body.

They take a seat on a rock beside the path. The darkness is dense, the only light is a glimmer of dew weighing down silky stalks of grass nearby. On the fringe, some chickens and haycocks linger peacefully, as if the hush and darkness were familiar friends.

Down below, the streets in town are almost deserted; the dancing outside the Castle has stopped, but there is a scattering of lights from night-owl windows.

"Shouldn't you be getting back?" asks Eirikur. "I mean, you ought to go to bed."

"No," says the girl, getting to her feet. "I don't live at the Castle. I'm staying with some people I know out here."

Even though she has asked him not to, Eirikur follows in her tracks; he doesn't want to lose her now, after being with her all evening, and it doesn't look as if she really wants him to go.

There is a garden around the house and they pause by

the gate in front, talking about the wonderful weather. She stares into his eyes, and Eirikur feels another surge of joy as he recalls the kisses that they have shared.

She opens the gate and Eirikur follows her down the garden path. "Let me come inside for a moment," he says. "If you don't mind? I don't want to go back to the boat just yet."

"Alright," she says in a whisper. "But you must tread very quietly, sweetheart. My landlady is sleeping upstairs and she gets so grumpy if she's woken in the middle of the night," the girl explains, as she opens the door quietly.

Eirikur promises to be as quiet as a mouse, and they slip inside. He takes off his boots in the hallway. The girl takes off her coat and pats down her hair in front of the mirror on the wall. Then they creep into the kitchen together.

Eirikur sits down on a chair and takes her on his lap. She presses her body against his; a woman's body so warm and alive, and her kisses send quivers down his spine, as if the girl in his embrace has become a part of himself. As he pulls her closer, her skirt rides up her thighs, and it is skin—naked skin—that he feels under his fingers, skin much softer than he would ever have imagined to be true. The girl presses her body closer, she is clinging to him, kissing him deeply, and the heat coming from this willing, womanly body is fire in Eirikur's veins. So this is what they were talking about in elaborate phrases, rude gestures and disgusting descriptions and dirty jokes—it's all nonsense—no more than the repulsive bragging of shipmates.

It was late in the night when Eirikur finally returned to the boat. The moon was still out, if only a sliver in the sky, waning swiftly, tidings of a shift in the weather—a turn for the worse—thought Eirikur. White banks of cloud clustered about the moon, as if something lurking in the dark was forcing its way to the surface.

When he made his way down to the harbour it was dead quiet on the main street, and only a single man was loitering under the eaves of a house on the corner. The air was cold now, and Eirikur shivered as he walked down the landing bridge. He noticed that there were two rowing boats tethered nearby, The others must have gone onboard already, but at least he wouldn't have to roam around the harbour on his own all night.

The man was resting against a stack of salt-fish, and as Eirikur approached he got to his feet and Eirikur recognised the rugged face of the Westlander.

"This is a fine time to arrive," he said. "Looks like someone got his leg over," he added, slapping his thigh. "Such is the way of the flesh, a man always ends up in the arms of a woman, or in the gutter, or under a stack of salt-fish… our goblets are empty… and I'm stuck here alone in the middle of the night, a man staring into a dying fire, watching the grey ashes grow cold. Arggh, I drank far too much last night and ended up down here. The Devil only knows where I've been, cause I can't remember a thing. But hey, what's done is done, besides, I must have been in excellent company because I'm still breathing," he smiles ruefully. "Are you going onboard now? There's an empty rowboat right here. Shall we go out together? Your boat is moored not far from mine."

"Why not," said Eirikur. He was not in the mood for talking, but thankfully, the Westlander said no more on their trip out to *The Rókin*, and when they arrived, there was no one on deck.

"Thank you kindly for the lift," said the Westlander, leaping aboard his boat.

"No thanks required," said Eirikur. "You're very welcome." He pushed off almost immediately, and swiftly rowed the few hundred yards towards his own boat, mulling over his trip to the so-called Paradise that everyone had so much to say about. God only knew why he felt so ill, and a bad taste lingered in his mouth, as if he were going to be seasick.

A weary wretchedness settled in his mind, and all the joy of the night before disappeared, giving way to the deep depression of his long days and nights at sea. He might as well go straight to H… and return to stormy seas… he thought.

He tethered the rowboat and clambered up onto deck, the last man to come onboard.

The cabin was cheerless: the fire had gone out; the rusty black tea kettle was still on the stove; a crumbling, half-eaten sea biscuit was discarded on the table; two rusty buckets of dirty dishes were abandoned on the floor; large black bags of rubbish and boots were slung in every corner; a cloud of petroleum smoke leaked from the oil lamp; not least, a cacophony of intermittent guffaws, bickering and loud bursts of laughter emitted from the bunkbeds, and one of the cook's bags of contraband lay at Eirikur's feet.

"Why does there always have to be such a confounded mess down here," Eirikur muttered under his breath, giving the rubbish bag a ferocious kick, which sent it flying across the cabin. The curtain in front of one of the bunks in the rear of the starboard side was yanked aside, and the dishevelled head of the cook appeared in the opening.

"Shame on you for abusing my property—it's just a few biscuits that were going to waste, they were still good for dipping into milk, a full house of children, I have. You've been so well-behaved and cordial on our trip, but now it's as if the Devil's got into you."

"I don't give a damn about your bloody bags of contraband!" Eirikur spat back. "You had better get your head back in your hole and shut your mouth, or I'll come over there and stuff one of your bloody bags down your throat."

The head of the cook withdrew behind the curtain again.

An odious feeling rose in Eirikur's chest. It felt as if everything that came his way was reprehensible and evil; it filled him with such rage that in that moment he could have committed murder… 'our goblets are empty', the Westlander said and he was right.

What was this spiritual malaise that followed in the wake of joy, right after your goblet is emptied? Eirikur could not define what he felt: a 'backlash', perhaps? It was the only word he could find for the overwhelming sadness he felt when all cords, every tethering pulled taut, suddenly went slack.

His mother used to say… what, exactly? He tried to recall her words… *Remember your maker when you are young, before evil sets in, and you no longer wish to be in this world…*

Eirikur was hungry and thirsty. He poured himself a cup of cold tea. Impaled the discarded sea biscuit with a dirty spoon, but he could neither eat nor drink. The vile taste in his mouth was still there and his belly lurched as if he would throw up, but it was empty.

He put down the spoon and cup. Discarded his sweater. *What was the point in going ashore?* he thought, as he pulled off his boots and threw himself onto his bunk.

He lay awake for a long time with the blurry image of a woman before his mind's eye. Her head bowed, her hair obscured her face, as she smoothed down her apron in utter exhaustion.

The Tree of Knowledge

by

Jørgen-Frantz Jacobsen

translated by Paul Russell Garrett

Tórshavn's old middle and *realskole* with its sweeping sod roof and low tarred wings, encircled by dense, bushy maples, and in the centre of the courtyard, a small, delicate rowan: 'The Tree of Knowledge of Good and Evil'… oh yes, this is where seven all-important years were spent, a lifetime, yes, an entire epoch, encompassing everything from the time you were a wee lad until you stood on the threshold of the adult world! The years were long back then, countless subtle changes occurred during this period. Each year had its own colour, its own tone. Only the intermediate years were tedious, the second and third years of middle school. Everything connected with the tedium of school, whitewashed windowpanes, varnished tables, measuring rulers, and cheerless penholders. There is something far airier to the final school years, the drizzly tediousness is beginning to lift, you are filled with expectation and springtime.

But those first few years! They hold a legendary splendour. They carry an imperishable butterfly dust on their wings. They have a distinct lustre, a misty smile, a splendid resonance. They live in your memories with the light of morn!

To this day you can still be filled with a filial gratitude towards the entire domain of the low tarred school, which the giant of a man, *Headmaster Lauritsen*, kept watch over with his stringent features. A mysterious dawn reigns over this Jupiter, over the Loki-like *Master Michelsen*, the god of thunder's craftily twisted foe, over the Apollonian *Skaalum*, whose attributes were leaf and spike, over the diminutive, but inescapable *Jacob Dahl*, brandishing the Bible's Old Testament lightning, and over the inscrutable Minerva *Miss Rafn* with Thyra Dannebod and Svantevit of the Wends in the background. With her pointed assessments and critical comments, and with her prodigiously scrupulous requirements for measuring wire and penwipers, she posed a distinctive filigree-like danger, worthy of a mythological world.

True, it was a Danish school, a Danish ideology, one that I find unsuitable for Faroese children. And yet there was plenty of honey-sweetness to gather in this Danish school amphibian, planted on Faroese soil.

Passing through the school gates, you entered a world of its own—one that you had neither imagined nor dreamed of in your hitherto, purely prehistoric cave-painting childhood. Here, for the first time, you made proper contact with reality. You were away from home, had duties and responsibilities under the brooding and elevated countenance of the headmaster. There was no pleading to Mummy here. No, by Jove! Here was only harsh reality and the true trembling and fear of God!

How infinitely small and insignificant you were. Above you was, everyone! The bumptious students of the first year of middle school, who liked to show off their might to a lad from the preparatory school, could offer golden sweets to the goddess Nina Helms, the youngest daughter of the district court judge! She was a superior being, who in all her splendour and elevation, would sometimes allow the lustre of her mercy to shine down upon one of us wretched little creatures for a fraction of a second. It was a wonder. There is no telling how much this fair and melodious girl of ten has meant to one's further sexual development.

Higher up the school ladder were various tough and depraved young men whom I have now forgotten. At the very top were the bearded heroes of the teacher training college. Then the celestial bodies, and finally, the headmaster. How infinitely far from a sheepish seven-year-old lad up to this legendary titan. And yet, you could come close to his power and divine might, yes, at times too close. But as the righteous avenging deity that he was, he mostly took it out on the older members of our community. Before him everyone trembled. How could a presumptuous and mighty boy from the final year fail to tremble and break down before his countenance!

Headmaster Lauritsen was assuredly an ingenious and brilliant educator. He was, quite simply, God. Treading on his doorstep was forbidden! That is how elevated his personage was. And if you accidentally smashed his window… well, the mere thought of it was enough to inflict on us a feeling of audaciousness that is simply without parallel in our later existence…

But hated he most certainly was not, there was neither grumbling nor griping, not even in the innermost recesses of one's heart. He was fully and completely accepted, the way you accept the ocean, the mountains, fate. Every disfavour was inexorably terrifying, and every favour was welcomed with trembling delight. No one kicked against these pricks! Before him even Miss Rafn quivered like a bird on a twig, and Skaalum was timid as a hare. Only Master Michelsen was so bold as to writhe, though keeping low to the ground, slavering with impotent venom.

No one had any doubts about the headmaster's elevated righteousness. If someone or other, guided by God knows which mystical power, were to forthrightly approach his flashing countenance, and with a clear and confident voice present their case—behold! then he was as friendly as in a fairy-tale, like the lion and the mouse, a man whose appearance, when it came down to it, no one could really describe, for no one dared look upon him with their eyes wide open.

But there was both goodness and beauty in the kingdom of the headmaster. It was a tremendously enthralling world that suddenly inundated your childhood. I remember with awe the first morning assembly, when the entire school sang:

Praise to the Lord, the Almighty, the King of creation!
O my soul, praise him, for he is thy health and salvation!

To start the school year with such a fundamentally Christian song, to offer it up as a glorifying acclamation to the work! A truly beautiful choice, which emphasised the school as a fundamental institution that has stood through all time, and that is now passed on to a new brood of the everlasting human race!

On the whole I am grateful to the headmaster for morning song. He was in fact the one who ushered you into the splendid world known as Danish hymnody. I remember

The Morning Hours Bring Golden Flowers, my first sense of school, autumnally golden and solemn. Then there were the bitterly low-spirited, doleful morning hymns such as *If Thou But Suffer God to Guide Thee*, others wintry and subdued: *The Waves, Mighty and Tall, Doth Tremble Before the Lord's Call*. Mystical: *He Shouts Abba Father, I Will Trust in Thee*. Most beautiful perhaps is the early Christian tone, exemplified in *Lord of Our Life* and *God of Our Salvation!*

At first I thought it was the headmaster himself who led the singing. Later I realised this would not be compatible with his elevated functions. But who could imagine morning song without him as a focal point? That would be like a church without an altar. Morning song was the solemn daily act by which the headmaster, in the most convincing manner, demonstrated that God was God of the world, and that he, the headmaster, was God of the school, with power extending far beyond the school gates. I don't say this in jest, but out of true admiration for his patriarchal and disciplinary genius. It was old-fashioned, but quite right to begin each day by demonstrating the natural order of things. It helps to understand the Middle Ages, the papacy, and the absolutism of God's grace. Undemocratic? Assuredly. And outdated. And not necessarily an example to emulate. But the school that Lauritsen took charge of was in a state of grievous decay and moral depravation. He managed to thoroughly rectify the morals—in his own emphatic way!

Moreover, the school was an *orbis mundi*, a world sphere, which you were surrounded by, but with threads leading out to everything, with knowledge of everything, a store of mystical knowledge that would open little by little. We began in the eastern corner, in the cranny Jacob Dahl and Miss

Rafn kept to. Jacob Dahl, the future rural dean and Faroese patriot, represented religion, and I will not forget him for the beautiful manner in which he ushered us into the New Testament's magnificent telling of Jesus. There is and always will be something fundamentally beautiful about the full sphere of one's consciousness, the foundations of which were established here. As teacher of religion, Dahl rose considerably above ordinary rote learning. This was far more valuable than Skaalum's strangely sciolistic dialectics in the later years. There was profound feeling and emotion in Dahl's teaching.

Miss Rafn represented Denmark, Danish geography and history. Residing in the corner for third year were technical science, physics and chemistry, electricity, and magnetism—it was all terribly enticing and exciting. The big cupboard that contained the lustre of the machines was fascinating. But best of all—you only discover that later—was the zoology and botany teacher Skaalum. For he represented *nature*. He kept to the east wing, in a small closet filled with peculiar creatures in spirit (something the school's bearded caretaker and handyman was occasionally wont to drink himself giddy on). And finally, Skaalum also had the small dark staffroom with the strange smelling stuffed seal. This could perhaps seem lowly and sombre, but all in all Skaalum represented precisely what would have to be considered vigour. The smell of distant fields clung to his raiment, at heart he was a good-natured, enormously engaged, and communicative little boy. He brought a breath of mountain air to the courtyard of the *realskole*. There was after all a devil of a lively vision within this man, who due to his ultra-reactionary political views so often incurred the scorn and derision of the more precocious students. He led us outside to the *haugen*[11] during physical education and showed us peculiar things. For by virtue of Skaalum, the courtyard was not a quagmire, but a place with its own refreshing echo, with a mystical view of mountains and moors, fields and meadows.

The third wing of the school was occupied by the headmaster. As a *teacher*, you didn't encounter him until a later age. But he was the best teacher, opening the door to literature and thereby the entire world. The best thing about him was that he never raised a finger to pontificate on literary history. He allowed literature to speak for itself, and eventually, through a story like 'Haldor Through the Mountains' you were far more enriched by *Hauch* than you would have been with the aid of a thousand literary pointers. Never did he speak a word of Holberg or Oehlenschläger, and for that I am grateful. Modern literary history teaching is artificial, pasted, borrowed opinions. An insulating layer of school idiocy is wedged in between the students and the works of poetry they are meant to benefit from, which, despite everything, are more important than the poet. At Tórshavn's *realskole* I learned a little about Danish literature. At Sorø Academy I learned a lot about Danish poets, but you couldn't see the wood for the trees. And at university, I generally slept through Vilhelm Andersen's brilliantly compelling lectures, though I have to concede the man could occasionally conjure up some magic.

The first years were, as previously mentioned, by no means boring. With a voracious appetite and wide eyes, we learned about geography, history and zoology. For me, school maintained its novelty long into the first year of middle school. Learning brought a smile to the lips. Even though the headmaster's English lessons could be tough, they were not lacking in poetry, thanks to the delightful Otto Jespersenian textbooks.

But then came the burden of school and the awkwardness. German was a confoundedly boring subject. Unbearably dull textbooks and readers, often characterised by a certain aggressive militaristic sentiment—*Das edle Blut*![15] Maths, too, failed to captivate, and overall, physics came as a big disappointment: futile swotting instead of experimenting.

Two new teachers arrived—*Arndal*, a clever fellow but strangely broken-down and listless, couldn't be bothered to open the cupboards containing the interesting testing equipment, which is difficult to forgive him for. At heart he really was a capital fellow, strong, sharp and (outside of school) full of vitality. Perhaps somewhat of a cynic. Towards interested students he was both willing and friendly, but he was, if possible, even more sick and confoundedly tired of all the stuffiness and burden of school than all of the bone-idle students combined.

The other new teacher, *Kristoffersen*, was indeed splendid. A new man of nature, like Skaalum. He was too tender-hearted and all too modest. He represented some of the most beautiful Danish qualities of all—the shy kindness and hospitality so prevalent 'in the countryside' where the arrogance of Copenhagen and the tedious provincial snobbishness have not glazed over true Danishness. That he was inordinately bashful and always in love was another matter, which incidentally does not make the man any less sympathetic.

Kristoffersen, who would be our German teacher, had something of Schubert's spirit about him. German natural romanticism, singing and springtime. *Wie scheint die Sonne, wie lacht die Flur.*[23] Freshness and gentleness. He encountered only meagre appreciation. All in all, the students at that time had developed into a stifling and crude audience. It was actually an appallingly stale and cynical atmosphere that arose in several of the student boarding houses in town. Stunted and scrubby, lewdly cunning youths, in whose midst Christian Matras' delicate soul went as unnurtured as a pale and overwrought asparagus. Most of them turned out to be humorous and kind people, good mates and decent fellows, but with little drive and interest caused by a premature nonchalance and a far too great preoccupation with sex.

The school's midmost years are by and large rank, stifling and dismal. But little by little new pleasures were discovered: borrowing books from the library, Danish lessons with the headmaster. And little by little, delicate and airy currents began to displace the foul smell that rose from the muddied confines of the *realskole*.

In the final years, the dawning summer of youth really took hold. It was a magnificent time, filled with an aura of expectation that can never be recreated. When I started year four of middle school, the Great War had well and truly broken out during the summer holidays. But its effect on me was if anything of something that was splendid and exciting. Our year is not part of the war generation. We experienced it all with carefree puerile minds and delighted in *Ship Ahoy* and *Tipperary* while we languorously longed to face this great unknown world.

The final years of *realskole* are where you start to become an adult, and for a time I was fully and completely smitten with a girl in this form. An unforgettable infatuation, an unforgettable year, and its equal can hardly be found in autumnal slush, wintry bleakness, and vernal delicacy. The year I left *Tórshavn Realskole*, the school had left the old building, moving outside the city. I moved to Sorø, which did not and never would have the same value for me as the old school in Tórshavn.

When I returned home three years later the headmaster was gone, Skaalum was gone, Arndal and Miss Rafn were gone, with Kristoffersen close to joining them. Jacob Dahl was now a priest out in Sandegjerde. The school was gone. There was nothing left.

Don Juan of the Cod Liver Oil Factory

by

William Heinesen

translated by Paul Russell Garrett

For Don Juan not only has luck with the girls, he makes them feel lucky too—and unlucky, but curiously enough, in such a way that they would have it thus, and it was a foolish girl who did not want to be unlucky in order just once to have been lucky with Don Juan.

Søren Kierkegaard

1

The scene of the events to be related here has to all intents and purposes been wiped off the face of the earth, as if ravaged by earthquake or other natural disaster, and yet this great upheaval stems from only the most peaceable and joyful reasons, namely the construction of a much-needed harbour with piers and a breakwater. Where these modern wharves and quays now extend, with their storehouses and office buildings, there was previously a solid rocky reef, that to the south, cut out into the open sea and formed a headland known as Stangenæs. This broad and bare ridge of rock, which to the east was crowned with the old ramparts and parapets of Skansin, lent itself perfectly to the drying of cod; here Consul Preisler had his drying yards and storehouses, and situated out on Stangenæs was his cod liver oil boiling house, a low stone building with a weather-beaten turf roof and a sooty fireplace at the end of the gable.

A strangely contradictory site, this Cod Liver Oil Factory; in winter deserted, dark and foreboding, ravaged by the elements; in summer transformed into nothing short of a living being, bubbling with life and full of warm breath, rich vapours, and rancid fumes, most often surrounded by a cloud of shrieking birds!

Cod liver oil is a remarkable thing: the sun's gift to all things living in the salty sea, an indispensably fortifying and warming ferment for all organic life in the cold water. A wonder elixir, also for people. Though loved only by a small minority of the children of the sea in the globe's northern polar region. Under more southerly skies subject to an inexplicable aversion that makes people grimace at the mere thought of this fluid.

Even among us inhabitants of the subarctic Faroe Islands, the relationship to cod liver oil is characterised by a certain distaste, at any rate an ambivalence, a love-hatred—not unrelated to the feelings with which sexual phenomena are also regarded by many. All things considered, some arcane connection between cod liver oil and sex may hold sway, something we will see examples of in this account of the Maltese, this strange ladykiller who here, at the Cod Liver Oil Factory on Stangenæs, had his stronghold and infallible trap.

2

The Maltese died five years before I was born, and I first became acquainted with him as a ghost. On moonlit winter evenings, when the Cod Liver Oil Factory was black and abandoned on its desolate headland, his face could be glimpsed in the small, high window that faced the shore. If you were particularly fortunate, you could also hear him singing and playing his zither in muted tones—a strange and sorrowful music, the kind that only restless spirits are capable of expressing in their colossal loneliness and regret.

As a restless spirit, the Maltese also had the habit of roaming about unseen and manifesting himself in inexplicable ways. Even after his death he had a bewitching power over certain women, such as the young fisherwoman, Laura, who as late as 1914 was said to have 'sensed him above her' in the Preisler drying yard, in broad daylight at that, before falling into a salacious swoon.

Of course the Maltese also came to people in their dreams, something I can personally attest to, as for a significant portion of my childhood, he was among my regular gallery of nocturnal disturbers. In the arena of dreams, however, he was one of the more peaceable players. Certainly he was dark and sinister and stank of rancid fish guts and other muck, but most often he kept humbly to the background, stooping under his burden of irredeemable sin and shame—except, as it happened, when he appeared in the company of Mad Mathæa and these two spectres came to blows and tried to wring the life out of each other. Mad Mathæa was one of my worst nocturnal tormentors.

You could hardly imagine a more terrifying sight than this Medusa, with her unblinking fisheyes and close-cropped hair. Alive, she had been so stark raving mad that the local authority had built her a small hut where she could be left to herself with her lethal rage. This hut, situated on one of the rocky ledges below Skansin's western bastion, after her death was used for the storing of explosives and bore a warning sign with one word: Dynamite. One fine morning, Mathæa was discovered in her hut, strangled. On that same ill-fated morning the Maltese was lost at sea. But to these tumultuous events we will return in due course.

3

During puberty, interest in the Maltese began to manifest itself in a new way. Some of my childhood friends related incredible things about the debauchery that had taken place at the Cod Liver Oil Factory during the Maltese's time there. Stoffa, son of the Evangelical cod liver oil boiler Kristoffer, who assisted his father at the factory, and who always stank of cod liver oil, was especially well-informed on this topic, and did not hold back when it came to factual particulars and hair-raising details. From what Stoffa claimed, the Maltese had, for instance, entertained a particular pleasure for rolling his victims in cod liver oil sludge, to make them as slimy and slippery as fish. One girl, who refused to be rolled about, he had simply thrown into the crucible, however its contents, on that occasion, had not been boiling, merely slightly heated, and then he himself had jumped into the cod-liver slush and sated his gluttony with her in there.

This warm slush made the girls rampageous, Stoffa claimed, they screamed and writhed like witches in flying ointment, some of them never recovered to be normal people again after being subjected to the Maltese's treatment but spent the rest of their lives in sin and savagery, and only stood to be saved if they converted to the Inner Mission and allowed themselves to be cleansed in the blood of the Lamb.

Being at the Cod Liver Oil Factory with Stoffa was exciting beyond measure, when he was out there on his own, tending the fire and keeping an eye on the boiling. The volume of liver moved slowly in the large vat, stirring below the steaming surface like living creatures turning in their sleep, now and then treacly venom-yellow bubbles rose to the surface, grew big and burst with a sound like a satisfied belch. The hotter the gushing mass in the vat grew, the livelier the movements became, tumefactions great and small arose here and there, coherent figures could be made out, faces appeared in the flesh-coloured slush, breasts and thighs and knobbly knees, backs, hips and stomachs, cleft bottoms and genitals, and the sounds grew strangely amorous, as if from idle cravings and unabashed concupiscence. The bubbles gathered in luxuriant clusters, like grapes or whale kidneys and burst with sounds resembling sumptuous kisses. Here and there it gave way to spasmodic contractions, and the clear, boiling cod liver oil squirted into the air in small spatters, like when flicking the slime out of a sea wrack's bladder.

We sat staring into this sorcery, spellbound and silent, filled with contradictory feelings: aversion and attraction, voracious curiosity and untold anguish.

That is how it was in the Maltese's world, simultaneously horrifying and frightfully fascinating, here where sin and lust grappled with delight and horror, and death had the final word.

Set against this backdrop, it really was no wonder the Maltese was long imagined as little short of the Devil himself: a prince of witches, the enormity of his infamy beyond comprehension, but at the same time practically awe-inspiring in the imperturbability of his lascivious wickedness. And yet, when it came down to it, a pitiful, pathetic existence, abandoned to merciless punishment and eternal damnation on the Day of Judgement.

Very slowly did this childish myth of fear and sorrow yield to more grown-up and objective aspects.

And yet—never would this old myth surrender its power entirely; its innermost core of mystery still obstinately refuses to allow itself to be laid bare.

4

During this present attempt to identify a rational connection in the Maltese's story, three sources have been particularly invaluable to me. Firstly, notations by the local historian, bookkeeper and organist Oscar Davidsen in his posthumous manuscript *Journal of Strange Misfortunes in my Hometown of Tórshavn*; secondly, Miss Yrsa Preisler's (future wife of Concertmaster Waldmüller) sporadic diary entries between 1893 and 1894, benevolently placed at my disposal by the editor of *Dagens Nyheder*, Ove Waldmüller; and lastly, information provided to me by the chief fish sorter Hans-Pauli

Alaih (1861-1941) during a sea voyage to the Azores in 1932 about the Maltese, whom he had known personally and had a number of dealings with. Naturally I've also taken a good deal of inspiration and poetic impetus from the many legends and anecdotes that circulated among ordinary people in my hometown during my childhood.

Of the Maltese's extraction and antecedents, practically nothing is known except that he went by the name *Adda Geraldi*. By his own account, he was born in the year 1870 on the island of Malta in the southern Mediterranean and had since boyhood served on British ships. His arrival in the Faroe Islands, he revealed, came as the sole survivor of a boat that capsized in the Norwegian Sea in March 1893, *The St Cuthbert's Duck*. He was notoriously saved by the people of the small island of Kolter, who brought him to Tórshavn with frostbitten feet and a badly inflamed gash across the small of his back.

As to the Maltese's rescue, Davidsen made the following notation:

'He was found in a completely enfeebled state, lying in the bottom of a dinghy that washed ashore on the pebbled beach in the small cove of Heljarsloka, discovered by pure chance by two eight or nine-year-old boys who were out collecting dead man's fingers. Of the island's male inhabitants on the said day, only these two young nippers and an old man were present, as the adult males had set off fishing early in the morning, but the women, with the help of the boys, managed to get the shipwrecked man inside. However he was so perished that only the heat of a human body, as was generally known, could save him from death, and as the two boys could not be induced to climb into bed with him, the decisive peasant woman Anna Zachariasen, along with her eighteen-year-old sister Sisal, lay down next to him, and these two resolute women, through their shared warmth, brought the unfortunate stranger back to life.'

At the hospital in Tórshavn, Adda Geraldi won over the hearts of everyone with his cheerful and endearing demeanour. The twenty-five-year-old Maltese bore many of the characteristic features often attributed to southern Europeans, he was of a small and slender build, with dark skin, dark-brown twinkling eyes and a row of strong white teeth; only his hair was not dark, but a reddish manila-blond; though an exceptionally thick and lush mane. His arms and legs were also particularly hirsute.

The Maltese gave the impression of having an infinite store of good spirits and zest for life, he smiled appreciatively at everything and everyone, and chatted congenially with the young storm spotter,[17] later chief fish sorter Hans-Pauli Alaih, who shared a room with him and could understand English and explain to the staff nurse Angelica what the Maltese said when he squeezed and kissed her hand, which he never missed an opportunity to do: 'Oh, Angelica! Here I lie, alive and kicking in a lovely bed, attended to by an angel—I, who should have lain at the bottom of the sea and been eaten by the fish!' Or: 'Oh Angelica, my lucky star, are you bringing me that delicious soup again, with prunes and cinnamon? I could kiss you right on your cinnamon belly!'

Even for the severe, black-clad ward sister Anna, the Maltese's smile had a disarming effect. He looked upon her as a nun and called her *Suora*. 'Pray for me, *Suora*, send greetings to our holy Mother and thank her for all her grace!'

Hans-Pauli Alaih, a man of a thoughtful nature, had his own quiet wonderings about his roommate. The cheerful and guileless manner this young stranger displayed—was it altogether genuine? Was there not a certain unease and worry lurking behind all this ostensible nonchalance? It was striking, at any rate, the Maltese's reticence when he was grilled about his birth and family circumstances, offering only deprecating hand gestures and evasive answers: 'Alas—a man who has been almost dead and has had his life returned by a pure stroke of luck, he has no past, he comes from everywhere and from nowhere, for he is born to life anew and has forgotten everything!'

Hans-Pauli realised it could certainly feel that way, to someone who had been through so much and been so near death. But still!

There was something else that didn't quite add up, namely that the weather conditions on the Norwegian Sea had not seemed nearly so turbulent at the time *The St Cuthbert's Duck* was meant to have capsized. On the contrary, the entire month of March had seen calm, cold weather. Had his ship truly capsized? Was it not far more likely that there had been a mutiny with bloody battles aboard? The gash on the Maltese's back could indicate this. Perhaps the young stranger had been marooned, had committed some serious breach of the law of the sea, and as punishment, been thrown overboard and abandoned to his fate?

5

Even as the Maltese lay in hospital, arrangements were being made in town to extend a helping hand to the destitute stranger and raise money for his kitting out and journey home. As so often was the case, this was undertaken at the initiative of the consul's wife, Jacobine Preisler, in the form of an evening of entertainment at Tinghuset.

Such evenings of entertainment with charitable aims were, according to bookkeeper Davidsen, a specialty of the consul's wife. She also had an uncommonly beautiful singing voice, a powerful and dark alto, and had trained at the conservatory and could have been an opera singer had she not been hindered by her imposing stature. The consul's wife was a giant of a woman, nearly half a head taller than the consul, who was a strapping and striking figure himself. The consul's wife' friendly and magnanimous nature was equal to her height.

The programme for the performance being prepared had in fact already been decided and partially rehearsed; it was meant to have been for the benefit of the old widow House-Marie, whose beggarly cabin had been ravaged by fire at Shrovetide, but the old woman had since passed away, and for that reason the benefit had been delayed. Now it was back on firm ground, and it was, Davidsen tells us, 'a most unforgettable evening.' The consul's wife sang arias from *Don Giovanni* and *Carmen*, accompanied on the lute (Tinghuset had no piano) by her equally musical daughter Yrsa; headmaster Prospersen read snippets of *Adam Homo*; the district court judge's two striking daughters, Kamma and Regina, appeared in tableaux as Orpheus and Eurydice; Hagbard and Signe and the girls from southern Jutland, along with Pastor Ewaldsen's men's choir sang *Farthest North* and *Dear Christians, One and All Rejoice*. But the evening's biggest surprise was a contribution completely outside the scope of the programme and was owing to none other than the beneficiary himself, Adda Geraldi, who despite not being discharged from the hospital, had been permitted to attend the performance, and near the end, he had jumped up onto the platform in his excitement, grabbed Miss Yrsa's lute and sung the popular Irish tune *Londonderry Air*.

The Maltese, who turned out to be a good string player with a clear and warm baritone voice, was greeted with rapturous applause and made to give an encore. He was wearing, Davidsen reports, 'a fetching sailor suit belonging to Hans-Pauli Alaih's younger brother and made a particularly good showing, and it can be presumed that as early as this occasion, the heart of many a young impressionable girl was set afire, thus sowing the seed for all the grief and harm that would later follow in the footsteps of this pernicious person.'

It might also be presumed that such a girlish heart throbbed in the bosom of young Miss Yrsa, and the series of unfortunate events that would eventually lead to the Maltese's own demise were also set in motion that evening.

The performance yielded a handsome profit, and the Maltese was informed that a tidy sum of money awaited him at Consul Preisler's office, and a steamship ticket had been booked for him aboard *The Otto Wathne*, which was expected from Iceland later that week.

Adda Geraldi went to the office, not to collect his money, but to report that his heart was not set on travelling, and that he, according to Davidsen: 'humbly beseeched and pleaded to be allowed to remain in the land of the Faroes, to which, notwithstanding his salvation, he owed such immense gratitude for the undeserved kindness he had been met with here, that he could feel at home as though in a new native land.'

The Consul, though he had a warm-hearted disposition, admittedly, could in a great many ways be a stringent and rigid man, not only permitted the Maltese to keep the money, but also promised to discover whether some form of suitable employment could be secured for him in his new native land.

Adda Geraldi was provided with temporary lodgings in the home of Madam Bærentsen in Myntestue, and when it was discovered that he was skilled in the art of ropemaking and splicing, and in addition that he had experience as a sailmaker, he was shortly after given a job at Preisler's sail loft in the so-called Consul Warehouse.

6

A couple of months now lapsed without the Maltese seeming to have made himself conspicuous in any way other than going about his work to everyone's satisfaction, and with his sociable nature, spreading general good cheer around him. But, as it would later turn out, certain concealed, yet for the future development of matters, key incidents took place during this time. This emerges more or less overtly from Miss Yrsa's diary entries during this period.

Yrsa Preisler, who had not even turned seventeen by this point, was as we will soon have the opportunity to see, an intelligent yet impressionable young lady with a rather significant poetic vein. She had accompanied her father on some of his frequent trips to Scotland and England, and, as it seems, been greatly enamoured of the British Romantics: Byron, Wordsworth, Coleridge, and more. The overwrought infatuation she harboured for the mysterious stranger from the sea can, in part, be explained as a result of the influence of this literary romanticism. Though only in part. As her diary reveals, there was talk of an all-consuming infatuation, the burning soul of a young girl and her first stormy encounter with the overwhelming demonic power of love.

The Maltese first features in Miss Yrsa's diary on 1 April 1893, under the pseudonym 'the Person' or 'P'. She writes: 'Met P today out by the bend, he stopped as if he wanted to talk to me, I gave a quick nod, hurried past, felt myself blushing. Oh, he is such a *dandy*! New clothes, bowler hat, a flower in his buttonhole, the peacock! He's leaving on Thursday, good. Why good? Perhaps I should have stopped, yet…'

A few days later she meets P again, this time 'out in Ålekjær, by the corner of the asylum garden,' writing: 'He stopped. The cheek! Told me he didn't want to leave, wanted to stay. Insufferable in his fancy clothes, looks like the Count of Monte Cristo or something! Probably fancies himself? Those eyes! I was cold as snow. Kamma says he looks like a blackguard. Truly.'

On 8 April she again meets P: 'He was in work clothes, which suited him, he almost looked like Robert Burns, he works in the loft of the warehouse out by the bend, had a big green lantern on his shoulder. We didn't stop, I pretended to be very busy. Those eyes!

So was it when my life began…

Goodness gracious!'

The entries for the following week are torn out of Miss

Yrsa's diary, but the seventeenth of April reads (in very thin, almost illegible writing): 'Same corner. He thinks it will do to speak openly with a lady on a public thoroughfare. Then he suggested we go into the garden! Should one have any more dealings with such a blackguard? Kamma has seen him with a nurse from the hospital. More suitable company, hm. Of no interest to me.'

Once again, a number of pages are missing from the diary. The next entry (28/4) is in English. Here it reads (inspired by a quote from Wordsworth): '...Is now so bright that no more. Lie awake, torn up (*harrowed*). Still nothing discovered... Fortunately H is still around me, seems distracted, people are talking about H and me. Poor H!'

This H—Hugo Waldmüller—was Miss Yrsa's cousin, Mrs Preisler's nephew from Copenhagen, who Yrsa Preisler would marry in September 1894.

From the above-mentioned quote, it seems the Consul's daughter has had some secret encounters with the Maltese, possibly making use of the old stone wall surrounding the asylum's overgrown and neglected garden for cover.

Early in the month of May, however, Miss Yrsa sets off for Scotland with her father to spend the summer at a finishing school for young ladies and to improve her already notable skills on the piano. Certain heartfelt pleas in her travel diary seem to indicate she is attempting to tear P out of her heart. Though as she admits, 'It is horrible and I dread it!'

It would later turn out that Miss Yrsa had every reason to dread it.

7

As for Adda Geraldi, he began to settle in as a citizen of his new native land and become a familiar and generally well-regarded figure in the small town. His work he carried out with diligence and skill, and he also made himself useful outside of his true competencies, as a carpenter, cooper and locksmith, yes, even as a piano tuner. He managed to fix up an old and damaged zither kept in Madam Bærentsen's box room so that it could be played. On quiet spring evenings, when the Maltese played and sang in his little gable room, usually by the open window, a group would congregate below the gable of Myntestuen, mostly children, but also adults, young women in particular.

Something of an acrobat also beat within the heart of the Maltese, he could walk on his hands and do sensational somersaults, and when one day the old rusty weathervane on the church tower went by the board, no one, apart from Adda Geraldi, dared climb the tall, flimsy iron pole, but with great dexterity, he climbed skywards and affixed the new top section.

As to the Maltese's participation in the town's public entertainments, Davidsen states with pointed irony: 'As dancer and mountebank, naturally there was no one who could surpass Geraldi, he soon became the chief gallant at Feliksen's restaurant, *The Rotunda*, where the youth of the day gathered for the so-called *Short Black Dance* (a Short Black being a coffee with spirits); here he instituted a new and fierce kind of galop, 'the Maltese Galop' named after him, which became particularly popular, even though as often as not it left the girls dazed and confused.'

The significant appreciation and enthusiasm apportioned to this foreign charmer naturally gave rise to certain countercurrents, as is always the case: bourgeois decency felt aggrieved, certain jealous rivals took to grumbling, and soon a web of tittle-tattle and indignant gossip arose around the Maltese, though it may not have been entirely without foundation.

Rumour had it he had turned the head of Madam Bærentsen's young daughter Augusta, causing her betrothal with the stout assistant lightkeeper Larsen to be aborted. Around the same time Adda Geraldi had dazzled this chaste virgin, he was meant to have been seen as a nocturnal visitor of the two young fishergirls Hanna and Hulda, who lived alone and led a notoriously loose way of life. Furthermore, the night watchman Hans Agranda was meant to have observed him one night at the churchyard with a woman, whom the watchman thought he recognised as Maja, the wife of the restaurateur Feliksen. And from yet another corner it was claimed with certitude that the Maltese did not shy from carrying out his unsavoury nocturnal activities on the consecrated soil of the churchyard (which incidentally abutted the small garden of Feliksen's restaurant), and the parish church council was reported to have had these disturbing rumours on its agenda.

One should not, however, believe that all of this gossip had a cooling effect on the young women of the town or made the Maltese a shady and shunned individual; on the contrary, his tarnished reputation had an even more stimulating effect on the girls, and when around midsummer of that year it became clear to all that Adda Geraldi was on the verge of linking his fate with one girl in particular, it caused amazement and disappointment among many, yes, in some cases verging on despair, such as with the aforementioned nurse from the hospital, Angelica Michelsen, who was one of the first young women the Maltese had courted. This Angelica later came to play a decisive role in the curious and fateful drama that gradually unfolded around Adda Geraldi.

On this topic, bookkeeper Davidsen writes: 'That the Maltese now seemed to have arrived at a more sensible thinking and resolved to replace his former dissolute lifestyle with a new, more demure one was received with general satisfaction and relief by all of the older and responsible people of Tórshavn. Unfortunately, as it later turned out, there was only talk of a brief hiatus, a calm before the storm.'

8

This hiatus merits its own particular mention, especially as it reflects certain human qualities in our Maltese, attributes that may divulge that he was not the heartless and unimaginable monster that the rigorous bookkeeper Davidsen makes him out to be.

The young woman who would seize Adda Geraldi's full attention and delight his heart and mind to the extent that he forgot everything around him, the reader has, earlier in this present account, if only superficially, already been introduced to: it was Sisal, who together with her sister, the peasant woman from the small island of Kolter, had with the warmth of her young body saved the shipwrecked Maltese from death. This Sisal had since travelled to the capital to take up the position of maid in Consul Preisler's home.

Bookkeeper Davidsen attributes to her the following rather harsh and unambiguous characteristics: 'Sisal Bergstok was in no way remarkable in appearance, a plain Faroese peasant woman, petite, medium blonde, very shy and slightly cross-eyed, but with a nature that was exceedingly steadfast and firmly anchored in her devout religious beliefs. She knew how it would end with the young man, who at her bosom had been called back from death to life, and she had felt genuine sympathy for him and done all she could to once more rescue him from ruin.'

Sisal did not participate in the town's public entertainments but joined the small devout group that came together in 'the Lodge' around the two Templars, the maths teacher Christiansen and the postmaster Nicodemussen. It caused general wonder among the small gathering when on one fine evening the quiet young girl from Kolter arrived at the lodge accompanied by none other than the young hothead Adda Geraldi. The Maltese appeared, contrary to his usual custom, highly respectful and sombre, sitting at the side of the devout young girl, taking great pains to take in and understand the Templars' urgent words, and during the hymns, he joined in on the melody with his sonorous voice, though naturally with his articulation he was less successful.

Many believed the Maltese's presence at the lodge could only be explained as a passing fad, or simply a ruse that the frivolous young man believed would assure him the favour of a girl who would otherwise be beyond his reach; but as the weeks passed and Sisal, night after night, arrived at the lodge with her Maltese companion, these grumblings had to be abandoned and the remarkable fact acknowledged that Adda Geraldi had changed his ways and been led down the path of redemption by the young girl. It could also be noted that the Maltese no longer frequented *The Rotunda*, and there were no indications of the young couple engaging in secret encounters; zealous observers could attest to the fact that every night after the meeting at the lodge, Adda Geraldi escorted the girl to the door of the consulate, took his leave in a seemly manner, to then return home to his lonely lodgings with Madam Bærentsen, whose daughter, incidentally, had in the meantime been happily reunited with her assistant lightkeeper.

It was also common knowledge that Mrs Jacobine Preisler very much approved of the beautiful relationship between the two young people that the Consul had taken into his service, which came fully to light when Mrs Preisler, at a small gathering for the Consul's workers and officials, personally announced the engagement between Sisal and Adda.

'News of this startling development,' Davidsen writes, 'positively moved our small town to tears. The shipwrecked man was united with the young woman who had saved his life; he had repented and abandoned his erstwhile frivolous existence and guided his storm-tossed craft into harbour. Their wedding was imminent. The Consul's wife, out of motherly care, had already obtained for the young couple a small, but beautifully situated house for them to live in: the so-called Sergeant House north of Skansin.'

To this the bookkeeper attaches the following embittered comments: 'Thus through underhand scheming, this unscrupulous rake managed to secure himself this victim too, and to bring shame and sorrow upon a warm-hearted and innocent young maiden.'

Here too there is cause to suppose that Davidsen is somewhat too rigorous and crude in his judgement. The details Hans-Pauli Alaih provided about Sisal Bergstok, rather poorly correspond with the image the bookkeeper has left of this young woman. She was, for instance, neither small nor unimpressive in appearance, but had a rather buxom figure, with thick dark hair and exceptionally warm and roguish eyes. In addition, she had, according to Hans-Pauli Alaih, a rather tempestuous and sarcastic personality, though still generally cheerful in nature and in possession of an amusing ability to imitate people, for instance and in particular the two unctuous and theatrical Templars of the Lodge. Her fiancé and future husband she was also adroit at copying, she made particularly merry with his halting language. That she was nonetheless deeply and passionately in love with him was beyond any doubt, and in many ways, it appears as though the Maltese has allowed himself to be bewitched and completely bowled over by this young girl's elementary charm. Likely the rootless adventurer has also had illusions that by her side he could devote himself to a new and better existence, free of the entanglements and troubles always connected with the life and activities of an untethered fop.

'On Saturday 12 August 1893,' Davidsen writes, 'the young couple were able to marry and move into the new home, which the Consul's wife, out of the goodness of her heart, had procured for them. Nor was there any lack of other favours on the part of the Consul, in the form of handsome and handy wedding gifts, as well as beautiful and stately entertainment during the wedding festivities, where the Consul's wife herself sang, among other things, Schubert's 'Pax Vobiscum', accompanied by the humming of Pastor Ewaldsen's men's choir, but also on a purely practical level, when the Maltese, upon Hans-Pauli Alaih's appointment to chief fish sorter, took over his post as storm spotter at the Preisler drying yards on the ridge of Skansin.'

'However,' the bookkeeper continues, 'it soon transpired that the blossoming matrimonial bliss, which one could but wish for the trusting young woman, was to be of the inconstant sort that quickly changes character and goes over to the opposite extreme.'

Were Davidsen to be believed, the unfortunate development in these matters is due solely to the 'innate wickedness and inferior mental faculties of the Maltese'—a perception that is shared by his contemporaries, but which in this present account, quite possibly for the first time, is cast in serious doubt.

For not only is it possible, but rather likely that Adda Geraldi could have, if not permanently settled down in this marriage, then at least as a husband and family man reasonably settled down in the small community that had so benevolently adopted him, had fate not subjected his capricious heart to a new and portentous strain.

9

Here Yrsa Preisler enters the picture again.

At the end of September, Miss Yrsa had returned home from her summer sojourn in Rock Manor near Loch Lomond. If her diary entries are to be taken altogether seriously, her stay at the Scottish finishing school had been practically one long unbroken chain of suffering and irreparable homesickness, not merely because of the strict and puritanical conditions at the school, but also, and in particular, because the warm feelings that the encounter with the Maltese had aroused in her heart had developed into a veritable obsession during her exile, which allowed her no peace, neither day nor night.

Of this, she confides in her diary with the entirely romantic overwrought fervour of a young woman's lovesick soul, often in direct address, such as on 3 June when she exclaims: '…My soulmate! If only you knew———! All, all, all this resplendent summer's day I have sat alone in my room, lost in thought of you, and in constant tears, yes, like a rain-soaked water lily, linked to the depths that provide her with nourishment and carry her on its surface, yet still a world closed off to her, a world that in her heart of hearts she desperately longs to dive into to become one with, but alas, it does not happen, perhaps not until the hour of death! Oh, my love, so distant over the great sea, now I look you in the eye! Come to me in dreams, drown me in the blissful depths of your love, let me not languish in this my dreadful solitude halfway between life and death!'

News (via a letter from her friend Kamma) of Adda Geraldi's betrothal with Sisal initially seems to have had a rather crippling effect on the unfortunate Yrsa. The diary page for 5 June contains only the single word '*Crushed*', and not until four days later does she seem to have recovered from her shock to the extent that she is again capable of writing—though in such frail writing that it can barely be read without a magnifying glass:

'Evening, 9 June 1893

Just returned from Mallard Inlet, where I sat hidden in the reeds in this interminable rain, soaked through, wanted to slip into the water and put an end to everything. Dared not. Or what? Not *mad* like Ophelia! Nearly though. Tried to *hate* him. Also thought: he does not exist, never has, is only in my dreams! But I *love* him! That is good to know.

> "*And meekly wait that moment, when*
> *Thy touch shall turn all bright again!*"

The letter from H [Cousin Hugo] that I crumpled up, I've unfolded again. *He*, at any rate, is not all there, the poor thing. So strange.'

The tone of the next entry is altogether different, indignant and childishly threatening, marked by a certain Gothic savagery *á la* Lord Byron: 'Enjoyed the thunderstorm last night, frightful sermon of the heavens, lay naked and bathed in the lightning! If you exist, snipe and wretch that you are, know that sooner or later punishment will strike you! Charred by lightning the first blush of dawn will find you at the bottom of the greenwood! Perhaps find us both, fused together in death, a pile of ashes, which mercifully the grass will soon grow over! PS Played Mozart's *Fantasia Sonata*, it soothes me, promises everything is not yet at an end.'

The entries for 13 September, the last day Yrsa Preisler spent abroad, are characterised by a similarly heightened romantic alteration, but it would seem, also by a certain ominous resolve: 'Be wary, I am still here. Know that you are threatened. *I shall overwhelm you and bring you to heel!*'

The page bears the postscript: 'Played ceaselessly, while I left the packing to Mary and Lizzie—*Sonata Pathétique* and others, Mozart's *Fantasia*, in particular, you exhale it, for everything here is merciful oblivion.'

According to Hans-Pauli Alaih, who was on the ferryboat that brought Miss Yrsa to shore from Preisler's merchant schooner, *The Jacobine*, the Consul's young daughter was much changed during her absence, she certainly did not appear to be returning from an enjoyable summer holiday, for she was pale, her face drawn, and had adopted cold 'lady-like' mannerisms. To the cheerful and good-humoured Kamma, who playfully elbowed her sullen friend in the side, she rebuked: 'Kamma, I am travel weary.'

Miss Yrsa's diary from the evening of her arrival (18 September) reveals a hint of her troubled and confused state of mind: '...it is perfectly natural for everyone to expect me to be cheerful and happy, but I cannot. Mother worried, wants Doctor Fredericia to examine my chest and my heart. My *heart*! I have no heart right now. Not for *him*, either. Ridiculous, all of it. Dare not see him again in case he proves not to be the air and nothingness he surely must be. Alas, if only he were not!!! But if he is (air and nothingness), then I myself am even more a nothingness. Have gone on too long with this stupid abscess in my heart, can no longer do without it.—P.S. Played Mozart's *Fantasia* for mother, she said that I astounded her ("plumbed the depths!").'

A week later, on 24 September, she writes: 'Finally saw P again, on my way home after an evening stroll with Kamma. He was whitewashing his house. Ridiculous! Much smaller than I remembered. Must have surprised him, he turned suddenly and saw us, greeted us respectfully, with a wry smile. Unshaven, white splashes on his face. Married and settled down, Lord help us, a perfectly ordinary, tedious fellow! Does not exist after all, I knew it! Went to bed early, lay crying, utterly foolish. Because he does not exist but has disappeared from my life, making the emptiness almost unbearable. However deep down in my heart of hearts I am indifferent, perhaps even happy, relieved, liberated? It is probably just a phase.—Letter from Hugo saying he expects me in the spring, indifferent to that, too! Indifferent to everything today, all things considered. Everything bores me to death, cannot be bothered to play the piano, go out, eat. Empty inside. Had a silly, solitary fit of laughter at the table. Everyone shook their heads, Father later took me aside, spoke earnestly, I took no notice, acted jolly, set him at ease.'

Miss Yrsa's entries over the following fortnight are brief, often only a single sentence ('Ground away at *The Diabelli Variations* eighteen times.' 'Drained and deathly tired.' 'I am a fool.'), sometimes utter nonsense ('Danced alone out by the bend to the silly part in the first movement of the *Hammerklavier Sonata*'), or short little sardonic rhymes:

For now the pussycat is dead, dead.
For now the pussycat is dead, dead.

Shortly after the simultaneously baffling and very telling diary pages, however, we have what would be Miss Yrsa's last entry for some time. From mid-October until 19 December she ceases to confide in her diary entirely. On the Wednesday evening of 14 October she writes (in her microscopic writing, in parts completely illegible): '...knew he was alone in the sail loft, went up and (...) did he truly believe he existed? (...) Told him he was a ghost, a Flying Dutchman, never returned to shore, still drifting in his boat (...) for I could not stand it anymore. For there is no one else I can love!!! Struck him and bit him, totally lost in indignation (...) Forgive! Then it went as I wished (...) in a state of beatitude. Nothing less. Happy at long last, no, not happy. Cannot be said. From now on I will no longer write, but live.'

What came to pass in the loft of the Consul Warehouse that fateful Wednesday afternoon is not difficult to reconstruct based on this diary fragment. Miss Yrsa, whose psychotic overwrought infatuation for the Maltese that not even the most reasonable remonstrances had been able to temper, has in desperation sought out the object of her untameable feelings; and as for him, as is no wonder, he ensured she did not leave having failed in her mission.

Nothing can be said, either, to the fact that bookkeeper Davidsen, who did not know of Yrsa Preisler's diary, ascribes Adda Geraldi the entire blame for the shocking and unfortunate incidents that followed. His contemporaries did likewise.

10

It is strange, almost inexplicable, that the Maltese and Miss Yrsa were able to pursue their secret relationship for an entire two months without being discovered. In all likelihood, the mere notion of an amorous liaison between the noble maiden from the consulate and the newly married scamp from the Sergeant House had been rejected as unimaginable and ridiculous.

Some have asserted that the clandestine lovers preferred to meet out at Skansin, where the Maltese had assumed the position of lamplighter, caretaker of the approach beacons located in the closed-off embankment area, (as well as the corresponding beacon on the other side of the bay), and that the 'boys' who used to assist him, were in fact, at least in some instances, Miss Yrsa in disguise, and in all likelihood, this is more than just one of the many fables people's imagination has put into circulation.

Another tale, one not entirely without foundation, has later been confirmed. It concerns the aforementioned Angelica Michelsen, the young staff nurse from the hospital that Adda Geraldi, promptly after his arrival in town, made advances to but later cast aside. This Angelica was one of those women whose heart the Maltese had completely bewitched, and in her despair at his desertion, she is meant to have secretly followed him and spied on his comings and goings so keenly that hardly any of his later manoeuvres have been able to escape her attention.

Hans-Pauli Alaih, who remembered this girl well, described her as being petite, mousy, and with a quiet smile, who would never dream of harming her fellow human beings. By all accounts, Angelica has kept her observations to herself for a long time, however in the end, tormented by grief and jealousy, has confided in Sisal what she knew about her husband and the Consul's daughter.

In doing so, little Angelica set in motion an extremely fateful series of events, and our account now enters into its final, unfortunate, and drama-packed stage.

11

'New Year's Day 1894,' bookkeeper Davidsen writes, 'was a day of consternation and sorrow, not just in my, but in the entire history of our little town.'

Davidsen, who has drawn a black cross above this chapter in his *Journal of Strange Misfortunes*, subsequently recounts the shocking events of the day with his usual meticulousness:

'It was around nine o'clock in the morning, and I had just sat down in the church to practise a prelude for the morning service, when my daughter Anna, completely aghast and dissolved in tears, arrived to tell me how that morning, a genuine attempt at murder was made out at the Sergeant House, as the Maltese's wife Sisal, wielding a woodchopper's axe (though not the edge, but the butt of the blade) had inflicted on her husband such a serious blow to the back of his head that he had been taken to the hospital in an unconscious state. However, this was not the only bit of bad news my daughter brought me, and horrible as it was, it was not the worst. For that same morning, she told me, still in tears, that our dear Consul had suffered a serious stroke and lay prostrate and unconscious, and that this had happened upon the arrival of Sisal, who, in a state of extreme shock, delivered the dismaying news to the Consul and his wife that their daughter Yrsa was fornicating with her husband and had been doing so for quite some time.'

'Since then,' Davidsen continues, 'more was revealed of this incident. The Consul's wife had taken Sisal's revelation with her characteristic composure and embraced her consolingly, as she earnestly entreated her not to wake Yrsa, still slumbering in her room, because her mother was likely anxious as to how her erratic daughter might react. As for the Consul, he turned quite pale and sat perfectly mute in his chair while his wife solicitously led the devastated and five-months-pregnant Sisal to a room so she could rest and take some fortifying drops. By the time Mrs Preisler returned to the front room, the Consul was lying on the floor, struck down by a stroke.'

Overcome by such oppressive memories, Davidsen enters in his journal the verse of a hymn:

'*Oh were our sins to be placed before Judgement,*
Then the fruit of the earth would spread like chaff.
Then, stricken and dazed,
We would be smitten into the dust.'

'The next day,' the journal continues, 'came the sorrowful news that our dear Consul J. O. Preisler had passed away quietly without waking from his merciful rest. I have written elsewhere with complete ineptitude about this exceptional man and great personality, who for forty years was my dear and propitious employer, and whose deeds and significance to our town are acknowledged in all quarters, and here all I can add is that his demise was not merely a difficult blow to everyone, but he also left behind a void that, as it turned out, would never be filled. He left behind no male heirs, and among his faithful employees there were none who possessed the personality and sense to lead his extensive enterprise forward in an effective manner.'

Here the bookkeeper adds modestly: 'In stating this, I fully realise that I am also directing an accusation against myself that is only too justified.'

He follows this with an exhaustive portrayal of the Consul's interment: 'As for the Consul's unfortunate yet brave wife, in the time that followed, she was forced to endure fresh trials, inflicted upon her by her daughter Yrsa, who, as it turned out, had ended up in circumstances that one would normally consider happy, but which here must be described using the exact opposite designation. By February, the Consul's wife had already departed for Copenhagen with her daughter. Miss Yrsa, thank the Lord, in high summer that very same year, was joined in the holy bond of matrimony with her noble-minded cousin, the musician Hugo Waldmüller. As for Adda Geraldi, after being discharged from hospital, he moved back to the Sergeant House, which at that point remained empty, since his wife Sisal had departed for the island of her birth, Kolter, never to return. Four months later she gave birth to a daughter.'

Seen through bookkeeper Davidsen's eyes, as already mentioned, the unfortunate business with Miss Yrsa and Adda Geraldi poses no great problem: *he* is the unscrupulous scoundrel, *she* the corrupted innocent. Were one to attempt to find a more accommodating picture of the emotional basis for the peculiar relationship between the Consul's daughter and the young seaman, however, certain peculiar complications are encountered, as so often is the case in dealing with the troublesome will-o'-the-wisp world of human love.

The resumed diary entries of Miss Yrsa from mid-December are in part presented in oracular style, which afford few fixed points. What is there to say about an utterance such as this from 18 December: 'Ninth and final time. Indifferent. *After us the deluge.* Unfortunately approaching zero. Then minus degrees.' Or (21 December): 'Longest night of the year. Flight and other insufferable and childish ideas and stupid tears, unsightly to see a man blubber. The namby-pamby. This is the worst to date. Now below zero.'

However, a longer notation dated 'The night before Christmas Eve' speaks in a somewhat clearer language. Here we have 'Reckoning. Always knew *he* did not exist, merely *a phantasma of my dreams*. Only myself to blame. Fortunately his crocodile blubbering makes me as ice. See through everything. The cold worsens. Carefree charade on the outside, lets me feel nothing, take everything without batting an eyelid, except mother's eyes! She truly believes I am wasting away in yearning for H! It's nearly true, for H is of course a man, good night, will properly cry myself to sleep.'

The forced calm reflected in these diary entries gives way, however, in the period between Christmas and New Year, to a veritable tornado of agonising outbursts, for the most part in a childish, romantic, and somewhat bombastic style, though often gripping in their untameable *furor poeticus*: '… walked alone by the beach again, shouting into the storm and the surf, oh! If anyone had heard me! Wished a flood would come to inundate everything. (The ending to Beethoven's *Appassionata*!) Be carried on dark waves, be engulfed... wander the depths, drowned but not dead, with eyes wide open, petrified and petrifying, like Medusa's.'

In light of this, the taciturn notes conveyed by Miss Yrsa's diary on 1 January 1894, the day before Sisal's atrocity and her father's death, seem strangely composed, nearly cool-headed: '...freezing, clear night. Deathly calm. What else would you expect than this lightning, this earthquake, so overwhelming and stupefying! Now all is quiet, here at the bottom, peace at long last. The peace of punishment.'

Later the storm breaks again; but we will let these be Yrsa Preisler's final words in the story before us, and return to the protagonist of our account, Adda Geraldi.

12

According to general accounts, the Maltese never fully recovered from the trauma Sisal inflicted on him in her wrath, and had become slightly deranged. Bookkeeper Davidsen however, does not share in this view, but remarks staidly moralising: 'Time and time again, wicked and felonious actions are sought to be excused on account of the perpetrators being of supposed unsound mind, but I, and many with me, find this to be a far too meagre pretext through which responsibility is evaded by the guilty party and is ascribed to—yes, who other than the very master of fate? Therefore he is to my mind an incorrigible rascal.'

Such an utterly uncompromising attitude towards the Maltese, the bookkeeper was not alone in taking. It is known, for instance, that headmaster Prospersen, leader of the parish council, applied significant pressure on Pastor Ewaldsen to have him pronounce from the pulpit the church's condemnation of Adda Geraldi's moral conduct, though the priest declined, citing John 8:7: 'Let any one of you who is without sin cast the first stone.'

Another of the Maltese's foes, Postmaster Nicodemussen, has, as archive studies reveal, gone to considerable lengths to have Adda Geraldi brought before the court on the charge of fornication—a step that the sheriff, Landfoged Kattentid, however, advised against, pleading that a potential hearing and the calling of witnesses could have extremely unwanted complications, unnecessarily bringing about harm to good men in prominent positions. It is likely similar considerations have been behind the council's dismissive attitude to a petition for the Maltese's speedy expulsion from the town, signed 'on behalf of many mothers,' by the midwife, Madam Olivia M. Davidsen, the bookkeeper's wife.

Not unexpectedly, the only punitive measure taken against Adda Geraldi also came at the hands of Bookkeeper Davidsen, who engineered the Maltese's dismissal from his job as handyman at the Preisler business, and from his position as caretaker of the approach beacons and quarantine flag. By thus depriving Adda Geraldi of his livelihood, the bookkeeper has likely hoped to make the recently arrived foreigner so fed up with life in his 'new native land,' that of his own accord, he would shake the dust off his feet.

Here, however, Davidsen has completely miscalculated. For a young and assiduous man such as the Maltese, who now only had himself to support, the matter of subsistence did not present much of a problem—by means of his fishing rod he could simply procure the dinner he needed, and mere steps from his door at that, and with his boat he could row out to one of the many fishing grounds in the Sound and like the other fishermen in town, he could return home to sell his catch on the quay.

And so, Adda Geraldi, with apparent peace of mind, took up the fishing trade, and there was no indication he had any intention to travel abroad, on the contrary, he tarred the Sergeant House and nailed a horseshoe above the door as a good omen. It was also generally expected that his wife would return and would do so once her anger and outrage had been given sufficient time to subside.

According to Hans-Pauli Alaih, whom the Maltese often visited during this time, usually with a hip flask in his pocket and in a rather inebriated state, this was also the outcome Adda Geraldi initially hoped for and imagined. But as time went by it became more and more clear that this hope was futile. In repentant and sentimental letters, which Hans-Pauli helped him compose and translate, Adda sought time and again to prevail upon his departed wife to return, but Sisal would not be moved. Only once did she contact him, and then to rather coolly and matter-of-factly inform him that she would never again have anything to do with him, and that he could abandon all hope.

The day the Maltese received this letter, he drunk himself to oblivion, and in the days and nights that followed he locked himself in his home and did not respond to either knocking or shouting. Hans-Pauli, who grew worried, gained entry to the Sergeant House through a back door he managed to prise open. He found Adda lying in bed, fully clothed, unshaven and red-eyed, in a strangely clouded and petrified state. After he had lain there for a while staring at his guest, as if only dimly recollecting him, the Maltese gave a deep sigh and proceeded to grope around the bed for a half-full bottle, which he found at long last and held to his lips. Gradually he came round, yawning and humming hoarsely while Hans-Pauli lit the fire and put the kettle on the stove.

After downing a few cups of strong coffee and picking at the dried fish his friend had brought him, the Maltese finally recovered to the extent that he regained the power of speech. He lay with his eyes shut, abandoning himself to a strangely long-winded and muddled, yet enraptured rambling. From this incoherent speech, however, Hans-Pauli, listening attentively, believed he had found distressing confirmation of what he had suspected from the very start: that Adda Geraldi was not at all the man he made himself out to be. He was apparently not from Malta, but from some or other Irish port town, and it seemed, the son of an Irishman and an Italian woman. Nor had he capsized with *The St Cuthbert's Duck*; a ship by that name certainly existed, but Adda had never seen it, only heard mention of it. The last ship he had sailed on, an American clipper, had a different name altogether, and it had not capsized, it had, as he put it, simply sailed without him 'in order to spare him the gallows.' What manner of offence he had committed on board was not clear from his ambiguous confession, it seemed to have something to do with fighting and killing.

The Maltese's speech grew more and more disjointed, but

before he was completely overcome by drink, he held his hand out to Hans-Pauli and spoke the dire and unforgettable words to the fish sorter: 'So now you know, Palle, I am not a living person but merely a drowned man, and for eternity I will be dead and gone!'

It was not clear to Hans-Pauli Alaih whether with this Adda wanted to express that as malefactor, he was better off considered dead, or whether he might be entertaining thoughts of suicide. Whatever the case, the dependable fish sorter resolved to keep him under close watch for the foreseeable future. But later that evening when Hans-Pauli returned to the Sergeant House, to his amazement he heard voices and women's laughter coming from the bedroom. The Maltese was in the company of a woman, possibly several, whomever they might be. Hans-Pauli decided not to disturb them, and shaking his head, he withdrew.

13

In the month of April 1894, what should happen but the Maltese obtaining steady work at the Preisler enterprise again, this time at the Cod Liver Oil Factory on Stangenæs. The old boiler, Oliver, who had been ailing for some time, needed a successor, and since the job of cod liver oil boiler is far from a coveted trade, it was difficult to find a replacement. With some reluctance, the fish sorter's proposal to employ Adda Geraldi, a man willing to undertake any kind of work, was accepted.

The Maltese, it seemed, had endured his crisis. But at the same time a noticeable change had come over him, externally as much as internally. He had let his beard and hair grow every which way, and of his former after-work-and-Sunday foppishness, nothing remained, he no longer appeared in a bowler hat or with a flower in his buttonhole, and the starched collar was replaced by a red-chequered scarf. Nor did he show himself at Feliksen's dance hall or other public places, he was, for the most part, rarely seen outside his place of work or home. He attended to his work with his usual care, he cleaned out the discharge pipes, plugged leaks, replaced cracked panes of glass, repaired shovels, scoops and other equipment painstakingly, cleared away old and worn-out drums and other rubbish, and scrubbed and washed liver sludge and other muck off the building.

It was also purported that, at his own expense, he carried out certain refurbishments, though the purpose of these was not immediately apparent, for instance, by the inside end wall of the Cod Liver Oil Factory, he is said to have constructed a bed-like bench, where he stored canvas and hessian—things that ought not be of any particular use at a cod liver oil factory, but that were intended for other and less functional purposes.

To illustrate this and related circumstances more closely, yet another quote from bookkeeper Davidsen's journal is presented:

'That summer of 1894 and late into the autumn, yes, right up until that fateful 21 December, when everything came to such a grievous end, the Maltese put his efforts into an enterprise whose unseemly and shameful character I am too ashamed to go into, but which concerns an ever increasing and eventually morbid inclination for women that bordered on obsession. One could hardly imagine that in this new state, both on the inside and out, the degenerate and sullied figure that he was, was any longer an adequate object of amorous attention; all the more one must marvel and take pity on the enthusiasm bestowed on him from various corners. Where it concerns lowly and simple-minded fishing shrews, or the numerous and regrettably fertile gadabouts with which our town was infested in those days, but whose numbers, thank the good Lord, are now considerably on the decline, one can just about account for such actions. However it is with both wonder and shame that it must be stated, for the sake of truth, that more often than not there has in fact been talk of women who would be seen to belong to more respectable circles.

Unfortunately the Maltese's enterprise was not without ignominious followers, and it is estimated that during the short span of time he spent in the Faroes, he was the cause of at least eleven pairs of eyes seeing the light of day for the first time. This man's power over the female sex seems to have risen in direct proportion to the increasing inflammation of his debauchery, and it is certainly no wonder there has been mention of a kind of devilish possession, nor would it seem to be utterly unfounded.

Alas, the unfortunate wretch received his punishment, and one can sigh to God that if not his soul, than his mortal frame has been lost.'

What the bookkeeper sidesteps for reasons of propriety, local lore spells out in disturbing detail, however, not all of it bears the mark of reliability. Claims that what most considered the exceedingly unsavoury atmosphere of the Cod Liver Oil Factory is said to have triggered erotic impulses among certain particularly predisposed females, can no doubt, as previously observed, hardly be rejected; but as to the number of female visitors the Maltese entertained at the factory and the frequency of their visits, a notorious propensity for exaggeration by the popular imagination is clearly to blame. The Maltese would simply not have been able to manage so great a number.

That the excesses mentioned here took place at the Cod Liver Oil Factory and not at the Maltese's home at Sergeant House has its own rather peculiar explanation: for this is where Angelica lived. This young girl, twenty-two at the time, whose jealousy has actually been the true cause of the whole wretched business with the Maltese, had moved into Sergeant House as a kind of housekeeper and kept the door shut to all unwelcome guests. Her passion for Adda Geraldi seems to have been of the sort that bears all burdens, even of the most multitudinous infidelities. In the humility of her abandonment she has contented herself with being both his maid and his bedfellow.

Following the Maltese's death, Angelica gave birth to twins, a son and a daughter.

14

The final chapter of the Maltese's saga is in truth not particularly merry.

As already mentioned, Adda Geraldi suddenly and unexpectedly disappeared from the scene where in the course of a mere two years, he had drawn such spectacular attention to himself that he is now among the local legendary figures, and he will not be forgotten for some time.

His demise and the shocking circumstances surrounding it are enveloped in a veil of secrecy that neither bookkeeper Davidsen nor any others have succeeded in lifting, but Davidsen notes in his journal with his usual meticulousness all that is known of these incidents.

'When the nightwatchman Hans Agranda,' it reads, 'whose duties also entailed watching over the stark raving Mathæa Magnussen, at eight o'clock in the morning on the fourth Sunday of Advent in 1894, passed the hut located below the ramparts of Skansin with his lantern, where the madwoman was confined, to his consternation he found the door wide open, and when he stepped inside, full of misgivings, he found the hut's unfortunate occupant lying dead on the floor. He immediately alerted Skansin's quartermaster Samuel Anthoniusen, who arrived at the scene with two of Skansin's trackers. A number of circumstances indicated there had been a scuffle with an intruder. The people of Skansin also noticed a line of footprints leading from the hut's entrance in the newly fallen snow, which in several places also bore traces of blood. The men followed these tracks in haste, down to the shore by the Cod Liver Oil Factory. Here they also found signs of a boat being dragged into the water, namely Adda Geraldi's dinghy, which had been stowed on the slope near the Cod Liver Oil Factory.

The quartermaster now assembled the entire staff of Skansin, and Skansin's two boats, *The Dronning Louise* and *The Politisten*, headed into the dark morning fully manned. By now the snow was falling so thick that not even the approach beacons were visible. Everyone was up that Sunday morning, standing out on Stangenæs and Thinganæs in expectant clusters. At daybreak the boats returned, one with the dinghy in tow, though it was empty, and of the Maltese there was no trace, apart from some blood in the water at the bottom of the keel.

Doctor Fredericia, who along with the sheriff, later examined Mathæa, ascertained that the girl had been strangled, evidently after a violent struggle. Her hands and fingernails were covered in blood.'

'In this pitiable manner,' Bookkeeper Davidsen concludes his account, 'the unfortunate Maltese ended his days. May God have mercy upon his sinful soul and temper His judgement on the Last Day.'

Row, My Boy, Row

by

Jens Pauli Heinesen

translated by Lindy Falk van Rooyen

The boy and his father sat and watched the houses on the shore shrink and disappear in the distance, one after another, as the motor of the boat worked steadily for them. A seal's head broke the surface, or perhaps it was a black cormorant riding a wave, and the father cursed aloud, wishing he had a rifle onboard. He turned to his son and pointed out the puffins as they dived off the cliffs, their wings beating the wind frantically—the guillemots like black ink strokes above the horizon—and the father aimed and fired his air rifle into the flock; he had never had enough money to buy a real one. Whenever a trawler came past, his eyes lit up. "Can you hear how hard that propellor is working? Nothing compared to the *Gloria Mundi*, though." His father had never got as far as a fisherman on a trawler, but he loved the simple life, and then he whistled a tune about the sea so wide, the islands everlasting green.

On days like these, it was good to be around his father. This was not always the case. For fifteen years he was a mechanic in the engine room of a large smack. But those days were over. If he stayed on land too long when the storms prevented him from going to sea in his eight-man boat, he started drinking, and when he did, it was best to stay clear of him—he became loud and bad-tempered, so bad others had to hold him back, else he'd start a fight.

A few nautical miles from shore his father killed the engine and cast out the nets as well as his fishing lines. Boats were drifting in the fjord, like sea birds sailing the waves; the water was dead calm and there was no more than a steady and long swell just under the surface. Other boats disappeared and reappeared, and the porpoises frolicked around them. But there weren't any fish, so they sailed back to shore a few miles, heading for a different fishing ground. They took their lunch tins and had a bite to eat along the way. Then they cast out their nets again, fished with the handlines for a while, and his father rolled himself another cigarette; as a rule, he had a cigarette clenched in the corner of his mouth, and the fingers on his right hand were stained yellow from nicotine—but when he was drunk he had so much to get off his chest that he forgot to smoke. His face and ears were blue from hunkering down in that old coffin ship, which, despite its eighty years of service, still chugged between Iceland and the Faroe Islands. The ship was called the *Gloria Mundi*, which means 'glory of the world'.

The father tipped the propellor and the motor lay idle as he let out the lines. As he watched his father work the boy suddenly noticed tiny tongues of fire unfurl at the base of the motor house; transparent, as if pale blue air. The boat shuddered, they heard a crack and then the motor burst into flames.

"Cut the fishing lines!" yelled the father, throwing an old

black coat over the motor house in the hope of smothering the flames, but puffs of smoke seeped through the holes, and the engine came to a coughing halt.

"Row, my boy, row!" yelled the father. "Get into the front compartment, my dear son, and row towards the other boats as hard as you can!" the father yelled as he did his best to dowse the fire in seawater, but the eight-man boat was just as old and saturated in oil as he was. Now the little tongues licked up around the motor house, and every crease, cranny and groove in the wooden boards leaked tendrils of smoke, which twisted into the air, as if a bonfire, and holes burnt through the coat, smoke and steam blackened the fibres.

"Row, my boy, row," said the father. "The other fishermen have seen us now, and they will come to our aid," he added calmly and quietly, his figure obscured by a bank of smoke, but every now and again his face reappeared, just for a moment. The father was coughing heavily, but he kept scooping water onto the fire; as if a seal ducking under a wave, the petrol drum dipped under the water and resurfaced almost immediately, but then the smoke swallowed it whole.

The father darted about in the flames at the bow—now fighting the blaze, now dowsing his son with seawater, and at last the petrol drum stopped its dunking over the side. The boy saw his father leap into the foremost compartment, and he was amazed that a man could walk through fire. Looking up, he was relieved to see the other boats come steaming towards them.

"Row, my boy, row," the quiet voice in the smoke cloud said.

With the sweat pouring from his brow and the heat scorching his face, the boy rowed the heavy eight-man boat as best he could. She was named 'Elsa' after his mother, but she was already battered and worn the day his father bought her. Squinting through the haze, the boy saw a sack being draped over the fuel tank, then everything was swamped by the sea.

"You are healthy and strong, my boy," said the quiet voice in the smoke cloud. "Just keep on rowing."

The bonfire had spread as far as the last bench but one; it was raging in the rearmost compartment, which was black as charcoal, and the boat whined in protest as the father battled the flames in the stern.

No one in the village understood this little man who, despite a house full of children to feed, would drink himself half to death. For years on end, he had toiled in the hull of the *Gloria Mundi*, a space so cramped a man could not turn without getting caught on some apparatus or another; the din down there was so loud you could not hear yourself speak, and the old man's skin was blue from the constant exposure to all that soot, oil, petrol, corroded rust and rotten bilge water, which no manner of scrubbing could remove from his face.

The first men to reach them were from a remote village, but Gullakur recognised them. They docked stern against stern, and the boy leapt onboard. When they asked about his father he pointed into the smoke cloud. The men started to scream and shout orders, some of them cursed out loud, yelling to the others to be damned careful not to get too close and risk setting their own boat on fire. Their rescue boat disappeared in the smoke, and not long after the men hauled something black onboard. Moments later, they backed away and set course for land at full speed. Gullakur sat behind the motor house, watching their eight-man boat go up in smoke. Two more fishing boats sailed up and circled round the wreck, then another came up in their wake. Not long after the smoke suddenly vanished altogether.

The men made a resting place for his father in the bottom of the boat and covered his body with an oil-skin coat. No one uttered a word. When Gullakur tried to come closer to see to his father, one of the men laid a hand on his shoulder and refused to let him pass. But once the boat was closer to shore, the same man came over to where he was sitting. The man was so out of breath that he barely got the words out: "Your father is alive. He asked where you were, and we told him that you're sitting right here, in the best of health."

Gullakur dropped his head to his chest. He noticed that his hands were covered in blood blisters, and he started to shiver with cold; he was soaking wet, drenched to the bone with seawater, and his hands hurt like hell. In the back of the boat, not a peep came out of his father. Gullakur smiled in relief because a man who doesn't utter a word of complaint after fighting fire and smoke was not a man in grave danger of dying.

A few months later his father was released from the hospital, and they got all dressed up for his return. Gullakur and his younger brothers knew how their father looked, because they had been to visit him once, but now they were curious to know how he would manage to eat his first meal at home.

Father had no fingers so mother spoon-fed him his dinner. He had no hair on his head, neither eyebrows nor eyelashes, and he sat at the table wearing sunglasses like a fine gentleman at a restaurant. When he was done with his dinner mother stuck a cigarette between his lips and lit it for him.

"The doctors are so clever these days," he said. "They're going to make me a pair of mechanical hands that are just as good as regular ones—with fingers and everything. I can't tell you how sick and tired I am of these bloody foreign cigarettes. It will be such a relief to be able to roll my own."

Heel!

by

Oddvør Johansen

translated by Marita Thomsen

He saw her shock at the merciless words, but they were out now, the words he had intended to say for so long, but kept trying to outrun.

It'll be rough, a friend had said, but Tórur wanted it to stop. He didn't want to carry on this duplicitous game of lies and flimsy excuses.

"I've fallen in love with another woman," he said in a sombre voice, "I want a divorce."

Ása stared at him, as if she hadn't understood the logic of what he was saying. Her lower lip wobbled as she stood there turning the wedding ring round and round and round. Then she burst into tears. Her voice was hoarse and unrecognisable.

"I don't want a divorce, I don't want a divorce, I don't want a divorce," she howled, "I want us to grow old together."

Her mascara dissolved and streamed down her cheeks, she let it drip, didn't even attempt to wipe off the black mess.

"You can't leave us, Tórur," she continued, "we belong together, you and I. What do you imagine the children and I will do, huh? What about us?"

"We have to talk to each other, Ása, like…"

"I'd rather you were dead," she burst out and started sobbing again.

There was a dark mad look in her eyes, and her face was swollen from crying.

Just to do something, he fetched the thermos and two mugs, poured them some coffee and asked her to sit down. He tore a piece of kitchen towel and handed it to her so she could blow her nose.

"We have to talk to each other, Ása, about everything."

"Divorce!" She sneered, "Like fuck you want a divorce! What'll you do without me?" She said coldly, "You're a ditherer, Tórur, an unrealistic manchild, when have you ever managed to even buy a shirt for yourself, eh? When have you ever put on the washing machine? No, right? I've waited on you hand and foot, cut your hair and washed the car, because you 'forgot', what a bloody fool I've been, eh?"

"You can have the car and the house," he blurted out, "it's your car anyway, you were the one who wanted that make and model in pink."

Why was he suddenly going on about the car, why was he such an idiot?

"Shut up about the car, it's mine."

"Ása, we have to talk to each other like civilised human beings."

"I don't want to be civilised. You're crushing me, don't you get that? You're having a midlife crisis, Tórur, so you decide to demolish my life in cold blood, *my* life, me who has worked myself to the bone, born you two wonderful children, knitted for you all and woven every single curtain in this damn place. Who else would have proofread your pathetic manuscripts? Have you no shame? Lecturing me about being civilised, when you're the one out on the streets chasing after anything in skirts like a dog in heat."

"Stop it, Ása!" He raised his open palms towards her.

"No, I won't stop. I just want you to stay here with me. I'll love you Tórur, we can start afresh."

She burst into tears again and shrieked like a toddler. He held her and rocked her back and forth, saying nothing, just rocking, rocking as she clung to him. It was like holding a sweet sister, he noted. Nothing more.

"If you leave me," she said, "you'll lose your kids too, make no mistake."

He didn't say anything. This wasn't the time to start discussing the children.

After, he was sitting in Beinta's little flat. It was so cosy and tranquil here. The little one was asleep in the bedroom, three candles flickered on the table.

"This peace and quiet does me such good, Beinta," he said, "you're so calm, and I need winding down, my nerves are shot and the whole situation is so upsetting."

She stroked his back. Listening.

"But," he said, "I don't want to lose touch with the kids, I intend to fight for my rights, no matter what."

"Tórur, you know I'll support you in everything, but you know you're in for a fight."

"I want to live my life with you, Beinta, isn't that what you want too?"

"Maybe we should take a break again first," she said, "maybe it isn't smart to rush into things."

"Yes, but we've had a break. Two whole months is a long time without contact. It felt like an eternity. We've tried to forget all about us, but I think about you all the time, and I miss you with every bone in my body. If all I get is ten years with you, Beinta, ten years, then I'll be satisfied."

"Give yourself time," she said, "you're so weighed down by this whole mess. The two of us we have time on our side, darling."

"We'll never come visit you." Sjúrður looked accusingly at his father, "if you leave us, then we'll hate you for real."

"Daddy hopes you won't, Sjúrður, daddy hopes that you and Andrea will visit me a lot. We will be together like always, and have a good time and play chess and play Wii and make dinner together."

"We're never coming. We hate that lady. Mum says she's mean. You have to come back to us."

The boy's words stung. They really made him feel like a big fat traitor. He felt the guilt dig in and could barely bring himself to look into his son's eyes. But he was determined to keep loving his children, he intended to be part of their lives and to be there when they needed him.

"You have to come back home to be with us," the boy repeated.

"You and mum can fall in love again."

Tórur felt helpless. How could you explain to a child that you had to leave them? How could you do it without second thoughts and nagging guilt?

Andrea started crying. Sweet little Andrea with the blonde silken hair.

"Come back home to us, daddy," she sobbed.

Tórur hugged her and rocked her on his lap.

"Daddy loves you so much, Andrea, you're daddy's girl, and daddy will never stop loving you."

"Will too, if you leave us, you don't really love us," she cried.

It was hopeless to explain anything at all to the kids. They shouldn't be involved anyway or be forced to take sides. Children will always think that everything has to stay the same and nothing gets to change, period.

Beinta was in the eye of a digital hurricane. The target of a barrage of scorn and humiliation night and day.

"Get your claws out of him," one text message read, "he's my husband, not yours."

"You're a nobody!"

"You think you and that little bastard of yours can replace us? You can't."

"Tórur was always a cheater, you don't know him at all. He's been sleeping around for years. I bet he hasn't told you any of that."

"I want him back. I love him the way he is."

Beinta was exhausted. She switched off and went to bed. Tórur was at a board meeting and that usually took a while. At two in the morning the phone rang. It was Ása.

"Tórur has spent the night here with me, and we made love in our old double bed." The phone cut out.

Beinta couldn't go back to sleep. Doubt set in. Was Tórur the man she thought he was? Was he leading a double life? Maybe there was no board meeting? Could she trust him?

Maybe she didn't actually know him? If she didn't there was no point in being with him, there was nothing to build a relationship on.

She tossed and turned in bed. Christ, she had to get up at 6:30 in the morning. Tomorrow would be a rotten day.

Ása was a real nightmare. Tonight it was the phone, yesterday an e-mail laying out how everyone knew that Tórur had started fooling around with a girl from work. And it went on to tell her how he spent his evenings drinking down at the Café Hvonn.

Why did Ása want him back so desperately if he was supposedly cheating on her all these years?

Was Tórur lying to her? The questions piled up and kept her wide awake.

She had never felt as safe or happy as she did in his arms. She would have to ask him. Ask him what was true and what wasn't.

The little one whimpered softly in his cot and gnashed his teeth, the way he always did. She loved how his little eyes lit up when Tórur came to visit. He probably missed having a dad with a deep voice and big hands.

Beinta drifted in and out of sleep. Her thoughts travelled back a couple of years. It would have been impossible if her mum hadn't stepped in when everything fell apart, and the boyfriend suddenly stuck his tail between his legs and asked for 'a break'. Only once did he come to see the boy, and then he asked to be excused. Said it made him feel so guilty.

Was she to go back to the same lonely humdrum routine here in the flat? Take the bus in the morning—over to the nursery—work until 16:30—back home to the flat. Stuck with the child every evening, only going out for fun once in a blue moon.

Tórur had revived her from a long princess slumber showering her in kisses and embraces. She had believed herself stone cold, sexually dead, but Tórur considered her beautiful and wise. Said she was a good mother with grit and the warmest hands in the world, he didn't want her to change a thing about herself for anyone. They would have a good life together.

Now she was lying here aching to believe him. That thought gradually soothed her mind and she nearly dozed off in the end.

At long last Tórur manages to spend some time with the kids. He attempts to explain gently to them that adults can grow apart and stop loving each other.

"Can they then also go cold and stop loving their kids?" Sjúrður asks.

Tórur was in no way prepared for all these questions. He replies a little startled that he doesn't think so. He will always love them, he says, always. He will always be there when they need him and plans to live just a stone's throw from where they live, because that's what he wants.

They kiss him goodbye when they leave.

His mother calls him.

"Good God, Tórur, what's all this Ása is telling me?"

"What? What is Ása telling you?"

"That you've been cheating on her for a whole year with some tart without breathing a word about it."

"Mum! You have to listen to me, ok? Sit down, all right,

and listen to me! I've met another woman, not a whore, mum, but a completely normal nice woman, who has a little boy, and I intend to leave Ása and get a divorce. That's the short and the long of it."

"Christ you're being selfish, Tórur, but you were always selfish and easily tempted, Ása says so too. And what about her? Don't you think about her at all? She is my daughter-in-law, and she has been for fifteen years."

"But mum, you don't have to stop being fond of Ása, not at all, and you will always be Sjúrður and Andrea's grandmother."

"But she says that you're scheming against her," she protests.

"What do you mean scheming?"

"Well, scheming to trick her out of her house and home and her car. You can't do that to her, Tórur, stop and think for a minute, boy!"

"Mum, please don't be so naïve, she's filling your head with stories. Of course I've absolutely no intention of tricking her, surely you know your son better than that!"

"She also tells me how that crazy tramp of yours won't leave her alone."

"What do you mean?"

"Well, she must be some piece of work, because she is bombarding her with e-mails and text messages and calling her night and day."

"I don't believe that for a second mum, I think that's a downright lie. You mustn't go believing everything Ása says, she's pretty out of it right now."

"Ása has been a good wife to you, remember that. She

bore you two lovely children and helped you with the accounts and everything. You're not doing right by her, and it's not long 'til Sjúrður's confirmation now..."

He had to get himself a lawyer, right now, this couldn't go on. They had to sort it out.

"Oh," said the lawyer, "it's all quite trite, banal really."

He was wearing a white top paired with yellow trousers, and was suitably stubbly. His ergonomic sandals were worn, and the place was untidy and dusty.

"Same tired old story," he continued, "a man or woman falls in love with someone other than the person they're married to and wants a divorce. And that's all folks. The end."

Tórur could hear the banality of the words once they were compressed into two sentences. Still, for him this wasn't banal at all, this was lived life, life or death. It was about pulling yourself together and starting over, before it was too late, it felt like a global sensation. His very own worldwide sensation that forced him to take stock of reality and assess his lived life, his very existence.

"Have you had a think about the estate? All the financial stuff?" the lawyer asked.

"Yes, I intend for my wife to get the house and the car, no share for me, we would split the cash and I want regular contact with the children."

The lawyer scratched his head and started drumming his fingers on the table.

"But think about it Tórur. That's slaughter. It's the usual whale slaughter, which all these men... Jesus, where is all the much-hyped equality? Many of these men end up languishing on some bench downtown. Do you realise how long it takes to get back on your feet… it takes years… and money… and a lot of grey hair.

"My income is better than hers," Tórur countered, "so I think it's reasonable."

The lawyer pondered this for a moment.

"I mean," Tórur continued, "I have more left to live on each month."

"Well, you certainly won't have more to live on, if you just give it away willy-nilly," the lawyer retorted. "I always say that at the heart of these cases is someone's guilty conscience."

"Well, I want a divorce without feeling too ashamed about it, and I'm thinking first and foremost about my kids, call it conscience if you will."

"If you say so, Tórur. Right, I'll cobble something together, then you can take a look at it."

Tórur is standing outside Hoyvík Church waiting for the congregation to come out. It was a nicer morning than expected, sunny with a light breeze. The ferry Ternan ploughs across the fjord with passengers bound for Nólsoy, and the church bells chime.

Down by the Tútakannutjørn pond kids in their Sunday best fling pebbles into the water, and somewhere beyond the church, in the carved up mountain fields where new houses gape half-finished, oystercatchers are calling.

He had been sitting on one of the last pews, because Ása didn't want him sitting with the family. And he shouldn't dare show up at the reception either, she had added.

Then they emerged. His mother had been allowed to join in along with his sister, who was on Ása's side, and Ása's entire family was there siblings, godfathers and godmothers.

Tórur approached Sjúrður and gave him a kiss. Then he handed the teenager an envelope from his jacket pocket.

"Congratulations my boy."

Sjúrður smiled, "Thanks a million, dad."

"Time to go Sjúrður," Ása was quick to interrupt.

Tórur turned to face the family, but he couldn't make eye contact with any of them.

So fucking cold. So painful. He had wined and dined this lot at regular intervals, hadn't he? He swallowed. Were human beings this small at the end of the day? Were they that easily manipulated? Was this really all it took for old friends to disown you?

Here he stood like an idiot with a fresh haircut in his best suit cradling this tiny hope that he would, after all, on this day be allowed to take part, and then it was just a vain pipe dream.

Ása wanted revenge. Even when she knew for certain that he was on his knees, he shouldn't be allowed any hope of anything at all. He was to be frozen out and could forget about having normal contact with the kids.

Had he never known the true Ása? Was it really possible that she—in such a short time—had become an entirely different person from the woman he was married to for fifteen years, or was this her true nature?

He got in the car but didn't bother to start the engine while the churchgoers gradually dispersed, some strolling down the road, most by car.

He felt tired. His heart was heavy. So tired, felt like he was about to doze off.

He was standing by the red gate, waiting for her. But,

weren't they divorced? Yes. No. He wasn't sure. She was so young and energetic, she always had been. Come with me! Why don't we hike up to the mountain fields of Bøllureyn, he said, and then we'll lie down in the heather and make love. Wait, something is wrong here. You're hopeless, she said, a hopeless make-believe-man. Anyway, you are the way you are, she carried on, not to worry though, I'll soon set you straight. Set straight. Set straight. The echo reverberated like in a church. You've become someone else, haven't you? This straightness is the end of you. Of feelings. Of love. And before you know it, she has you straightened out and turned into someone else. You talk in her village dialect, she directs and modulates, she makes schedules, and you, you're her nice, trimmed poodle. 'Jump,' she says, and you jump. But you don't want to. You escape to the boat moored in Álaker or to the mountains, because it heals you and makes you whole again. Why is her hair grey? Where are the kids? There. Sjúrður is only six, and oh, he loves that boy more than anything in the world. He's terrified of losing him, scared that he'll have an accident. Nothing must happen. Oh God, he's sweating anxiously, but Sjúrður sends him one of his dazzling smiles.

He woke up. The car park was empty and the church doors locked. He was drenched in sweat.

The papers were on the table. Ása had one of the best lawyers in the country, who without so much as a sideways glance, worked for his client and nobody else, as is right and proper. Next time Tórur needed legal advice he would ask this guy.

He read the document: Ása would stay in the house.

The car loan was strung around his neck. The furniture?

Who cared. He got the old family chatol, Wiinblad lamp and a divan bed. He could forget about the books, except for the lexicon he purchased at eighteen from the Red Cross shop. He mustn't forget the little silver spoon, the christening gift from his godfather Alfred, it had followed him his entire life.

The children would not want for anything materially, and his half of the house would be transferred straight to their ownership, forthwith. The bloke in the yellow trousers couldn't do any more for him and shrugged.

For the entire hour leading up to this Ása had worn him out on the phone. She wanted double-child alimony. Okay! Tórur didn't want to hang up now so close to the finish line, but listened one more time to all the accusations. It was extortion, pure and simple. If he paid for this or that, then he could see the kids a little more, maybe.

He suddenly sensed a plan: Ása wanted to make things so hard for him, that the new relationship wouldn't stand a chance.

His blood pressure. He had forgotten his morning meds and hurried to swallow the pill. Moments away from signing the damn papers that would release him from marriage, all he felt was drained.

There was no return. His life with Ása was over, and this was no happy divorce. In a way it felt sad, empty after all these years. They had experienced so much together. A long period in life had ended, an era, which, no matter what, would always be a significant part of who he was.

In the last year, he had tried to imagine if it would be possible to go back home and take up where he left off, but in the same breath every fibre of his being bristled. It would have been a big fat lie, and it would also have been a betrayal of Beinta. She was his angel of salvation, she brought out the best in him, because she let him be who he always had been: the happy boy who loved to tinker with an old wreck of a boat in Álaker, who loved to hike in the mountains with his friends, and who loved to experiment in the kitchen.

Oh Beinta, darling, we will make it through my love. It was a wonder to love again. She didn't want to change him, she just made him young and happy and gave him an appetite for life. He was okay.

Tórur looked out the window and noticed that the landscape had turned white. The mountains sparkled, it was exquisite. Like a Christmas card. But wasn't it summer, midsummer, he was about to start a new life with his angel… his ears rang. Was he passing out? Probably best to crouch.

In the act he glimpsed a spray of rain on the car window. It was crimson. He clawed for his mobile and managed to press 'Beinta'.

Then he lost consciousness.

The Cocks are Crowing

by

Hanus Kamban

translated by Lindy Falk van Rooyen

I walked into town slowly. The streets were deserted. Not a soul was about. I felt as if I were a stranger, a lonely traveller returning from an arduous journey to another village—in New Zealand, Brittany or some Spanish isle—the tiled roofs, gables and dormer windows made a deep impression on my mind, as if I had never seen them before. The old Post Office, the hair salon, the fish shop and stores on the main street were swept up into my fancy, hovering somewhere between reality and dream. On the outskirts, our house seemed magnificent, despite the crushed shells in the herb garden in front, the white-washed flagstone and carved windowsills, as if they were a mirage or vision of a star on the fringe of the Milky Way, which would disappear as soon as daylight broke.

The girl had told me to come over, if I liked. Even so, I was afraid. It is not a big deal. But I had never done it before. For me, it was merely an act. Like diving into the sea or standing on a podium before a crowd. Everybody had a girl. It went with the territory. Like wearing a shirt-and-tie on Sundays, or owning a shaver, a wrist-watch, a cigarette lighter.

The weather was dry. It had been for days and weeks,

and there wasn't a breath of wind. A scent of mould and dust lingered in the air. Paper, peels, flasks and rubbish bags whirled through the streets. Every dip and hollow parched to the bone. Warped by the arid heat, buckthorn peeped through the cracks in the doorframes. Beyond town, the sun glowed like a midnight lamp, and I knew that in less than five hours the street cleaners would arrive, laden with shovels, scoops and wheelbarrows.

Flat, tarred roofs and tufts of peat meant that I had reached the old town. As if a stray dog, I skulked through the narrow streets, stole up a flight of crooked stairs and took a short-cut through a building I had never set foot in before. It was almost impossible to walk upright in the corridor. Who lived in this building, anyway? Fairy-tale dwarves? Hunch-backed geriatrics? A tribe of extraordinarily short-legged beings? Someone obviously lived here, because the window frames were white-washed, herb pots stood on the windowsills and the front steps bore the tell-tale traces of a broom.

I had come to a more modern part of town. Here, the houses were three storeys high, iron railings barred the balconies, windows and rooftops. I descended a steep hill. The houses were still old, if not ancient; here, I had been hundreds of times before. Each house had a private, well-kept herb garden and meticulously pruned trees. They revealed themselves, naked in the white night, but I had never noticed the herb gardens before; how could that be? It was here that the children played during the day, women shook out carpets and grannies sat on benches in the shade.

I came into another narrow lane. Now I knew I was close. Here I saw the first signs of people, and Rasmus was at his post in the window; peering down the street, still as a statue. I had heard from friends that he preferred boys to girls. That he spied on them from his window. I had no idea if this was true. He had never said anything of the kind to me. I quickened my pace, and as I came past him, I realised that he was staring up at the third storey of the building opposite. His eyes burnt into my back. I cast a glance over my shoulder, but Rasmus looked down from the window. I couldn't see his eyes; nonetheless, an image of them were cast on my inner mind: evil, hard, envious perhaps.

Making my way through the old town, a strange calm had come over me. I had tried to draw the sensation out, stretch this paltry half-hour of peace into an eternity. Rasmus disappeared from the window, so this was it; the moment I was waiting for. The house rose before me—brown paint, elongated, three storeys high with two dormer rooms. The second window was hers. Would someone spot me when I went inside? Would someone wake up when I stole up the stairs? Would she even open the door? And what would I say if she did?

I slipped inside the entrance and crept up the stairs. First floor. Second floor. I was standing outside her door. I knocked. Once. Twice. After the third knock, I heard a scrape behind the door. At last, it opened. "Oh, it's you?" the girl said, blinking against the light. She was wearing her pyjamas. I followed her inside and closed the door behind me as she put on a lamp on her desk.

Her room was small. She slept on a convertible sofa bed, I noticed. Her furniture was sparse: apart from the desk, she had a bedside table and a sideboard. On the desk stood a radio, a record player, a few books on accounting and business. On the partition wall hung a picture of a dark-haired girl—a Roma-girl, perhaps—and on the sideboard there was a colourful crow carved out of wood.

What do people talk about the first time they are alone together? She told me about her parents and siblings, what they did for a living. I responded in kind. She talked about her classmates. I told her that I was in my final year of school, that I hoped to take my exams in the summer.

Her face was pale, her hair black, her eyebrows dark, her nose large, almost Gallic, even so, I doubted that I would have recognised her if I passed her on the street. The lampshade cast a red glow over everything in the room. I was grateful to her for that; I felt somehow protected by the glow, as if she had given me a mask.

She only owned one record. I didn't have a record player myself. But I knew the song. It was a single-LP—everyone, who was young back then, knew it: '*With your sweet lips a little closer to the phone...*'

We listened to it.

"What does the English word 'pretend' mean?" she said after a while, breaking the silence. She was looking up at me as if I were some kind of seasoned professor.

"'Pretend'? It means to play, to make as if, to be something you're not," I translated.

The song ended. I could have sworn I heard a sound in the stillness that followed. A cock crowing? On a fence—far away in the outfield?

We sat for a while, each of us lost in our own thoughts. She broke the silence again: "What would you like to study at university?"

I wondered what I should say. Medicine? Engineering? Philosophy? Literature?

"I want to study to become an engineer," I said with conviction in my voice. "I want to make a difference." I explained. Told her that I wanted to transform desert sands into fertile, cultivated fields, but I get my tongue in a knot; I saw myself standing on the bank of a river in Egypt, in a white lab coat, taking charge, with a sun hat shading my sunburnt face. Hungry children looked up at me with hope in their eyes. Crowds of people thanked me for the food they now had in their bellies.

Once we had covered the future and I had done my bit for the Aswan and many other far flung places besides—testimony of my sheer guts and creative imagination—we agreed to lie down because I had school the next day, and she had to be up in time for college.

Two hours later, I started awake. The girl was still fast asleep. I considered leaving a note before I left. But I had no idea what to write; I was afraid that whatever I wrote, it would sound ridiculous or inappropriate, so I just scurried out and closed the door behind me.

I went back down the stairs the way I came; the edges were rounded off, as if trodden down over half a century. The steps creaked under my feet. I pondered over the people living in the house. The girl had mentioned some of them, but I got the impression that she didn't know any of them very well: on the ground floor, an elderly couple that owned the complex; the first and second floor was let out. The girl's room was sandwiched between two unmarried, middle-aged men. Who were these people, really? I knew that each of them would have their own story to tell. Their own dreams and worries in this world. The residential complex was dead quiet, but I fancied that I could hear the boarders turning in their sleep, muttering in confusion, snoring. It occurred to me that the town was full of people renting—seamen, labourers, students—but most of all, lonely young girls sleeping in attic rooms. Were they happy? *Un*happy? Waiting for the haze to clear, in limbo somewhere between indecision or despair? My thoughts were interrupted by a cock crowing. The sound burst through an open window in the hallway. Obviously, it was coming from the property next door.

I made for the main door leading outside. But as I put my hand on the door handle, I was struck by a thought. What if the people living in this building were to meet? Every morning, they went their respective ways; every evening, they came back and disappeared into their respective rooms. But what if they didn't? What if, instead, they said: *let's go to the bakery and buy ourselves a big cake and get together for a chat? What if we make the best out of our time spent under the same roof?* But I pushed the fancy aside as quickly as it came. Some ideas are feasible; you can say them out loud, people will support them, get used to them. But other ideas are simply impossible, ridiculous or foolish, they get relegated to the past, or delayed to the future, banished to another time and place which has no room for them either.

The walk home went quicker. Rasmus was still at his window. This time we made eye contact; his expression was neither wary nor leering. Just dark. And sad. Perhaps there was nothing forbidden about his dreams. Perhaps he was just one of those people who was awake by night, asleep by day. I took the same route home. As I came through the final alley of the old town, I saw the sun rise over the sea, as if a glittering hot lid of a pot. I heard another cock crowing, but this time, it sounded like a war cry. Right next to me.

I opened the gate, walked down the garden path, up the steps and opened the front door. Everything was quiet inside. Sometimes, my mother waited up for me, leaving the door ajar. When I arrived, she would peer at me with tired, sleepy eyes; it was my worst nightmare. But on that morning, the house was still. It was so quiet that I thought I could hear the silence; my parents' breathing and snoring, my siblings spying through the keyholes. I opened the door of my room in the attic that I shared with my brothers. It smelt of oil and tar; they were both apprenticed ship mechanics. Dawn was breaking and the wind picked up. I don't know why, but I felt sorry for myself. Not just for me, but for my parents, and all those lonely girls in town, who were just sitting around in their bedrooms, sleeping on a sofa that converted into a bed at night with a cock carved out of wood on the sideboard, waiting.

Heartbreak

by

Gunnar Hoydal

translated by Marita Thomsen

At thirteen I decided to write a novel about heartbreak. It was to be so spellbinding and magnificent that I felt compelled to write in a foreign language, to make sure it would get far enough in the world. To my knowledge, there was also so little heartache in the Faroes that it wouldn't suffice for a novel as great as this one.

The heartbreak wasn't actually mine, it belonged to my brother. What I had experienced paled in comparison; it was when we were leaving the Faroes, and I watched Rannvá gradually shrink to a blur in the quayside crowd. A tiny bright speck of a face, which it was hard enough not to lose in the throng, and I was moved for a moment, because nobody could say when we would be back, if ever, or if we would even survive! And by then Jógvan would for sure have snatched her.

No, I reasoned later, my own lover's chagrin was so small that it would only stretch to a Faroese short story. But Egil's! Lord knows if Danish would be enough. Perhaps German or English would be better suited, I had picked up enough at school to walk home from town singing to myself in these world languages. And then there was Spanish, an option now that we had moved to South America.

To Ecuador, a little country out west facing the Pacific where the sun rises perpendicular to the ocean. In a photo taken north of the capital Quito, Egil stands astride, aged fifteen, shadowless, in front of a monument erected on the Line itself. Left leg in the northern hemisphere, right leg in the southern. It appears to be a big moment, because his eyes hold a rather serious gaze, and his chin is raised a little higher than normal, he is broad-shouldered. A little mob of ogling kids encircles him; they don't see many adults wearing shorts up here in the Andes. Diddan, the youngest of us, is in the photo with him, pale as chalk compared to the other kids; Kjartan and I didn't get into the shot, I had declared those shorts a huge embarrassment, and Kjartan would always do what I wanted. But this was around the time of that new turn. I had noticed that he was starting to outgrow me, and it pained me, because I had always had those fifteen minutes on him, the age gap that entitled me to tell him what's what.

Another photo featuring Egil, perfectly posed. Now he is in swimming trunks, because we have descended from the highlands to the coastal town of Manta, to live. He is holding his right arm across his torso, clasping the wrist with his left hand, and is flexing his arm and chest muscles; it's clear that he is in good shape. Not better than Espinales though, who is standing in the background. The grooves between his muscles run down his chest and across from the hips. Egil is visibly straining with a chest full of air, while Espinales flashes a broad smile, hands on hips, and just *is* like this. A little to one side I am doing a handstand. I told Kjartan that he shouldn't bother to be in the photo, because all he can do is roly-polies, so he was the one who took the snap.

Espinales must have been twenty, maybe twenty-one, and though he sometimes looked a little tough, he was easy-going and quick to lend a hand. But some blood disorder kept him from going fishing with the others. Every day, except Sunday, he would help out on the square where the big market was, and where most shopping in town took place. There was the odd regular shop with a counter and shelves like in Tórshavn, mostly run by some German or Italian who had arrived after the war, from what we could gather, to get out of trouble. We shopped there, because pápi had recently lost his appendix and it hadn't made him any less squeamish about food than he already was. The stuff in tins, well, one knew what it was, he insisted; whereas the wares they hawked at the market, produced straight out of nature, well, there was no way of knowing how they had been handled. He had recurring visions of himself laid out, poisoned, with his widow and orphans standing over him, forsaken and forgotten in a foreign continent. That explained why he would pull us aside from time to time to tell us what we were to do when this happened, how we were to get ourselves home again, and how we were to deal with his remains.

We lived in the poor end of town. Somehow a four-floor concrete building had wound up among the rickety huts. Fronted by a colonnade, which is sort of like a pavement with a ceiling and columns facing the road. This was the most populated part of the house, and when we wanted to get inside at noon or at night we often had to step over people who had decided to rest there. Other than them, the massive building only housed one German, who locked his door whenever he heard us on the staircase. And then his wife, who had growths protruding from her hair like little horns, a bit like the budding studs on a wether lamb. With empty windows the house overlooked the shacks, perhaps it gained a new little eye when pápi screwed in the UN sign, which he had been given when we came, but seemed otherwise quite uninterested in seeing any of the goings on around it.

At the top was a flat roof with a water tank replenished by half-grown boys every morning. They struggled to transfer sloshing barrels from mules to their own backs and then up all the flights to pour into the cistern that fed our tap down below. This water teemed with life, its surface topped by a permanent crust of mosquitos vying for a gap to lay their eggs. Other than that a low wall encircled the roof, which was our lookout over the dusty town, down to the beach and out across the bay: there was always a grey mist shrouding the landscape. We could also see the white canvas of the open-air cinema from here, and you could rely on dusk to arrive at the same time every single evening, falling like a lid over the houses, until a projector cut a hole in the darkness and sent galloping sheriffs and lovers from Hollywood into the night.

We were never told outright, that we weren't to go to the square on our own, and we knew that Egil was there all the time with Espinales. For about two months mamma and pápi believed that he went swimming every afternoon. My curiosity ballooned, and one day I decided to go after him and find out what he was up to. Kjartan said that he was coming too, I wondered if it was really okay, but he gave me a look, and it became clear that we were the same height. Besides, I would keep a firm eye on him.

We set out to find Egil, just to see him, even if he didn't see us. We knew that Espinales' mum and sisters had a fish stall where they sold what his brothers and father caught. We often watched them landing their catch, small fish netted in the bay and larger fish, mostly tuna, caught in the open sea from little wooden sailboats that floated out on the morning breeze and returned around noon, when the wind direction changed landwards.

We looked everywhere, but it was a pandemonium of yelling, clatter and scents. Fruit, vegetables, fish, all manner of sausages, bread, boiled tripe, flies and a web of bugs surrounding anything edible, while ground beetles and skin beetles and the odd scorpion stalked below. Shouting little boys dashed between stalls hawking brushes, lottery tickets or homemade ice-lollies out of wooden crates with lids, frosty little multi-hued cubes wrapped in sodden newspaper. Their cries fused with music from a cacophony of radios by the sound of it, each stall had not only its own smell and colour, but even its own tune.

Shaggy grey pigs squealed and zigzagged between everyone's legs, pestering the beggars. Kjartan slipped something into the tin of a little girl with withered legs, even though I told him that all the others wouldn't leave us alone if he did. As soon as I said it, something pecked viciously at my foot. I jumped up thinking that maybe somebody had overheard. But a hen was all it was, it had spotted my blasted wart, and I kicked it under a table generating a spray of tail feathers that lingered in the air. This wasn't much liked, in an instant I was surrounded by people shouting at me, fortunately Kjartan had his wits about him and managed to get across that we were buying that particular hen for dinner, that's why. An angry lady rummaged under the table, cut the hen's head off and hurled the flapping carcass at us, and there was no haggling, the price was what we had in our pockets.

"Let's go!" I snapped and decided to bury the hen in the sand somewhere, there was no way I was lugging it home, I would have to explain everything. But he wouldn't come, promising to wait until I was back. When I had got away from the market din, I threw the carcass to a couple of vultures eyeing a rat. Barely had I turned, before other birds of the same ugly sort swooped from the sky. So that was one good deed done.

Kjartan had vanished when I returned, or maybe I had taken a wrong turn. But I ran straight into Espinales' stall, he and his father were carrying crates into the back tent. I asked after Egil. No, he wasn't there. But didn't he usually come here? Espinales grimaced at me to shut up, I didn't quite get it. The father glared at me, when I asked again. Espinales was standing behind him, and it dawned on me that he wanted me to clear out of there.

So I wandered around the entire square, but found neither of my brothers. I grabbed a mango and bit into it, until I remembered that I hadn't a *centavo* in my pocket. I put it back, but an older boy had seen and grabbed hold of me. People crowded around, I had to break loose, ran and managed to escape unscathed except for something sticky flung at my ear; there was no time to check if it was the fruit I had bitten into too soon.

In a rotten mood I made my way home, where the family thought little of my exploits. Diddan asked if I'd started chasing girls at the square too now. I didn't understand why Kjartan gave her such a shove, or why Egil went rigid. Mamma searched one face after the other, while pápi, who as so often was sitting in his own thoughts, neither heard nor saw.

Afterwards, when the three of us were on our own, I let loose, especially on Diddan, demanding to know what it was they were up to.

"Are you blind?" asked Kjartan, "can't you see anything?"

"See what?" I scowled more than usual, thinking of those fifteen minutes of mine and how dare he talk to me like that.

"Don't you see that Egil's got a girlfriend?" Diddan exclaimed, "Egil and Gracia!" she added in a teasing singsong.

I burst out laughing. What did they know, pair of babies, about stuff like that? I, who was experienced, I who had strolled through the park in Tórshavn, listening to babbling ducks and the sighing wind in the trees hand in hand with Rannvá in the dark, *I* knew, what this meant, but they, what did they know about life?

"He's afraid too, he's scared," Kjartan said.

"He's too scared to tell mamma and pápi!" Diddan added, it sounded almost like the little scamp was trying to teach me something.

"He's started sneaking out at night," Kjartan said. I had to laugh again. I slept next to him every night, Kjartan on this side, Egil on that, he wouldn't get anywhere without me knowing.

"Poor Egil!" Diddan sighed, "he cries!"

Cries? I had noticed that his eyes had been reddish lately and small. And the other night he had woken me up, though I was usually a heavy sleeper.

"He coughs," I protested, "he's got a cold!" And suddenly I noticed that I wasn't feeling too well myself.

It gave me lots to think about. This much was clear, something was going on, and, as the oldest after Egil, I had a responsibility to shoulder now that he seemed lost in some parallel universe. I observed him on our morning trudge to school; he fixed his eyes on the sand trail, a slog of a walk, only glancing up at passers-by, a person, a donkey. And in the classroom, which was no more than a bamboo shed, I could see that he barely scribbled down our Spanish dictation:

El aire está formado principalmente de oxígeno y de nitrógeno en la porción de veintiún partes de oxígeno y sesentainueve partes de nitrógeno. Air is mainly made up of oxygen and nitrogen, twenty-one parts oxygen and sixty-nine parts nitrogen.

He couldn't sing the anthem right either: "*Salve oh Patria, mil veces! Oh Patria!*" Light filtered between the bamboo slats and the teacher, who was tutoring us separately because we had made so little progress, blew his nose, fanned away the flies, and was not pleased.

This went on for a while. I thought about Rannvá and concluded that it was serious. Mamma and pápi had reached roughly the same conclusion, and they took him aside for talks, but he refused to say a word. I overheard mamma in the sitting room saying something has got to be done, and then pápi saying twaddle! He knew what it was like at that age, and he had been exactly the same with a girl from Hvítanes, when he was fifteen, it was part and parcel of growing up, trivial really, like a cold. My unspoken inclination was to agree, except for that last bit about it being trivial. I pondered what

Jógvan might be up to, given that fortune had favoured him and I had been sent to foreign lands, one day, though, I would be back!

We were nearing Lent, and the town was getting ready for the big carnival. New stalls sprung up at the market with magicians, cripples and soothsayers, and in front of a freshly erected tent flanked by five smaller tents men were queuing up at a table where a bejewelled, though somewhat faded, lady knitted and took their money. The tents were emblazoned with intricate hand-painted signs announcing girl's names; I knew full well what this meant, but was a little embarrassed that Kjartan might too.

I observed Gracia, Espinales' sister, who was selling fish nearby, filleting and weighing by hand before fixing a price. Like a girl suddenly and unexpectedly grown. The sun silhouetted her, lighting up tiny golden hairs along her arms all the way up to a flash of softer and dimmer growth. She had a dark complexion and black eyes like her sisters, but her skin was more golden, it had a glow, I could see that she irradiated light. From time to time she glanced my way, as if I held some importance above and beyond the rest, though she was unsure if she should smile at me, attempted it, but her eyebrows didn't quiet unfurrow.

Chaotic days ensued. The men went on a binge and mamma tried to keep us at home. But the wether lamb lady had bought herself new hair and was terribly pleased with herself. "For the twins!" she announced in English, and brought us a big box of balloons. Kjartan blew his up and released them, it wasn't much fun, so I stuck mine on the tap and they bulged like fat drops. We then carted them to the roof and I got Kjartan and

Diddan to hurl them at anyone walking by below.

We got caught that very evening. I tried to tell the truth, that it wasn't me, but we both got a dose of itching powder under our shirts and down our backs, and people bellowed at us that we had no business here, and that we should push off back to the US, bloody *gringos*, instead of harassing decent people. Kjartan, who somebody had spotted throwing them, had his trousers pulled off and was thrown into the street. I managed to escape, crawling under tables and crates, through clutter and rubbish. Until I found myself facing the Espinales stall!

"Show us then!" Espinales scoffed, "show us what you're made of, you little snitch!" Luckily Gracia was standing next to him and took me in to her sisters. I couldn't get a word out, I was on fire. They undressed me, doused me in buckets of water, laid me out on a bench that smelled like summer coalfish, and I immediately fell into a deep sleep.

Gracia was watching over me when I woke up. I thought she looked like Rannvá. There was something soft and pretty about her eyes, she sat there gazing into space, gently swaying, as if she had a melody inside she was singing to herself. When she noticed that I was awake, she bent down, smiled and placed her cheek against mine. Caught up in a turmoil of feelings, I cried.

Time went by and things were more out in the open. Mamma made pápi take it more seriously, as for me, a great aching had come into the mix. The pair had progressed to the occasional stroll hand in hand on the beach; Egil flexed every muscle and lifted Gracia up in the air, while all I could muster were some handstands on the margins. Kjartan sat in front with a gentle smile and had his own thoughts; I could see that he was my equal, even just sitting down.

Egil was more self-assured now, but when I swam past their spot, or spied on them, I had the impression that Gracia could be so pale, the light I had seen around her was fading, I looked and I looked and suffered, because I couldn't do anything about it; the sighing winds from the park in Tórshavn drifted through me, and I knew that in life hope is intertwined with great trepidation. Gracia was shy and never knocked at our door, but she and Diddan became friends, perhaps because she picked up Spanish the fastest. And when Diddan returned we bombarded her with questions, what had Gracia said, where had she been, and what had she been doing.

Everything changed overnight. Pápi was working on setting up a fish processing plant in the scrubland north of the town. The investments in buildings and equipment had become so significant, that a young guard was hired to stand watch. One morning he was killed. What we could glean from adult conversation was that he had been seeing a girl, but her father had said no, and then her brothers had hacked him to pieces with a machete.

That was when pápi took notice. And a few days later it came like a shot: us kids were to be sent away to school as soon as possible. The tickets were already bought, and our parents would accompany us as far as Quito, everything had been arranged with the embassy there to ship us back across the world.

A decision had been made, everyone was upset. But I, who was responsible now that Egil could not be relied on, realised that it was the only option. Do it quickly and minimise the pain. I tried talking to Egil about it, but he wouldn't listen, as he was busy pacing his room, and now it was Kjartan's eyes that looked like he had a cold.

One night I woke with a start and realised that Egil was gone. Diddan and Kjartan stood whispering by the window, just as I was about to say something, they jumped me, and before I knew it they had me tied down with a blanket wrapped around my head. I saw red and managed to make enough noise to wake the adults who rushed to us.

We were all questioned, but the pair of them clammed up. Pápi was furious and decided to start the search immediately. I, who understood the gravity of the matter, hurried to dress and join him. We strode through a darkened town and across the barren square, only its smell lingered in the air, there was a nocturnal rustle in the rubbish, other than that it was silent. Then we paced up and down the beach sweeping dunes and low shrubs with our torches. To no avail.

Pápi thought it ill advised to wait, and first thing in the morning he went to talk to Espinales and his parents. Neither Espinales nor his sisters knew anything, in a rage the father railed against the *gringos*, didn't they get their fill plundering and torturing people for money and land? But the brothers still joined in the search, and a gaggle of kids followed the search party. Pápi was drenched in sweat, he was dizzy from heat and fear and this curiosity that brought out the entire neighbourhood.

It got to me too, so I set out searching on my own. And mid-afternoon I found them. The guard's shack had suddenly sprung to mind, it had been empty for a while. The door was locked, but when I pushed hard it budged just a little, as if it had been barricaded from the inside, the slim crack was enough to spot movement inside. The instant I howled that I had seen them, the door burst open and I was hit so hard that I tumbled backwards in the sand. It was Kjartan who stood over me.

Egil did nothing. He stood there with the baguette Kjartan had brought them, holding it sort of like a weapon, but he despaired now realising that there was nothing they could do. I didn't see Gracia, I was so dazed that I fled, half crawling, and with my heart pounding so hard that my ears nearly burst. It was like a massive wave had come crashing down and dragged me out along the seafloor, swept me up in a maelstrom of sand, light and sound, and as my lungs filled with brine, I knew that only Gracia could bring me back ashore.

But I never saw her again. Within a week we departed. On a grey day after torrential rains. It was doubtful if the two little planes would be able to take off, the unpaved strip was drenched and viscous, and the tyres dug into the sand. Pápi, Diddan and Kjartan took the front plane, from the back one we watched it lurch along the strip and take off.

Egil looked neither up nor down as we took off, mamma had taken one of his hands in hers, but it was lifeless. I looked towards the little fleck where the others were floating, a tiny mosquito over the rainforest homebound back across the world. I thought of Rannvá, but was certain that I would forgive Jógvan. Because I would be so busy. I knew all about life now, and was going to write a novel about heartbreak. Maybe it should be in Spanish, so it could travel further afield. And up there, as the Andes rose slowly from the horizon, I decided that it would be titled 'Secret tears'.

The Last Fishing Trip

by

Magnus Dam Jacobsen

translated by Marita Thomsen

He had been young and light-footed once. Everything had seemed like child's play and had anyone truly lived, it was him. All the countries he had read about and longed to see, he had seen, and then some. Though there had been many a close call, his health had never failed him and all his limbs were intact. He had been both shipwrecked and stranded, yet somehow made it back to a rolling deck every time. Thrice he had been torpedoed, twice north in the Atlantic and once in the Pacific, and he would never forget the cutting arctic cold, there were no words for it, only experience could convey its sting. But he stayed in fortune's favour and always chanced on a raft. That third time he had rowed the last two days and nights on his own, the other five had succumbed to exhaustion, and he had laid them so that gulls and other birds of prey wouldn't get to their eyes. A terrible image was etched in his brain, from when a sailor had told him about how seafarers, powerless and defenceless, had their eyes pecked out while they were still alive. He said it happened so quickly that you never noticed until your sight was robbed.

They had enough food and water, liquor too, but that he

had tossed overboard, he knew the havoc drink could wreak. And he remembered his father, who taught him currents and navigation, between flashes of past perils on fishing boats and freightliners. That time in Greenlandic waters when they caught the tail of a breaker, which in one fell swoop peeled off the entire portside gunwale from stem to stern. And wartime convoys when submarines sent death chasing after them. He could hear the explosions and saw the chaos, flames and smoke. *Full speed ahead!* That was the order and on they would plough through the drowned, who they had chatted, drunk and brawled with in the last port. One night he couldn't stomach any more, he was losing his mind to the tune of pleading howls and horrific screams from the wretches battling death—scorched by fire, mowed down by sterns and propellers or simply drowning because they never learnt how to swim. He tore into the mess and smashed his right hand sideways down on the steel table rim. He looked down at the hand where the scar ran deep, it had given him some relief.

Then the war ended and free from bodily harm he roamed the streets of Chicago again. Went down to Basin Street where he met Louis Armstrong. He spent a few years living in San Francisco, there he had taken up karate and got a black belt, knowing self-defence could come in handy and it was good exercise, plus it kept him from wasting time. On shore he had worked as a stevedore. Then he grew restless once more and he signed back on. He said goodbye to that blonde, he was so used to saying goodbye, still, this time felt different, he knew he would be back.

And he remembered the girls in Japan and the bears on Kodiak and the leaping salmon up in Alaska. That vast land with its mountains and fjords, icescapes and forests, lakes and rivers he wanted to revisit. And he remembered one night in dire straits in Port Said. Thieves had made it into the hold on his watch. There were three of them and they pulled knives on him, and one of them managed to stab him, but then he fired and two went down, the third got away. He patted his belly where the long scar framed his ribs. Thinking back now, he regretted doing it. Christ! what were dirt poor and downtrodden people to do other than steal? But, he had lived a rough life, and such was their reality.

When he set out sailing at fourteen, first on smacks and then with the merchant marine, he had by the age of twenty not touched tobacco, booze or women. By forty he had bought girls with their hymen unbroken, but by then he was tired of chasing new countries and new experiences, and he had been forced to quit the bottle. Drink made him dangerous, it brought on the wildest deliriums and made him punch anything in his way in a blind frenzy, one day he would kill someone or get himself killed. He signed off in San Francisco. The blonde still worked at the same place and lived at the same address. They bought a house and moved in together. Kids weren't on their mind, but if any should come they would be welcome. No little ones came, though, and they lived just as well regardless, they were probably too old for babies anyway, they both thought it best to be young with your children. He returned to Alaska to go salmon fishing. He loved fishing, it was exciting, well paid work and so fresh, and he got to use his body. They sold their home in San Francisco and built another up in Alaska. These years at her side were the best he ever had.

They were both experienced, mature people and spoke little

of the past. If they did bring anything up it was for comparison or to underscore a point, and there was never an angry word between them. Though they had scant interest in politics, they always voted for the Democrats. The salmon expeditions were short and highly profitable. When he was home they just spent time together, talking, playing chess, hiking for days through mountain forests, along waterfalls and lakes. On those trips they lived off fish, bread and water. Huddled together in the evenings they gazed into the fire, until only the stars lit up the night. Then they would slip into their sleeping bags under the slopes of the light tent, which rolled up to fit into the palm of a hand. They read papers and books, helped each other clean and cook, they felt good together. They didn't seek out other company, happy to be together and have the chance to live their own lives.

And he marvelled at how much she had changed since he first got to know her. He had judged her by the company she kept. It made her appear the way he believed her to be and he behaved and talked to her accordingly thereafter, which resulted in her calling him the most merciless, brutal, hard and cynical person she had ever met. As was typical of him, that just spurred him on and he had severed all ties with her in one swing of the axe. Later he had reconsidered, wondering if he hadn't misjudged her. At the end of the day, he had no idea who she truly was, so he had pulled himself together and had gone back to her place to see her. She was startled when he appeared, scared, she hadn't expected to see him again. He explained to her *why* he had come, that he would like to get to know her without other people around, and that he believed he had formed the wrong impression of her.

And just as hard, rough and bloody-minded as she had seemed to him before, she was now just as lovely, womanly and wise when he got to know her. He had utterly misjudged her. She wasn't just pretty and graceful and meticulous with herself and her affairs, she was also profoundly mature and taught him, perhaps unknowingly, a lot about what it meant to have character. He never asked anything of her. He had no right whatsoever to demand anything of her. He was just blissful that he was lucky enough to get to know her so well. That he was in love with her went without saying, but he, who had been with so many women, ladies of pleasure, didn't dream of sleeping with her. That seemed insignificant, he was content just to talk to her, and be where she was. One evening while walking her home, he said that he would be signing back on again now. She stopped and looked at him. And he vividly remembered the red brick wall, steeple and bell backdrop. He explained to her that compared to her he was a bloody-minded, tough and brutal bastard, but that he loved her, but he was also aware that she was a person who all men simply *had* to love, so he didn't in any way intend to bind her with these words, he just wanted her to *know* before he buggered off.

She hadn't said anything while he was talking, just stood there, poised in the sealskin coat that reached down to the gleaming brown leather boots she was wearing. Her blonde locks, shiny and smooth with a straight fringe, caressed her shoulders. It was winter and a damp cold evening. Then he lifted his eyes, and she was laughing and covering her mouth, the way she always did when she laughed. He glanced at her a little insecure and asked what she found so amusing. With a more serious look she tilted her head in shy self-assurance, and she said, "Have you never considered that I might also be in love with you?" No, he hadn't, truth be told, ever considered that. He, like an idiot, had spent all these months without even contemplating that the reason why they were spending so much time together was as simple as she liked being with him. He stayed that night, and many nights after that, until his ship weighed anchor. He had to take this trip as he wanted to prove to himself that he could easily do without her. But no, she reeled him in without even trying, and then they moved to Alaska.

Life during those years had been like lying back in a rowboat slowly drifting down a wide stream. On both banks was the forest, so friendly, dense and safe, and above rose the homely mountains and firmament. Still and starry and moonlit. Within them reigned the same quiet tranquillity. They were like two eternal images grown into each other. After a decade had passed in this Garden of Eden, she died. A drunk driver was the cause. She was killed on the spot, while he was off fishing. He didn't understand, couldn't comprehend it. He had faced death so often, but never like this. His first thought was grief and rage, to get his hands on that driver and tear him to pieces. But no, was that any way to remember her, she who had given him so much good, who had taught him how necessary it was not to make life any harder than it already was. Instead he visited the driver, the way he knew she would have wanted him to, and he found a wretch in greater agony than himself or his love, who was dead.

Afterwards he lived alone, he didn't need any other woman. And he pondered his foolishness; taking *her* for the men she had gone out with. The crowd she had been part of when they met, just happened to share such snippets of her past with him. And from this tittle-tattle he had fashioned her into something she was *not*. Yes, she had taught him a lot. He had, when it came to human insight and treating and handling other people, been an ignorant fist-crushing, mouth-shooting barbarian until she entered his life. She had softened him, never on purpose, just by being herself. And yet! Hadn't it been on purpose? Yes, of course she knew what she was doing, she was too wise to ignore it. She had done it, because she knew that she was the only person he truly listened to and took seriously. Not just out of love, no, but also respect for her wisdom and character, for her thoughts and insights, how she had welcomed life's ups and downs. And he sat by the window and looked out into the bright, sprawling garden, which she had planted and tended to. His contribution had been a bit of heavy lifting. All he had planted was a pigeon apple tree, his apple of choice, and six white lilacs, *Syringa Lemoine* he believed the label had read. And those he had tended well, the way he tried to take care of everything else. But, it had taken willpower, in great measure. To her, it seemed, everything came easy.

There were meadows and trees, shrubs and vegetable plots, a greenhouse and a pond. The house overlooked it all. Out there he saw the sea and the summits, and a Russian song sprang to mind, one he heard while sailing in those parts:

Where were you my eagle on blue wings,
where were you for so long my eagle…

He fished, the way he had while she was alive. Took care of the house, tended to the plants. And though she was dead, she was everywhere. She kept him alive and saw to it that he looked after himself. He couldn't quite tear himself free from this place where they made so many memories. And he sat by her grave and listened and reminisced and dreamed. He heard her talking to him, looking at him with her beautiful smiling eyes, and saw her shaking her head and laughing. The flyaway hair, irises, contour of her chin, colours, mouth and teeth, shoulders, chest, body, the firm shapely limbs, and sometimes this distant expression on her face, like a deep sorrow, as she looked over at him, caressed him, and was happy and smiling again. He saw her amble through the house, the garden, by the pond, their daylong hikes and evenings and nights. They would chat and play chess, and she usually won, or they would just sit and be one with the sea, forest and air. He yearned for her, both in body and soul, and he fathomed how much she had given him, and how much he had lost. He missed her and cried, realising that he would never see her again, he also understood that he had to get away from there, she wasn't *there* anymore, she was part of him now.

Five years had passed since she was gone. He was now fifty-five-years-old, and he had never felt as grief-stricken, but he was not weakened. There were times when he had considered returning to the bottle, but no, he didn't want to cause her the grief of disintegrating into a jabbering wreck, who would die adrift on some wave of liquor. He signed on again, but so much had changed at sea, and so much had changed in him.

For five years he sailed again, then he moved home. He had never sailed as a navigator or captain, he didn't like to study, and he had no interest in becoming an officer, life as a boatswain had suited him fine. He had always been up on deck and was used to sailing forward of the mast, it was where he felt best. This open free deck, and this open free life between often stubborn, rough and wild men, who also had the warmth of more or less fixed and loyal friendships. He was an able-bodied seaman and boatswain and perfectly content with that. He had never dreamt of any middle-class job with power and responsibility. Nothing was further from him. What he had craved and sought was life itself, experience, action, being, and it had been bestowed upon him.

He signed off in Guam and headed for Alaska. Sold the house and moved home to the motherland. He didn't want to get rid off their things, not a teacup, he had it shipped home in containers. He didn't want for money, by chance. He had never possessed any financial sense himself, but he had always been good at earning his keep, equally at blowing it in a wink, then back out to tack. She wasn't like that, she looked after money. At first he thought she was mean and tight-fisted. It had troubled him, he had always despised stinginess and love of money. But he had been wrong on that count too. She wasn't stingy, she just had respect for money. She wasn't used to the life of ease he was. Her upbringing and childhood bore no comparison. Whenever he was back to digging lint out of his pockets he would just take a berth somewhere, which meant shelter, work, pay and food. She had with her example taught him how earnings should be managed, without letting it turn him into a dollar-bill-counting zealot.

This made him today, by ordinary accounts, well off. He had to laugh, that *he* was to become a moneyed man, who just wrote figures on a cheque and then got the money through thin air or straight into his palm. But he had to admit that here too she had been wiser. Having enough made life easier, created freedom. And it was again clear to him that he hadn't started thinking at all until he met her. Before her arrival, he had just lived haphazardly, following urges, desires and whims. And he didn't regret it either. He had lived a rich, varied, colourful and exciting life, and he had also experienced truly loving a person and leading a secure middle-class life with her, without ever becoming the worst of all, a petit-bourgeois.

He was a citizen, yes, of life. He had the means and he had the experience, longing, love, yearning, zest and health. Back home he purchased a house, not too far from the docks, and a motorboat. Since then he had lived off the interest from his money, which had piled up in bank accounts and bonds, and off the catch he landed after his fishing trips as he went out fishing every day the weather permitted. It was his boat and his memories that kept him alive. He, who used to have to pull himself together just to sit still for one second, could now sit for hours here in the kitchen with a quiet, distant smile as dusk filled the house. Sometimes he played Louis' records while reminiscing about Chicago and Basin Street and countless other places.

He tended the house, boat and sea, his fishing gear and tools, the shotgun and rifle and harpoon. *He* would never go into any respite or care home or fade away in some hospital bed. He was determined to partake until the end in this swirling current that was life. Always feel the engine reverberate through the timber planks and into the body. The sea and air, cloud drift and birds, watch the sun shimmer in wave crests, as he stood shotgun in hand observing the spot where he knew a shag's neck would bob up again. He wanted to see the splashing silvery cod emerge hooked and thrashing from the deep, the tug on the line and the haul. Haddock and pollock, ling and cusk, halibut and cod gleaming white, brown and red. Cast anchor below the headland, shoot guillemot, and when that season came, catch fulmar. He wanted to live and die on his boat, *Mary Lee*, namesake of the golden-haired girl resting between Alaska's peaks who shared in his every breath. The sea, the breakers and the pulling tide. The sharp air, saturated with brine and wind from every direction on the compass. The ocean, which he and *Mary Lee* and all humankind belonged to. For everything came from the sea and returned to the sea.

He was no longer fourteen, he was eighty-four, and this was to be his last day of fishing. He had decided it. His legs were starting to falter, his hearing too, but he still had his eyes, like the eagle, like the gannet and the flying falcon. He knew that he also had cancer in his belly. He smiled, odd that precisely he, who always had a stomach of iron, would get stomach cancer. Luckily he had the boat. A spasm came over him, he seized up in pain, this time it kept rolling, sweat poured down his forehead, stopped at his eyebrows, rounded his eyes and ran down his cheeks, before it came to an end. Best to get out there immediately, you never knew where the limit was when you were truly *ill*. He might faint, be found before coming round again and taken to hospital. That would make it hard to get out fishing. He didn't want to die in a bed.

His will was written. His sister was his next of kin, but they were like cat and dog, and she had enough to live on. But she had a granddaughter who was married and they weren't that well off. Not that they suffered any outright hardship, but he would like to make life easier for them, because they were precisely the right people, the money could give them freedom. He wanted to play his part in liberating them from workplaces and employers and authorities and Lord knows what else people had to suffer and be saddled with on their earthly journey. He had left them all of his possessions, which constituted more than a trifle. Insurances he had none of, except for the ones he was obliged to take out as a landowner. He was pleased that he had such a nice sum, lawfully earned and secure. And then there was the house, it was a good size and in very good repair. A house wasn't something the young ones had, so it would stand them in good stead. They would never have to grovel before banks or other money institutions, on the contrary. He didn't begrudge them any of it, they were very likable young people, got him thinking of himself and the blonde, who was with him now on his final fishing trip. Before leaving he made sure to lock up carefully and as usual, he took the key. Out of engrained habit, he had always been fastidious about keys. He vividly recalled the moment over there in Malaysia, when he hadn't locked up and nearly got his throat slit. Were it not for his light sleep and fine-tuned ears, he wouldn't have managed to tackle the killer. His niece, who regularly cleaned his house, had a spare key.

Soon he was pushing out. The well-oiled engine clanked merrily, buried its snout and danced with glee. The boat glistened and shone, in fine repair and fresh paint. He hadn't brought the shotgun along today, it hung at home flanked by the rifle and harpoon. He would, on occasion, shoot a porpoise for himself and harpoon it immediately. When the foaming wake was past the last house, he pulled out the bottle. He hadn't had a drop for forty-four years now. He had spent twenty years drinking and sixty-four sober. He held the bottle up against the clear air. This beautiful colour, like golden syrup, filled with heather and memories of Scottish shores, Highland Queen! He pulled out the cork, sniffed and drank and swallowed, breathed deeply! Oh he felt good. He had another taste, deep and long, gazed up into the clouds travelling along the clear azure sky. Everything became shimmering bright and limpid, like when he was a little boy, fresh and new, like when he had his very first drink. He took in the shore, fields, and pastures, rocky beach and crags, mountains and summits, cliffs and skerries and islets and seaweed, and shellfish. As he reached Skarvsurð Scree six shags dived into the waves.

Blood pumped through his body and mind, every vein bursting with frothing life. The world was flooded with new light and sound. He steered past the headlands towards the *Báran*[24] swell. Remembering the first time his father had explained its fierce tidal incarnation, *Vestbáran*, to him. Today he would make her acquaintance, meet her terrible power and pull. Today she would rise, he was sure of it. Had *he* not grown up with the sea and its currents. The tide was pulling hard today, tonight the moon would be plump, soon it would turn. The sun lay low, it beamed through crests spraying light frothy foam. He was inside the *Báran* now, landwards loomed the towering cliff and seawards the low broad-shouldered island. And there came the breaker, towering and foaming, a curling mane propelled by ground swells and all of the ocean's might. Blue, green and white, booming, roaring, crashing. It simmered, swirled and sang, and he was carried away by unfathomable forces. Old habit had him fighting, then his chest filled, gave up heaving, his lifeless arms drooped. He had returned to the sea.

At a Café

by

Arnbjørn Danielsen

translated by Marita Thomsen

No man is an island, entire of itself...
John Donne

I'm sitting at a café reading a paper. Yes, I was meant to hurry, but it's always a drag to get up again once you've made yourself comfortable.

A waitress and I are the only ones here.

It's quiet, no music and no chatter.

There isn't much for the waitress to do just yet, but there probably will be when people start leaving work. It's the middle of the day. She looks bored. Can't fault her. But why? Everyone gets bored once in a while. Isn't that some established truth? Let's say it is. Still, she picks up a dishcloth every so often, sort of to underline her domestic virtues to herself. No harm in that. She probably has a lot on her mind. Kids? A husband? She does look maternal. Bordering forty, plump with a sprinkling of freckles under her eyes. She wears a knee-length blue dress.

It's the uniform at this establishment. All the women working here wear it, but it suits her. Anyway, enough about that. She looks thoughtful. What's hubby doing? Or, are the kids home from school yet? Maybe they ran into the road to play. That's not a comforting thought. And here she sits unable to really do anything about all that needs doing. That's how she appears to me. But my assumptions may be well off the mark. I'd love to know what she's thinking right now. What she's feeling. But if I asked her, she'd think me mad. In any case, it seems to me that something about her husband weighs on her mind today. "What's he actually up to at work? Comes home late all the time and then when I ask him why, he gets cross and shrugs, like it's none of my business. Best not ask about it," she frets. Still, you don't always need questions. Examine the brow and the wrinkles cupping eyes and chin and search the dark furrowed eyebrows. Words hang there in fat clusters that sometimes burst and wash over her and into her eyes, nose, ears, mouth, hands and legs. And nobody gets it but her, even in a room full of people. The bigger the crowd, the harder it is for others to understand. The pair of them—husband and wife—become a twosome walled off from the world. Except for the kids, of course. But everyone else is eons away. They don't understand the wordless language between them. Or the panic that they should somehow misjudge each other and catch a whiff of adultery. Some sort of life necessity lies ahead, which is to be satisfied day after day, year after year.

I light up. The paper fell on the floor. I pick it up, but can't be bothered to read it.

Oh, a new customer just walked in, a tall grey-haired man in a suit and tie with a briefcase under his arm. Surely a white-collar worker. Perhaps on his way to the bank. Or the post office? He buys a cup of coffee with sugar. Smiles at the lady. But doesn't say much. Asks her to sell him a cheroot. She obliges. He takes a seat in a corner. Guess he's a regular. Must be about half a century old. He rummages in the briefcase. What did he forget this time? Whatever it is, he doesn't appear to find it. Sets the case back down. Looks straight ahead and gulps a mouthful every now and again. He looks unmarried. Like someone most at ease in his own company. Not prone to escapism though by my estimate. Has a car and an apartment outside of town. Or maybe owns a house. What might he be thinking about? Mozart? Buñuel? The Common Market? It would be amusing to know. Or about any lady friends? How they sometimes surprise him and occasionally let him down. I think he's an even-tempered man, happy in his own skin, someone who doesn't get all worked up about such things. Goes home after office hours without much thought. Not one to be thinking about his own life necessities at the workplace. Isn't in thrall to his emotions. Does his job well. Doesn't let his mind roam through thoughts about everything under the sun. The tasks on the desk need tending to. You're in the red or in the black, and that's that.

But as he sits here on his own, snippets of days gone by come to him. Gain on him slowly. There is the Mediterranean. Sun, sand and sea. People bathing. All his friends with him in Spain, it was indeed fun. The drink was cheap. There will be another summer yet. And then they will bathe and watch the bullfighting.

He rises suddenly. Searches the briefcase again. Looks like he has forgotten some paperwork. Receipts, bills? Just then a new customer enters, a Spaniard working in Denmark.

The customer who might be a clerk or an accountant smiles and nods to the waitress before making his way out. The Spaniard heads to the counter and buys himself supper. He's black-haired, like most Iberians. He wears a suit and a tie, like a clerk. Also carries a briefcase. His Danish is accented. He takes a seat at a table by the window. Considers which side to pick; but finally decides and positions himself with a view of the traffic outside. He eats unhurriedly. Looks like he has plenty of time. Could well be one of the hopefuls trying to secure a new job. Visiting factories every day in the hope of landing a cushy well-paid position. He's a man in his prime. Has a charismatic face. Casts the occasional glance around the empty café. Then carries on eating until his plate is clean.

He lights up a cigarette. Stares through the window. The cars pass at dizzying speeds. Driving forwards, only forwards.

But what about the Mediterranean. The sun, sand, sea.

The birds, the mountains?
Women, children?
His course is set for the peak.
Now he's pining at its foothills. Watching cars speed by.

Why is it such a slog to walk uphill? The diversion is so long. First to Copenhagen. To factories. Hydrochloric acid, sulphuric acid. Why this endless bloody detour. I hate detours.

The summit casts its colossal shadow across the base of the mountain. And yet hope lives in all humans, in some form or other.

When he has turned this cigarette to ashes, he lights another. Then gazes back out of the window.

He probably shares a bedsit with other Spaniards, crammed together, locked away. And that's not all. Somewhere in the distant horizon Spain beckons, the land of white sands against azure seas.

And the breeze swirls across Europe. New, longer detours are forged. And for these detours other detours are constructed, and so on it goes.

In come the labourers. And I take my leave. Have been idling here long enough. Best get home.

I walk past lit houses. People have just come home from their work. Some are slumped in front of the telly. Others are still busy with the housework.

It snowed this morning and the frost lingers. There is a crunch underfoot.

The streetlights are on, thankfully, because the path is now suddenly one with the white earth. And we love the earth, the soil.

Where our feet are firmly planted.

Somewhere above me houses rise. Resting on earth they reach for the firmament.

A sudden waft of dry-fermented *ræst* lamb catches me. Can't be far now. And *Midnight Rambler* too in the same gust.

I run to the door and let myself into the warmth.

Breath of Light

by

Oddfríður Marni Rasmussen

translated by Lindy Falk van Rooyen

Light from outside. Lighter than an eye. Today. Soft and playful. I have to wash the floor. If I don't do it now, I'll have to wait three months and then it will be Christmas. The light from outside lifts my head, which is resting in my hands. Today I will get up. Maybe I'll wash a load of dirty underwear. Maybe. But when I try to get up, I can't lift my head out of my hands.

An image emerges from the light. Stop! Let me look at it more closely.

I see a man in a dark-red sweater and shorts go into a perfume shop. Further down the road, a sunbeam points into the open window of a living room. Inside, a girl is watching a beer commercial on television:

The man asks his son if there is anything to drink in the house.

Clip.

The son says he'll look in the fridge and see.

Clip.

The man drinks out of a dark bottle.

Clip.

"Bloody hell?! This is a soda-pop, my boy!"

My legs fall asleep. I cannot move, because if I do, the image will disappear. My legs sting but the light is soft. There's a knock at the door. I yell 'come in!'

"You've bought yourself a new pair of shoes," a voice in the hall says.

I make no reply. If I do, I will lose my grip on the light; so clear now that it fills my entire field of vision.

I wake to someone clapping me on the shoulder. They ask where I bought my shoes? Rigid in my seat, I say I got them overseas. Under my breath. The light is inside. The pins-and-needles in my legs dissipate.

The image loops in my head. I wake up.

"From now on," I say. "From this day on."

The Return

by

Carl Jóhan Jensen

translated by Marita Thomsen

My last recollection is of a tree. A maple tree. I remember throwing my head back in a fit of laughter perhaps. For one breath I look up between branches and clearings in the leaves. Up into the noon blue. A bird spirals skywards above the crown. Circle after circle. Ever widening. Winds itself up, as I gawp like an idiot with my nose in the air. Winds itself over to the tree planted right by the white gate to the graveyard *undir Svínaryggi*, known as the old cemetery, near the extensive stretches of greenery in central Tórshavn. But as I stare backwards bent under the canopy, recently returned from five years abroad, as I sense the strain on the sinews under my chin, and pins and needles in my neck, as I hear the sounds of the town, the streets, the bay, as I feel a lightness in my soul, right there under the maple tree because I am back home, as I gaze after this bird winding itself up circle by circle, and have an inkling of concord and coalescence, as I feel instantly elated, uplifted, why nearly aglow with the new context in our history, the change that appears underway, a sudden disquiet rears its head. Discord. Despair. A deep pull inside. Wafting like a reflection of the foliage. The twisting, twirling leaves. The bird spiralling heavenwards. Circle after circle. It is as if something snaps. As though something loses its hold. Lets go. A centrelessness. A malaise drowns the day. Drowns out sanctity and innocence. The erstwhile distance holding it all together. Moments ago. In exile. That set the course. Unequivocally. For everything. Circle within circle. Held differences. Proximities. Proportions. Held them tight. Held on. Held to. Held up. Everything comes apart. I don't know what is causing this. Perhaps the knobs standing to attention side by side all along the fence on both sides of the gate. Troubling signs, which, when traced back through a long tradition, refer to an aesthetic that separates life from its *sine qua non*. Ending. Dissolution. Perhaps it is the thick perfume of freshly cut grass. Perhaps the memorial slabs. The half-forgotten past. I don't know. This disquiet is so abrupt. It sends a shock, a jolt, through me. Still. I catch myself quickly. Steady my nerves. Worry not. I manage to deflect it. This time. Before doubt clouds this clearing in my mind, and my heart is overcome with unbridled dread.

Across the street my wife is waiting impatiently with my eldest son. The other one tugs at my jacket sleeve and tells me to come along now. Why we stand here, he asks with a frown. He yanks my sleeve. He wants a balloon. He wants to see the boat races. Chomping at the bit.

It's the eve of St. Olaf's Day.

We were on our way to the town square for the opening ceremony.

I gather my thoughts. I take my son's hand and we cross the street. But afterwards. Afterwards, as we walk down Grímur Kamban's Street, I know somewhere deep inside of me that everything is different. Changed. Now. It has come to that, no getting around it, it has come to that point where everything shifts mood. And later, in the following weeks, months, while recent days simmer in the mind, the disquiet returns, with a vengeance. Time and again.

It will not yield. The malaise.

On several occasions I catch myself unwittingly under the maple tree again by the west corner of the old cemetery right across from Pól Restorff's shop. Out of the blue, there I stand staring up into the branches, into the gradually reddening and withering canopy. At leaves that fall off. Stand there like an idiot. Like a madman. Gawping. To no avail. Everything remains asunder. Grows even further apart. The foliage bidding farewell, the black branches. The bird is nowhere to be seen either. The bird that wound itself up, up and up. Spiralling in widening circles. Only the odd crow comes flapping. Not the bird I half expect to make the difference. Perhaps. It will wind itself down again. Leisurely. Someday. Down into the tree crown. Then shoots will surely stir. Then all will coalesce anew into common identity, vision and concord.

Alas, no. Far from it.

An evening not long ago, I unwittingly placed myself once again under the maple tree at the southern border of the old cemetery. Nasty hail showers punctuate a stiff wind. It's dark too. My last entirely conscious act was to head down to the SMS Shopping Centre for the papers, and indeed I have three newspapers under my arm. One Icelandic and two Faroese. As I dawdle there absent-mindedly peeping up into the bare branches clawing at the howling wind, there is suddenly a thud. A bang. A slam. It startles me. I see that the gate is open. A looming dark shape emerges through the fence, and it's heading straight at me. My hair stands on end. My knees wobbled. I will admit a howl was building inside, but in that instant a deep coarse voice says in Icelandic, *hvurn andskotan*, it says, why are you gawking here in the dark in this weather.

I know that voice.

It's Malakoff. No mistaking him. The Icelandic classicist I told you about, the one who ripped into our old Prime Minister Dam and the socialists at Lyngsøe's barbershop down on Áarvegur Road. There he stood, Malakoff, draped in an ankle-length black raincoat and balaclava.

My shaking subsided and I bade him good evening.

Calmly.

Hvurn andskotan, he repeated. The Koff (as I call him). *Hvurn andskotan ert tú að thveilast?* He was asking me what the hell I was doing here.

I could, of course, have asked in return what brought him from Hvannasund to Tórshavn to wander between the graves in the old cemetery, especially this late on a Friday evening in a showery north-easter. But it is what it is. He is an oddball, The Koff, there is no hiding that, and someone once confided in me that it was rumouired that he was an occultist in his youth and dabbled, and still does, some will have it, in all shades of the occult. So I just shrug.

We stand there a moment shuffling at the ground and looking past each other. In silence, as so often happens when you chance upon someone and suddenly feel hesitant and hampered by consideration and politeness.

In the end The Koff asks if I'd like to come along with him to Tórshøll for a drink. That proposition seemed to me both misplaced and misjudged, so I countered that, well, I really ought to have headed home a while ago. The Koff scoffed, and I heard him mutter angry words about *kvennmenn* and *skass*, which I don't care to repeat.

I hemmed and hawed.

He insisted.

It wouldn't take long to count the coins in my pocket. But then it occurred to me that I might be missing out. This man was no fool. Far from it. Perhaps I ought to bring it up with him, I thought, this thing about coming asunder, all this I have been torturing myself with for so long and can find no words to express. No need to tell you, of course, I know how he gets when he drinks, what a piece of work he can be. It was a gamble. I risked getting caught up with him when one of his moods set in, and either he would get loud-mouthed, sneering and nasty, or wallow in pessimism and depressing babble. I thought, well I won't stay after my money's gone, and so off we went.

We took the road down Dr. Jakobsen's Street.

As we walk along, I bring up this thing with him about the disquiet that came over me under the maple tree that time. Last summer. I worked myself up. I blurted it all out, I did. I am, regrettably, prone to that, rattling on.

The Koff said nothing. He does that sometimes, clams up with an air of I couldn't care less what anyone is saying. Can't even hear it. He hummed to himself and dug his hands into his coat pockets. Still, he did nod now and then, if I let up. Nodded a couple of times and pulled one hand out of its pocket, but as soon as I spoke, he stuffed it back in and resumed the humming.

Luckily it's a short walk from the old cemetery down

to Tórshøll.

I had never been inside Tórshøll before. The Koff insists that it's because of my fear of the people and that I haven't the stomach for anyone but the better-heeled crowd in Kaggin. I take his remark in good humour, but I do know that the place is of mixed repute.

We enter. Head straight up a flight of stairs. Cross a set of double doors into a squat oblong hall. Bays line the long wall at both ends. Scattered tables wait encircled by chairs in red steel and varnished plywood, the like of which I hadn't seen since cub meetings at the YMCA in the sixties. I half-expected old scoutmaster Álvheygg to greet us, but no. Quite the opposite. Clusters of beer bottles and rank tobacco. At the far end of this den of perdition a bartender is leaning on the counter, half-dozing, a roll-up clings to the corner of his mouth and he exudes a blend of cold despair and irony. A band, somewhere out of sight, is playing Norwegian pop. Old Doodle Bugs tunes.

The Koff buys us beer, Black Sheep, and Schnapps. Two each.

We pull up at a long table right by the double doors. Not much of a crowd tonight. A couple of men are sitting on the window side. Still in workman's clothes and mostly silent. At our end of the table presides a buxom woman with her legs crossed. She is wearing stripy trousers. And a white and lime green jacket bursting at the seams. Her thinning hair is rumpled. Her pouting lips sort of lose their shape when they split into something probably meant as a smile. In the middle of the table, diagonally across from me, a long-jowled guy with a receding hairline hitches his elbows on the surface and stares vacantly into space. A couple float across the dance floor. Not too steadily. He in his gumboots and she in her sleep. For a while we are lost in our own thoughts. The Koff and I. Pour beer in the glasses. Drain the dark brew.

Without a word.

The Koff finally broke the silence, it's the return, he suddenly exclaimed, only now removing his balaclava and pulling up his coat sleeves.

I flinch.

I say, the return, I say. Unconvinced. As if to imply, I'm not that easily duped. But The Koff just indulges in a sardonic smile. He digs a fag end out of his shirt pocket and lights up.

"It's a poem," he says. A little touchy. "A poem by Yeats, a couple of lines came to me earlier. Surely you've read Yeats?" With an expression verging on contempt.

I shrug, but don't deny it.

The Koff half shuts his eyes and drones. Turning and turning, he drones, "*...in the widening gyre,*
the falcon cannot hear the falconer."

He pauses for a moment.

I make no response.

"Consciousness," says The Koff and opens his eyes, "with Yeats consciousness is like a circle, do you understand, for the Irish, and whether it expands, the circle, it has a centre, and whether it holds, the centre, it has the potential to, but for the Faroese, on the contrary, for the Faroese consciousness is bicentric, and the Faroese always fret that neither centre will hold. The Faroese never gyre around one, inwards or outwards, without being painfully aware of the other. As has become apparent." The Koff downs one Schnapps. Grimaces.

"Christ, the Faroese are even scared of mastering their own language," he resumes, "too afraid to grasp it even passably, they immediately worry about what will happen to the Danish, whether that centre will hold and vice versa. And now they are even talking about sovereignty," snorts The Koff, "the Faroese, heavens above, and identity, they want to enter a new millennium with self-reliance, say the Faroese, but then a couple of Danish suits float down from the sky, tread black and magnanimous onto these skerries and put it to the people what a pity it is that they should want such a thing, and in their wake slithers a path to hell *extra regnum*, a rump, if you will, of crystallised conceit, and it is unabashed and blunt, it says that it is not up to the Faroese what their future should hold, it is in good hands, it is in Danish hands. And then there is also the fact that unfortunately sovereignty is out-of-stock in Europe, everyone has already had their share, and he shrugs and reiterates his regrets a couple of times, before ascending back into the heavens. And the Faroese are left on their inclement cliff. Without a word of protest, on the contrary, they just lower their eyes, crestfallen and sheepish," says The Koff and gulps the other Schnapps.

"And the Faroese," he says, "the Faroese call themselves a nation in Faroese, yet still consent, whether it's just to be on the safe side, to not being one in Danish," rounds off The Koff, with another drag of the fag end. And blows a lingering wisp.

The long-jowled man suddenly rises with a clatter and crash. His crotch is very clearly wet, so the inside of his thighs. He teeters. For the blink of an eye. Then he draws himself up and says with abrupt absurdity: "*Ich bin ein Berliner*," and slumps back into his chair.

No one takes any notice. Harmony reigns. Inside.

The Koff strokes his stubbly chin. "The Faroese," he says, "are the ones who leave this place and move away, they appear to avoid this dual-centre maelstrom often becoming, temporarily at least, more Faroese, more whole so to speak, abroad, they brave spinning in wider circles, intellectually and linguistically, certain that the centre will hold, manage to delude themselves that the Faroese is a monocentric consciousness, just as for Yeats, the Irishman, take that inky cap poet, for example, the one on the radio of late, the guy seems to harbour no doubt that there is only a single centre in Faroese conscience."

I attempt no response. Nurse the beer glass, turn it in my hands half thinking of something else, but give a start, because jowls-in-a-box on the other side of the table springs up again and declaims, in the same tone as before, merely louder, "*Ich bin ein Berliner*," and pounds his fists on the table, before he plonks back down again.

The Koff turns his chair and his back on long-jowls. He straightens his legs, gives a little stretch and then crosses one over the other. Calmly.

He says, "The *angst*, *kjeiri* friend," and draws the final puff from the roll-up, "the *angst* that pained you that day in the old cemetery, it stems, are you listening to me, it stems from the fact, that you sensed the dual-centre state again then, as you stood there gazing into the tree branches, you glimpsed it, but refused to acknowledge that, because unwittingly you are, of course, scared that if there are two centres, then neither will hold, not any more, not after all these years spent abroad, and that's that, *alt og sumt*."

I thought, perhaps, to myself I thought, yes perhaps. I don't know.

And I have thought the same since, though many a moon has passed after that tipsy evening spent at Tórshøll in The Koff's company, and I think it now. Perhaps, I think, perhaps, because once again, unwittingly and in this precise moment, I have positioned myself under the maple tree on the west side of the southern border of the old cemetery, and from here you are hearing these words of mine.

Perhaps.

To Those Who Think They Know It All

by

Tóroddur Poulsen

translated by Lindy Falk van Rooyen

retrospectively
your continuous time is
just slipping away

I see   I only see   The light   Pure light   The tunnel
I pass through
    Light   I am crying in my mother's arms for the first time   Images in light just as I am light   And pápi is smiling as he takes me in his arms and says *trullinulli*   How can I express this solitude   Like a lonesome trip to the cinema with images twirling around you   The cinema is made of light too   Now I am crawling along the floor   I have shat in my nappy and it needs to be changed and my bum is a little bit raw   I am dressed in a christening robe   I am christened and given a name   I cry   Mamma's boobs as delicious as juicy baby toes   I never knew milk to taste so good   *omma* and *abbi*[25] from when they were young   I can move about easily now   Mamma is pushing me in a pram   We are on our way to town   The Butcher Shop   Minced meat   We pop in at the dairy with

a pail for milk I long to reach deep into the light But all longing is light Pápi and a cement mixer I am getting in his way He is building a wall around our house Pápi ties me to a post firmly I put sand in my mouth Sand is lovely stuff Mamma is hanging the washing out on the line So many colours When I was a child I thought everything was black and white and flecks of blue and grey I am sat at the table and must eat on my own but I am playing with my food and my mash potato is spread over the table and onto the floor so mamma grabs the spoon and starts to feed me I am in a field with *omma* and *abbi* I lose my dummy in a big pile of sheep shit *Abbi* dips it in a river Happy again I get up and run and jump and trip and fall and tumble and cry again We find a good seat on a big flat rock and *omma* has brought out a homemade cake and the gulls cry and cry but the woodcocks above make the strangest noises of all I am fascinated by a Lepidoptera and *abbi* is singing the song of the butterfly so fine Mamma tucks me into the pram but I will not sleep Her song is so sweet I reach up to her and finally fall fast asleep in her arms Now I am old enough to say all the words and go into town on my own But by the time I get home the loaf has been hollowed out at one end Mamma is furious it looks like a rat has been at it my boy she says but can't stay cross with me long and puts jam on my slice and lets me go play with the others but then there's a ruckus outside as I have smashed a glass pane next door I did not want to smash the window I just wanted the others to know how good I could throw a big stone I get a smack on my bottom and sent up to bed and I cry myself to sleep On my first day of school I am told what I can and cannot do But as one of the boys you don't do what you're told you do all you want So I'm kept in school I long to be home with mamma Pápi is in an engine room far out to sea By the time he comes home the days are much shorter and darkness is falling but just maybe he's carved a toy boat for me Time rushes in a flurry in this tunnel of light I have no feelings My feelings are the stuff of light too My memories glimmer dark I remember once waking up scared in the middle of the night and I dare not go back to sleep and I get up and creep down the hall to cuddle with mamma and pápi but find them there moaning and groaning I have fallen in love with Helga She kissed me one night we were kicking some cans down the road A tingle goes down my spine Helga's eyes are blue but her hair is black and when she flashes her smile everything inside me starts to smile as well I'm a little bit shy and I worry that someone will take her away from me Once after a game of hopscotch with the others I kissed her in parting and the smile that she smiled was so wide I was sucked inside and almost drowned School is going badly but all I wanna do is play football and chase after girls I'm a good swimmer Not only in school time but afterwards too All girls with yellow tags and the boys with red ones are called out of the pool as our time is up and we make for the showers but Illi-Ivan shoves me aside god forbid you use all the hot water and that's exactly what I've just done Now I'm eleven and drunk the first time We've stolen a bottle of brandy from Per's father and pissed as coots we're out on the town and the next day mamma is mad she starts to cry and I cross my heart and hope to die and promise never to touch the stuff again And I don't get drunk again till I'm about thirteen and we're hanging out in

The Club and a band is playing Led Zeppelin songs and *Ten Years After* I get a Schnapps from a drunk man in the men's room and throw up in the urinal but he gives me another and I chase it with a can of Elephant Beer that is still warm from the pocket of his jeans And I dream I'm playing the Led Zeppelin song *Livin' lovin'* I have no interest in getting confirmed and mamma is sad so I say if I get a guitar I'll go and get confirmed so I do and the priest lays a hand on my head and asks me some questions that I have to answer and I hated cutting my hair but luckily it grows back quickly because no one can play the guitar properly with a crew cut And I get given the blue volume of the New Testament I've skimmed through I strum I strum I strum Playing the guitar is going well and the last thing I need is to go to school to listen to some dumb teacher or other talking except for in German because that teacher is hot as hell I blush bright red whenever she asks me a question And when I have my first climax under the covers it's her I'm thinking of and I'm a little ashamed but I still keep thinking about her Mamma is very unhappy that I've started to smoke and she's confiscated the pack of fags she found in my pocket and threatened to scrap my pocket money for good if I don't give it up at once I steal twenty kroner out of mamma's purse I need to buy cigarettes a teacher catches me smoking in the loos at break time and he tells me to fish the stubs out of the toilet and calls up mamma but when I tell her he made me fish cigarette stubs out of the urinal mamma starts to fume and calls back to give him a piece of her mind and the teacher never catches me smoking in the loos again Now I'm in love with Elspa Elspa can smoke at home if she wants to and she gets much more pocket money than I do and we bum a fag off some creep after school and Elspa's the first girl I shag and it's so embarrassing because I come too soon but a few nights later we try again and then it goes better and we use a condom that Elspa has stolen from her parents but not long after it's over between us Elspa says all I care about is my guitar and my heart is broken and I steal a bottle of gin from pápi and I get shit-faced and I don't remember it myself but I wake up in hospital and they tell me I stole a moped and ran over a cop and crashed into a car by the roadside and I'm lucky to get away with a broken arm and a bang on the head   Whatever are we going to do with him I heard mamma say in tears to pápi   I cannot be bothered to go to school but I get a job baiting fish lines in the afternoon to pay off the debt on the new amp I've bought for the guitar   Andi is the name of the guy I've become good friends with and he has his own set of drums he's pretty good at playing them too and we've been jamming a little with another guy I know from class called Símun and he plays the bass and Waterball is what we call ourselves and then we jam and jam every single day till we're asked to play at a dance at Losjuni centre and it goes really well   The girls in our class are mad about us they say we're amazing and we play *White Room* and *Fire* and *Something* and *Whole Lotta Love* and *Sunshine Of Your Love* and *House Of The Rising Sun* and *Hey Joe* and *Child Of The Moon* and *Jumpin' Jack Flash* and *Love Like A Man* and *Lola* and *Born To Be Wild* and *Sweet Jane* and *Tú og eg á ástartingi* and *Tađ stóđ eitt hús i Grønulíđ* but that one we only play at small gigs because we learnt it in Sunday school and later they ask us to play at The Club in town and one time Andi is so drunk and stoned he falls off his chair and we switch to one of my own songs called *You Said I Was Boring* and luckily there's this other guy called Hanus at the dance that happens to play the drums in an orchestra and we ask him to step in for Andi who's fallen asleep in a heap on the stage and shortly thereafter Andi goes off to sea and I stop going to school altogether and mamma gives up on me entirely and I start working at the timber yard near the quay and later at Pihl & Sons as here I can earn more money also at night and then I try delivering bread for the baker but that doesn't work out very well and finally I find work splitting stones for the dynamite boss who comes from Iceland and then Andi comes home from the sea and we fall off the wagon with a vengeance and end up in Copenhagen and Christiania in a drug haze and now everything's gone black but I know that we came home again after squandering every penny we don't have and we've got withdrawal symptoms in a big way with the shakes and sweat baths and we hadn't slept in days because our brains were high on speed and pickled in alcohol and finally things settle down and we start playing a little music again and I even try to translate a few rock songs into Faroese but then Andi goes off the deep end and loses interest in jamming with us but then he gets a job at the shipyard and I start an apprenticeship with a timber man named Boylin god only knows why but only six months later I get sacked because it's too hard to get up for work Monday mornings and I toy with the idea of going to music school but then I start filleting fish at Bacalao's fish factory instead because I really need the money despite the fact that I'm still living with mamma and pápi who is almost never at home so I'm the one who has to paint the roof of our house and I wouldn't mind doing it if only the weather wasn't so bad and I lose heart halfway through but then I pull myself together and I remember mamma was so happy she said I'm almost as hard-working and determined as my father and she brought me pastries from the bakery and there's so much that has to do with girls and I'm becoming a real cool cat but I end up cutting my hair because it stinks so awfully of fish at Bacalao's and then there's this communist guy who works at the factory with me and he tries to get me to go to a meeting and he gives me this pamphlet on class conflict or something along those lines and I say that we'll be just fine as long as we've got a job and he says the capitalists are making a filthy profit off our backs and I don't want to end up in Siberia either and then he says I need to come to one of their meetings to get informed and I say I've had more than enough of that kind of thing at school and I can take care of myself thank you very much but we become good friends all the same and sometimes we go out in Tórshavn together because also he likes to party and I end up at some or other meeting after all and its dead boring but I meet a hot girl there and another time I manage to drag Andi along to a study group and it turns into nothing but one big hash ring and the council finds out and then we're not invited to join the study group again but at one point I read *The Communist Manifesto* and it's not half bad but I stick to playing the guitar and I teach a little music at night school and I start playing in Tórshavn with the Men in Sunglasses and I don't need glasses at all but when we play in The Club I do so with sunglasses and we strum everything under the sun even a couple of songs we've written ourselves and by now I've met Jórun and she's the one who took the initiative that night at the Jazz Club I was standing around dreaming and she touched me on my arm and said why don't we go for a ride and I thought this was so terribly kind of her and now I can see her before me as we go for a walk to Tinganes and find a good place to rest on a rock and then our lips meet and our tongues entwine and it's almost as if we were breathing the same breath not least when we end up in bed back at her place

Marigold

by

Sólrun Michelsen

translated by Marita Thomsen

It's past eight when Tóra wakes up. She blinks at the ceiling, then looks around. Why is she in the living room? It comes to her. Ah, yes.

So she dozed off after all. Must have slept a couple of hours. Like the dead. She didn't dream a thing, not that she can remember.

It's gloomy where she lies. Those thick olive green velvet curtains never let the living room have any light, even when they aren't drawn. They just sag gathering dust and with every passing day they seem heavier and darker to her. Doing their damnedest to shut out any light.

Well, they were his choice those curtains, back in the day.

She had already picked out a pair of bright airy ones, but he stood his ground.

He always did stand his ground.

She usually knows what the weather is like when she wakes up, by looking at the clock and gauging the light in the room. But she isn't in the bedroom this morning. Still, she thinks she can tell that it's either rain or fog today. She shoves the plaid aside, gets up off the couch, stiff in every joint, and passes the closed bedroom door on her way to the bathroom. There she puts on the same clothes she took off last night.

It reeks of vomit in here. The dark blue towel she used as a mop is still tossed on the heated bathroom floor. She bends to pick it up and dumps it in the laundry basket.

In the kitchen she hears the rain hit the window. There is also an odd sigh in her head. A whispering silence. She flicks on the coffeemaker and fetches the magazine she was reading last night.

She pours herself a mug and leafs quickly through its pages, without really looking. She can't concentrate. Shuts the magazine again. Tries to smooth the glossy cover. It feels bulkier than a moment ago.

Then she gets up and goes into the bedroom. Without looking at the bed she pulls out the top drawer in the chest. The one with underwear. Moves something inside it and rummages. Stands there for a while staring at nothing. Has forgotten what she came in here for.

When the coffee pot is empty, she looks at the clock. They will be expecting her at the pool at nine. As usual.

Three times a week she meets up there with her friend Anna. And all the others, of course.

"Lord knows this is keeping us alive," drones Henny every time they are in the sauna and the chat gets going. Every single time.

Tóra looks out of the window and notes that it has cleared up. Outside is a big pot with dazzling yellow blossoms. The last of the flowers that bloomed from his hands all summer long. Marigolds. His marigolds.

She gets up and glances over at the kitchen clock again.

Not long to nine. Time to hurry. She has to pack her swimming gear. She usually gets it ready the night before.

She picks up the brush and runs it through her dark hair. Struggles to untangle the knots. She stares at herself in the mirror for a moment. Not a grey streak in sight. Odd. Then she plaits her hair into a tight braid.

She heads out, locks the door behind her and gets into the car. On the passenger seat sits a white plastic bag with something in it. It's tied at the top. She stares at the bag for a moment. Wrenches it suddenly towards her, gets back out, unlocks the front door and flings it into the hallway. Turns the lock again, gets back in, and tries for a moment to steady herself.

She takes the ring road, though that route is a little longer than cutting straight through town. At the traffic lights she stops next to a little red car. The exhaust is fuming. A young woman is at the steering wheel. Beside her sits an unshaven man. He leans over and kisses her. The woman turns the mirror with one hand and inspects herself. With the other she fixes her hair. The man says something and the young woman turns laughing to the side window and looks straight into Tóra's face.

The smile jolts through Tóra. Then the lights are green, and the little car disappears around the corner spewing smoke behind it.

She parks outside the swimming pool. Inside are other marigolds, she muses. They have always called them marigolds here, the early risers, the ladies who swim every morning. She takes a deep breath and gets out.

The chatter hits her at the entrance as her pool card is punched in exchange for a key with a brown strap. She checks the tag. Number 67 today.

"Hello," chirps Anna in nothing but knickers. She got locker number 69. Anna is a good friend. So naïve. Or feigns to be. Always thinking the best of everyone. Maybe she truly casts no shadow.

Tóra senses the dead waters ripple as she looks at her friend's beaming face. But then her mind flashes an image of how Anna always makes a beeline for the garden when he is outside, and they share a laugh and chat. She has watched them many times.

"Everything is so pretty and well kept at yours," enthuses Anna. "He is so hardworking. Wish mine were as handy as he is." And then there's how she always insists on saying goodbye to him before leaving.

Tóra takes a deep breath and starts undressing. She hears water gushing from the showers, and then Karin's voice. Singing her heart out, as usual.

Some ladies are already in the pool, while others are lounging in the sauna.

"It's better for the muscles to get warmed up first," declares Henny. She also says that every single time. Has claimed the monopoly on knowing it all on behalf of them all. Perched there on the top rung of the sauna in all her naked plumpness, like some sort of Buddha pouring out her wisdom.

"That's for sure," is the refrain that concludes most of her sermons.

Christ what a bore! Prattling incessantly, not letting anyone get a word in edgeways. Tóra has more than once felt an urge to get up and stuff a towel in her mouth, see if that will shut her up. They're all thinking it, but nobody dares to say anything.

Tóra is really not in the mood for her today.

Karin's soprano fades when the door to the pool swings shut. Tóra dives straight in. Swims underwater until she is nearly out of breath. Then emerges in a splutter. Counts the laps as she turns: "Ten, fifteen, twenty, twenty-five, thirty..."

Suddenly she feels sick. Down at the deep end what happened last night crowds her mind, forces her to get her head above water and cling to the side of the pool. The fragments reel through her mind like a hazy short film.

She sets the table. She has fried some fish fillets. She likes fish. She watches him. Willing him to start, before she picks up her own knife and fork.

She sees his face sour. Take a turn. The same procedure every time. A cycle on repeat. Dusk washes out the room.

She stares at his scrunched up face. The expression of an animal caught in headlights, one blink away from a hit and run.

The scowl of a primate. Not a trace of forbearance or any kindred emotion. No desire to reconcile or patch things up. Nothing but chest thumping.

She battles the fear, the vice that has gripped her for so long. The companion she was always trying to keep in check.

He clears his throat. He always clears his throat first before saying anything. Wants to make sure that his words ring loud and clear. Leave no scope for misunderstanding.

"Do you think you're in charge here?" he says in a quiet voice.

A tense giggle bubbles inside her chest. It would be no use replying, even if she wanted to. The receiver is switched off. Impossible to talk your way out of it. He is incapable of normal conversation. If only he knew how to talk to her about these little incidents, which are quite trivial really, but grow, straw upon straw, into stacks blocking the road. Haystacks that obscure the horizon and are declared off limits, preserved in black safety nets, rather than shaken out and hung to dry, so they might at least be of some use. If only he were capable of conversation, of letting her get a word in. So they could just talk to each other instead of suffocating under the ash cloud of silence that sets in after these episodes. A silence that paralyses the house for weeks on end, and makes her feel forced into a coat five sizes too tight if she even has to set foot in the same room as him. All these meals at the table, where the food just swells up in her mouth are killing her.

A force burns inside. Like one of those black holes that suck everything up, insatiable. Yearning to cast itself over shrubs and saplings, anything within reach. It will probably end up like a centrifuge that breaks loose from its ties and disappears into space.

But she must try to hold it back. Reign it in.

She has lost count. Swims towards the ladder and gets out again. She washes her hair in the shower and heads to the sauna to dry off.

"I thought you'd never come out again," Anna smiles.

"Your place for coffee?"

"Not today," she replies curtly. She turns away and pretends not to notice her friend's bewildered expression. But Anna asks no questions. Leaves her be.

In there they also let her be. Gazed at her with sympathy. Asked if she would like to phone anyone.

She just sat and looked at him, lying there so peaceful, while tears streaked her cheeks. There was no holding them back. They rolled down her chin and dripped on the white duvet cover with that narrow blue stripe proclaiming the name of the hospital. In the whiteness her tears made two damp stains a few shades darker. She sat motionless. Looking at the stilled face. His expression seemed naked somehow. Like he was sad about something. It wouldn't change again. And his hands. She spent a long while watching his still hands with their pristine manicured nails. Every time he came in from the garden he would stand there scrubbing his nails clean. Scrubbing and scrubbing. Cleanliness was next to godliness.

She couldn't bring herself to touch his hands. They had always looked so big to her. Overgrown. Now she could see that they were completely normal. Smallish even, for a man. She held them in her gaze until they shrank to nothing.

When she finally rose, a nurse handed her the white translucent bag of clothes to take home.

She dresses quickly, grabs the bag with the wet swimsuit, leaves and gets in the car. Takes the ring road again, but at the roundabout she exits towards the hospital. In the car park she turns off the engine and just sits there staring at the looming structure.

He is behind one of all those windows. Or maybe not. He has probably been shoved in some basement. Perhaps underground. Don't they put them in a cold store or drawer or something? She saw that in a film. No need for a window when there is no life anyway.

No life.

She sits for a while and studies her hands clutching the steering wheel. Fresh drops on the pane draw a shadow pattern that makes them look so scarred.

She stares at the entrance where glass doors open and close automatically as soon as anyone approaches. Stares, as if she were expecting him to walk out at any moment.

A young couple emerges. The man is cradling an infant swaddled in a blue blanket. He gazes into his arms with a smile.

It always felt like an ambush. All it took was a casual reply. Or nothing at all. She was never prepared.

"There was nothing wrong with the food," she hears herself saying. "There never was."

She shifts her gaze to the rear-view mirror and is startled by her own reflection. She sees a pale naked face entangled in unkempt wet hair. Bags under the eyes.

"Who are you?" she whispers and hides her face in her hands.

She drives home. Looks around as she drives. Everything is the same. Everything is changed.

Back home she unlocks the door. The white bag is there at her feet. She picks it up in a two-finger pinch, goes out and tosses it in the bin. Back inside she slowly closes the front door. She pauses on the mat, motionless. Then fetches a roll of black bin liners and heads for the living room. She takes all the pictures off the walls and throws them in a black bag. She stares at the wedding photo for a long time, before returning it to its nail.

In the bedroom she pulls the soiled covers off the duvets and pillows. Carries them to the washing machine and starts the cycle. She hesitates before she grabs his duvet and pillow and shoves them in another bag. Empties the wardrobe where his clothes hang.

She lugs it all to the car and drives to a skip, where she dumps the lot.

Back in the bedroom she notices that she has forgotten the little painted picture hung between the windows. An image of yellow flowers. She unhooks it and studies it. They could be marigolds, but they aren't. These are sunflowers. He bought the painting one time when he was abroad. He had seen sunflowers growing there. He said that in a book by Simon Wiesenthal there was such a lovely story about these flowers. After that trip he tried to get them to grow in the garden, without luck. Instead he sowed marigolds. He tended them oh so tenderly and they grew like weeds.

He also got her to read that story about the sunflowers on the soldiers' graves, but she thought it contrasted too starkly with what had gone on outside the graveyard for anyone to call it lovely. How big would the field have to be if every person turned to ash in the concentration camps should have their own sunflower? Or the piles of bodies they had buried? An endless sea of sunflowers? No. There was nothing lovely about it. It had made her cry.

She hurls the picture into another bin bag.

It takes her several trips.

An impulse makes her go cold and ties her stomach in knots. Dinner. She hasn't done the shop yet. Deep breaths eventually steady her nerves. She will never have to make dinner again.

Her thoughts return to the meal the night before. Just like that, the words had been there. The words that spun in her mind every time it happened. They had become a mantra. Only this time she startled herself by saying them out loud.

"I wish you'd disappear!"

He had been leaving the table, but froze mid-rise, staring at her in disbelief. Without thinking she had also risen. All of a sudden he crumpled back into the chair and slumped forward on the table with both hands clutching his skull. The fish platter was shoved aside. His empty plate tumbled to the floor and smashed into a thousand pieces.

"My head hurts," he moaned.

"Just disappear," she whispered.

When she is finally done, Tóra steps into the shower. She scrubs every inch of her skin until her legs buckle, and she sinks into a sobbing heap. She sits there for ages, huddled with her arms around her knees, rocking back and forth under cascading water.

She gets dressed again and dries her hair. Takes a seat at the kitchen table.

He has cheated her. Gave her no notice. No warning. She sits for a moment staring out at the marigolds.

The shadow she concealed all these years has broken free and is sitting next to her.

Then she gets up again, pulls a pair of scissor from the top drawer and steps outside. She cuts all the marigolds, carries them inside and arranges them in a vase in the middle of the kitchen table.

Fond farewell.

She rinses the scissors under the open tap. Then she dries the scissors and returns them to the drawer. Stands then facing the window. The garden.

"You have to understand that I'm doing this for your own good, because I love you so much," he used to say, after he had taken her into the bedroom and showed her how much he loved her. Had showed her stars and moons. Had taught her to see the entire Milky Way.

But first he untied her hair from the ponytail and fanned it out on the pillow.

She would wash it every day, to be certain that it smelled right.

"It was this beautiful hair that first caught my eye," he would say, winding a thick lock around his hand.

Now there is no one who loves her anymore.

She cries. Her whole body shakes.

"People who've been good together, who've had a good marriage don't grieve as much as people who've lived like cat and dog."

That was something Henny said once, when they were sitting in the sauna.

Tóra dries her eyes with one hand. With the other she moves the pepper mill behind the saltshaker.

"Like *that*," she says in an obstinate tone. Then she eyes the marigolds for a while, gets up, yanks them from the vase and crushes them into the already overflowing bin bag. She rinses the vase and puts it back in its place.

She sits immobile at the kitchen table as dusk falls. Stares into thin air or down at the tablecloth. Absently brushes some crumbs from the tablecloth into her palm. The only sound is the ticking of the kitchen clock.

She looks at the empty chair that always groaned when he sat down, looks at the door frame where the white paint is peeling on the spot he always used as a hand-rest, and at the stove, which will now go practically unused.

She remembers when that hand caressed her, and she liked it. Remembers how she would often lie and stare pleadingly, hungrily at his back. Remembers how she would reach her hand over, let it nearly graze him, sensing his warmth before pulling it back again. Sometimes she would satiate herself, so quietly that her breathing didn't betray her, because she also had to monitor that his breathing didn't change.

Afterwards she would lie for a long time gazing into the darkness, occasionally broken by a ray of light along the ceiling from a passing car.

Her eyes fall on the slippers left beside the chair, she forgot all about them. She stretches her foot over, nudges them closer and puts them on. They are far too big. Smooth inside. Worn. A flutter of tenderness billows through her. She lets her feet slide back and forth a couple of times. Like a child playing at being an adult. It feels safe.

She seeks out the sounds. Of how he drags his feet across the floor. Clears his throat at the table. Snores in the armchair and in bed through the night.

The low singing and whistling when he was gardening outside. He wanted her to come out and look every time a shoot pushed through. And she would stand there and marvel, while in her mind she moved one foot forward and trampled it.

It's dinnertime. She gets up and paces restlessly in the kitchen. Opens the fridge door. Brings something to the table, eyes it for a while then returns it to the fridge. Boils the kettle, hesitates a little, but then sets a mug for him too. Her hand trembles as she pours the water for him. She looks at the tea and wants to say something to him. Now she can. She tries, but the words won't come, they will, surely.

It's so quiet here. Much too quiet. She glances at the front door. It's possible to wish for something. To dream. She doesn't wish fervently, but like a person wondering if wishes are arranged according to whether you deserve them or not. Now perhaps one will come true.

She runs a hand through her long, thick locks. She is going to get her hair cut tomorrow. She is going to go from salon to salon until she finds a hairdresser, who can take her straightaway. She intends to have it cropped very short.

But the velvet curtains she can't get rid of just yet. It wouldn't seem decent somehow.

And perhaps someone will soon knock on her front door and offer her a new life.

"Come along," they will say. And they will get paintbrushes and freshen up the doorframe and the entire kitchen along with it, all the well-meaning people, and she will get up and help them.

And she is going to look forward to the weekends.

Tomorrow is mid October. She is bone tired.

The day is so short. Dusk comes along halfway through the day, and then it's dark.

She will miss him.

She hears the bus drive past outside and looks at the clock. The last departure of the night. She opens the front door and steps outside. Stands on the doorstep for a moment. Turns her face up to the darkness. It's drizzling. The darkness is empty, but when she looks over her shoulder at the house, where there is light in every window, it's also dark inside.

The house is so big. Far too big.

But hasn't she spent countless waking nights here? And inside her it was neither winter nor summer. No. Too many fragments of the person she was are scattered here.

Not easy to part with something like that.

Something she once read comes to mind. In Africa somewhere there is a tall mountain. Locals say that the vultures nesting at the summit fly so high that they can see into the future.

In the end she is too exhausted to keep herself awake any longer. She heads to the bedroom. Stops a moment and looks at the double bed. Only one half is made.

The room smells of soap.

She takes the duvet and pillow and makes up the sofa in the living room. The forlorn wedding portrait hangs here. She notices that the picture is crooked and straightens it a little, before she flicks off the lights.

She is going to sleep now, and until she dozes off she is just going to lie and search the night for sounds that are no longer here.

The Seal Woman

by

Marjun Syderbø Kjelnæs

translated by Lindy Falk van Rooyen

The door shuts behind her. Ever so slowly, the nurse begins to climb. The stairway is high. A tower of grey steel over her head. Her rubber-soled shoes thud on the steps, but the sound cannot reach the ceiling before it fades into nothingness. To her left, she grips onto the shiny black handrail that runs all the way to the top floor, as if a twisting black ribbon of mourning inside her soul. She holds onto the rail tightly and hauls herself upwards.

Outside the metal door on the top floor she comes to a halt. Despite twenty years of experience, the feeling still surfaces once in a while: an icy fear which creeps up her throat and trickles down into the tips of her fingers, as if the future gradually steals away her life; clairvoyance does not sit well with the scientific nature of her profession. But she has learnt to live with her gift. When she was younger, the premonitions were stronger and more intense. Heaven knows she cried countless tears over events only *she* knew were going to happen. It made her feel unbearably exposed. When she trembled with fear, her colleagues thought she was too thin-skinned, or simply lacked the necessary endurance for the job.

"You can never give up," an elderly, more experienced colleague once told her when she confessed that she was considering a change of profession. "A nurse can *never* give up!"

She is still not convinced that the matron with bushy eyebrows and a bun at the base of her neck had a patent on the truth. But that day, she chose to do as matron said. She chose not to give up; she makes the same choice again every day, and with time her nerves seemed to have been invigorated. Now she just lets the fear course through her veins. So she takes a deep breath, as if to fill her lungs before diving several fathoms down, and launches herself into an all-white world, ensconced in white.

"Rocka, rocka, my baby…"

The sound is coming from behind a grey screen at the far end of the ward. She folds it back and smiles at Marin, the little old lady resting in the bed in the corner. According to her file, Marin is close to ninety years old. Till now, she has lived in a retirement home, but they could no longer take care of her there. A few weeks ago, Marin fell and broke her hip, so they sent her here, to the hospital. Her family is now hoping for a referral to an alternative institution. Marin herself is oblivious to both time and place.

Her eldest daughter, who is about seventy years old, visits Marin faithfully. She has forbidding stories to tell about her mother's retirement home: "It's like getting letters from Bethlehem," she says. The home is cramped and no one takes any proper care of her frail mother. She would have liked to do so herself—she has done so before—but she's not up to the task any more, due to a bad back. She has worked at the fish factory for most of her life, her husband needs care as well, her younger sisters can't help either, her own children have far too much on their own plates, same goes for her grandchildren, who have to concentrate on getting an education, not to mention everything else that goes along with being young these days, some of them live in Denmark anyway, but every time she visits her mother it feels like she has a physical burden on her back, weighing her down.

The nurse tells the woman that she understands perfectly and lets her rattle on. She knows that it would help to ease her bad conscience.

The tip of Marin's pointy red nose peeks out from under the large duvet that she has pulled right up under her chin. Her wispy hair is chalk-white and her eyes are pale-blue as pools of water. "Rocka, rocka, my baby," Marin says tenderly, as she rocks herself back and forth in her bed.

"Are you rocking the child to sleep?" she asks, pulling up a chair and gently taking one of the old lady's hands in hers. She gives it a squeeze; Marin's hand is ice-cold.

The old lady cocks her head. Looks at her kindly. "Ssh," she whispers. "He just won't settle down tonight." Then she begins to sing a Faroese lullaby:

"*Rocka, rocka, my baby,*
The witch is now in chains,
Mamma is threshing corn,
Pappa is blowing the lur-horn

Creep out of your crab's shell,
The hag is here no more;
Without her wicked wand,
She failed to get a single bite..."

Marin's words falter mid-stanza. She forgets the lines, jumbles them up. Finally, she falls silent altogether, but it's as if her body recalls the lullaby's rhythm, and it keeps rocking her back and forth, back and forth. Marin has a pillow in her arms. Here, listening to the gentle beat of her mother-heart, nine children found peace and comfort in her warm embrace. She has drifted into a dream: she is a young girl once more, walking along the cattle tracks on the green mountain slopes. The proud leader of the flock, Marin has a milk pail strapped on her back, her chin lifted to meet the spring breeze. The cheerful laughter of the other milkmaids mingles with the call of a bird building its nest in the heather. The scent of peat, moss and crowberry lingers... the damp corn fields quiver with the promise of summer in the air. The lush village nestles in the beautiful valley with a sea view, like a contented cat purring, curled up on a warm stone in the sun. Now Marin kneels by the stream with her mother. They are washing a huge pile of clothing. The water is clear and bitterly cold, turning her small fingers blue. Her mother's eyes search the horizon, but there is no sign of a boat, not yet; it's too soon to expect the fishermen home. They fold their wet washing into a basket and get to their feet. Best they hurry home to prepare dinner, she thinks.

The ward is empty around them. In one corner, three steps lead up to a glass cage. Computers and medical apparatus, blinking lights, slim green lines showing the vital signs of patients resting elsewhere.

"Your hands are so cold, Marin," she smiles and lays a hand on the white scarf wrapped around the old lady's head.

"Get up and stoke the hearth for me, Sámal," Marin says. "There's a good boy."

In the final embrace of the sun, the evening sky like a deep red canvas depicts charcoal clouds that are gradually dissolving into the air until darkness whips her black cape over the islands. The ward is peaceful. White coats move slowly through the corridors, whispering to one another, checking in on the patients. Someone in a distant ward finally stops moaning and falls into an unfeeling, dreamless sleep instead.

In the distant pitch darkness, wet windowpanes shatter, young dreams escape, flee from the car and depart into death. Sorrow and black steel shred souls asunder. One moment, squeals of laughter, the next, showers of glass shards, an almighty crash, then… silence. Broken hearts.

The car flips several times, comes down hard on the asphalt and skids sideways. The rear wheels wedge in a stream by the roadside. The headlights blink aimlessly into the fjord.

Resting her forehead against the cool glass, she is standing by the window on the top floor of the hospital. Everything is ready: beds, instruments and medication. All they can do now is wait—with trembling hearts—for the ambulance to arrive. Half an hour ago, just after the call came in, the car accident seemed distant and unreal. But the man's voice still rings in her mind: "Multiple deaths at the scene… they were just kids. We're heading for Tórshavn now."

Two nurses dab the corners of their eyes as they bring out the oxygen lines. Another has a face like stone. In the middle of the night, lab assistants, doctors, porters and anaesthetists called in from home and other departments filter down the corridor. Everyone asks the same questions—*When*? *Where*? *How*?—as they check the instruments, register vital signs, point and give a series of instructions. Everyone is saying their prayers.

Her mind is elsewhere: her youngest son is fourteen years old. He desperately wants a scooter and he keeps nagging her to buy one for him. Her eldest son has just turned 18. He already has a driver's licence. She hopes and prays that both her sons are sound asleep in their beds. "Please, dear God, don't let it be one of mine," she prays under her breath. She knows it's selfish, but she can't help it; a protective, maternal instinct. It's the same for everyone, and she can see a similar prayer written in the faces of her colleagues.

The lift arrives and two yellow jackets on either side of a gurney rush in. She knows that terrible images from the accident are still fresh in their minds, slowly burning into memories, which they will try to forget. But the images will return. In their nightmares they are still on their knees in the mud, rain and blood, looking for signs of life.

The body on the gurney is jostled about involuntarily, it's a young woman—no, just a girl—badly smashed up. Her hair is wet, her face is disfigured and her dark, brown eyes stare vacantly into space.

"One, two, three." Many hands work in unison to transfer the battered body onto a bed. Now a hopeless battle against the clock begins. Doctors prick holes into bloodless vessels, nurses pump air into collapsed lungs. The limbs of the body jerk under the shocks administered to it. They *will* the heart to beat. Just once. But there is no life to save. No soul to keep.

An intern refuses to give up. His face is smeared in tears and sweat, his arms hang loosely by his side. He grabs the defibrillator again and yells at the nurse: "Clear! Clear!" The nurse takes him by the shoulders: "Put it down, now," she says gently. "She's gone. We've lost her." The surgeon looks up at the clock on the wall: "Time of death: 4:36 am." His words send a shiver through the team. They look up. Recognise the powerlessness reflected in each other's eyes. A monotone sound comes from an instrument behind them. The seconds that follow in silence feel unbearably long. Then a restlessness descends. The doctors yank off their blood-soaked gloves, disinfect their hands, wish each other good night. Everyone disperses in their separate directions.

The intern takes a seat on the step up to the glass cage. Buries his face in his hands.

A foreign doctor on the team goes to the window. Stares gloomily into the darkness outside, lost in thought. He has a hard time understanding the locals. The Faroes is such a beautiful country. And its people are free. They have no wars and no hunger, no deprivation to speak of, but most of them don't seem to appreciate what they have. Where he comes from, death is a daily occurrence. Civil war, hatred and mayhem are so close to home that they grate on him. He has lost two brothers. And his mother, a gentle and kind old lady. She spent the last moments of her life on her knees, begging for mercy, her fingers still sticky with the dough of the bread she was baking. He found her in their kitchen when he came home.

Now he feels as if he's still on the kitchen floor, tears pouring down his face, holding her lifeless body in his arms. *Dear, beloved mother!* And now he is here, a windswept archipelago in the far North Atlantic. A stranger, alone in a foreign country. He feels as if he's on the fringe of the world. The people on this island have been more than hospitable, he cannot deny that, but it's as if the welfare and surplus of their society has made them… indifferent. As if their vision is drowned in victory, or saturated in boredom. And they waste their lives on expensive cars. No, he does not claim to understand the Faroese people, but he understands his own people even less. The world we live in is incomprehensible.

The foreign doctor turns away from the window and walks over to the nurse to talk to her about what has happened. Little by little the ward empties.

Now she is alone with the dead girl. It is incredibly peaceful, a death silence. She fills a small, steel bowl with soapy water. Prepares the disposable cloths for cleaning the dead body. It's as if all the sounds around her accumulate and resound in her head; her feet shuffling to and from the bed, her own shallow breathing, the metallic chime as she puts the bowl down. The water turns red-brown as soon as she starts: first, she wipes around the closed eyes of the corpse. Then she dabs the forehead. Her skin is cool and pale like ivory under the mud.

So young—w*hy*? *why*?

The thoughts of the intern on the step interrupt her own.

The foreign doctor is talking to her colleague: "Why would they gamble with their lives like that?"

She mulls over his question. Could it be something

particular to the Faroese, which is difficult for a foreigner to understand? No, she can't say that she understands it either; she cannot comprehend why death came for this girl so early. Taking stupid risks could be one explanation. Could it be a case of a lack of community, no common sense of identity? This was the suggestion offered by a historian whose lecture on Faroese history she once attended. He proposed that the Faroese society has undergone so many significant and wide-reaching changes in the last century that the nation itself has lost its identity; the Faroese soul has been lost in an evolutionary process. We have no sense of who we really are, he said. This is why we are overly courageous. And why we play with our lives.

But she knows better than trying to fit things into neat little boxes. There's no point in trying to understand all the connections in the world at once. This is not the right place. And definitely not the right time.

"Dearest, child," she whispers, once again horrified at how young this girl was. Slowly she brushes the long, dark hair, as if a mother preparing her daughter for school. Once in a while, she takes a break. Sighs. Starts brushing again. A wave rises in her chest, threatening to overwhelm her, and she closes her eyes. A biblical passage she once learned by heart comes to her lips, and she mouths the words silently: "The Lord is my shepherd… though I walk through the valley of the shadow of death, I will fear no evil, for… for…" She forgets… suddenly, it feels all-important to recall the words—right now—as if only they can save her from the rough seas in her mind. "For… she holds her breath. For… thou art with me." Relieved, she exhales and continues her work.

The girl has a muddy silver heart locket around her neck. She unfastens it and washes the chain under hot running tap water. When she dries it with a white cloth she sees the engraving: *For Sára, with love, dad.*

*

The rain is pounding on the window. The sound sucks her back in time, as if dropping down the chute of childhood memory: "Listen how hard it is raining outside."

She is at home with her parents in the pitch dark. The rain is so hard it sounds as if waves of wind and water are thrashing against the roof. A constant rush of water from above. But they are snug and warm in their living room below. Wrapped in a woollen blanket, she snuggles up to her mother beside her.

"Oh, it's so lovely to be indoors when it's raining," her mother says to her father. "Yes," he replies. "Or caught in a downpour outside—as long as you have the right clothing for it—walking back in the dark, bowed against the wind with the knowledge that soon you will reach the comfort of your home," he adds with a smile. She knows what he means, appreciates his humble patience and gratitude; this is the soul of her father. His memory is a stab in her gut. And without him it's as if she's suspended naked over an eternal void; it's been with her for a long time, but all that remains is a gaping sense of loss.

*

Now she is done preparing the head of the dead girl so she moves to the other end of the bed. Little feet in white socks are sticking out from beneath the white sheet that covers the body. As she carefully removes the socks, she notices that one of the legs is lying at an awkward angle. She tries to ease it into a more comfortable position. Taking hold of the heel, she lifts the leg, but only the part below the knee moves; the thigh bone is crushed. Her hand flies to her mouth and she flees out of the room.

Two other nurses come in and take over. They cut off the remainder of the girl's clothing and bind her body; the leg is so shattered they have to hold it together with large strips of gauze and medical tape. The sight of congealed blood and a sweet, rancorous smell will remain in their minds long after they get home. In a heavy silence, tender hands do for the girl what little can be done: her body is dressed in clean, white clothing, and laid out on a clean, white bed. They fold the hands over her chest and light a dim lamp by her bedside.

Even though she has done a nurse's report hundreds of times before, she lets someone else write it. Nor can she face calling the parents. Not tonight.

"What is the best way to give the parents the news?" asks her distressed young colleague, who has been assigned the task in her stead.

"Come, I will help you," she says, in spite of herself.

They take a seat in their nurse's station to make the call together. After the difficult conversation with the parents, she puts her arms around the young nurse: "I woke them up," she says in a trembling voice. "Their voices sounded so peaceful. At first, I thought they had misunderstood me."

"Yes, I know," she says, trying to comfort the young nurse. "But you mustn't give up," she hears herself say, even if her tone is different to the matron's.

A short while later they can hear that the parents of the dead girl have arrived in the corridor. They go out to greet them, shake hands and offer their condolences. Words seem so base and utterly meaningless. Sára's father is a tall man. He takes a seat on a chair against the wall. Stares at the linoleum floor, hugging himself, as if his entire body is in physical pain. Sára's mother is pacing back and forth along the corridor. She does not want to shake hands with anyone, but immediately asks to see her daughter.

They show the parents into the ward.

Later, more relatives arrive; siblings, the grandmother and grandfather. The white coats try to comfort them. There are many questions, few answers. Stories about Sára are quietly shared: Sára was in her final year of High School and wanted to become a vet one day. Her loved ones listen to each other, remembering Sára. She wanted to travel the world. Now her dreams are broken. The parents pour cups of coffee and pace the corridor. They are grateful that they have one another. The parents sit on hard chairs and recall their beloved daughter's childhood, her first steps. And now the tears come. They cry for a long time. Silently. The parents hug each other, inconsolable. No one in the world knows the pain they feel at this moment. Their tears come from deep inside. Beseeching tears, as if they were calling their daughter back to the cold, pale body that lay on the bed before them.

It is good that they cry like this, she thinks. When she was in nursing school, she secretly used to take books home with her from the library. She would spend hours on her couch, reading musty old books about the human psyche, looking for answers to the questions that plagued her. And now she recalled an ancient Jewish parable: Adam and Eve were banished from the Garden of Eden, but God could see that they were sorry for their sins. He took pity on them and said: "My dear children! I have punished you for your sins, and banished you from the Garden of Eden, where you have lived a carefree life. Now you will go out into a world of grief that cannot be described in words. But you should know that I am gracious, and that my love for my children is eternal. I know the hardship you meet will make you bitter, so now I will give you a precious gift, the divine pearls known as tears: whenever your agony becomes unbearable saltwater will pour from your eyes, and the moment the tears come, your burden will feel lighter to bear."

Adam and Eve were amazed by what they heard. Tears poured from their eyes and fell onto the dry earth at their feet; these tears were the first moisture to quench the earth. Adam and Eve passed this precious gift onto their children. And ever since, whenever human beings experience great pain or sorrow, salt tears will escape from their eyes. And yes, they will feel some relief from their awful burden of sorrow.

She chided herself for thinking about beautiful stories in the terrible reality of the moment.

"Rocka, rocka, my baby." Marin has woken up behind the screen.

During the course of the night, she checked on her from time to time, but always found the old lady fast asleep. When news of the car accident was reported, the staff transferred her to a different ward; her frail body was taken away in silence, in the dark, by the hands of strangers, the sum total of her possessions transported on a gurney.

Now she stands by Marin's bedside. The old lady looks at her tenderly, as if she would like to say something, but cannot find the words. Instead, she begins to sing the lullaby again, and somehow, it comforts her soul.

Marin has wet her bed so she starts changing the sheets. The lady's old body is rigid and awkward so it's difficult to move her in the bed. She lays out a crisp, white sheet. Marin has been watching her all the while, her eyes wide open, but now her glance shifts to the window. She looks across the Sound to the neighbouring island. A boat is heading out of the fjord and its sail billows out in the wind. Marin begins to cry.

"I'll be done in just a minute, Ma'am," she says. "Then you can lie down in peace."

The night shift is almost over. She takes a seat in the office with the other nurses. On the wall is a board where all the names and birthdates of the patients are written in a black, felt-tip pen. They rub the names out as soon as the patients are well enough to be discharged. She notes that there are almost 80 years' difference between the birthdates of Marin and Sára; it seems somehow wrong and strange that the youngest name should be erased first.

Shift change is at seven o' clock. As the sun rises, the town awakes, as if stretching its limbs in the pale morning light. Her colleagues have just woken up, and now they are standing before her, ready to take over the patients in the ward.

Whilst she is bringing the new nurses up to speed they hear voices singing a hymn; its coming from Sára's room. She stops talking for a moment. Listens. Then continues her handover report; it's a relief to tell the others what has happened.

She goes down the stairway again. Now the black ribbon of mourning is on her righthand side. Lady night brought her legend, fate and mystery. As if a selkie in a white skin, she swam through the dark water, between portent, rocks and skerries. That story has always fascinated her; the fate of being caught between two worlds. The selkie lived two lives, and so does she. In her grey skin, the selkie swims free in the wide oceans, with her own kind, and this appears to be her favoured choice. But on the Thirteenth Night, the seals swam ashore and danced on the rocks in front of the seal cave. Naked in the moonlight. Perhaps her freedom exists in the choice itself? But as the legend goes, the man from Mikladalur stole her skin while she danced. She was the most beautiful and passionate woman he had ever seen, so he took her seal skin. And this was the reason why she was unable to return to the sea. The choice was taken from her.

She recalls one summer, many years ago, when she and her husband took the children on a daytrip. The boys wanted to see if they could catch some baby coalfish, so they took a drive to the rocky shore. The boys were still small and they had to lead them by hand over the sharp, rocky steps. She remembers their happy faces with their bright-red noses as they sat on the rocks, fishing with their dad. There was a cove nearby, and she decided to go for a walk along the rocks, deep into the black mountain gorge. High above her, the white waterfall roared. It gushed over the edge of the cliff and plummeted onto the wet stones below. She stood there for a long time, as if caught in a thunder cloud, letting pearls of moisture cling to her face, hair and clothing.

Joyfully, she made her way back down to shore, but about twenty minutes later, she came upon a seal cave. She sat down on a large rock that was raised above the spray of water. Silent, listening. All at once she saw a grey head stick up above the sea, directly in front of her perch on the rock. It was a seal, scanning the coast, it's head swivelling like the periscope of a submarine that checks to see if it's safe to surface. More heads appeared above the water. Long nose hairs and opal eyes. The seals hauled themselves up onto a skerry and made themselves comfortable in the warm sun. The largest male seals secured the best seats in the sun for themselves, the females stayed on the edge, closest to the water, but the cubs didn't venture out of the water, simply fooled around in the surf in between the skerries.

An old man from the village once told her that the cubs were so curious and playful that many of them were caught and killed before they were a year old. She sat watching them frolic in the waves for a long time, entranced. Then she heard one of her boys yell in the distance.

The image of the cave, the seal woman's story and the silver-grey creatures in front of the cave that day, the entire scene, became a recurring dream in her life ever since. She recalls the particular thickness of the seal skins. Under their coats they have a generous layer of fat, which is essential for their survival in the ice-cold sea.

The nurse takes a seat on a step for a moment. It's as if her soul is reaching upwards, restless and agitated.

Catching her breath, she remembers an anecdote about a tribe in darkest Africa. They were nomads, who take flight on foot, but along the way they like to sit down from time to time, waiting for their souls to catch up before forging ahead on their journey. For her, it feels as if she were coming up to the surface to fill her lungs with air. Then she goes home to get some sleep, only to dive into the deep again at night.

A hand gently rests on her shoulder: "Rough night?" a voice asks. She looks up, nods. Manages to bring a sad smile to her lips.

When she finally reaches the cellar, exhausted, she sheds her white coat.

On Location

by

Katrin Ottarsdóttir

translated by Lindy Falk van Rooyen

The ferry sailed out of the fjord and headed into open sea. All morning they pretended that nothing was wrong and conversed in single syllable words. Tea, egg, boil, soft, hard, cheese, jam, roll, toast, yes, no, thanks. No unpleasantries. The pigsty is not even mentioned. Nor, for that matter, the night we spent in the hotel. It's as if yesterday never happened.

They were sitting at the breakfast table. He, chomping on his food and slurping on his coffee. She had no appetite whatsoever, agonising over yesterday instead: *How can you sit there, in silence, pretending that nothing has happened?! You cannot possibly have forgotten your loathsome behaviour?! Infinitely condescending. Nothing is below you. Are you* really *so adept at forgetting what you don't care to dwell on?*

She has decided that the best course of action is simply to pretend that nothing happened, because she knows what he's like. He can wriggle out of any awkward situation; he turns everything in his favour. She refuses to give him the satisfaction of thinking that he can manipulate her, make her doubt everything, especially herself; she will not let him make her believe that she is mistaken, that she is just another paranoid little girl.

But here they are, onboard the ferry, on their way home again. In three hours, she will no longer have to be near him, no longer have to listen to him. She hitches up her camera equipment and adjusts the straps over her shoulders; she loves the weight of it, loves the feel of it. She should never have gotten herself into this situation. She should have insisted on her right to leave. Even though he has the power; someone like him always does.

Why does she have to be here at all? Why is she not in the comfort of her own flat? She closes her eyes for a moment. Allows herself to be drawn back in time, determined to know whether her brain is playing tricks on her, whether she can do it, can turn the camera around, inwards.

So she closes her eyes and delves into her mind, opens memory's door and locks it behind her.

Still blissfully ignorant, she accompanies him to the pigsty which, till moments before, he had not mentioned to her. The road is newly paved and it feels as if they're driving on a polished dining room floor. The Volvo is old, but it's the best car that the radio station owns. The Sony camera equipment is safely stowed in the boot; she packed it herself, of course.

She loves driving, loves to feel the pistons working for her—the harder the better—but right now she would rather be any place other than in the car with this balding, would-be anchorman who is half-asleep on the front seat next to her, straining his seatbelt, exuding sticky bad breath.

He made her take this trip with him, just because he'd suddenly had the brilliant idea to film a documentary about some ill-fated pigsty on a deserted island. And she had done everything she could not to end up alone with him at the little hotel—the only hotel on the island, but he was the one who called the shots, and with a snap of his fingers, he could have her replaced. They arrived at the terminal just in time to see the last ferry depart. It was like feeling her lifeline slip through her fingers, as she watched the ferry cast off and head for the horizon in a cloud of steam. All the while, she felt his eyes burn into her cheek, knowing, smug. It was all she could do to grin and bear it.

She knew that he could see the look of dismay on her face. He was aware of her misgivings about his motives, but he just smiled his trademark hollow, condescending smile. Not to her, not even to himself, but to the waves, sea and earth. She had no doubt that he could taste it; the sweet sensation of his own power.

She had to keep a cool head and resolved to find strength in her own powerlessness.

When she looks up the ferry is no more than a dot on the horizon. Her head feels as if it were about to burst with pent up anger and fear. The lust for revenge surges inside her. He leans back against his seat, glancing at her through half-closed eyes. He wets his lips with the tip of his tongue and smoothes down the edges of his toupee.

"Do you think that our little community needs all your fine learning and education?"

Yes, as a matter of fact, she does. Every community in the world could stand a little erudition.

"Most friends left the island to stuh-dee," he says with

a scornful snort. "They pissed off to bigger towns on other islands, or Copenhagen. I could've done the same, of course, but I chose to stay behind and read books which I chose myself—not to mention sleep with as many women as I choose," he adds, winking at her. "I've bedded more women than all those men with their fancy papers put together."

An exasperated sigh almost escapes her lips, but she manages to bite it back.

Why the hell was she here, anyway?! Why should she drive this man around on a godforsaken island when she could be back home with someone else? The entire scene is ridiculous.

"Impressive," she says, doing her best to keep her voice even.

The trademark smile slithers over her. She shudders, feels as if a jellyfish has latched onto her face and neck.

"I can assure you that I've read many more books than all those people who call themselves journalists just because they've studied at the right schools and went to university."

"You mean people like me?"

She's unwilling to look at him, does not want to see his side-parting, which is etched into his toupee, straight as an arrow, his white scalp-line littered with dandruff. Someday she ought to ask him if he uses a ruler. She trains her eyes on the road, focuses on the markings in the centre.

They're descending into a beautiful valley, and ordinarily, she would have let her eyes feast on the sight. But today—with this man in the car—it's impossible.

He snorts again. Asks how many books *she* has read.

"I've no idea," she says honestly. "I wasn't keeping count. I've been devouring books from the moment I learnt how to read; as soon as I finished one, I began the next. I'm twenty-three years old, learnt to reading for pleasure when I was six, and read at an average speed. Then I went to school and university, and worked my way through everything that was prescribed by the curriculum. You can do the maths yourself."

He says he's not inclined to do the maths. But he asks what she's reading at the moment.

She hesitates, not sure what to tell him; she has no desire to share any personal information with this man.

"Or maybe you'd rather tell me how many men you've slept with?" He snorts again. "And *of course* you have to keep count, my dear. Including how many times you've been taken from behind. Remember *that* the next time you're on your knees with your arse in...

She grits her teeth.

"Damn Dostoevsky," he says instead. "His letters. Right now, I'm reading about his gambling habit... roulette, his debts, and... nervous breakdown." He spits out the words 'nervous breakdown' as if the syllables were globs of bitter chewing tobacco in his mouth. "It's ridiculous. Men don't have nervous breakdowns... but what about you?" he asks. "How many nervous breakdowns have you had?"

She puts her foot down, and the car speeds up, plunging them into the mouth of a black tunnel. She smiles to herself when she sees his knuckles go white on the door handle. He's audibly grating his teeth, too, but apart from this, he doesn't make a sound. In the distance, the light at the end of the tunnel appears like an alluring, white eye, but a dark object obscures it almost immediately. For a moment, all daylight is extinguished by an otherworldly fiend on wheels. The headlights of their

Volvo only illuminates a short stretch of the road before them, beyond their beam the tunnel is pitch black, but just before absolute darkness engulfs them, a line of bright, colourful bulbs appear, and she recognises the monster for what it in fact is: a glittering amusement-park truck approaching from the opposite end.

She switches to the oncoming lane, speeds up even more, waiting for a reaction from the man in the seat next to her—a curse, a word, anything to puncture his bloated condescension. At last she hears a gasp escape from his lips. Satisfied, she grits her teeth and swerves the Volvo back into the right lane. The truck roars past, and the piercing sound of its horn rings in their ears as their car bursts into the daylight at the other end.

She takes her foot off the accelerator, the car gradually slows down, and the landscape opens up before them. In a barely audible voice, he asks her to stop the car because he needs to take a pee; so he says.

She pulls over next to some boulders that jut into the road. Tells him he can go and do whatever he needs to behind them. He winks at her and gets out of the car. Outrageously, he takes two steps and pees against the rocks, directly in front of the fender. She doesn't flinch and watches him relieve himself, a bland expression on her face.

A violent gust of wind shakes the chassis. Her eyes remain fixed on him, marvelling over the fact that his toupee remains in place, as if cemented onto his skull. She can't understand why he doesn't just shave it all off? Then no one would know he was bald. What little hair he does have is a greasy, black band circling his head, just above his ears. *Why should she care if he insists on making a fool of himself?*

Her gaze drifts to the horizon, but there is nothing to be seen out there. Neither ferry nor any other boats. No cars either. *Has the world stopped turning?* It's as if the asphalt has turned into sand. That's just perfect. The last thing she wants is to be stuck in a time warp—whether real or surreal—with this man that she cannot stand.

He gets back into the car. The smile is back. With an added twist of deceit. It makes her suspicious, furious, tired. He tells her that he once had sex with a woman behind those rocks.

"A lecherous filly, she was," he says. "Married, too. I didn't have the heart to ruin a good memory by pissing on our bed of passion."

She makes no comment. He changes the subject. Asks if she missed the Faroese landscape when she was away studying or whatever the hell it was she did. She laughs it off. Says he would know better than her.

They travel in silence for a while. Then he asks if she has read all Dostoevsky's books?

She admits that she hasn't. For example, she says, she hasn't had a chance to read *A Day in the Life of Ivan D*...

The words are out of her mouth before she can stop them. She could have bitten her tongue in half. She's done it again. For some reason, she always mixes up Dostoevsky with Solzhenitsyn. Perhaps she ought to make a point of reading Solzhenitsyn's book, so she doesn't keep confusing him with Fyodor... of course the would-be anchorman is eager to point out her ignorance.

"I knew it, missy," he says smugly. "I knew you were one of those college girls who can't distinguish one great novel from another. Confuses the Russians. I've met many of your sort. Rest assured, you're not the first."

She reckons that her best strategy is just to let him think that she's less intelligent than he is. Then he'll become obsessed with educating her, and revel in the pleasure of one-upmanship. In the meantime, she'd hopefully be spared from hearing any more graphic details about his sex life.

She feigns surprise.

"What? That wasn't Dostoevsky?!"

He eyes her for a moment, gently, overbearingly. "No, it wasn't, pussycat. Dostoevsky didn't write that one. Solzhenitsyn did. You ought to know the difference."

He's enjoying himself immensely, she can tell.

"You must be mistaken," she says, bone tired of this conversation.

"No, I'm not. You're welcome to come over to my place tonight, so I can show you. I'll let the wife know you're coming in the meantime." All at once saccharine-sweet, he flashes her a genuine smile.

"There's no need for that. I know I'm right. Remember that *I'm* the one who's been to university, after all," she snaps.

He laughs at her. Tells her not to fret her pretty little head about that. It will only give her wrinkles on her brow. Pretty young lasses shouldn't have worry-lines on their forehead from thinking too much.

They've arrived at their destination. He looks eager as a schoolboy now, and the smile is back as he tells her to hurry up and bring the camera equipment with her. Soon she will see the light, he assures her. Then he gets out of the car and disappears into the barn.

The moment she sets foot inside, laden with the bulky

equipment, the acrid stench of piss hits her in the solar plexus in a full-frontal onslaught. She steels herself, knowing that he is watching her, even as he stands chatting with the pig farmer on the far side, sniffing for her tiniest hesitation, the merest sign of weakness. She tightens the brace around her waist, taking comfort in the restraint of the girdle about her hips, it helps her to keep it together; grounding her, keeping her centred. Flexing her abdominal muscles, she lifts the 7 kg camera and positions it on her shoulder. With practised ease, she pulls back her shoulders and thrusts out her chest. Then she takes a deep breath through her mouth and marches over to the two men who are languidly watching her every move.

She turns her back on the would-be anchorman and extends her hand to the farmer in greeting. He has a bear grip, as one might have expected from a man who lives off the land. She has a sense that he sympathises with her, however, and his smile is genuine, not in the least bit hollow and it reaches his eyes. She returns his smile in kind. Tells her anchorman that she's ready to roll.

"Just tell me when you'd like me to begin filming?" she says in a professional tone.

She hears a hefty grunt from one of the stalls. She turns her head and she sees a huge hog mount a sow standing in front of him in the pigsty. The anchorman chuckles to himself and wets his lips again. He asks her to come along, prodding her ahead of him with one of his fat—surprisingly hard—little sausage fingers.

The hog appears to be struggling. With every attempt, he flounders, slips off the back of the sow. The anchorman tells her to start filming immediately. She starts rolling and adjusts her lens. No sooner has the hog succeeded in getting his front legs up, than the battle to penetrate the sow begins. The anchorman rests a hand on her shoulder, points directly at the pigs, tells her to zoom in. Keep zooming, keep zooming, he says, tells her to get a little closer still, on her knees.

Her lens trained on the pigs, she complies without thinking, puts her knee down, feels the cold as the soggy surface seeps through the fabric of her jeans.

More than anything else, she wants to knock this idiot over the head with her camera, pull down his pants and shove his arse into the stall with the rest of the pigs; so he could get taken from behind by that hapless hog and its useless snake-like penis. But she resists the impulse, and lets him rest two fingers on her camera and push it down to get a close-up on the mating pigs. Despite the seven kilogrammes of electronic equipment on her shoulder, she can feel the pressure of his fat sausage finger on the camera, and her arm is aching. She knows he won't let her stop filming until the hog has spent his energy in every sense. As if a robot, she continues filming the mating pigs. Sees nothing, hears nothing, not even the anchorman's panting breath, probably in sync with every thrust and squeal coming from the hog. Instead, she thinks about the letters of Dostoevsky. Reminds herself of all the strife and struggles that he met in his life. If Fyodor could endure it, the least she could do is survive filming on location with this swine and his brothers.

He's standing in the hotel reception, boasting about the pigsty documentary to anyone who cares to listen. She tries to slip past unnoticed, laden with equipment, her earphones in place, which at least helps to drown out some of his voice. But of course she's not going to get away that easy; she almost makes it to the stairs, but unfortunately at that point, she drops a camera pole, which clatters down the steps behind her.

Barely getting the chance to berate herself for her clumsiness, he's already there, at the foot of the stairs, offering to give her a hand. He picks up the pole and takes the two steps up to her level, a ridiculous grin all over his face. He reminds her to take better care of the property of the National Radio Broadcaster that the Faroese taxpayers have paid for with their own blood, sweat and tears.

She gives him an indulgent smile. Accepts the pole and tucks it under her arm awkwardly, doing her best to juggle all the remaining equipment which is hooked, strapped and girded to various parts of her body. Then she turns on her heel and tries to get the hell away from him. But he puts his hand on her arm. Reluctantly, she stops in her tracks. He asks what she has planned for the rest of the evening.

"I think I'll get an early night," she says. "You ought to do the same. The ferry leaves early tomorrow morning," she reminds him. "And right now, I'd like to put away this equipment, before it breaks me in half."

He shrugs, and she takes her chance to leave. But he follows her down the corridor and up to the first floor. When they get as far as his door, her composure fails and she gives him a piece of her mind: she asks him what the hell he was thinking?! Who is interested in a 'documentary' about copulating pigs!? Or was this trip purely for his own amusement?! It was absolutely unacceptable that he should bring her on such a ludicrous assignment!

He leans on his door, opens it and pauses on the threshold, looking at her with bloodshot, swollen puppy-dog eyes, which were starting to water now.

"If you knew how wretched I've been, you wouldn't talk to me like that," he says sulkily.

Fumbling in his inner jacket pocket, he draws out a flask. Helps himself to a little Dutch courage. Takes another big gulp and offers her some. She shakes her head. He snorts at her and screws the lid back on.

"I'm not a successful man, even though I might look like one," he goes on. "My wife just upped and left me. Took the kids with her. She's turned them against me. I haven't had contact with them for years." He sinks onto his knees, and to her dismay, starts to cry. She can't bear the thought of this asinine moron confiding in her, just because he's had too much to drink. Not to mention make her life at the station miserable just because he has the upper hand. *She will not let him get the better of her!*

She lets her equipment slide to the floor—in the middle of the corridor—and pulls him to his feet. Helps him to get into his room and take a seat on his bed. This is no mean task; he's overweight and it's difficult to move his flabby body. *How could he let himself go like that*? A shudder of revulsion runs down her spine and she's at pains not to let it show.

He sneezes, hard, says he has no joy in his life. He'll never get over his family deserting him. He looks up at her with pleading eyes and starts to ramble, asks her to stay, help him get through the night, they were the worst, the long, lonely nights, and she's so pretty, so strong, and he needs her youth and energy, which is so fresh and utterly irresistible.

She lets him talk. Helps him to lie down. Takes off his shoes. Covers him with a blanket and makes for the door.

"Please don't leave me, dear. Please stay with me, *you* are the only one who can help me tonight. Your precious Dostoevsky is not the only one having a nervous breakdown… the smarter the man, the greater the nerves… the strength needed to calm them… I'm terrified it will happen again… a breakdown… please, you must not…"

She closes the door behind her, hitches the heavy equipment onto her shoulders and hurries to her own room, which is only two doors further down. She locks the door and bolts it. Checks the handle, but she cannot make it more secure. Nothing can make her feel safe.

She plugs in the camera battery so it can charge overnight. Gets into bed, fully-clothed. She lies there, waiting, listening through paper-thin walls, both knowing and not knowing what she is waiting for. Her only solace and sense of reality in the darkness is the faint, blinking signal of the battery charging on the table against the wall; red and green blinks with a little blue in-between. The camera equipment. Her shield. Always.

And then she hears what she has been waiting for. The footsteps. Lurching down the corridor. They stop outside her door. He fumbles with the handle. She hears the door jamb rattle. The handle clicks down, several times, as if he cannot comprehend that the door is actually locked. Then he starts to knock and he keeps knocking. She tries to block out the sound, pretends—to herself, to him, in the face of the entire, shitty situation—that she's already gone to sleep.

In a raspy whisper, he calls her name through the key-hole. Then his voice breaks and he starts to sob, begging her to open the door. He says that he means her no harm, that he just wants to be with her, that they can have a beautiful night in each other's arms, he needs her, *she* needs him and she knows it, he pleads…

After this has gone on for at least a quarter of an hour, she can't take it anymore. She tells him to go back to his room, that everything will be better tomorrow, he just needs a good night's rest.

He keeps banging on the door.

She reminds him that he's still married after all, that his wife might be waiting for him at home, right now, eager for his return.

He changes tack. He's angry now. Tells her that she knows she wants him. That she's too afraid to give in to her desires. He kicks the door to make his point, so hard that the camera equipment shudders, the battery lights stutter and begin to blink in irregular beats. At long last the fool runs out of steam. Everything is quiet.

She closes her eyes and sleeps like a stone.

"Now! Are you lost in your own world?! We're at work, you know. And I said come here."

He wants her to capture him on film with the lonely pigsty on the green slopes in the background, so she follows him onto the deck. She is at his disposal. Everything she has to offer is strapped to her body; a defence against him, a wall against everything in this world. Her equipment. Indestructible, supportive and comforting.

He and his toupee have long since found their rightful place. He takes up a stance, the parting deftly faced away from the lens. He reaches out his hand, impatiently.

She gives him the microphone and he begins to talk immediately, not knowing that she hasn't connected it yet.

He starts to say a few words about pigs, their ability to survive, their potential to provide meat and sustenance to mankind. Then he winks at her and says that pigs can be utilised for much else besides, that they can liven up frigid young women with nothing but 'technical skills' at their disposal.

She zooms up to the talking mouth. Cracked lips moving, revealing his uneven teeth and something from his breakfast that is stuck between his front teeth. A seed of strawberry jam, perhaps.

The weather is fine with clear skies above. He says he wants her to shoot something for the optics—people love that kind of thing after all. She keeps her mouth shut, knows better than to give her opinion on fluffy pictures for aesthetic effect, sound journalism vs. sloppy craftmanship. Soon, they are sailing on the open sea, surrounded by the heavy swells, teasing and playful waves at the bow.

They move towards the stern. He wants a shot of himself with the railings in the background. He positions himself at the base of the ferry's steam pipes, in relative shelter from the wind. The toupee stays nicely in place, rigid on his scalp. He does his best to hold his head at a favourable angle that doesn't make it too obvious, though.

She keeps filming, doesn't bother to focus or adjust the contrast. He keeps talking into the microphone, explaining god-knows-what because she can hear the drone of his voice only, not the words themselves. Now he wants to move to the railing with the glittering wake whipping up behind him. Absolutely, this could work very nicely, she tells him. She's onboard one hundred percent. Inspired, she asks him to turn his body a little more towards her, so she can get a better angle. He hesitates, but his vanity gets the better of him. He twists towards her, looks directly into the lens. She asks him to back up a bit. Walks slowly towards him, passes the steam pipes, her feet sliding their way forward on the deck.

He keeps her eyes on her, and she asks him to back up a little more, tells him it's a great shot, he makes an extremely fine figure, this is exceptional reporting journalism, and he smiles, encouraged by her words. He keeps backing up, carefully; she keeps advancing, excited and terrified all at once. He's smiling at her, and his smile is neither hollow, condescending nor mean. In fact, he looks rather proud, victorious. She keeps advancing, foot by tentative foot, all she knows is what she can see unfolding before the lens, oblivious to all else.

Why has he stopped walking? she wonders and asks him to keep moving for the camera.

Someone is yelling something at them, loudly. It's a man's voice, a tone with innate authority. It might be the captain making an announcement over the loudspeaker. She resents his smug assumption of authority, just like the anchorman's. But she won't let them stop her now. She watches the anchorman watching her, his eyes open wide and she stares through the lens in surprise; there is a look in his eyes that she has never seen before. Perhaps he is seeing her properly for the first time, she thinks, and finally acknowledges her professionalism and superlative technical skills. But perhaps she's mistaken? And why is he coming towards her now?

She dodges him, tenses her muscles, corrects the familiar movement of her equipment, the ever-comforting weight bearing down on her body. She grits her teeth, he can go to hell. He is and always will be a pig. She keeps the lens trained on him, determined to document this man, even if it's just for herself, she thinks, as she steps into thin air.

The last thing she sees through the lens is the toupee, rising on end; it dovetails into a tiny, flapping firewall on the back of his head. It looks hilarious, and she laughs to herself, inwardly, as the weight pulls her down into the deep and everything goes black.

Disappearing Men

by
Firouz Gaïni

translated by Lindy Falk van Rooyen

One fine summer morning the bodies washed up on the shore. First one, then another. The third appeared in the surf around noon. The fourth soon followed with the tide. It was right here, just south of the new beach hotel with a sea view from the boulders that a little girl found them the following weekend; the corpses of four young men. The police soon arrived on the scene, hastily loaded them into a van and drove away. Someone made enquiries. But the media did not broadcast the incident. Then it happened again. This time, a young couple, tourists who had arrived on the islands the night before, came upon the lifeless bodies caught in the skerries off the coast. It was their first walk along the beach, and it was the first trip they had taken together. They had saved up for months in advance and booked an entire week in a large hotel on the paradise island. Their room had a large balcony jutting over the heavenly blue ocean. The sea was terrifying. And then this: hand in hand, shocked to the core, staring at three naked corpses. The woman burst into tears and yelled for help. Then she felt faint and keeled over. People who had heard the woman's call came running. The police were sent for. They arrived promptly and whisked away the dead. The next day, the young couple broke off their holiday early and went home; the woman could not bear to stay on the island.

Every week, additional corpses washed up on the shore. In the neighbouring town, which also boasted grand hotels for rich foreign tourists, they had hired trawlers to spread nets fifty metres from the shore—to prevent the bodies from being driven onto the land. It did not work very well. Even if the trawlers managed to gather them in the net temporarily, the sharks tore them apart in the water. No one ever knew what happened out there; people enjoyed themselves on the beach, without a thought about what was happening out at sea. The awkward problem of the tide of corpses grew day by day. Once, the net ripped and half-eaten body parts scattered and washed up right next to a group of children who were building sandcastles on the beach. The town council reacted swiftly and took measures to keep the tide of undesirables at bay: two policemen armed with binoculars and loaded rifles combed their coastline day and night. As soon as they spotted the bodies floating in the water, they closed the beaches and scooped up the corpses in a large net. No one knew about the clean-up operation. Indeed, most of the work was done at night. Dogs were also brought in to search the rocks along the shore. 'Tide-men' the policemen called themselves when they joked about their clandestine clean-up operation.

One fine summer morning five brothers boarded a flimsy, unpainted rowboat that was tethered to the landing bridge. They loaded a sack of food and a cask of water for their journey. The youngest brother, who was only nine years old, was not happy. He was afraid to go and tried his best to hold back his tears as he cast a sorrowful look over his shoulder at his mother. She was standing on the landing bridge amongst a group of relatives with grave expressions on their faces. The eldest brother, who had bought the boat for the journey, made a short speech to their family: he promised to take good care of his brothers and send word as soon as they arrived at their destination. He thanked his parents for everything they had done for him and his brothers. He assured them that they were strong and brave young men who were looking forward to setting out to sea. They would earn a living and send money back home to their family; they were leaving out of necessity. Before they cast off to sea, the brothers sang a lovely hymn about their homeland. They looked back at the small village where they were born and raised, the towering cliffs and deep valleys; they knew every cove, every stone, every tree. And when the village disappeared behind the horizon, it was the last time these men saw their homeland.

The storm broke on their very first day on open water. They saw two other boats capsize and sink into the vast bowels of the ocean. Two brothers, the youngest and the weakest, were washed overboard and disappeared under the massive crest of a wave. A few hours later, the remaining brothers succumbed to the storm; the sea swallowed the boat and dragged the men into the deep. The oldest and strongest brother, who had two daughters of his own, had locked an arm around each of his brothers by his side as they sank deeper and deeper into the darkness. The nameless graveyard. Later, the dead travellers washed up on the shore like driftwood. Naked, weather-beaten bodies that rolled ashore up north. The eldest brother lay on the sand with his two younger siblings on either side, his large, black hands still locked around their middles. The birds had long since pecked their eyes out. His head was swollen by the relentless pressure of the salt water. Even so, a hint of a smile lifted the corners of his mouth. As if he had simply drifted off to sleep with a pleasant thought at the moment of death. Or perhaps he took comfort in dying in the company of his beloved brothers, who he had taken care of ever since their father disappeared on a fishing trip up north. The father rested in peace with his own brothers in the nameless graveyard. Now only the women and small children of their family remained in the village.

The parents of the distressed young couple came to meet them at the airport. Somewhat unexpectedly, a few friends also came to welcome them home. Only two days had passed since they had waved their friends and family goodbye at the very same boarding gate. Laughing and joking, they promised to send a card for Christmas—should they decide that they weren't coming back before winter! Alma was wearing a new red dress that reached all the way down to her white, high-heeled sandals. The young man wore a straw hat pulled down over a pair of black sunglasses. They were ecstatic, enthusiastic and excited about their holiday, an unforgettable experience which they'd be bragging about to their friends at dinner parties for years to come. But nothing goes as planned. Now, all they wanted to do was return to their daily routine. The three blackened corpses on the beach had given them the shock of their lives. At first, Alma was the one who was particularly upset by the chain of events. But now the man was the one struggling to stay sane. He barely managed to greet his parents at the airport. He did not utter a single word in greeting and avoided eye contact, plagued by guilt.

On the paradise island life goes on as usual. But there has been a troubling development: it seems that many of the bodies are not corpses, but men still breathing! As it turns out, these experienced seafarers are so resilient that many of them—putting to shame all theories and expectations of certain death at sea—are still alive when they are washed ashore. Somehow, these men were able to keep their heads above water. They overcame even the most challenging battles against stormy seas during the night. The small airport on the island saw a sharp rise of foreign travellers, arriving in all seasons of the year. A steady stream headed north, filling the local hotels and beaches and creating prosperity for the shops and the local business community. All around the island, new hotels sprang up. But the tide of bodies from the south kept rolling in. And as I mentioned, sometimes they were still breathing. It was not feasible to scoop the live ones up in a net, so here a different solution had to be found. Nature alone could not stop them from coming ashore, so what could we do to protect our beaches against these uninvited guests? This was the question people discussed in reception halls and conference rooms all around the island.

Fatherless girls help their sick mothers to wash clothing in the river that runs through the village with the broad cove, which are known to be the best fishing grounds in the whole Faroese archipelago. Mothers tell stories of the days when the men used to go out fishing early in the morning, coming home with their nets full of fresh fish at sunset. Now there are neither fish nor strong men left in the village. The only men who haven't gone are the sick and the wretched, who barely have the strength to walk, and a host of exhausted foreign fishermen, who, more often than not, merely land at the bridge briefly, before heading north in their boats. Some end their days in their village. After a journey walking barefoot through a desert they are barely alive, knocking at death's door. Only the strongest survive. And we know that few find a new life beyond the horizon: most of the men end up washed ashore as a corpse. Some of them are washed back to the island on the tide, the remainder rest in the nameless graveyard, which once used to be the rich fishing grounds that sustained us all. The girls ask about their fathers every day. Mothers say that their fathers are well, that they will soon come home and visit. When his work is done, they say. Your father wants you to have a better future than ours. The children clapped their hands and kissed the mouths of their fathers in a picture frame which hung on the living-room wall; a tattered photograph of a strong man with bloodshot eyes that hid his shattered dreams.

One beautiful summer morning, five brothers get into a boat which disappears at sea. And no one ever hears from them again.

Two of Seven Short Prose Texts

by

Lív Maria Róadóttir Jæger

translated by Marita Thomsen

My face/by the sink: I remember noticing suddenly one morning between now and then, that the body always changes. Noticing how it pulls like fuck on the glistening surface, as it breaks ice-cold each morning with my face. A ripple in the water. On a wave I am prettier; blurred and without detail. Every morning I see it, that I am relentlessly becoming something else, as nights and days jump rope, time and I skip, and on occasion I feel a bit of a laughingstock. Who is that? I ask staring into the mirror to know, if it is really me reflected there. Or someone else. I remember when I met you for the first time. Your contour alive in the night. Your body new to the world.

*

Nightmare: I remember waking in the middle of the night with palpitations. Dreaming something, without recall. A dream that lingers as an eerie sensation in a horror film, a creepy sound quivering through the veins. Deep in the ear a tone blares: the flat is a still-life, the past day a forgotten winter, the dream a disappearance, and yet crystal clear in my pulse, in my breath, in my body. How can it be in me, the dream? Where did it come from? Where did it go? I glimpse a nightmare about teeth: my teeth detaching from the gums, one after the other. Did I grow old overnight? A dead metallic taste develops in my mouth as I spit my teeth out into the sink. The brain a shower of sparks. I wish I could see inside it, into the malleable matter that is me—and understand something. Look, there it is, the dream and tang of iron. Look. In the mirror I see two eyes and one everyday. Outside snow falls, white and typical, a quiet repetition on the pavement. As if it were hiding something from me. White solace. White solace.

Fennel

by

Annika Skaalum

translated by Marita Thomsen

Impatiently I queued at the back of a long line for the till near the shop entrance. Of course the queue had to be long, and me at the back of it, on a beautiful day like today—a solitary bright, still fair weather day in the long line of spitting, dark, gusty bad weather days. To numb my resentment, I watched the people coming and going through the wide automatic glass doors in front of us. Adults on errands hurried ceaselessly in and out after work, listening and sniffing intently—all with the same vacant hunting expression that indicates blood sugar at rock bottom, and that they on their daily chase at the eleventh hour have spotted, or sunk their claws into, today's prey. And the rest of us breathe easier, as this probably, yet again, has prevented witless, famished customers from tearing each other apart in frenzied bloodlust in the aisles.

In my own basket I had something branded Giant Smokin' Dawgs, and a pack of hotdog rolls. So high were my expectations for these products, that it would certainly prevent me from lunging at my neighbour in the queue, slashing their coronary, and tearing off a fresh hunk of meat for myself. On the other hand—Giant Smokin' Dawgs… is that meant to be interpreted as enormously hot—in the sense of spicy or popular, both? Time will tell, I think to myself, not that I have any intention of suing the company, if the sausages fail to live up to such a brazenly self-congratulatory name. My fangs are itching now, I do hope that the queue will pick up the pace, and keep me from losing control and executing my aforementioned, abominable, beastly plans.

A slender man in his mid-thirties, who I had noticed, because he slipped into the shop so nimble and quick, was now panting right on my heels in the queue. His warm breath on my neck caused me to glance over my shoulder in surprise. At the end of his khaki jacket sleeve, where his hand poked out, I spotted—not a hand grenade—but that he was buying only a single item, which he clutched so tight that his knuckles were pale.

It was a bulb of fennel.

Bright green as spring hope and white as the knuckles of the hand holding it.

Here stood the first human I had ever seen purchase a fennel bulb, and in a store that really doesn't have much of a vegetable selection—why, it was nothing short of a minor miracle to find fennel in this place. And at that thought, I felt quite a dose of adrenaline rush through my sugar-poor bloodstream, which unsettled me to such a degree, that I couldn't suppress an urge to stir and take a few involuntarily steps without really moving, so I wouldn't lose my spot.

The line was long now and had ground to a halt. The payment system was down, again, and the boy at the checkout had already made repeated calls over the PA system for someone to man the other till. To no avail. I felt sorry for him, though it looked like he was managing to keep cool. A bleak situation at a bleak food shop with bleak customers, staffed with school kids, who proudly and solemnly try their hardest to do their first ever job well, while the seasoned, disloyal and lazy colleagues are off in the storeroom every five minutes smoking, chatting, texting and Lord knows what else.

It meant that we would be in this queue plenty long enough for me to steal, with a little guile, the occasional glance over my shoulder, purely by chance, of course, feigning boredom, and systematically study my fennel man more closely.

I decided to work my way up and noted that he was wearing house shoes.

One should be cautious not to over interpret slippers on such a beautiful day, many types of slippers are well suited as summer sandals. These however were worn and faded. I surmised that they had been black once, but that was probably a long time ago. A strap was also loose, so he had definitely been at home, when the decision was made to go out and purchase the blessed fennel, because the shoes were too shabby to have been worn here straight from work. If he was, indeed, in work.

It was possible that he couldn't afford to buy new slippers precisely because he was unemployed. On the other hand, in that case he would most probably have other things than a silly fennel bulb to spend money on. So the preliminary conclusion was that he was not unemployed, had been home, had started cooking dinner and then rushed out, in his slippers, to the shop to buy this fennel, and in my mind I could vividly imagine how he, or a potential partner, was making dinner from a new exciting recipe, where fennel was suddenly listed as required for this rare delicacy. Fennel, which no one in this country just happens to have in their pantry on an ordinary midweek afternoon—and in this culinary cultural crisis my dear friend in the queue had dashed off, and against all the odds, found the required fennel bulb, which he now clutches so hard his knuckles whiten.

My nostrils were now picking up the firmness of his grip. A fresh whiff of celery mixed with the sugary aniseed of *kongabomm*[26] sweets wafted gently up the queue, and made me turn to look, and I noted, yes, yes, a wedding ring on one of the five white-knuckled fingers squeezing the poor fennel.

Well, then it was perhaps the wife who had dispatched him to the shop.

Of course she had to have fennel, if the recipe called for it—and though hubby had only just got his slippers on, she had probably asked him to hurry out and come back quick.

And here he stood, so close to the finishing line of his successful errand, totally oblivious to the fact that this shop doesn't sell fennel, just your ordinary boring products, which they are certain they can sell to their many, ordinary boring customers—ordinary boring vegetables like carrots, onions, cucumbers, tomatoes, peppers. Actually, I remember when peppers weren't boring, but so new, unknown and exciting that only the bravest souls dared to buy them, and I also remember how they gradually turned ordinary and boring like all the other boring vegetables. No, he didn't know that if you are looking for a rarity, you should stay away from here, because only anyone oblivious, or a lunatic, would come in here actually intending to buy fennel. He was blissfully unaware of all this.

But I knew it, and I wouldn't dream of coming here to buy that fennel he is now slowly strangling. What I really want is to turn around and ask him to relax a little with that fennel for Christ's sake. Nobody in their right mind would be standing there squashing a vegetable like that. Then again, he may not be in his right mind, seeing as he came here for the sole purpose of buying that bloody fennel. And perhaps he thinks it will run off, if he doesn't grip it like a vice. No wonder his wife sends him to the shops as soon as he sets foot in the house.

Little by little I grow more and more offended that the shop, with which I am so intimately familiar, has betrayed me like this. I feel mocked, because had anyone asked me, I would have advised against coming here to buy such an uncommon vegetable, I would. And so they would have thought me a liar at best, spiteful at worst.

And the fennel man behind me has no notion how lucky he is. He surely thinks it is completely natural to be able to dash off to any old shop in slippers, and find enticing, sumptuous fennel bulbs heaped on the vegetable shelf waiting—just for him, the way the rest of us know that our trusty old carrots and leeks await us steadfast and patient week after week, year after year after year after year…

I have a go at him under my breath, tell him to count his lucky stars that he found this fennel, which he is now crushing to fennel pulp, and that he most probably has human error to thank for the unlikely success of his errand.

Because it is most definitely a mistake that fennel was ordered in for this shop this week. Human error. Not big or serious, like when airplanes crash and hundreds of people die, and there is a search for a black box to reveal the human error. This error may appear so minute that perhaps nobody will ever notice, which means that the vegetable wholesaler will forever more order extra fennel destined to make the long journey here from far-flung countries—fennel that nobody will buy, except the odd lost, panting, numpty, because fennel bulbs are not today's peppers and will never become ordinary and boring like all other ordinary, boring vegetables, nor *smokin'* like my self-congratulatory sausages, hence most of them will go up in flames, as rubbish, at the incinerator plant and transform into dark, polluting, clouds of smoke floating in the skies for all eternity, thereby increasing the dangerous greenhouse effect, leading the ice-caps to…

And at long last a nicotine-reeking teen is making her way to the other till.

Kongabomm

by
Malan Poulsen

translated by Marita Thomsen

Strings dangled above the bed, they looked like spider webs. Sometimes they would be lowered, so the woman could hoist herself up to sit against a jumble of pillows.

The girl also noticed that the bed had bars, which the hands wanted to pull at, but the adults said no!—and meant it.

The woman filled the bed. Her white angel hair cascaded down the pillows, and her eyes peered from deep inside the darkness that flanked her high nose. Her voice was stern, but a sudden smile would warm everything in a flash. And the hands that caressed the girl's hair, when she would slip into the sitting room in the mornings, were long, tired paws lacking the strength to claw.

"Look in the drawer, pet, you can have a sweet from the pack. Only one, mind."

She rushed over and yanked open the drawer, there was the pack of shimmering red sweets. It rustled when she picked one out, and they were often so stuck together that it was a struggle to free one from the lump. She wanted to take more, but didn't dare—those eyes saw everything—and if she as much as tried, then the stern voice would come: "Only one, I said."

With the aniseed sweet stuffed in her mouth, she was Gretel in that story about the gingerbread house, before the witch arrived, her tongue traced the candy contours of a royal crown. *Kongabomm* were the king's sweets, that's proper fancy, and as she sneaked back out of the sitting room she felt chosen.

It was strange, with the woman in the sitting room they had to keep quiet, because she was ill.

Sometimes they would go in and sit with her. Quietly. The adults would speak clearly in that same tone they used with her, but they wouldn't scold. It was boring; the hands wanted something to do, like pull at the levers that made the back of the bed go up and down, so the woman also went up and down. But then they would nag: "Stop it! Be a good girl now and don't tire granny."

So the legs starting kicking the bed while the mouth sang words that broke free with every kick: "*Konga-bomm, konga-bomm, konga-bomm, konga-bomm.*"

And in a blink they would grab her, hard, and shove her into the kitchen with a hiss.

"Be still in there then!"

Waiting in the kitchen was no fun, it wasn't fun in the sitting room either—but everyone else was in there.

One morning there was no woman in the sitting room; she could take as many *kongabomm* as she liked, but the sweets had congealed into a grey-red lump. Untouchable, like the slugs in the jar, that time.

A slime trail shimmered in the grass behind the little grey and brown slugs. She collected them in a jar and screwed the lid on tight, wanting to own them, and hid them right at the back under the stairs.

By the time she rediscovered her hoard and unscrewed the lid, it was all a slimy slop. Suddenly breathing felt impossible. She hurled the jar as far as she could and ran back inside, choking back the tears. They asked: "What's the matter?" And the sobs welled out, ferociously, but no words. So they shook their heads and gave each other looks.

They said the woman had gone into hospital.

The hospital. It had rows of windows and rows of people in beds. She wasted away in there; all she wanted was to get out again.

They walked the long corridor and into the room where the woman was lying, quiet, in the white bed.

She had to get to the window high above, she climbed onto one knee, hooked her fingers on the sill and hoisted herself up.

On tiptoe she stood looking out.

Beautiful Life I Have Been Given

by

Trygvi Danielsen

translated by Marita Thomsen

In a far-flung place where nature still blooms unhindered, untouched by mankind's devastating hand, flies a dainty azure butterfly.

In play it chases an emerald slope all the way to a calm clear lake that reflects its extraordinary colour. As the butterfly delights in its own beauty, the mirror is dashed by the silvery arch of a freshwater fish leaping to swallow the butterfly.

The freshwater fish, pleased with its catch, senses its highest jump ever as its curve extends through the air. Before the giddy fish plunges back into the water, an overgrown and exquisite white-tailed eagle dives and buries its talons in the fish with the butterfly in its belly.

On regal wings the eagle draws breezy intricate movements and hoists itself up above the green canopy in a race to the sky. There is no mistaking its satisfaction with the quarry, or its ignorance of a nearby hunter's eye looking straight at its beak through the telescopic sight on his rifle. A deafening blast paints the sky black, and the eagle spirals down through gap-toothed crowns that let the sun dapple golden hues on the stone dead bird of prey, until it collides with the ground. Its talons are nailed so eagerly in its catch that the fish and the fowl, in spite of the long fall and crash landing, remain inseparable. In the melancholy of death's throes the freshwater fish recalls the moment only a few seconds ago, when it was swimming free in crystalline waters and executed the highest most dexterous jump of its life to catch the pretty butterfly.

The very instant
its last breath
sighs across the dewy grass,

the butterfly finds its way out of the fish gut and propels itself with sweeping flaps out into the wild through the sea creature's mouth. In this moment the blue wings set in motion a breeze that travels over magnificent mountains, down deep valleys and across mighty oceans as it relentlessly gathers force.

The wind
conquers multiple challenges,
battles cold fronts, hot fronts and countercurrents,
and by the time it has crossed half the globe,
it has grown to a raging hurricane.
It was in this hurricane,
I came into being.

*

The pair lies intertwined in a filthy bed in the corner of a three-room flat with a minimalist cosy feel. The wind lashes the panes in sharp gusts, at times it sounds like a banshee trying to shatter the glass with her formidable natural voice. Scented candles mask the cloying stench of decay suffusing the mould-colonised flat. Used syringes are strewn around the record player, which is playing the only album they own:

The Motion Picture Soundtrack from
Top Hat
(1935)

Their favourite film. Whenever they're separated, he always calls her on sleepless nights and sings *Cheek to Cheek* over the phone until she drifts off. I'm not comparing him to Fred Astaire, but he can hold a tune, he really can. Vónbjartur. Dad.

He's a sculptor. With special focus on the female form, he creates sculptural art of people in coitus. Chiselled haphazardly in anything carveable he comes across and uses. Sometimes his mates help him carry big rocks up to his seventh floor flat. He sells the sculptures on the street, and occasionally he exhibits. He's talented, unfortunately the world of sculpture is a bit niche. He often declares that it's better to be broke and happy than unhappy and loaded. All he wants to do is cut stone.

"I think the storm should be called Isabella," dad murmurs.

She gazes at him with a hazy smile. Naked, she rests her chin on his manly chest, she's caressing the curls on his sternum.

* pearls of sweat *

"I think we're at D in the storm alphabet. So it's the fourth one this year. There are just more and more of them," she replies hushed.

Lív. Mamma. She has long blonde hair and a distinctive face. There aren't many who consider her beautiful, but she has a natural face, free of make-up. Her body shape is reminiscent of the quintessential 1960s pinup with healthy soft forms. It's the shape of every woman Vónbjartur sculpts. She creates arty shorts with close ups of bugs and amphibians. She adores colourful insects playing on green foliage. In contrast with biodiversity, she conveys images of colourless bugs in grey and poor areas. A friend composes dreamy original scores for the films, and sometimes she gives the insects voices and spins stories from them. She also paints, but only trees, some struck by autumn, ghostly, colourless
and morose,
    others magnificent
    in dazzling spring bloom.

They

stand on the street every day and sell their art. Sometimes her films are shown at underground bars and alternative galleries. The smattering of money they scrape together is all destined to pay for their next fix.

Vónbjartur, "Food we can pinch, and rent we can pay later."

Now they lie there, in the polluted love nest, my intoxicated parents so aptly named: *Bright Hope*, aka, Vónbjartur, and *Life* aka Lív. Fate's irony will have it that they haven't much of a life, but optimism and hope they possess by the bucket load.

"D… Diana? No. I think the storm should be called something grandiose. Maybe Diamanta. Diaphanous, indomitable and mighty Diamanta."

She lets out a tender teasing laugh.

"Diamanta isn't a name," she playfully asserts.

His smile muscles teeter on a U-turn.

"It's a name if I say it is."

Silence sets in while he lights a fag, smokes it down and stubs it out in the ashtray he made himself. The record crackles softly as it broadcasts the harmonies of dancing angels.

Vónbjartur, "Dance with me." (insistent)

The high is nearing its peak and so are Fred and Ginger, circling under the needle.

"Dancing shadows in storm Diamanta," she sings, before she gets up and with a flourish offers him her hand.

They dance naked and tenderly. He holds her close and gazes so intently in her eyes that he sees the colours and shapes of her soul. Her soul is colourful and like a bird's silhouette, he muses. Perhaps a crow, but not black or mean. A bright and hopeful crow flying passionately in place

like when it's blustery
and the birds look
like paintings
nailed
paintings
nailed to the sky.

He spins her around in lazy circles, sends her away, catches her again and bends her over backwards; all the while their pupils pierce each other's soul. In the end he lays her on the

table, knocking two sculptures off to shatter on the floor.
Warm shared laughter. (Close-up)
He kisses her eagerly,
first her whole face,
her ears,
then her neck
then further down.

He gently licks his way down her breasts, stomach, legs and inner thighs, then sucks the skin edging her labia. He feels her craving surge.

He
kisses,
sucks,
licks
and caresses her entire body, until lost in aching hunger she begs him to fuck her. His mighty pulsating dick is on the edge of exploding, but he doesn't give in. Her body is his playground and every last square millimetre is to be explored and played in. She tries pulling him inside, but he stops her. Lust sends tiny shockwaves from the marrow of her bones to the tip of the down on her silky skin. They breathe in heavy rapid unison. At last he lets his soft silver tongue gently trace her cunt until it locks in on its clitoral home. She moans deeply as he lovingly sends her on a dream journey to the furthest reaches of the universe and home again. His sweat and her cum glitter on his face as he re-emerges with the expression of a great warrior. He gently lets his dick slide into her dripping flesh, centimetre by centimetre, advancing until he reaches her body's deepest recess. She pants softly staring

into his burning eyes and clinging to his body of sweat as he accelerates his travels in and out of her. The firmament opens and gifts her wave after wave of radiant technicolour orgasms, while the candles send humble light rays across their sweat-soaked fused skin. With the same force the storm throws at the quaking flat, he occupies her with ferocity and grace, until he feels a life-giving primeval seism gather strength up through his shaft and with a

Hiroshima
Supernova
test dummy
head breaks
*** explosion! ***
fills her with his manhood.

*

My time has come now.
Getting to the goal is what matters.
While my drenched parents, shattered and drained, cling to each other on the floor where they doze off in safe skins, my race begins to become the sperm cell that merges with the egg. The journey is long and competition ferocious. In all directions spermatozoids are struggling to break through the membrane cloaking the life-giving egg. We all know what's at stake. This is our shot at existence.
Still some seem to slip behind on purpose,
as if blessed with an omniscience,
telling them,
this is not their life

to be given.
In frenzied burrowing I tear my way through the firm tissue until I see the light. It is bright, alluring and magnificent.

The light of life.

I glow!

I twinkle!

Look at me!

It feels like it's sucking me in, like it has chosen me over every other cell fighting as fervently as I to win the only available seat of existence. The sensation of becoming one with the egg is like the deepest, purest, truest breath ever drawn.
The primeval breath.
The moment when you know that you exist.
When for the first time you feel the life you have been given.

*

Vónbjartur stirs. Strange dreams have visited his realm of rest, and in the haze he wonders where he is, but then he recognises her smell. The scent of safety. He couldn't put her aroma in words, but it's

unmistakable.

Vónbjartur thinks, "*She is its only carrier.*"

The dreams were long, strange and vivid. Immense and beautiful beings were stretching and broadening Vónbjartur several metres this way and that, like he was made of rubber. When they let go of his skin, it twanged back into its original position. For the beings this was more of an inspection than entertainment. Then they tried teaching Vónbjartur how to carve. The odd thing was that they carved in fire. With ordinary knives in rust-free steel they cut flames into shapes and objects. One being designed a tiny little willy, another a body-sized helicopter, and a third formed the letter U and the number 6.

U

*　　　6　　　*

Vónbjartur carved an unfamiliar face in the flame, and when the creatures saw it they started shrieking at him. Their mouths fell to the floor and turned into massive holes emitting otherworldly sounds. Their eyes took on the shape of the unknown carved face, while they started to run around manically. Suddenly one fell on its arse and burst into tears. The others watched it morosely for a moment, before they launched into

Feathers
by
Man Man

This comforted the being, it dried its eyes and listened with a rapt smile. In the dream dad was moved to tears by the sight of the singing beings comforting the crying one.

He's lying on the floor with Lív in his arms staring at the ceiling. He glances at the clock he inherited from his grandmother, which leans against the wall at the opposite end of the room. It's in limbo between night and morning.
He gently kisses mum's forehead. She smiles in her sleep.

He gets up heavily and soundlessly without waking her, puts on the first crumpled garment he comes across on the floor and heads out the front door. Pangs of hunger are driving him down to the corner shop (100% service 24/7) a stone's throw away. The storm has metamorphosed into a deadly calm. The sidewalks are deserted and hushed. The distant dawn gifts the city rousing cloudbreaks, like promises of brighter times ahead.

He loves the calm on these habitually stressed streets.

Higgs Boson Blues

@ Nick Cave and the Bad Seeds

and the tune plays in his head as he ambles.

Suddenly he feels a violent shock to the nape of his neck and collapses.

A teenager has taken a baseball bat to him. From the darkness four more emerge. They're all wearing hoodies with no distinctive markings. They hit, kick and trample dad, who lies unconscious, helpless. One is wearing heavy safety boots. He stamps on dad's head and it looks like he snaps.

In a frenzy

he tramples harder

and harder and harder and harder

and harder and harder and harder (harder),

as the skull shatters underfoot. He feels like an almighty god turning stone into liquid. He feels powerful and big.

Hoodie #2: "FUCK'S SAKE! UR KILLING HIM!"

His pack tries to tear him away, but he keeps stomping as he cackles and cries, cackles and cries senselessly. In the end they prise him off and he tumbles back on top of one of his mates. They all stand there for a heartbeat looking in horror at the man crumpled in a puddle of blood on the road with a skull so smashed he might as well have been decapitated. He is

stone cold dead.
They run, spooked.

*

Life
in
the womb
Shelters
is tough in this time of sorrow.
I thrive here, it's cosy and safe, but it affects me deeply that mamma has fallen into paralysing depression.

Under the darkening star of despair she cries endlessly.
At times
(Soulless Hollywood C film)
she curls into a howling longing,
as she wraps herself in clothes
that still carry his scent.

Her eyes stream like a primal river that has flowed ceaselessly for aeons, dug itself into the earth's crust slicing grooves and deep scars in her soul. When she isn't crying she just lies in bed, listening to the record and staring into the void. Sometimes she smiles for a nanosecond when she thinks about dad.
Lív (manic), "He just went down to the corner shop. He'll be right back," she comforts herself in an imaginary mirage, before bursting into tears again.

She barely eats. She's using more, though. The missed rent piles up. She hawked the clock and other stuff, but hasn't the strength to stand in the street and sell their art. (Theme song)

I'm hungry. Mamma is just about my only food source, and she isn't exactly a rich blossoming well. But I get her, because I miss dad too,
I love her,
she's my mamma.

The womb is a wondrous place. Snug, but not too tight. I try not to tumble, so I won't tire mamma. I explore my surroundings, feel how all the threads are tied and twined. I marvel at the interconnections and tissues all working together to nourish me, that is their shared purpose. I'm humbled when it dawns on me that this is all just for me. It's magnificent! The vitality, the intricate whole labouring to give tiny little me a shot at life.

*

At first the high was scary. It made me sick. I felt weak and rotten, like the needle was a vampire sucking the life out of me. Gradually I got used to it,
until it
eventually
became
essential.
Now I need it.
I love watching the preparations. I love the wafting scent when

she lights up under the tablespoon. The sight of the liquid she squirts out of the syringe to make sure that no nasty air bubbles cause trouble. The feeling of strangled blood flow when she tourniquets her veins. Then I know that the high will come soon. All I have to do is wait until she picks up the syringe, slides it gently into the vein and…

* Ah *

The craving is satisfied.

In triumphant bliss I stretch and softly caress the tissue cradling me to convey my satisfaction. Now we lie there, in our sullied lonely nest, the intoxicated mother and daughter twosome, Lív and me.

*

Banging at the door. Mamma pretends not to notice. She's lying in bed. Banging turns to pounding. She wraps her head in a pillow to muffle the sound.

"Open
the fuck up!
Open now,
or I'll do it myself!"
It's the landlord, Lýðar.
He's in his mid thirties, but his looks make him seem a decade older. He's flabby, black-haired, hairy and has a deformed nose, probably the result of his combative nature coupled with

his want of fighting skills. He slavishly wears tank tops with yellow stained armpits. Occasionally he tosses a checked shirt over them.

He isn't carrying the keys to the flat, so he jangles some random keychain against the door, as loud as he can manage.

Mamma comes round and sits up in bed.

The window is ajar and welcomes echoing police sirens and drifting smog inside.

"Coming, I'm coming. Chill!"

She gets up and steers towards the door. Her legs wobble a little as she walks. A dribble of vomit adds character to her grey t-shirt and the unconcealed white panties aren't exactly white anymore.

She opens the door.

"Well, fancy meeting a fine woman such as yourself here," he sneers, as he lumbers into the flat trailing a stinking halo of cheap booze. He locks the door behind him.

With indifferent irony she waves him in, before she pulls dad's old leather jacket off the peg, puts it on, pulls a cigarette from the pocket and lights up. She sits down at the table and sets her numb eyes on Lýðar.

"You're three months behind." (That smile)

She maintains eye contact and smokes in silence.

"Three months!!!

That's no way for me to run a business, now is it?"

Hands clasped behind his back, the man creeps in circles a few times, hushed, before he takes the seat across from her.

"Haven't you got anything to say for yourself?

How d'you intend to solve this problem?

I don't suppose you've got any cash,

still, there has to be some way to arrange payment."
He adds that last bit.

She stubs, observes the dead fag for a moment and looks straight into his eyes again.
Lív (in a flat tone),

"I'm sure we can work something out."

Neither doubts what she's alluding to.
His laugh is like a thousand snakes hissing.
"That so?" he asks aroused. "Work something out, you say. Sounds interesting. *But it'll have to be something veeery special if you intend to pay off three months' rent!"*
He lets out another sickening hiss.

* Sssssssss *

I'm about to hurl, and I can feel mamma is too.

He undresses and reveals his full naked ugliness. With the slithering smile on his mug he dumps his ass on the bed and waits for mamma. His puny penis and shrivelled balls barely get a look out from under the gut throwing shade on the genitals. He lies back, and the sight of him becomes even more repulsive

"MAKE ME HARD,"

he orders with authority.

She crouches at the foot of the bed and starts to touch him. I cover my eyes with my little hands and feel them drenched in tears. I get what's happening.

She's doing this for us.

I feel her head move up and down with his little limb in her mouth. She seesaws sluggishly, while her lost eyes stare blindly into his soulless glare. He lets out a low moan and hisses sharply.

"You've tried this before, YOU WHORE, I can feel it.
Suck slower.
Yeah...
That's more like it."

Mamma's nausea cuts like a scalding knife. I wish I had four hands to cover both my eyes and ears.

Too long later a fat grunt comes out of him. Mamma walks over to the sink, spits and drinks a few drops from the tap. He grins as he gets dressed.

"Three months is lots of dosh. Expect plenty of visits if we're to break even," he declares icily as he goes out the door.

Mamma throws herself on the bed. We cry in unison into the realm of rest.

*

MORNING

Mamma feels rested. She gets up, parts the curtains and opens the window. It's a brilliant autumn day. The massive ball of fire radiates in utter solitude on the peaceful cobalt dome and casts its warm love down on the kids playing in the dazzling streets. Mamma takes a lingering shower with scolding water and fragrant milk soap that softens the skin. Then she puts on her favourite clothes: the yellow-blue woolly jumper, which makes her eyes pop, the tight black trousers with diagonal pocket zips, and the old brown leather boots that match the belt. She emerges into a clear crisp autumn breeze that's pushing out the polluted city air.

The sun's invigorating energy seems to have sowed a smile in the city's soul that now sprouts in every single person in the streets mamma walks. She comes across a cosy café that serves brunch. She eats her fill and rounds off with a juicy red watermelon slice. This is one of the few public places where smoking is permitted inside, so she lights up and relaxes in the chair for a bit. The radio announces that a combo of clear skies and solar flares will make for exceptionally bright northern lights tonight. Mamma nods contented.

The air is cleaner the closer you are to the sea. Herring gulls flock in orderly patterns above the pier constantly calling out.

*** karr * karr ***

Mamma walks along the pebble beach and sits on the shore, where it's quiet. The waves lap the beach with a soft healing sigh that gently seeps into mamma's mind. She closes her eyes and becomes one with the splashing, lets it massage the breath flowing through her. Giddy butterflies flutter in her belly as she hears each wave fulfil its destiny by ending its existence in a mild explosion that sends it back to its source where the journey begins anew. It's as if this simple meek sighing reveals the most tangled secrets of the universe, if you're a good enough listener.

Mamma feels like a glowing light. An unbridled urge comes over her. She stands up, takes all of her clothes off, carefully puts them down and walks step by step into the ocean. The cold water revitalises her naked body. When it's deep enough she dives in.

She feels free floating through the water molecules, which move aside in friendship to let her body travel.

(The water molecules move aside for her:
some of them have known her before
as raindrops and snowflakes:
they recognise her,
greet her with kindness)

Though industry in the area has polluted the water to the point that the local authorities advise against children playing on the beach, all she feels is purity. As if she is shielded by a sparkling source of light, which only lets unspoiled water touch her human skin.

She emerges and draws a deep breath.

*

Night comes and darkness takes over where the light let go. We're lying wrapped in a warm blanket on the roof. No winds stir tonight and the sky is star bright, the way an infant soul is pure. The northern lights gleam miraculously
across the dome like
an innocent ballerina
whose reflection
is a bright light
in a
dead
ballroom.

I feel the needle prick. Mamma decided to use all she had left. I instantly feel that this high is paralysing.

We sit in silence for a moment as we watch the universe's free soul dance in the sky.
"Tell me about daddy," I blurt out.
She gently caresses her belly and says nothing.

"Some people glow," she slurs tenderly.
"They're surrounded by an invisible light, infectious like laughter. It spreads joy and tranquillity to its surroundings. Your dad was one of them. He had that. He took me from that godforsaken place. He took me to a place where I was just me. He taught me to understand *it*. Understand ***it***. Do you get it? To fathom truths and to fathom *the* truth."
I think I get it.
"Can't you light a cig?" I ask.
I love it when she smokes.
"This one time we took the bus south. We had no clue where we were going or what we'd do when we got there, she explains between drags. He suddenly felt like going, so we went. We ended up in a little town way south. Where the crows turn, or maybe where they start their journey."

* Short laugh *

"We were broke, so we pinched food from a shop. They found out, of course, so we had to run from an old hag, who looked like she was about to explode with rage. He was laughing his arse off as we ran. He loved a thrill.
Then we got to a lake outside of town. We had a blanket with us, which we wrapped ourselves in. We lay there all night talking while we looked up at the sky. That was the first time I

told him I loved him."
She talks in slow motion, but the words are clear and filled with love.
"I wish it were different. I wish that I…"
She stops talking.
"Mamma don't say that. We'll make it together. You and me."
My voice sounds to me like it's coming from someone else. I'm cold.
"Mmm," she hums hopefully, "We'll make it. Destiny's on our side."
I smile, moved, with distant eyes.
She's panting and sweating profusely.
"When darkness befalls you
and obscures all the living
all joy and respite,
destiny opens the door
to the truest light
of them all
If you know how to look.
It's your soul shining through."

The giant shimmering ballerinas twirl swift and graceful along the firmament. They glimmer in every hue and for fractions of seconds they take on the shapes of faces and stills from snippets of memories.
Mamma smiles feebly.
"Look… can you see? That's him. Definitely. That's his soul dancing there."
She falls quiet. The usual steady rise and fall of her belly stops. A chill besets our body, no truce. White froth bubbles from

mamma's mouth. I see the soul of the universe dance, until all goes dark.

Narrator #2,
"*A man in an office dreams*
that he swims in pristine
seawater.
A fish dreams
that it flies
high up
up above jade canopies.
A bird dreams that it's an ancient tree rising steadfast and secure in harmony with the origin of breath.
Earth dreams
that she's an enormous rain cloud,
caressing lonely deserts with drops of life.
Sun dreams
that she's a budding flower
in a sprouting meadow.
Universe dreams
that it's a minute
azure butterfly,
who flies daintily
scattering pollen
from bloom to bloom."

I, "*I dream that I'm a little girl sitting on a blanket in a forest under a sun, belly laughing with my parents.*"

I open my eyes and see that I'm surrounded by light. On each side of me drifting love beams twinkle and smile at me. One

light is colourful and looks like the silhouette of a bird. Like a crow, but not black or mean. A bright and hopeful crow, who flies passionately without getting anywhere, like in a storm, when the birds seem like paintings nailed to the sky. The other glitters exquisitely like an innocent ballerina, whose reflection is a bright light in a dead ballroom.
I smile back at them overjoyed.

Now we lie here,
in purity's soul nest,
a family high on joy.

Me. Vónbjartur & **Lív**

***

Notes

Little Kálvur

by Jakob Jakobsen
translated by Marita Thomsen

Page 36

1... Little Kálvur translates as Little Calf. Historians believe there is a kernel of truth to this account in that it portrays a priest, who lived in Sandoy in the second half of the 13th century.

2... *Bøur* is an infield, cultivated land or pasture within village walls, as opposed to *hagi*, which is uncultivated mountain land.

3... in the original the following text is inserted here in parenthesis: 'known as *norðuri á Bø* to the locals'.

4... *Roykstova* is the front room in old Faroese houses with an open fire. It served as kitchen, workroom, living room and sleeping quarters.

Page 37

5... if this phrasing sounds a little odd, it is because it mirrors the original. Certain expressions in this text have become engrained in Faroese language and literature. And, though the text has been edited slightly for the sake of clarity and flow, I have attempted to remain faithful in the English to the most widely known expressions.

6... in the original the following text is inserted here in parenthesis: 'Slavansdalur is a valley in Fjalshagi.'

Page 38
7...*Toft* is common in place names, it means ruin.

Page 39
8... *Drýlur* is unleavened bread.

9... *Náðinsgarður* is an annexe farm bestowed on a clergyman's widow.

The Dream

by Andrea Reinert

translated by Lindy Falk van Rooyen

Page 80
10... *huldrelands* in the broadest sense denote a hidden or secretive place. In Norse mythology, the *huldra* or *hulder* were mythical forest creatures, usually women, who appeared to men and seduced them with their beauty. In a Christian context, folklore evolved to portray the huldra as a demon or a fallen creature in need of salvation.

For Now

by Maria Mikkelsen

translated by Marita Thomsen

Page 100

11… *omma* means grandmother.

Page 101

12… Jakke is a common shortening of Jákup.

Page 114

13… Ernst Moritz Arndt, hymn, Danish translation by F. Hammerich.

14… Aurelius Prudentius Clemens (4th Century), Hymn 529 '*Med sorgen og klagen hold måde, Guds ord*', Danish version Peder Hegelund, 1586, C.U. Sundt 1840.

Page 115

15… N.F.S Grundtvig, Hymn 325 '*Jeg ved et lille Himmerig,*' 1837 and 1853.

16… J. Larsen, Danish hymn.

Page 120

17… Faroese traditional ballad refrain '*Trøðum lættliga dansin*', meaning 'Lightly tread the dance'.

Page 122
18… Danish traditional ballad '*Hr. Tidemand*'.

19… Danish traditional ballad '*Sorte Plov*'.

Page 127
20… Danish traditional ballad '*Vind op, vind op i Rå*'.

The Homecoming

by Martin Joensen

translated by Lindy Falk van Rooyen

Page 163
21… is an old Danish drinking song: *Tonight we would drink, if only there were beer to be had; tomorrow we would sail, if only a favourable wind would blow*

Page 165
22… is an extract from an old viking hail to King Ragnar: *We wield our swords in mighty battle*

The Tree of Knowledge

by Jørgen-Frantz Jacobsen

translated by Paul Russell Garrett

Page 182
23… *How the sun sparkles! How the field laughs!*

The Last Fishing Trip

by Magnus Dam Jacobsen

translated by Marita Thomsen

Page 277

24… *Báran* is a named wave formation

To Those Who Think They Know It All

by Tóroddur Poulsen

translated by Lindy Falk van Rooyen

Page 296

25… *abbi* means grandfather

Fennel

by Annika Skaalum

translated by Marita Thomsen

Page 363

26… *kongabomm* are red aniseed-flavoured boiled sweets. A crown is usually printed on both sides. Tradition has it that they were first prepared for King Christian V by his court physician. They came about as a remedy for the King's sore throat, because the King refused to take the pure aniseed oil first prescribed. The royal physician then resorted to adding aniseed oil to sugar paste with a drop of beetroot juice for colour. The King was reportedly delighted and the sweets became known as *Kongen af Danmark bolcher*, King of Denmark sweets.